ROBERT SILVE
THE PLEASURE OF YOUR COMPANY
AT THE CONGLOMEROID COCKTAIL PARTY

You are about to witness a gathering unlike any you have ever attended. You'll see half a dozen travelers in time and space, including a pair of faithless lovers, a man who misplaced his past, and a resurrected Rennaissance musician. You'll encounter several novel lifeforms, including religious apes, helpful dinosaurs and the latest in exotic plagues. And you'll meet a brace of remarkable personages such as Will Shakespeare, the Archduke Ferdinand and the Emperor of San Francisco. The attire is informal—a ritual mask or the latest bodysculpture will do—and a remarkable time is guaranteed for all.

ROBERT SILVERBERG is one of science fiction's most accomplished authors. He creates characters of overpowering realism, set against a dazzling array of fantastic settings. His brilliant SF novels such as *Thorns*, *Dying Inside* and *The Book of Skulls* are modern classics. He is acclaimed for his recent historical fantasies *Lord of Darkness* and *Gilgamesh the King*. And his bestselling Majipoor Trilogy (*Lord Valentine's Castle*, *Majipoor Chronicles* and *Valentine Pontifex*) has established him as one of science fiction's most popular authors. This book, containing never-before-collected stories since 1980, confirms Silverberg as an author whose short fiction compares to Le Guin and Bradbury in its elegance, imagination and emotional power.

The Conglomeroid Cocktail Party

Robert Silverberg

BANTAM BOOKS
TORONTO · NEW YORK · LONDON · SYDNEY · AUCKLAND

*This low-priced Bantam Book
has been completely reset in a type face
designed for easy reading, and was printed
from new plates. It contains the complete
text of the original hard-cover edition.*
NOT ONE WORD HAS BEEN OMITTED.

THE CONGLOMEROID COCKTAIL PARTY

*A Bantam Book / published by arrangement with
Arbor House Publishing Company*

PRINTING HISTORY
Arbor House edition published June 1984
*A Featured Alternate of the Science Fiction Book Club,
June 1984*
Bantam edition / July 1985

ISBN 0-553-25077-9

Published simultaneously in the United States and Canada

---

*Bantam Books are published by Bantam Books, Inc. Its trade-
mark, consisting of the words "Bantam Books" and the por-
trayal of a rooster, is Registered in U.S. Patent and Trademark
Office and in other countries. Marca Registrada. Bantam
Books, Inc., 666 Fifth Avenue, New York, New York 10103.*

PRINTED IN THE UNITED STATES OF AMERICA
H   0 9 8 7 6 5 4 3 2 1

Acknowledgments

"The Far Side of the Bell-Shape Curve," "Waiting for the Earthquake," "The Palace at Midnight" and "Our Lady of the Sauropods" first appeared in *Omni*.

"At the Conglomeroid Cocktail Party," "Gianni" and "Needle in a Timestack" first appeared in *Playboy*.

"The Pope of the Chimps" first appeared in *Perpetual Light*, edited by Alan Ryan.

"The Man Who Floated in Time" first appeared in *Speculations*, edited by Isaac Asimov and Alice Laurance.

"How They Pass the Time in Pelpel," "Not Our Brother" and "A Thousand Paces Along the Via Dolorosa" first appeared in *Twilight Zone*.

"The Trouble with Sempoanga" first appeared in *Beyond*.

"The Regulars" first appeared in *Isaac Asimov's Science Fiction Magazine*.

"The Changeling" first appeared in *Amazing Stories*.

"Jennifer's Lover" first appeared in *Penthouse*.

For   *Ben Bova*
      Robert Sheckley
      George Scithers
      Alice K. Turner

The right people in the right place at the right time.

Contents

Introduction

I had given up writing short stories, for one thing. The last one I did was in 1973, an item called "In the House of Double Minds," and I decided to call it quits with that one. Short-story writing is hard on the nerves: you have no room to make any real mistakes, by which I mean that every word has to count, every line of dialogue has to serve three or four simultaneous purposes, every scene has to sweep the story inexorably along toward the culminating moment of insight that is the classic short-story payoff. In a novel you can go off course for whole chapters at a time and no one will mind; you may even find yourself being praised for the wonderful breadth of your concept. But a short story with so much as half an irrelevant page is a sad, lame thing, and even the casual and uncritical reader is aware that something's wrong with it.

Having been through the tensions of short-story creation inordinately often over a twenty-year period—I don't know how many of them I've written, and perhaps not even my bibliographer, bless him, has the exact count, but a quick glance at my office shelves shows me nearly two dozen volumes of them, each containing five to fifteen stories—I resolved to excuse myself from further struggle with the form. In a collection of my stories published in 1978 I wrote in the introduction, "I suppose I might someday write another short story, but it has been almost five years since the last and I still see no sign that the impulse is coming over me. So be it."

In truth I was, at the time I wrote that introduction, feeling no impulse to write long stories either: I was wholeheartedly weary of fictionizing in general, and some years previously I had (publicly, vociferously and, as it turned out, somewhat prematurely) announced my retirement as a writer. But midway through 1978 I found myself suddenly planning the lengthy novel that I was to call *Lord Valentine's Castle*, and there went my retirement. Apparently I had only been on sabbatical leave.

Nevertheless, I gave no thought to returning to short-story writing. They still seemed like damned nuisances to me. You needed a stunning idea, for one thing—the ideal science-fiction short story, I think, should amaze as well as delight—and you had to develop it with cunning and craft, working on the edge of your nervous system every moment, polishing and repolishing to hide all those extraneous knees and elbows. It meant a couple of weeks of nasty work, for which the immediate cash return, incidentally, was likely to be about $250, and then maybe $100 every year or two thereafter if you had written something good enough to be anthologized regularly. Though cash return is not the most important factor in a writer's life (if it were, we'd all be writing *Love's Purple Pitfalls* books, or whatever else happens to be the hot thing of the moment), it *is* a consideration, especially when a good short story takes fifty or a hundred working hours, as mine were tending to take. At $2.50 an hour I often felt I'd enjoy some other kind of work.

But then came a magazine called *Omni*.

It was slick and shiny and its publishers understood more than a little about the techniques of promotion, and it started its life with a circulation about six times as great as any science-fiction magazine had ever managed to achieve, plus a raft of expensive ads. After some comings and goings in the editorial chairs the job of fiction editor went to my old friend Ben Bova, who began to hint broadly that it would be a nice idea if I wrote a short story for him. He mentioned a sum of money. It was approximately what I had been earning for my novels circa 1968. Though cash return is not the most important factor in a writer's life, the amount of money Ben mentioned was at least capable of causing me to rethink my antipathy to short-story writing.

By the time I was through rethinking, however, Bova had moved upstairs and was *Omni's* executive editor. He had brought in as fiction editor another old friend of mine, the veteran science-fiction writer Robert Sheckley. Sheckley also thought I ought to be writing stories for *Omni*. All through 1979 he and Bova sang their siren song to me, and in the first month of the new year I gave in. I phoned Sheckley and somewhat timidly told him I was willing to risk my nervous system on one more short story after all. "He's going to do it," I heard Sheckley call across the office to Bova. It was as though they had just talked Olivier into doing one more Hamlet. So much fuss over one short story!

But for me it was a big deal indeed: at that moment short-story writing seemed to me more difficult than writing novels, more difficult than learning Sanskrit, more difficult than winning the Olympic broad jump. I had promised, though; and I sat down to try. Though in an earlier phase of my career I had thought nothing of turning out three or four short stories a week, it took me close to a week to get the opening page of this one written—it was the story called "Our Lady of the Sauropods"—and I assure you that that week was no fun at all. But then, magically, the barriers dissolved, the words began to flow, and in a couple of days the story emerged.

Whatever had frightened me about doing short stories was gone. A month later still another old friend, Harlan Ellison, upon finding out that I seemed to be capable of writing them again, asked me for a story for a book he was editing. He had asked me for the same story in 1975, and I had refused then on grounds of inability to produce; but his project was still open here in 1980, and I had no excuses any longer. I did "Waiting for the Earthquake" for him, and let *Omni* publish it also. Then George Scithers, who was editor of *Isaac Asimov's Science Fiction Magazine*, called with an idea that became the little story called "The Regulars." Next I tried the tricky and difficult "Far Side of the Bell-Shaped Curve" for *Omni*, and brought it off. And so on and so on. I was back in business.

Story after story tumbled out. I became a crazed short-story writer. A look at the copyright listings will indicate that all the stories in this book were written between January of 1980 and April of 1982—seven in 1980, seven in 1981, two in 1982. It's almost as though they were stashed in the computer all those dry years, waiting for me to push the right button to let them out.

Bova and Sheckley of *Omni* were the parties most responsible for getting me started again. (Neither of them works there now, but I have gone on writing stories for Ellen Datlow, Sheckley's successor as fiction editor.) When suddenly I found myself producing stories faster than a single magazine could absorb them, I turned to *Playboy* as well, and wandered into one of the most rewarding editorial relationships of my life with their brilliant fiction editor, Alice K. Turner. Not only did she publish three of the stories in this collection ("Gianni," "At the Conglomeroid Cocktail Party" and "Needle in a Timestack"), but she has somehow managed to teach me a new trick or two, when I thought I knew them all. Kathy Green of *Penthouse*, Ted Klein of *Twilight Zone* and Judith Sims of *Beyond* were the other magazine editors with whom I worked on stories for this book; I also must mention Alan Ryan, who commissioned "The Pope of the Chimps" for his book *Perpetual Light*, and Alice Laurance, who invited me to contribute "The Man Who Floated in Time" to her anthology,

Speculations. I am grateful to them all for leading me back to short-story writing.

Not that writing them has become any easier, or that it is in any way fun. I still think that doing short stories is rough work. I get paid princely sums for writing them, and I love looking at them once they're finished; but line by line they call from me an outpouring of energy that novels do not seem to require. The degree of compression required, the architectonic demands, the anxieties that are evoked by the need to get everything absolutely right—I quail at all that. I back away in horror from new projects. I mutter. I procrastinate.

In fact, this introduction was written between pages 14 and 15 of my latest story, one summer morning when page 15 seemed utterly unattainable. Undoubtedly I *will* get to page 15, and on beyond it to the end this afternoon, tomorrow, next Tuesday, whenever. A professional doesn't give up midway, however much he may whimper or scream or moan or stall. When I have run out of excuses, I will get on with the job. I wish writing short stories held more pleasure for me, but I don't expect that wish to be granted. But at least *reading* my stories, once they are finished, gives me great delight. And, I devoutly hope, not only me.

Robert Silverberg
Oakland, California
July 1983

The Far Side
of the Bell-Shaped
Curve

Sarajevo was lovely on that early summer day. The air sparkled, the breeze off the mountains was strong and pungent, the whitewashed villas glittered in the morning sunlight. Reichenbach, enchanted by the beauty of the place and spurred by a sense of impending excitement, stepped buoyantly out of a dark cobbled alley and made his way in quick virile strides toward the river's right embankment. It was nearly 10:30.

A crowd of silent, sullen Bosnian burghers lined the embankment. The black-and-gold Hapsburg banners fluttered from every lamppost and balcony. In a little while the archduke Franz Ferdinand, the emperor's nephew and heir, would come this way with his duchess in their open-topped car. Venturing into dangerous territory, they were, into a province of disaffected and reluctant citizens.

The townsfolk stirred faintly. The townsfolk muttered. Like puddings, Reichenbach thought, they awaited in a dull, dutiful way their future monarch. But he knew they must be seething with revolutionary fervor inside.

1

Reichenbach looked about him for dark taut youths with the peculiar bright-eyed look of assassins. No one nearby seemed to fit the pattern. He let his gaze wander up the hills to the dense cypress groves, the ancient wooden houses, the old Turkish mosques topped by slender, splendid minarets and back down toward the river to the crowd again. And—

Who is she?

He noticed her for the first time, no more than a dozen meters to his left, in front of the Bank of Austria-Hungary building: a tall auburn-haired woman of striking presence and aura, who in this mob of coarse, rough folk radiated such supreme alertness and force that Reichenbach knew at once she must be of his sort. Yes! He had come here alone, certain he would find an appropriate companion, and that confidence now was affirmed.

He began to move toward her.

His eyes met hers and she nodded and smiled in recognition and acknowledgment.

"Have you just arrived?" Reichenbach asked in German.

She answered in Serbian. "Three days ago."

Smoothly he shifted languages. "How did I fail to see you?"

"You were looking everywhere else. I saw you at once. You came this morning?"

"Fifteen minutes ago."

"Does it please you so far?"

"Very much," he said. "Such a picturesque place. Like a medieval fantasy. Time stands still here."

Her eyes were mischievous. "Time stands still everywhere," she said, moving on into English.

Reichenbach smiled. Again he matched her change of language. "I take your meaning. And I think you take mine. This charming architecture, the little river, the ethnic costumes—it's hard to believe that a vast and hideous war is going to spring from so quaint a place."

"A nice irony, yes. And it's for ironies that we make these journeys, *n'est ce pas?*"

"Vraiment."

They were standing quite close now. He felt a current flowing between them, a pulsating, almost tangible force.

"Join me later for a drink?" he said.

"Certainly. I am Ilsabet."

"Reichenbach."

He longed to ask her when she had come from. But of course that was taboo.

"Look," she said. "The archduke and duchess."

The royal car, inching forward, had reached them. Franz Ferdinand, red faced and tense in preposterous comic-opera uniform, waved halfheartedly to the bleakly staring crowd. Drab, plump Sophie beside him, absurdly overdressed, forced a smile. They were meaty-looking, florid people, rigid and nervous, all but clinging to each other in their nervousness.

"Now it starts," he said.

"Yes. The foreplay." She slipped her arm through his.

Not far away a tall, young, sallow-faced man appeared as if he had sprung from the pavement—wild hyperthyroid eyes, bobbing Adam's-apple, a sure desperado—and hurled something. It landed just behind the royal car. An odd popping sound—the detonator—and then Reichenbach heard a loud bang. There was a blurt of black smoke and the car behind the archduke's lurched and crumpled, dumping aides-de-camp into the street. The cortege halted abruptly. The imperial couple, unharmed, sat weirdly upright as if their survival depended on keeping their spines straight. A functionary riding with them said in a clear voice, "A bomb has gone off, your highness." And Franz Ferdinand, calm, disgusted: "I rather expected something like that. Look after the injured, will you?"

Ilsabet's hand tightened on Reichenbach's forearm as the bizarre comedy unfolded: the cars motionless, archduke and duchess still in plain view, the assassin wildly vaulting a parapet and plunging into the shallow river, police pursuing, pouncing, beating him with the flats of their swords, the crowd milling in confusion. At last the damaged car was pushed to the side of the road and the remaining vehicles rapidly drove off.

"End of act one," Ilsabet said, laughing.

"And forty minutes until act two. That drink, now?"

"I know a sidewalk café near here."

Under a broad turquoise umbrella Reichenbach had a slivovitz, Ilsabet a mug of dark beer. The stolid citizens at the surrounding tables talked more of hunting and fishing than of the bungled assassination. Reichenbach, pretending to be casual, studied Ilsabet hungrily. A cool, keen intelligence gleamed in her penetrating green eyes. Everything about her was sleek, self-possessed, sure. She was so much like him that he almost feared her, and that was a new feeling for him. What he feared most of all was that he would blunder here at the outset and lose her; but he knew, deep beneath all doubts, that he would not. They were meant for each other. He liked to believe that she came from his moment, and that there would be a chance to continue in realtime, when they had returned from displacement, whatever they began on this jaunt. Of course, one did not speak of such things.

Instead he said, "Where do you go next?"

"The burning of Rome. And you?"

"A drink with Shakespeare at the Mermaid Tavern."

"How splendid. I never thought of doing that."

He drew a deep breath and said, "We could do it together," and hesitated, watching her expression. She did not look displeased. "After we've heard Nero play his concerto. Eh?"

She seemed amused. "I like that idea."

He raised his glass. *"Prosit."*

"Zdravlje."

They snaked wrists, clinked glasses.

For a few minutes more they talked—lightly, playfully. He studied her gestures, her sentence structure, her use of idiom, seeking in the subtlest turns of her style some clue that might tell him that they were co-temporals, but she gave him nothing: a shrewd game player, this one. At length he said, "It's nearly time for the rest of the show."

Ilsabet nodded. He scattered some coins on the table and they returned to the embankment, walked up to the Latin Bridge, turned right into Franz Joseph Street. Shortly the royal motorcade, returning from a city-hall reception, came rolling along. There appeared to be some disagreement over the route: chauffeurs and aides-de-camp engaged in a noisy dispute and suddenly the royal car stopped. The chauffeur seemed to be trying to put the car into reverse. There was a clashing of gears. A gaunt boy emerged from a coffeehouse not three meters from the car, less than ten from Reichenbach and Ilsabet. He looked dazed, like a sleepwalker, as if astounded to find himself so close to the imperial heir. This is Gavrilo Princip, Reichenbach thought, the second and true assassin; but he felt little interest in what was about to happen. The gun was out, the boy was taking aim. But Reichenbach watched Ilsabet, more concerned with the quality of her reactions than with the deaths of two trivial people in fancy costumes. Thus he missed seeing the fatal shot through Franz Ferdinand's pouter-pigeon chest, though he observed Ilsabet's quick, frosty smile of satisfaction. When he glanced back at the royal car he saw the archduke sitting upright, stunned, tunic and lips stained with red, and the boy firing at the duchess. There was consternation among the aides-de-camp. The car sped away. It was 11:15.

"So," said Ilsabet. "Now the war begins, the dynasties topple, a civilization crumbles. Did you enjoy it?"

"Not as much as I enjoyed the way you smiled when the archduke was shot."

"Silly."

"The slaughter of a pair of overstuffed simpletons is ultimately less important to me than your smile."

It was risky: too strong too soon, maybe? But it got through to her the right way, producing a faint quirking of her lip that told him she was pleased.

"Come," she said, and took him by the hand.

Her hotel was an old gray stone building on the other side of the river. She had an elegant balconied room on the third floor, river view, ornate gas chandeliers, heavy damask draperies, capacious canopied bed. This era's style was certainly admirable, Reichenbach thought—lavish, slow, rich; even in a little provincial town like this, everything was deluxe. He shed his tight and heavy clothing with relief. She wore her timer high, a pale taut band just beneath her breasts. Her eyes glittered as she reached for him and drew him down beneath the canopy. At this moment at the other end of town, Franz Ferdinand and Sophie were dying. Soon there would be exchanges of stiff diplomatic notes, declarations of war by Austria-Hungary against Serbia, Germany against Russia and France, Europe engulfed in flames, the battle of the Marne, Ypres, Verdun, the Somme, the flight of the kaiser, the armistice, the transformation of the monarchies—he had studied it all with such keen intensity, and now, having seen the celebrated assassinations that triggered everything, he was unmoved. Ilsabet had eclipsed the Great War for him.

No matter. There would be other epochal events to savor. They had all history to wander.

"To Rome, now," he said huskily.

They rose, bathed, embraced, winked conspiratorially. They were off to a good start. Hastily they gathered their 1914 gear, waistcoats and petticoats and boots and all that, within the prescribed two-meter radius. They synchronized their timers and embraced again, naked, laughing, bodies pressed tight together, and went soaring across the centuries.

At the halfway house outside imperial Rome, they underwent their preparations, receiving their Roman hairstyles and clothing, their hypnocourses in Latin, their purses of denarii and sestertia, their plague inoculations, their new temporary names. He was Quintus Junius Veranius, she was Flavia Julia Lepida.

Nero's Rome was smaller and far less grand than he

expected—the Colosseum was still in the future, there was no Arch of Titus, even the Forum seemed sparsely built. But the city was scarcely mean. The first day, they strolled vast gardens and dense, crowded markets, stared in awe at crazy Caligula's bridge from the Palatine to the Capitoline, went to the baths, gorged themselves at their inn on capon and truffled boar. On the next, they attended the gladiatorial games and afterward made love with frantic energy in a chamber they had hired near the Campus Martius. There was a wonderful frenzy about the city that Reichenbach found intoxicating, and Ilsabet, he knew, shared his fervor: her eyes were aglow, her face gleamed. They could hardly bear to sleep, but explored the narrow winding streets from dark to dawn.

They knew, of course, that the fire would break out in the Circus Maximus where it adjoined the Palatine and Caelian hills, and took care to situate themselves safely atop the Aventine, where they had a fine view. There they watched the fierce blaze sweeping through the Circus, climbing the hills, dipping to ravage the lower ground. No one seemed to be fighting the fire; indeed, Reichenbach thought he could detect subsidiary fires flaring up in the outlying districts, as though arson were the sport of the hour, and soon those fires joined with the main one. They sky rained black soot; the stifling summer air was thick and almost impossible to breathe. For the first two days the destruction had a kind of fascinating beauty, as temples and mansions and arcades melted away, the Rome of centuries being unbuilt before their eyes. But then the discomfort, the danger, the monotony, began to pall on him. "Shall we go?" he said.

"Wait," Ilsabet replied. The conflagration seemed to have an almost sexual impact on her: she glistened with sweat, she trembled with some strange joy as the flames leaped from district to district. She could not get enough. And she clung to him in tight feverish embrace. "Not yet," she murmured, "not so soon. I want to see the emperor."

Yes. And here was Nero now, returning to town from holiday. In grand procession he crossed the charred city, descending from his litter now and then to inspect some ruined shrine or palace. They caught a glimpse of him as he entered the Gardens of Maecenas—thick-necked, paunchy, spindle-shanked, foul of complexion. "Oh, look," Ilsabet whispered. "He's *beautiful!* But where's the fiddle?" The emperor carried no fiddle, but he was grotesquely garbed in some kind of theatrical costume and his cheeks were daubed with paint. He waved and flung coins to the crowd and ascended the garden tower. For a better view, no doubt. Ilsabet pressed herself close to Reichenbach. "My throat is on fire," she said. "My lungs are choked with ashes. Take me to London. Show me Shakespeare."

There was smoke in the dark Cheapside alehouse too, thick sweet smoke curling up from sputtering logs on a dank February day. They sat in a cobwebbed corner playing word games while waiting for the actors to arrive. She was quick and clever, just as clever as he. Reichenbach took joy in that. He loved her for her agility and strength of soul. "Not many could be carrying off this tour," he told her. "Only special ones like us."

She grinned. "We who occupy the far side of the bell-shaped curve."

"Yes. Yes. It's horrible of us to have such good opinions of ourselves, isn't it?"

"Probably. But they're well earned, my dear."

He covered her hand with his, and squeezed, and she squeezed back. Reichenbach had never known anyone like her. Deeper and deeper was she drawing him, and his delight was tempered only by the knowledge that when they returned to realtime, to that iron world beyond the terminator where all paradoxes canceled out and the delicious freedoms of the jaunter did not apply, he must of necessity lose her. But there was no hurry about returning.

Voices, now: laughter, shouts, a company of men entering the tavern, actors, poets perhaps, Burbage, maybe, Heminges, Allen, Condell, Kemp, Ben Jonson possibly, and who was that, slender, high forehead, those eyes like lamps in the dark? Who else could it be? Plainly Shagspere, Chaxper, Shackspire, however they spelled it, surely Sweet Will here among these men calling for sack and malmsey, and behind that broad forehead Hamlet and Mercutio must be teeming, Othello, Hotspur, Prospero, Macbeth. The sight of him excited Reichenbach as Nero had Ilsabet. He inclined his head, hoping to hear scraps of dazzling table-talk, some bit of newborn verse, some talk of a play taking form; but at this distance everything blurred. "I have to go to him," Reichenbach muttered.

"The regulations?"

"Je m'en fous the regulations. I'll be quick. People of our kind don't need to worry about the regulations. I promise you, I'll be quick."

She winked and blew him a kiss. She looked gorgeously sluttish in her low-fronted gown.

Reichenbach felt a strange quivering in his calves as he crossed the straw-strewn floor to the far-off crowded table.

"Master Shakespeare!" he cried.

Heads turned. Cold eyes glared out of silent faces. Reichenbach forced himself to be bold. From his purse he took two slender, crude shilling-pieces and put them in front of Shakespeare. "I would stand you a flagon or two of the best sack," he said loudly, "in the name of good Sir John."

"Sir John?" said Shakespeare, blank-faced. He frowned and shook his head. "Sir John Woodcocke, d'ye mean? Sir John Holcombe? I know not your Sir John, fellow."

Reichenbach's cheeks blazed. He felt like a fool.

A burly man beside Shakespeare said, with a rough nudge, "Me-thinks he speaks of Falstaff, Will. Eh? You recall your Falstaff?"

"Yes," Reichenbach said. "In truth I mean no other."

"Falstaff," Shakespeare said in a distant way. He looked displeased, uncomfortable. "I recall the name, yes. Friend, I thank you, but take back your shillings. It is bad custom for me to drink of strangers' sack."

Reichenbach protested, but only fitfully, and quickly he withdrew lest the moment grow ugly: plainly these folk had no use for his wine or for him, and to be wounded in a tavern brawl here in A.D. 1604 would bring monstrous consequences in realtime. He made a courtly bow and retreated. Ilsabet, watching, wore a cat-grin. He went slinking back to her, upset, bitterly aware he had bungled his cherished meeting with Shakespeare and, worse, had looked bumptious in front of her.

"We should go," he said. "We're unwelcome here."

"Poor dear one. You look so miserable."

"The contempt in his eyes—"

"No," she said. "The man is probably bothered by strangers all the time. And he was, you know, with his friends in the sanctuary of his own tavern. He meant no personal rebuke."

"I expected him to be different—to be one of *us*, to reach out toward me and draw me to him, to—to—"

"No," said Ilsabet gently. "He has his life, his wife, his pains, his problems. Don't confuse him with your fantasy of him. Come, now. You look so glum, my dear. Find yourself again!"

"Somewhen else."

"Yes. Somewhen else."

Under her deft consolations the sting of his oafishness at the Mermaid Tavern eased, and his mood brightened as they went onward. Few words passed between them: a look, a smile, the merest of contacts, and they communicated. Attending the trial of Socrates, they touched fingertips lightly, secretly, and it was the deepest of communions. Afterward they made love under the clear, bright winter sky of Athens on a gray-green hillside rich with lavender and myrtle, and emerged from shivering ecstasies to find themselves with an audience of mournful scruffy goats—a perfect leap of context and metaphor, and for days thereafter they made one another laugh with only the most delicate pantomimed reminder of the scene. Onward they went to see grim, limping, austere old Magellan sail off around the world with his five little ships from the mouth of the Guadalquivir, and at a whim they leaped to India, staining their skins and playing at Hindus as they viewed the expedition of Vasco da Gama come sailing into harbor at Calicut, and then it seemed proper to go on to Spain in dry, hot summer to drink sour white wine and watch ruddy freckled-faced Columbus get his pitiful little fleet out to sea.

Of course, they took other lovers from time to time. That was part of the game, too tasty a treat to forswear. In Byzantium, on the eve of the Frankish conquest, he passed a night with a dark-eyed voluptuous Greek who oiled her breasts with musky mysterious unguents, and Ilsabet with a towering garlicky Swede of the imperial guard, and when they found each other the next day, just as the Venetian armada burst into the Bosporus, they described to one another in the most flamboyant of detail the strangenesses of their night's sport—the tireless Norseman's toneless bellowing of sagas in his hottest moments: the Byzantine's startling, convulsive, climactic fit, almost epileptic in style, and, as she had admitted playfully at dawn, mostly a counterfeit. In Cleopatra's Egypt, while waiting for glimpses of the queen and Antony, they diverted themselves with a dark-eyed Coptic pair, brother and sister, no more than children and blithely interchangeable in bed. At the crowning of Charlemagne she found herself a Frankish merchant who offered her an estate along the Rhine, and he a mysteriously elliptical dusky woman who claimed to be a Catalonian Moor, but who—Reichenbach suddenly realized a few days later—must almost certainly have been a jaunter like himself, playing elegant games with him.

All this lent spice to their love and did no harm. These separate but shared adventures only enchanced the intensity of the relationship they were welding. He prayed the jaunt would never end, for Ilsabet was the perfect companion, his utter match, and so long as they sprinted together through the aeons, she was his, though he knew that would end when realtime reclaimed him. Nevertheless, that sad moment still was far away, and he hoped before then to find some way around the inexorable rules, some scheme for locating her and continuing with her in his own true time. Small chance of that, he knew. In the world beyond the terminator there was no time-jaunting; jaunting could be done only in the fluid realm of "history," and history was arbitrarily defined as everything that had happened before the terminator year of 2187. The rest was realtime, rigid and immutable, and what if her realtime were fifty years ahead of his, or fifty behind? There was no bridging that by jaunting. He did not know her realtime locus, and he did not dare ask. Deep as the love between them had come to be, Reichenbach still feared offending her through some unpardonable breach of their special etiquette.

With all the world to choose from, they sometimes took brief solo jaunts. That was Ilsabet's idea, holidays within their holiday, so that they would not grow stale with one another. It made sense to him. Thereupon he vaulted to the Paris of the 1920s to sip Pernod on the Boulevard Saint-Germain and peer at Picasso and Hemingway and Joyce, she in epicanthic mask of old Cathay to see Kublai Khan ride in triumph through the Great Wall, he to Cape Kennedy to watch the great Apollo rocket roaring moonward, she to London for King Charles's beheading. But these were brief adventures, and they reunited quickly, gladly, and went on hand in hand to their next together, to the fall of Troy and the diamond jubilee of Queen Victoria and the assassination of Lincoln and the sack of Carthage. Always when they returned from separate exploits, they regaled each other with extensive narratives of what had befallen them, the sights, the tastes, the ironies and perceptions, and, of course, the amorous interludes. By now Reichenbach and Ilsabet had accumulated an elaborate fabric of shared experience, a richness of joint history that gave them virtually a private language of evocative recollection, so that the slightest of cues—a goat on a hill, the taste of burned toast, the sight of a lop-eared beggar—sprang them into an intimate realm that no one else could ever penetrate: their unique place, furnished with their own things, the artifacts of love, the treasures of memory. And even that which they did separately became interwoven in that fabric, as if the telling of events as they lay in each other's arms had transformed those events into communal possessions.

Yet gradually Reichenbach realized that something was beginning to go wrong.

From a solo jaunt to Paris in 1794, where she toured the Reign of Terror, Ilsabet returned strangely evasive. She spoke in brilliant detail of the death of Robespierre and the sad despoliation of Notre Dame, but what she reported was mere journalism, with no inner meaning. He had to fish for information. Where had she lodged? Had she feared for her safety? Had she had interesting conversations with the Parisians? Shrugs, deflections. Had she taken a lover? Yes, yes, a fleeting liaison, nothing worth talking about; and then it was back to an account of the mobs, the tumbrils, the sound of the guillotine. At first Reichenbach accepted that without demur, though her vaguenesses violated their custom. But she remained moody and oblique while they were visiting the Crucifixion, and as they were about to depart for the Black Death she begged off, saying she needed another day to herself, and would go to Prague for the premiere of *Don Giovanni*. That too failed to trouble him—he was not musical—and he spent the day observing Waterloo from the hills behind Wellington's troops. When Ilsabet rejoined him in the late spring of 1349 for the Black Death in London, though, she seemed even more preoccupied and remote, and told him little of her night at the opera. He began to feel dismay, for they had been marvelously close and now she was obviously voyaging on some other plane. The plague-smitten city seemed to bore her. Her only flicker of animation came toward evening, in a Southwark hostelry, when as they dined on gristly lamb a stranger entered, a tall, gaunt, sharp-bearded man with the obvious aura of a jaunter. Reichenbach did not fail to notice the rebirth of light in Ilsabet's eyes, and the barely perceptible inclining-forward of her body as the stranger approached their table was amply perceptible to him. The newcomer knew them for what they were, naturally, and invited himself to join them. His name was Stavanger; he had been on his jaunt just a few days; he meant to see everything, *everything*, before his time was up. Not for many years had Reichenbach felt such jealousy. He was wise in these things, and it was not difficult to detect the current flowing from Ilsabet to Stavanger even as he sat there between them. Now he understood why she had no casual amours to report of her jaunts to Paris and Prague. This one was far from casual and would bear no retelling.

In the morning she said, "I still feel operatic. I'll go to Bayreuth tonight—the premiere of *Götterdämmerung*."

Despising himself, he said, "A capital idea. I'll accompany you."

She looked disconcerted. "But music bores you!"

"A flaw in my character. Time I began to remedy it."

The fitful panic in Ilsabet's eyes gave way to cool and chilling calmness. "Another time, dear love. I prize my solitude. I'll make this little trip without you."

It was all plain to him. Gone now the open sharing; now there were secret rendezvous and an unwanted third player of their game. He could not bear it. In anguish he made his own arrangements and jaunted to Bayreuth in thick red wig and curling beard, and there she was, seated beside Stavanger in the Festspielhaus as the subterranean orchestra launched into the first notes. Reichenbach did not remain for the performance.

Stavanger now crossed their path openly and with great frequency. They met him at the siege of Constantinople, at the San Francisco earthquake, and at a fete at Versailles. This was more than coincidence, and Reichenbach said so to Ilsabet. "I suggested he follow some of our itinerary," she admitted. "He's a lonely man, jaunting alone. And quite charming. But of course if you dislike him, we can simply vanish without telling him where we're going, and he'll never find us again."

A disarming tactic, Reichenbach thought. It was impossible for her to admit to him that she and Stavanger were lovers, for there was too much substance to their affair; so instead she pretended he was a pitiful forlorn wanderer in need of company. Reichenbach was outraged. Fidelity was not part of his unspoken compact with her, and she was free to slip off to any era she chose for a tryst with Stavanger. But that she chose to conceal what was going on was deplorable, and that she was finding pretexts to drag Stavanger along on their travels, puncturing the privacy of their own rapport for the sake of a few smug stolen glances, was impermissible. Reichenbach was convinced now that Ilsabet and Stavanger were co-temporals, though he knew he had no rational basis for that idea; it simply seemed right to him, a final torment, the two of them now laying the groundwork for a realtime relationship that excluded him. Whether or not that was true, it was unbearable. Reichenbach was astounded by the intensity of his jealous fury. Yet it was a true emotion and one he would not attempt to repress. The joy he had known with Ilsabet had been unique, and Stavanger had tainted it.

He found himself searching for ways to dispose of his rival.

Merely whirling Ilsabet off elsewhen would achieve nothing. She would find ways of catching up with her paramour somewhen along the line. And if Ilsabet and Stavanger were co-temporal, and she and Reichenbach were not—no, no, Stavanger had to be expunged. Reichenbach, a stable and temperate man, had never imagined himself capable of such criminality; a bit of elitist regulation-bending was all he had ever allowed himself. But he had never been faced with the loss of an Ilsabet before, either.

In Borgia, Italy, Reichenbach hired a Florentine prisoner to do Stavanger in with a dram of nightshade.

But the villain pocketed Reichenbach's down payment and disappeared without a care for the ducats due him on completion of the job. In the chaotic aftermath of the Ides of March, Reichenback attempted to finger Stavanger as one of Caesar's murderers, but no one paid attention. Nor did he have luck denouncing him to the Inquisition one afternoon in 1485 in Torquemada's Castile, though even the most perfunctory questioning would have given sufficient proof of Stavanger's alliance with diabolical powers. Perhaps it would be necessary, Reichenbach concluded morosely, to deal with Stavanger with his own hands, repellent though that alternative was.

Not only was it repellent, it could be dangerous. He was without experience at serious crime, and Stavanger, cold-eyed and suave, promised to be a formidable adversary. Reichenbach needed an ally, an adviser, a collaborator. But who? While he and Ilsabet were making the circuit of the Seven Wonders, he puzzled over it, from Ephesus to Halicarnassus to Gizeh, and as they stood in the shadow of the Colossus of Rhodes, the answer came to him. There was only one person he could trust sufficiently, and that person was himself.

To Ilsabet he said, "Do you know where I want to go next?"

"We still have the Hanging Gardens of Babylon, the Lighthouse of Alexandria, the Statue of Zeus at—"

"No, I'm not talking about the Seven Wonders tour. I want to go back to Sarajevo, Ilsabet."

"Sarajevo? Whatever for?"

"A sentimental pilgrimage, love, to the place of our first meeting."

"But Sarajevo was a bore. And—"

"We could make it exciting. Consider: our earlier selves would already be there. We would watch them meet, find each other well matched, become lovers. Here for months we've been touring the great events of history, when we're neglecting a chance to witness our own personal greatest event." He smiled wickedly. "And there are other possibilities. We could introduce ourselves to them. Hint at the joys that lie ahead of them. Perhaps even seduce them, eh? A nice kinky quirky business that would be. And—"

"No," she said. "I don't like it."

"You find the idea improper? Morally offensive?"

"Don't be an idiot. I find it dangerous."

"How so?"

"We aren't supposed to reenter a time-span where we're already present. There must be some good reason for that. The rules—"

"The rules," he said, "are made by timid old sods who've never moved beyond the terminator in their lives. The rules are meant to guide us, not to control us. The rules are meant to be broken by those who are smart enough to avoid the consequences."

She stared somberly at him a long while. "And are you?"

"I think I am."

"Yes. A shrewd man, a superior man, a member of the elite corps that lives on the far side of society's bell-shaped curve. Eh? Doing as you please throughout life. Holding yourself above all restraints. Rich enough and lucky enough to be able to jaunt anywhen you like and behave like a little god."

"You live the same way, I believe."

"In general, yes. But I still won't go with you to Sarajevo."

"Why not?"

"Because I don't know what will happen to me if I do. Kinky and quirky it may be to pile into bed with our other selves, but something about the idea troubles me, and I dislike needless risk. Do you believe you understand paradox theory fully?"

"Does anybody?"

"Exactly. It isn't smart to—"

"Paradoxes are much overrated, don't you think? We're in the fluid zone, Ilsabet. Anything goes, this side of the terminator. If I were you I wouldn't worry about—"

"*I* am me. I worry. If I were you, I'd worry more. Take your Sarajevo trip without me."

He saw she was adamant, and dropped the issue. Indeed, he saw it would be much simpler to make the journey alone. They went on from Rhodes to the Babylon of Nebuchadnezzar, where they spent four happy days untroubled by the shadow of Stavanger; it was the finest time they had had together since Carthage. Then Ilsabet announced she felt the need for another brief solo musicological jaunt—to Mantua in 1607 for Monteverdi's *Orfeo*. Reichenbach offered no objection. The instant she was gone, he set his timer for the twenty-eighth of June, 1914, Sarajevo in Bosnia, 10:27 A.M.

In his Babylonian costume he knew he looked ridiculous or even insane, but it was too chancy to have gone to the halfway house for proper preparation, and he planned to stay here only a few minutes. Moments after he materialized in the narrow cobble-paved alleyway, his younger self appeared, decked out elegantly in natty Edwardian finery. He registered only the most brief quiver of amazement at the sight of another Reichenbach already there.

Reichenbach said, "I have to speak quickly. You will go out there and near the Bank of Austria-Hungary you'll meet the most wonderful woman you've ever known, and you'll share with her the greatest joy you've ever tasted. And just as your love for her reaches its deepest strength, you'll lose her to a rival—unless you cooperate with me to rid us of him before they can ever meet."

The eyes of the other Reichenbach narrowed. "Murder?"

"Removal. We'll put him in the way of harm, and harm will come to him."

"Is the woman such a marvel that the risks are worth it?"

"I swear it. I tell you, you'll suffer pain beyond belief if he isn't eliminated. Trust me. My welfare is your welfare, is this not so?"

"Of course." But the other Reichenbach looked unconvinced. "Still, why must there be two of us in this? It's not yet my affair, after all."

"It will be. He's too slippery to tackle without help. I need you. And ultimately you'll be grateful to me for this. Take it on faith."

"And what if this is some elaborate game, and I the victim?"

"Damn it, *this is no game!* Our happiness is at stake—Yours, mine. We're both in this together. We're closer than any twins could ever be, don't you realize? You and me, different phases of the same person's time-line, following the same path? Our destinies are linked. Help me now or live forever with the torment of the consequences. Please help. *Please.*"

The other was wavering. "You ask a great deal."

"I offer a great deal," Reichenbach said. "Look, there's no more time for talking now. You have to get out there and meet Ilsabet before the archduke's assassination. Meet me in Paris, noon on the twenty-fifth of June, 1794, in the rue de Rivoli outside the Hôtel de Ville." He grasped the other's arm and stared at him with all the intensity and conviction at his command. "Agreed?"

A last moment of hesitation.

"Agreed."

Reichenbach touched his timer and disappeared.

In Babylon again he gathered his possessions and jaunted to the halfway house for the French Revolution. Momentarily he dreaded running into his other self there, a malfeasance that would be hard to justify, but the place was too big for that; the Revolution and Terror spanned five years and an immense service facility was needed to handle the tourist demand. Outfitted in the simple countryfolk clothes appropriate to the revolutionary period, equipped with freshly implanted linguistic skills and proper revolutionary rhetoric, altogether disguised to blend with the citizenry, Reichenbach descended into the terrible heat of that bloody Parisian summer and quickly effected his rendezvous with himself.

The face he beheld was clearly his, and yet unfamiliar, for he was accustomed to his mirror image; but a mirror image is a reversed one, and now he saw himself as others saw him and nothing looked quite right. This is what it must be like to have a twin, he thought. In a low, hoarse voice he said, "She's coming tomorrow to hear Robespierre's final speech and then to see his execution. Our enemy is in Paris already, with rooms at the Hôtel Brittanique in the rue Guénégaud. I'll track him down while you make contact with the Committee of Public Safety. I'll bring him here; you arrange the trap and the denunciation; with any luck he'll be hauled away in the same tumbril that takes Robespierre to the guillotine. D'accord?"

"D'accord." A radiance came into the other's eyes. Softly he said, "You were right about Ilsabet. For such a woman even this is justifiable."

Reichenbach felt an unexpected pang. But to be jealous of himself was an absurdity. "Where have you been with her?"

"After Sarajevo, Nero's Rome. She's asleep there now, our third night: I intend to be gone only an instant. We go next to Shakespeare's time, and then—"

"Yes, I know. Socrates, Magellan, Vasco da Gama. All the best still lies ahead for you. But first there's work to do."

Without great difficulty he found his way to the Hôtel Brittanique, a modest place not far from the Pont Neuf. The concierge, a palsied woman with a thin-lipped mouth fixed in an unchanging scowl, offered little aid until Reichenbach spoke of the committee, the Law of Suspects, the dangers of refusing to cooperate with the revolutionary tribunal; then she was quick enough to admit that a dark man of great height with a beard of just the sort that M'sieu described was living on the fifth floor, a certain M. Stavanger. Reichenbach rented the adjoining room. He waited there an hour, until he heard the footsteps in the hallway, sounds next door.

He went out and knocked.

Stavanger peered blankly at him. "Yes?"

He has not yet met her, Reichenbach thought. He has not yet spoken with her, he has not yet touched her body, they have not yet gone to their damned operas together. And never will.

He said, "This is a wonderful place for a jaunt, isn't it?"

"Who are you?"

"Reichenbach is my name. My friend and I saw you in the street and she sent me up to speak with you." He made a little self-deprecating gesture. "I often act as her—ah—go-between. She wishes to know if you'll meet her this afternoon and perhaps enjoy a day or two of French history with her. Her name is Ilsabet, and I can testify that you'll find her charming. Her particular interests are assassinations, architecture, and the first performances of great operas."

Stavanger showed sudden alertness. "Opera is a great passion of mine," he said. "Ordinarily I keep to myself when jaunting, but in this case—the possibilities—is she downstairs? Can you bring her to me?"

"Ah, no. She's waiting in front of the Hôtel de Ville."

"And wants me to come to her?"

Reichenbach nodded. "Certain protocols are important to her."

Stavanger, after a moment's consideration, said, "Take me to your Ilsabet, then. But I make no promises. Is that understood?"

"Of course," said Reichenbach.

The streets were almost empty at this hour. The miasma of the atmosphere in this heavy heat must be a factor in that, Reichenbach thought, and also that it was midday and the Parisians were at their *déjeuner;* but beyond that it seemed that the city was suffering a desolation of the spirit, a paralysis of energy under the impact of the monstrous bloodletting of recent months.

He walked quickly, struggling to keep up with Stavanger's long strides. As they approached the Hôtel de Ville, Reichenbach caught sight of his other self, and with him two or three men in revolutionary costume. Good. Good. The other Reichenbach nodded. Everything was arranged. The challenge now was to keep Stavanger from going for his timer the moment he sensed he was in jeopardy.

"Where is she?" Stavanger asked.

"I left her speaking with that group of men," said Reichenbach. The other Reichenbach stood with his face turned aside—a wise move. Now, though they had not rehearsed it, they moved as if parts of a single organism, the other Reichenbach pivoting, pointing, crying out, "I accuse that man of crimes against liberty," while in the same instant Reichenbach stepped behind Stavanger, thrust his arms up past those of the taller man, reached into Stavanger's loose tunic to wrench his timer into ruin with one quick twist, and held him firmly. Stavanger bellowed and tried to break free, but in a moment the street was full of men who seized and overpowered him and dragged him away. Reichenbach, panting, sweating, looked in triumph toward his other self.

"That one, too," said the other Reichenbach.

Reichenbach blinked. "What?"

Too late. They had his arms; the other Reichenbach was groping for his timer, seizing, tearing. Reichenbach fought ferociously, but they bore him to the ground and knelt on his chest.

Through a haze of fear and pain he heard the other saying, "This man is the proscribed aristocrat Charles Evrémonde, called Darnay, enemy of the Republic, member of a family of tyrants. I denounce him for having used his privileges in the oppression of the people."

"He will face the tribunal tonight," said the one kneeling on Reichenbach.

Reichenbach said in a shocked voice, "What are you doing?"

The other crouched close to him and replied in English. "We have been duplicated, you see. Why do you think there are rules against entering a time where one is already present? There's room for only one of us back in realtime, is that not so? So, then, how can we both return?"

Reichenbach said, with a gasp, "But that isn't true!"

"Isn't it? Are you sure? Do you really comprehend all the paradoxes?"

"Do *you*? How can you do this to me, when I—when I'm—"

"You disappoint me, not seeing these intricacies. I would have expected more from one of us. But you must have been too muddled by jealousy to think straight. Do you imagine I dare run the risk of letting you jaunt around on the loose? Which of us is to have Ilsabet, after all?"

Already Reichenbach felt the blade hurtling toward his neck.

"Wait—wait—" he cried. "Look at him! His face is mine! We are brothers, twins! If I'm an aristocrat, what is he? I denounce him too! Seize him and try him with me!"

"There is indeed a strange resemblance between you two," said one of those holding Reichenbach.

The other smiled. "We have often been taken for brothers. But there is no kinship between us. He is the aristocrat Evrémond, citizens. And I, I am only poor Sydney Carton, a person of no consequence or significance whatever, happy to have been of service to the people." He bowed and walked away, and in a moment was gone.

Safe beside Ilsabet in Nero's Rome, Reichenbach thought bitterly.

"Come. Up with him and bring him to trial," someone called. "The tribunal has no time to waste these days."

The Pope of the Chimps

Early last month Vendelmans and I were alone with the chimps in the compound when suddenly he said, "I'm going to faint." It was a sizzling May morning, but Vendelmans had never shown any sign of noticing unusual heat, let alone suffering from it. I was busy talking to Leo and Mimsy and Mimsy's daughter Muffin, and I registered Vendelmans's remark without doing anything about it. When you're intensely into talking by sign language, as we are in the project, you sometimes tend not to pay a lot of attention to spoken words.

But then Leo began to sign the trouble sign at me, and I turned around and saw Vendelmans down on his knees in the grass, white-faced, gasping, covered with sweat. A few of the chimpanzees who aren't as sensitive to humans as Leo is thought it was a game and began to pantomime him, knuckles to the ground and bodies going limp. "Sick—" Vendelmans said. "Feel—terrible—"

I called for help, and Gonzo took his left arm and Kong took his right and somehow, big as he was, we managed to get him out of the compound and up the hill to headquarters. By then he was complaining about sharp pains in his back and under his arms, and I realized that it wasn't just heat prostration. Within a week the diagnosis was in.

Leukemia.

They put him on chemotherapy and hormones, and after ten days he was back with the project, looking cocky. "They've stabilized it," he told everyone. "It's in remission and I might have ten or twenty years left, or even more. I'm going to carry on with my work."

But he was gaunt and pale, with a tremor in his hands, and it was a frightful thing to have him among us. He might have been fooling himself, though I doubted it, but he wasn't fooling any of us: to us he was a memento mori, a walking death's-head-and-crossbones. That laymen think scientists are any more casual about such things than anyone else is something I blame Hollywood for. It is not easy to go about your daily work with a dying man at your side—or a dying man's wife, for Judy Vendelmans showed in her frightened eyes all the grief that Hal Vendelmans himself was repressing. She was going to lose a beloved husband unexpectedly soon and she hadn't had time to adjust to it and her pain was impossible to ignore. Besides, the nature of Vendelmans's dyingness was particularly unsettling because he had been so big and robust and outgoing, a true Rabelaisian figure, and somehow between one moment and the next he was transformed into a wraith. "The finger of God," Dave Yost said. "A quick flick of Zeus's pinkie and Hal shrivels like cellophane in a fireplace." Vendelmans was not yet forty.

The chimps suspected something, too.

Some of them, such as Leo and Ramona, are fifth-generation signers, bred for alpha intelligence, and they pick up subtleties and nuances very well. "Almost human," visitors like to say of them. We dislike that tag, because the important thing about chimpanzees is that they *aren't* human, that they are an alien intelligent species; but yet I know what people mean. The brightest of the chimps saw right away that something was amiss with Vendelmans, and started making odd remarks. "Big one rotten banana," said Ramona to Mimsy while I was nearby. "He getting empty," Leo said to me as

Vendelmans stumbled past us. Chimp metaphors never cease to amaze me. And Gonzo asked him outright: "You go away soon?"

"Go away" is not the chimp euphemism for death. So far as our animals know, no human being has ever died. Chimps die. Human beings go away. We have kept things on that basis from the beginning, not intentionally at first, but such arrangements have a way of institutionalizing themselves. The first member of the group to die was Roger Nixon, in an automobile accident in the early years of the project long before my time here, and apparently no one wanted to confuse or disturb the animals by explaining what had happened to him, so no explanations were offered. My second or third year here, Tim Lippinger was killed in a ski-lift failure, and again it seemed easier not to go into details with them. And by the time of Will Bechstein's death in that helicopter crack-up four years ago the policy was explicit: we chose not to regard his disappearance from the group as death, but mere going away, as if he had only retired. The chimps do understand death, of course. They may even equate it with going away, as Gonzo's question suggests. But if they do, they surely see human death as something quite different from chimpanzee death—a translation to another state of being, an ascent on a chariot of fire. Yost believes that they have no comprehension of human death at all, that they think we are immortal, that they think we are gods.

Vendelmans now no longer pretends that he isn't dying. The leukemia is plainly acute, and he deteriorates physically from day to day. His original this-isn't-actually-happening attitude has been replaced by a kind of sullen, angry acceptance. It is only the fourth week since the onset of the ailment and soon he'll have to enter the hospital.

And he wants to tell the chimps that he's going to die.

"They don't know that human beings can die," Yost said.

"Then it's time they found out," Vendelmans snapped. "Why perpetuate a load of mythological bullshit about us? Why let them think we're gods? Tell them outright that I'm going to die, the way old Egbert died and Salami and Mortimer."

"But they all died naturally," Jan Morton said.

"And I'm not dying naturally?"

She became terribly flustered. "Of old age, I mean. Their life cycles clearly and understandably came to an end and they died and the chimps understood it. Whereas you—" She faltered.

"—am dying a monstrous and terrible death midway through my life," Vendelmans said, and started to break down and recovered with a fierce effort, and Jan began to cry, and it was generally a bad scene from which Vendelmans saved us by going on, "It should be of philosophical importance to the project to discover how the chimps react to a revaluation of the human metaphysic. We've ducked every chance we've had to help them understand the nature of mortality. Now I propose we use me to teach them that humans are subject to the same laws they are. That we are not gods."

"And that gods exist," said Yost, "who are capricious and unfathomable and to whom we ourselves are as less than chimps."

Vendelmans shrugged. "They don't need to hear all that now. But it's time they understood what we are. Or rather, it's time that we learned how much they already understand. Use my death as a way of finding out. It's the first time they've been in the presence of a human who's actually in the process of dying. The other times one of us has died, it's always been in some sort of accident."

Burt Christensen said, "Hal, have you already told them anything about—"

"No," Vendelmans said. "Of course not. Not a word. But I see them talking to each other. They know."

* * *

We discussed it far into the night. The questions needed careful examination because of the far-reaching consequences of any change we might make in the metaphysical givens of our animals. These chimps have lived in a closed environment here for decades, and the culture they have evolved is a product of what we have chosen to teach them, compounded by their own innate chimpness plus whatever we have unknowingly transmitted to them about ourselves or them. Any radical conceptual material we offer them must be weighed thoughtfully, because its effects will be irreversible, and those who succeed us in this community will be unforgiving if we do anything stupidly premature. If the plan is to observe a community of intelligent primates over a period of many human generations, studying the changes in their intellectual capacity as their linguistic skills increase, then we must at all times take care to let them find things out for themselves, rather than skewing our data by giving the chimps more than their current concept-processing abilities may be able to handle.

On the other hand. Vendelmans was dying right now, allowing us a dramatic opportunity to convey the concept of human mortality. We had at best a week or two to make use of that opportunity: then it might be years before the next chance.

"What are you worried about?" Vendelmans demanded.

Yost said, "Do you fear dying, Hal?"

"Dying makes me angry. I don't fear it; but I still have things to do, and I won't be able to do them. Why do you ask?"

"Because so far as we know the chimps see death—chimp death—as simply part of the great cycle of events, like the darkness that comes after the daylight. But human death is going to come as a revelation to them, a shock. And if they pick up from you any sense of fear or even anger over your dying, who knows what impact that will have on their way of thought?"

"Exactly. *Who knows?* I offer you a chance to find out!"

By a narrow margin, finally we voted to let Hal Vendelmans share his death with the chimpanzees. Nearly all of us had reservations about that. But plainly Vendelmans was determined to have a useful death, a meaningful death; the only way he could face his fate at all was by contributing it like this to the project. And in the end I think most of us cast our votes his way purely out of our love for him.

We rearranged the schedules to give Vendelmans more contact with the animals. There are ten of us, fifty of them; each of us has a special field of inquiry—number theory, syntactical innovation, metaphysical exploration, semiotics, took use, and so on—and we work with chimps of our own choice, subject, naturally, to the shifting patterns of subtribal bonding within the chimp community. But we agreed that Vendelmans would have to offer his revelations to the alpha intelligences—Leo, Ramona, Grimsky, Alice and Attila—regardless of the current structure of the chimp-human dialogues. Leo, for instance, was involved in an ongoing interchange with Beth Rankin on the notion of the change of seasons. Beth more or less willingly gave up her time with Leo to Vendelmans, for Leo was essential in this. We learned long ago that anything important had to be imparted to the alphas first, and they will impart it to the others. A bright chimp knows more about teaching things to his duller cousins than the brightest human being.

The next morning Hal and Judy Vendelmans took Leo, Ramona and Attila aside and held a long conversation with them. I was busy in a different part of the compound with Gonzo, Mimsy, Muffin, and Chump, but I glanced over occasionally to see what was going on. Hal looked radiant—like Moses just down from the mountain after talking with God. Judy was trying to look radiant too, working at it, but her grief kept breaking through: once I saw her turn away from the chimps and press her knuckles to her teeth to hold it back.

Afterward Leo and Grimsky had a conference out by the oak grove. Yost and Charley Damiano watched it with binoculars, but they couldn't make much sense out of it. The chimps, when they sign to each other, use modified gestures much less precise than the ones they use with us; whether this marks the evolution of a special chimp-to-chimp argot designed not to be understood by us, or is simply a factor of chimp reliance on supplementary nonverbal ways of communicating, is something we still don't know, but the fact remains that we have trouble comprehending the sign language they use with each other, particularly the form the alphas use. Then, too, Leo and Grimsky kept wandering in and out of the trees, as if perhaps they knew we were watching them and didn't want us to eavesdrop. A little later in the day, Ramona and Alice had the same sort of meeting. Now all five of our alphas must have been in on the revelation.

Somehow the news began to filter down to the rest of them.

We weren't able to observe actual concept tramsmission. We did notice that Vendelmans, the next day, began to get rather more attention than normal. Little troops of chimpanzees formed about him as he moved— slowly, and in obvious difficulty—about the compound. Gonzo and Chump, who had been bickering for months, suddenly were standing side by side staring intently at Vendelmans. Chicory, normally shy, went out of her way to engage him in a conversation—about the ripeness of the apples on the tree, Vendelmans reported. Anna Livia's young twins, Shem and Shaun, climbed up and sat on Vendelmans's shoulders.

"They want to find out what a dying god is really like," Yost said quietly.

"But look there," Jan Morton said.

Judy Vendelmans had an entourage too: Mimsy, Muffin, Claudius, Buster, and Kong. Staring in fascination, eyes wide, lips extended, some of them blowing little bubbles of saliva.

"Do they think she's dying too?" Beth wondered.

Yost shook his head. "Probably not. They can see there's nothing physically wrong with her. But they're picking up the sorrow vibes, the death vibes."

"Is there any reason to think they're aware that Hal is Judy's mate?" Christensen asked.

"It doesn't matter," Yost said. "They can see that she's upset. That interests them, even if they have no way of knowing why Judy would be more upset than any of the rest of us."

"More mysteries out yonder," I said, pointing into the meadow. Grimsky was standing by himself out there, contemplating something. He is the oldest of the chimps, gray-haired, going bald, a deep thinker. He has been there almost from the beginning, more than thirty years, and very little has escaped his attention in that time.

Far off to the left, in the shade of the big beech tree, Leo stood similarly in solitary meditation. He is twenty, the alpha male of the community, the strongest and by far the most intelligent. It was eerie to see the two of them in their individual zones of isolation, like distant sentinels, like Easter Island statues, lost in private reveries.

"Philosophers," Yost murmured.

Yesterday Vendelmans returned to the hospital for good. Before he went, he made his farewells to each of the fifty chimpanzees, even the infants. In the past week he has altered markedly; he is only a shadow of himself, feeble, wasted. Judy says he'll live only another few weeks.

She has gone on leave and probably won't come back until after Hal's death. I wonder what the chimps will make of her "going away," and of her eventual return.

She said that Leo had asked her if she was dying, too. Perhaps things will get back to normal here now.

* * *

Christensen asked me this morning, "Have you noticed the way they seem to drag the notion of death into whatever conversation you're having with them these days?"

I nodded. "Mimsy asked me the other day if the moon dies when the sun comes up and the sun dies when the moon is out. It seemed like such a standard primitive metaphor that I didn't pick up on it at first. But Mimsy's too young for using metaphor that easily and she isn't particularly clever. The older ones must be talking about dying a lot, and it's filtering down."

"Chicory was doing subtraction with me." Christensen said. "She signed, *You take five, two die, you have three.'* Later she turned it into a verb: *'Three die one equals two.'"*

Others reported similar things. Yet none of the animals were talking about Vendelmans and what was about to happen to him, nor were they asking any overt questions about death or dying. So far as we were able to perceive, they had displaced the whole thing into metaphorical diversions. That in itself indicated a powerful obsession. Like most obsessives, they were trying to hide the thing that most concerned them, and they probably thought they were doing a good job of it. It isn't their fault that we're able to guess what's going on in their minds. They are, after all—and we sometimes have to keep reminding ourselves of this—only chimpanzees.

They are holding meetings on the far side of the oak grove, where the little stream runs. Leo and Grimsky seem to do most of the talking, and the others gather around and sit very quietly as the speeches are made. The groups run from ten to thirty chimps at a time. We are unable to discover what they're discussing, though of course we have an idea. Whenever one on us approaches such a gathering, the chimps very casually drift off into three or four separate groups and look exceedingly innocent—"We just out for some fresh air, boss."

Charley Damiano wants to plant a bug in the grove. But how do you spy on a group that converses only in sign language? Cameras aren't as easily hidden as microphones.

We do our best with binoculars. But what little we've been able to observe has been mystifying. The chimp-to-chimp signs they use at these meetings are even more oblique and confusing than the ones we had seen earlier. It's as if they're holding their meetings in pig-Latin, or double-talk or in some entirely new and private language.

Two technicians will come tomorrow to help us mount cameras in the grove.

Hal Vendelmans died last night. According to Judy, who phoned Dave Yost, it was very peaceful right at the end, an easy release. Yost and I broke the news to the alpha chimps just after breakfast. No euphemisms, just the straight news. Ramona made a few hooting sounds and looked as if she might cry, but she was the only one who seemed emotionally upset. Leo gave me a long deep look of what was almost certainly compassion, and then he hugged me very hard. Grimsky wandered away and seemed to be signing to himself in the new system. Now a meeting seems to be assembling in the oak grove, the first one in more than a week.

The cameras are in place. Even if we can't decipher the new signs, we can at least tape them and subject them to computer analysis until we begin to understand.

Now we've watched the first tapes of a grove meeting, but I can't say we know a lot more than we did before.

For one thing, they disabled two of the cameras right at the outset. Attila spotted them and sent Gonzo and Claudius up into the trees to yank them out. I suppose the remaining cameras went unnoticed; but by accident or deliberate diabolical craftiness, the chimps positioned themselves in such a way that none of the cameras had a clear angle. We did record a few statements from Leo and some give-and-take between Alice and Anna Livia. They spoke in a mixture of standard signs and the new ones, but, without a sense of the context, we've found it impossible to generate any sequence of meanings. Stray signs such as "shirt," "hat," "human," "change" and "banana fly," interspersed with undecipherable stuff, *seem* to be adding up to something, but no one is sure what. We observed no mention of Hal Vendelmans nor any direct references to death. We may be misleading ourselves entirely about the significance of all this.

Or perhaps not. We codified some of the new signs, and this afternoon I asked Ramona what one of them meant. She fidgeted and hooted and looked uncomfortable—and not simply because I was asking her to do a tough abstract thing like giving a definition. She was worried. She looked around for Leo, and when she saw him she made that sign at him. He came bounding over and shoved Ramona away. Then he began to tell me how wise and good and gentle I am. He may be a genius, but even a genius chimp is still a chimp, and I told him I wasn't fooled by all his flattery. Then I asked *him* what the new sign meant.

"Jump high come again," Leo signed.

A simple chimpy phrase referring to fun and frolic? So I thought at first, and so did many of my colleagues. But Dave Yost said, "Then why was Ramona so evasive about defining it?"

"Defining isn't easy for them," Beth Rankin said.

"Ramona's one of the five brightest. She's capable of it. Especially since the sign can be defined by use of four other established signs, as Leo proceeded to do."

"What are you getting at, Dave?" I asked.

Yost said, "'*Jump high come again*' might be about a game they like to play, but it could also be an eschatological reference, sacred talk, a concise metaphorical way to speak of death and resurrection, no?"

Mick Falkenburg snorted. "Jesus, Dave, of all the nutty Jesuitical bullshit—"

"Is it?"

"It's possible sometimes to be too subtle in your analysis," Falkenburg said. "You're suggesting that these chimpanzees have a theology?"

"I'm suggesting that they may be in the process of evolving a religion," Yost replied.

Can it be?

Sometimes we lose our perspective with these animals, as Mick indicated, and we overestimate their intelligence; but just as often, I think, we underestimate them.

Jump high come again.

I wonder. Secret sacred talk? A chimpanzee theology? Belief in life after death? A religion?

They know that human beings have a body of ritual and belief that they call religion, though how much they really comprehend about it is hard to tell. Dave Yost, in his metaphysical discussions with Leo and some of the other alphas, introduced the concept long ago. He drew a hierarchy that began with God and ran downward through human beings and chimpanzees to dogs and cats and onward to insects and frogs, by way of giving the chimps some sense of the great chain of life. They had seen bugs and frogs and cats and dogs, but they wanted Dave to show them God, and he was forced to tell them that God is not actually tangible and accessible, but lives high overhead although His essence penetrates all things. I doubt that they grasped much of that. Leo, whose nimble and probing intelligence is a constant illumination to us, wanted Yost to explain how we talked to God and how God talked to us if He wasn't around to make signs, and Yost said that we had a thing called religion, which was a system of communicating with God. And that was where he left it, a long while back.

Now we are on guard for any indications of a developing religious consciousness among our troop. Even the scoffers—Mick Falkenburg, Beth, to some degree, Charley Damiano—are paying close heed. After all, one of the underlying purposes of this project is to reach an understanding of how the first hominids managed to cross the intellectual boundary that we like to think separates the animals from humanity. We can't reconstruct a bunch of Australopithecines and study them; but we *can* watch chimpanzees who have been given the gift of language build a quasi-protohuman society, and it is the closest thing to traveling back in time that we are apt to achieve. Yost thinks, I think, Burt Christensen is beginning to think, that we have inadvertently kindled an awareness of the divine, of the numinous force that must be worshipped, by allowing them to see that their gods—us—can be struck down and slain by an even higher power.

The evidence so far is slim. The attention given Vendelmans and Judy; the solitary meditations of Leo and Grimsky; the large gatherings in the grove; the greatly accelerated use of modified sign language in chimp-to-chimp talk at those gatherings; the potentially eschatological reference we think we see in the sign that Leo translated as "jump high come again." That's it. To those of us who want to interpret that as the foundations of religion, it seems indicative of what we want to see; to the rest, it all looks like coincidence and fantasy. The problem is that we are dealing with nonhuman intelligence and we must take care not to impose our own thought-constructs. We can never be certain if we are operating from a value system anything like that of the chimps. The built-in ambiguities of the sign-language grammar we must use with them complicate the issue. Consider the phrase "banana fly" that Leo used in a speech—a sermon?—in the oak grove, and remember Ramona's reference to the sick Vendelmans as "rotten banana." If we take *fly* to be a verb, "banana fly" might be considered a metaphorical description of Vendelman's ascent to heaven. If we take it to be a noun, Leo might have been talking about the *Drosophila* flies that feed on decaying fruit, a metaphor for the corruption of the flesh after death. On the other hand, he may simply have been making a comment about the current state of our garbage dump.

We have agreed for the moment not to engage the chimpanzees in any direct interrogation about any of this. The Heisenberg principle is eternally our rule here: the observer can too easily perturb the thing observed, so we must make only the most delicate of measurements. Even so, of course, our presence among the chimps is bound to have its impact, but we do what we can to minimize it by avoiding leading questions and watching in silence.

Two unusual things today. Taken each by each, they would be interesting without being significant; but if we use each to illuminate the other, we begin to see things in a strange new light, perhaps.

One thing is an increase in vocalizing, noticed by nearly everyone, among the chimps. We know that chimpanzees in the wild have a kind of rudimentary spoken language—a greeting call, a defiance call, the grunts that mean "I like the taste of this," the male chimp's territorial hoot, and such—nothing very complex, really not qualitatively much beyond the language of birds and dogs. They also have a fairly rich nonverbal language, a vocabulary of gestures and facial expressions. But it was not until the first experiments decades ago in teaching chimpanzees human sign-language that any important linguistic capacity became apparent in them. Here at the research station the chimps communicate almost wholly in signs, as they have been trained to do for generations and as they have taught their young ones to do; they revert to hoots and grunts only in the most elemental situations. We ourselves communicate mainly in signs when we are talking to each other while working with the chimps, and even in our humans-only conferences, we use signs as much as speech, from long habit. But suddenly the chimps are making sounds at each other. Odd sounds, unfamiliar sounds, weird, clumsy imitations, one might say, of human speech. Nothing that we can understand, naturally: the chimpanzee larynx is simply incapable of duplicating the phonemes humans use. But these new grunts, these tortured blurts of sound, seem intended to mimic our speech. It was Damiano who showed us, as we were watching a tape of a grove session, how Attila was twisting his lips with his hands in what appeared unmistakably to be an attempt to make human sounds come out.

Why?

The second thing is that Leo has started wearing a shirt and a hat. There is nothing remarkable about a chimp in clothing; although we have never encouraged such anthropomorphization here, various animals have taken a fancy from time to time to some item of clothing, have begged it from its owner and have worn it for a few days or even weeks. The novelty here is that the shirt and the hat belonged to Hal Vendelmans, and that Leo wears them only when the chimps are gathered in the oak grove, which Dave Yost has lately begun calling the "holy grove." Leo found them in the toolshed beyond the vegetable garden. The shirt is ten sizes too big, Vendelmans having been so brawny, but Leo ties the sleeves across his chest and lets the rest dangle down over his back almost like a cloak.

What shall we make of this?

Jan is the specialist in chimp verbal processes. At the meeting tonight she said, "It sounds to me as if they're trying to duplicate the rhythms of human speech even though they can't reproduce the actual sounds. They're playing at being human."

"Talking the god-talk," said Dave Yost.

"What do you mean?" Jan asked.

"Chimps talk with their hands. Humans do, too, when speaking with chimps, but when humans talk to humans, they use their voices. Humans are gods to chimps, remember. Talking in the way the gods talk is one way of remaking yourself in the image of the gods, of putting on divine attributes."

"But that's nonsense," Jan said. "I can't possibly—"

"Wearing human clothing," I broke in excitedly,

"would also be a kind of putting on divine attributes, in the most literal sense of the phrase. Especially if the clothes—"

"—had belonged to Hal Vendelmans," said Christensen.

"The dead god," Yost said.

We looked at each other in amazement.

Charley Damiano said, not in his usual skeptical way, but in a kind of wonder, "Dave, are you hypothesizing that Leo functions as some sort of priest, that those are his sacred garments?"

"More than just a priest," Yost said. "A high priest, I think. A pope. The pope of the chimps."

Grimsky is suddenly looking very feeble. Yesterday we saw him moving slowly through the meadow by himself, making a long circuit of the grounds as far out as the pond and the little waterfall, then solemnly and ponderously staggering back to the meeting place at the far side of the grove. Today he has been sitting quietly by the stream, occasionally rocking slowly back and forth, now and then dipping his feet in. I checked the records: he is forty-three years old, well along for a chimp, although some have been known to live fifty years and more. Mick wanted to take him to the infirmary, but we decided against it; if he is dying, and by all appearances he is, we ought to let him do it with dignity in his own way. Jan went down to the grove to visit him and reported that he shows no apparent signs of disease. His eyes are clear; his face feels cool. Age has withered him and his time is at hand. I feel an enormous sense of loss, for he has a keen intelligence, a long memory, a shrewd and thoughtful nature. He was the alpha male of the troop for many years, but a decade ago, when Leo came of age, Grimsky abdicated in his favor with no sign of a struggle. Behind Grimsky's grizzled forehead there must lie a wealth of subtle and mysterious perceptions, concepts and insights about which we know practically nothing, and very soon all that will be lost. Let us hope he's managed to teach his wisdom to Leo and Attila and Alice and Ramona.

Today's oddity: a ritual distribution of meat.

Meat is not very important in the diet of chimps, but they do like to have some, and as far back as I can remember, Wednesday has been meat-day here, when we give them a side of beef or some slabs of mutton or something of that sort. The procedure for dividing up the meat betrays the chimps' wild heritage, for the alpha males eat their fill first while the others watch, and then the weaker males beg for a share and are allowed to move in to grab, and finally the females and young ones get the scraps. Today was meat-day. Leo, as usual, helped himself first, but what happened after that was astounding. He let Attila feed, and then told Attila to offer some meat to Grimsky, who is even weaker today and brushed it aside. *Then Leo put on Vendelmans's hat* and began to parcel out scraps of meat to the others. One by one they came up to him in the current order of ranking and went through the standard begging maneuver, hand beneath chin, palm upward, and Leo gave each one a strip of meat.

"Like taking communion," Charley Damiano muttered. "With Leo the celebrant at the Mass."

Unless our assumptions are totally off base, there is a real religion going on here, perhaps created by Grimsky and under Leo's governance. And Hal Vendelmans's faded old blue work hat is the tiara of the pope.

Beth Rankin woke me at dawn and said, "Come fast. They're doing something strange with old Grimsky."

I was up and dressed and awake in a hurry. We have a closed-circuit system now that pipes the events in the grove back to us, and we paused at the screen so that I could see what was going on. Grimsky sat on his knees at the edge of the stream, eyes closed, barely moving. Leon, wearing the hat, was beside him, elaborately tying Vendelmans's shirt over Grimsky's shoulders. A dozen or more of the other adult chimps were squatting in a semicircle in front of them.

Burt Christensen said, "What's going on? Is Leo making Grimsky the assistant pope?"

"I think Leo is giving Grimsky the last rites," I said.

What else could it have been? Leo wore the sacred headdress. He spoke at length using the new signs—the ecclesiastical language, the chimpanzee equivalent of Latin or Hebrew or Sanskrit—and as his oration went on and on, the congregation replied periodically with outbursts of—I suppose—response and approval, some in signs, some with grunting garbled pseudohuman sounds that Dave Yost thought was their version of god-talk. Throughout it all Grimsky was silent and remote, though occasionally he nodded or murmured or tapped both his shoulders in a gesture whose meaning was unknown to us. The ceremony went on for more than an hour. Then Grimsky leaned forward, and Kong and Chump took him by the arms and eased him down until he was lying with his cheek against the ground.

For two, three, five minutes all the chimpanzees were still. At last Leo came forward and removed his hat, setting it on the ground beside Grimsky, and with great delicacy he untied the shirt Grimsky wore. Grimsky did not move. Leo draped the shirt over his own shoulders and donned the hat again.

He turned to the watching chimps and signed, using the old signs that were completely intelligible to us, "Grimsky now be human being."

We stared at each other in awe and astonishment. A couple of us were sobbing. No one could speak.

The funeral ceremony seemed to be over. The chimps were dispersing. We saw Leo sauntering away, hat casually dangling from one hand, the shirt in the other, trailing over the ground. Grimsky alone remained by the stream. We waited ten minutes and went down to the grove. Grimsky seemed to be sleeping very peacefully, but he was dead, and we gathered him up—Burt and I carried him; he seemed to weigh almost nothing—and took him back to the lab for the autopsy.

In mid-morning the sky darkened and lightning leaped across the hills to the north. There was a tremendous crack of thunder almost instantly and sudden tempestuous rain. Jan pointed to the meadow. The male chimps were doing a bizarre dance, roaring, swaying, slapping their feet against the ground, hammering their hands against the trunks of the trees, ripping off branches and flailing the earth with them. Grief? Terror? Joy at the translation of Grimsky to a divine state? Who could tell? I had never been frightened by our animals before—I knew them too well, I regarded them as little hairy cousins—but now they were terrifying creatures and this was a scene out of time's dawn, as Gonzo and Kong and Attila and Chump and Buster and Claudius and even Pope Leo himself went thrashing about in that horrendous rain, pounding out the steps of some unfathomable rite.

The lightning ceased and the rain moved southward as quickly as it had come, and the dancers went slinking away, each to his favorite tree. By noon the day was bright and warm and it was as though nothing out of the ordinary had happened.

Two days after Grimsky's death I was awakened again at dawn, this time by Mick Falkenburg. He shook my shoulder and yelled at me to wake up, and as I sat there blinking he said, "Chicory's dead! I was out for an early walk and I found her near the place where Grimsky died."

"Chicory? But she's only—"

"Eleven, twelve, something like that. I know."

I put my clothes on while Mick woke the others, and we went down to the stream. Chicory was sprawled out, but not peacefully—there was a dribble of blood at the corner of her mouth, her eyes were wide and horrified, her hands were curled into frozen talons. All about her in the moist soil of the stream bank were footprints. I searched my memory for an instance of murder in the chimp community and could find nothing remotely like it—quarrels, yes, and lengthy feuds and some ugly ambushes and battles, fairly violent, serious injuries now and then. But this had no precedent.

"Ritual murder," Yost murmured.

"Or a sacrifice, perhaps?" suggested Beth Rankin.

"Whatever it is," I said, "they're learning too fast. Recapitulating the whole evolution of religion, including the worst parts of it. We'll have to talk to Leo."

"Is that wise?" Yost asked.

"Why not?"

"We've kept hands off so far. If we want to see how this thing unfolds—"

"During the night," I said, "the pope and the college of cardinals ganged up on a gentle young female chimp and killed her. Right now they may be off somewhere sending Alice or Ramona or Anna Livia's twins to chimp heaven. I think we have to weigh the value of observing the evolution of chimp religion against the cost of losing irreplaceable members of a unique community. I say we call in Leo and tell him that it's wrong to kill."

"He knows that," said Yost. "He must. Chimps aren't murderous animals."

"Chicory's dead."

"And if they see it as a holy deed?" Yost demanded.

"Then one by one we'll lose our animals, and at the end we'll just have a couple of very saintly survivors. Do you want that?"

We spoke with Leo. Chimps can be sly and they can be manipulative, but even the best of them, and Leo is the Einstein of chimpanzees, does not seem to know how to lie. We asked him where Chicory was and Leo told us that Chicory was now a human being. I felt a chill at that. Grimsky was also a human being, said Leo. We asked him how he knew that they had become human and he said, "They go where Vendelmans go. When human go away, he become god. When chimpanzee go away, he become human. Right?"

"No," we said.

The logic of the ape is not easy to refute. We told him that death comes to all living creatures, that it is natural and holy, but that only God could decide when it was going to happen. God, we said, calls His creatures to Himself one at a time. God had called Hal Vendelmans, God had called Grimsky, God would someday call Leo and all the rest here. But God had not yet called Chicory. Leo wanted to know what was wrong with sending Chicory to Him ahead of time. Did that not improve Chicory's condition? No, we replied. No, it only did harm to Chicory. Chicory would have been much happier living here with us than going to God so soon. Leo did not seem convinced. Chicory, he said, now could talk words with her mouth and wore shoes on her feet. He envied Chicory very much.

We told him that God would be angry if any more chimpanzees died. We told him that *we* would be angry. Killing chimpanzees was wrong, we said. It was not what God wanted Leo to be doing.

"Me talk to God, find out what God wants," Leo said.

We found Buster dead by the edge of the pond this morning, with indications of another ritual murder. Leo coolly stared us down and explained that God had given orders that all chimpanzees were to become human beings as quickly as possible, and this could only be achieved by the means employed on Chicory and Buster.

Leo is confined now in the punishment tank and we have suspended this week's meat distribution. Yost voted against both of those decisions, saying we ran the risk of giving Leo the aura of a religious martyr, which would enhance his already considerable power. But these killings have to stop. Leo knows, of course, that we are upset about them. But if he believes his path is the path of righteousness, nothing we say or do is going to change his mind.

Judy Vendelmans called today. She has put Hal's death fairly well behind her, misses the project, misses the chimps. As gently as I could, I told her what has been going on here. She was silent a very long time—Chicory was one of her favorites, and Judy has had enough grief already to handle for one summer—but finally she said, "I think I know what can be done. I'll be on the noon flight tomorrow."

We found Mimsy dead in the usual way late this afternoon. Leo is still in the punishment tank—the third day. The congregation has found a way to carry out its rites without its leader. Mimsy's death has left me stunned, but we are all deeply affected, virtually unable to proceed with our work. It may be necessary to break up the community entirely to save the animals. Perhaps we can send them to other research centers for a few months, three of them here, five there, until this thing subsides. But what if it doesn't subside? What if the dispersed animals convert others elsewhere to the creed of Leo?"

The first thing Judy said when she arrived was, "Let Leo out. I want to talk with him."

We opened the tank. Leo stepped forth, uneasy, abashed, shading his eyes against the strong light. He glanced at me, at Yost, at Jan, as if wondering which one of us was going to scold him; and then he saw Judy and it was as though he had seen a ghost. He made a hollow rasping sound deep in his throat and backed away. Judy signed hello and stretched out her arms to him. Leo trembled. He was terrified. There was nothing unusual about one of us going on leave and returning after a month or two, but Leo must not have expected Judy ever to return, must in fact have imagined her gone to the same place her husband had gone, and the sight of her shook him. Judy understood all that, obviously, for she quickly made powerful use of it, signing to Leo, "I bring you message from Vendelmans."

"Tell tell tell!"

"Come walk with me," said Judy.

She took him by the hand and led him gently out of the punishment area and into the compound and down the hill toward the meadow. I watched from the top of the hill, the tall, slender woman and the compact, muscular chimpanzee close together, side by side, hand in hand, pausing now to talk, Judy signing and Leo replying in a flurry of gestures, then Judy again for a long time, a brief response from Leo, another cascade of signs from Judy, then Leo squatting, tugging at blades of grass, shaking his head, clapping hand to elbow in his expression of confusion, then to his chin, then taking Judy's hand. They were gone for nearly an hour. The other chimps did not dare approach them. Finally Judy and Leo, hand in hand, came quietly up the hill to headquarters again. Leo's eyes were shining and so were Judy's.

She said, "Everything will be all right now. That's so, isn't it, Leo?"

Leo said, "God is always right."

She made a dismissal sign and Leo went slowly down the hill. The moment he was out of sight, Judy turned away from us and cried a little, just a little; then she asked for a drink; and then she said, "It isn't easy, being God's messenger."

"What did you tell him?" I asked.

"That I had been in heaven visiting Hal. That Hal was looking down all the time and he was very proud of Leo, except for one thing, that Leo was sending too many chimpanzees to God too soon. I told him that God was not yet ready to receive Chicory and Buster and Mimsy, that they would have to be kept in storage cells for a long time until their true time came, and that was not good for them. I told him that Hal wanted Leo to know that God hoped he would stop sending him chimpanzees. Then I gave Leo Hal's old wristwatch to wear when he conducts services, and Leo promised he would obey Hal's wishes. That was all. I suspect I've added a whole new layer of mythology to what's developing here, and I trust you won't be angry with me for doing it. I don't believe any more chimps will be killed. And I think I'd like another drink."

Later in the day we saw the chimps assembled by the stream. Leo held his arm aloft and sunlight blazed from the band of gold on his slim hairy wrist, and a great outcry of grunts in god-talk went up from the congregation and they danced before him, and then he donned the sacred hat and the sacred shirt and moved his arms eloquently in the secret sacred gestures of the holy sign language.

There have been no more killings. I think no more will occur. Perhaps after a time our chimps will lose interest in being religious, and go on to other pastimes. But not yet, not yet. The ceremonies continue, and grow ever more elaborate, and we are compiling volumes of extraordinary observations, and God looks down and is pleased. And Leo proudly wears the emblems of his papacy as he bestows his blessing on the worshipers in the holy grove.

The Changeling

In Memoriam: PKD

Just as the startling facade of the Temple of Quetzal-coatl came into view on the far side of the small pyramid, Hilgard felt a sudden touch of vertigo and swayed for a moment, as though a little earthquake had rippled through the Teotihuacan archaelogical zone. He leaned against a railing until the worst of the queasiness and confusion had passed. The heat? The altitude? Last night's fiery dinner exacting its price? Down here in Mexico a tourist learned to expect that some kind of internal upset could strike at any time.

But the discomfort vanished as quickly as it had come, and Hilgard looked up in awe at the great stone staircase of the temple. The jutting heads of the feathered serpents burst like the snouts of dinosaurs from the massive blocks. Traces of the original frescoes, perhaps fifteen hundred years old, glinted here and there. Hilgard took eight or nine photos. But he was too hot and dusty and weary to explore the wondrous building with any real vigor, and he still felt a little shaky from that dizzy spell a moment ago. The pressure of time was on him also: he had promised to meet his driver at two o'clock at the main parking lot for the return trip to Mexico City. It was nearly two now, and the parking area was at least a mile to the north, along the searing,

48

shadeless thoroughfare known as the Avenue of the
Dead. He wished now that he had started his tour here
at the awesome Quetzalcoatl Temple instead of consum-
ing his morning's energy scrambling around on the two
huge pyramids at the other end.

Too late to do anything about that. Hilgard trudged
quickly toward the parking lot, pausing only to buy a
tepid beer from a vendor midway along the path. By
quarter past two he was in the lot, sweaty and puffing.
There was no sign of his driver and the battered black
cab. Still at lunch, probably, Hilgard thought, relieved at
not having to feel guilty about his own tardiness but
annoyed by yet another example of Mexican punctual-
ity. Well, now he had time to get a few more shots of the
Pyramid of the Sun while he waited, and maybe—

"Señor? Señor!"

Hilgard turned. A driver—not his—had emerged
from a shiny little Volkswagen cab and was waving to
him.

"Your wife, señor, she will be here in two more
minutes. She is taking more pictures on the top of the
big pyramid, and she says to please wait, she will not be
long."

"I think you want someone else," Hilgard said.

The driver looked baffled. "But you are her husband,
señor."

"Sorry. I am not anybody's husband."

"Is a joke? I am not understanding." The driver
grinned uncertainly. "A blonde woman, dark glasses. I
pick you and she up in front of the Hotel Century, Zona
Rosa, ten o'clock this morning, you remember? She said
to me, ten minutes ago, tell my husband wait a little, I
go take more pyramid pictures, just a few minutes. And—"

"I'm staying at the Hotel Presidente," Hilgard said.
"I'm not married. I drove out here this morning in a
black Ford cab. The driver's name was Chucho."

The Mexican's grin, earnest and ingratiating, stayed
on his face, but it grew ragged, and something hostile
came into his eyes, as though he was beginning to think

he was being made the butt of some incomprehensible gringo prank. Slowly he said, "I know Chucho, yes. He took some American people down to Xochimilco this morning. Maybe he was your driver yesterday."

"He met me outside the Presidente. We arranged it last night. The fare was seventeen hundred pesos." Hilgard glanced around, wishing the man would show up before things got even more muddled. "You must be mistaking me for a different American. I'm traveling alone. I wouldn't mind meeting an interesting blonde, I guess, but I don't happen to be married to one, and I really am certain that you're not the driver I was with this morning. I'm very sorry if—"

"There is your wife, señor," said the Mexican coolly.

Hilgard turned. A trim, attractive woman in her late thirties, with short golden hair and an alert, open face, was making her way through the clutter of souvenir stands at the entrance to the parking area. "Ted!" she called. "Here I am!"

He stared blankly. He had never seen her before. As she drew closer he forced a smile and held it in a fixed and rigid way. But what was he supposed to say to her? He didn't even know her name. *Excuse me, ma'am, I'm not actually your husband.* Eh? Was there a television program, he wondered, that went to elaborate lengths to stage complicated hoaxes with hapless, unsuspecting victims, and was he at the center of it? Would they shower him with home appliances and cruise tickets once they were done bewildering him? *Pardon me, ma'am, but I'm not really Ted Hilgard. I'm just someone else of the same name and face.* Yes? No.

She came up to him and said, "You should have climbed it with me. You know what they've been doing up there for the past half hour? They're celebrating the spring equinox with some kind of Aztec rite. Incense, chanting, green boughs, two white doves in a cage that they just liberated. Fascinating stuff, and I got pictures of the whole thing. Hold this for me for a minute, will you?" she said casually, slipping her heavy camera bag from her shoulder and pushing it into his hands. "God, it's hot today! Did you have fun at the other temple? I just didn't feel like hiking all the way down there, but I hope I didn't miss—"

The driver, standing to one side, now said mildly, "It is getting late, Missus. We go back to the city now?"

"Yes. Of course." She tucked a stray shirttail back into her slacks, took the camera bag from Hilgard and followed the driver toward the Volkswagen cab. Hilgard, mystified, stayed where he was, scanning the parking lot hopelessly for Chucho and the old black Ford and trying to construct some plausible course of action. After a moment the blonde woman looked back, frowning, and said, "Ted? What's the matter?"

He made an inarticulate sound and fluttered his hands in confusion. Possibly, he told himself, he was having some sort of psychotic episode of fugue. Or perhaps that moment of dizziness at the Temple of Quetzalcoatl had in fact been a light stroke that had scrambled his memory. Could she really be his wife? He felt quite certain that he had been single all his life, except for those eight months a dozen years ago with Beverly. He could clearly envision his bachelor flat on Third Avenue, the three neat rooms, the paintings, the little cabinet of pre-Columbian statuettes. He saw himself at his favorite restaurants with his several lovers, Judith or Janet or Denise. This brisk, jaunty blonde woman fit nowhere into those images. But yet—yet—

He had no idea what to do. His fingers began to tremble and his feet felt like blocks of frozen mud, and he started to walk in a numbed, dazed way toward the Volkswagen. The driver, holding the door open for him, gave him the sort of venomous look of contempt that Hilgard imagined was generally given to gringos who were so drunk at midday that they were unable to remember they were married. But Hilgard was not drunk.

The woman chattered pleasantly as they zipped back toward Mexico City. Evidently they were planning to visit the Museum of Anthropology in Chapultepec Park that afternoon, and tomorrow morning they would move on either to Cuernavaca or Guadalajara, depending on which one of them won a low-keyed disagreement that had evidently been going on for several days. Hilgard faked his way through the conversation answering vaguely and remotely and eventually withdrawing from it altogether by pleading fatigue, a touch of the sun. Before long, gray tendrils of smog were drifting toward them: they were at the outskirts of Mexico City. In the relatively light Sunday traffic, the driver roared flamboyantly down the broad Paseo de la Reforma and cut sharply into the Zona Rosa district to deposit them in front of the slender black-and-white tower of the Hotel Century. "Give him a nice tip, darling," the woman said to Hilgard. "We've kept him out longer than we were supposed to."

Hilgard offered the glowering driver a pair of thousand-peso notes, waved away the change, and they went into the hotel. In the small lobby she said, "Get the key, will you? I'll ring for the elevator." Hilgard approached the desk and looked imploringly at the clerk, who said in fluent English, "Good afternoon, Mr. Hilgard. Did you find the pyramids interesting?" and handed him, without being asked, the key to room 177.

This is not happening. Hilgard told himself, thinking of his comfortable room on the seventh floor of the glossy Hotel Presidente. This is a dream. This is a hallucination. He joined the blonde woman in the elevator; she pressed 17 and it began to ascend slowly, pausing dismayingly for a fraction of a second between the tenth and eleventh floors as the power sagged. Room 177 was compact, efficient, with a semicircular double bed and a little bar unit stocked with miniature bottles of liquor, mixers, and such. The woman took a brandy from it and said to him, "Shall I get you a rum, Ted?"

"No. Thank you." He wandered the room. Feminine things all over the bathroom sink, makeup and lotions and whatnot. Matching his-and-hers luggage in the closet. A man's jacket and shirts hanging neatly—not his, but the sort of things he might have owned—a book on the night-table, the new Updike novel. He had read it a few months ago, but in some other edition, apparently, for this had a red jacket and he remembered it as blue.

"I'm going to grab a shower," she said. "Then we go out to get lunch and head over to the museum, okay?"

He looked up. She padded past him to the bathroom, naked; he had a sudden surprising glimpse of small round breasts and dimpled buttocks, and then the door closed. Hilgard waited until he heard the water running, and took her wallet from her open purse. In it he saw the usual credit cards, some travelers' checks, a thick wad of well-worn Mexican banknotes. And a driver's license: Celia Hilgard, thirty-six years old, five feet five, blond hair, blue eyes, 124 pounds, married. *Married.* An address on East 85th Street. A card in the front of the wallet declared that in case of emergency Theodore Hilgard was to be notified, either at the East 85th Street address or at the offices of Hilgard & Hilgard on West 57th Street. Hilgard studied the card as though it were written in Sanskrit. His apartment was on East 62nd Street, his gallery two blocks south of it. He was sure of that. He could see himself quite sharply as he walked down Third every morning, glancing toward Bloomingdale's, turning east on 60th—

Two Ted Hilgards? With the same face?

"What are you looking for?" Celia asked, stepping from the bathroom and toweling herself dry.

Hilgard's cheeks reddened. Guiltily he tucked her wallet back in her purse. "Ah—just checking to see how many pesos you have left. I thought we might want to cash some travelers' checks when the banks open tomorrow."

"I cashed some on Friday. Don't you remember?"

"Slipped my mind, I guess."

"Do you want some of my pesos?"

"I've got enough for now," he said.

They had lunch at the hotel. For Hilgard it was like

sitting across the table from a keg of dynamite. He was not yet ready to admit that he had gone insane, but very little that he could say to her was likely to make any sense, and eventually she was bound to challenge him. He felt like someone who had come into a movie in the middle and was trying to figure out what was going on, but this was worse, much worse, because he was not merely watching the movie, he was starring in it. And found himself lunching with a total stranger to whom he had been married, it seemed, for years. But people who have been married for years have little new to say to one another at lunch, usually. He was grateful for the long silences. When she did speak, he answered cautiously and briefly. Once he allowed himself the luxury of calling her by name, just to show that he knew her name; but his "Celia" provoked a quick frown in her that puzzled him. Was he supposed to have used some pet name instead? Or was there a name other than Celia by which everybody called her—Cee, perhaps, or Cele, or Charley? He was altogether lost. Lingering over his coffee, he thought again of that dizzying moment at the Temple of Quetzalcoatl, when everything had swayed and swirled in his head. Was there such a thing as a stroke that affected one's memory without causing any sort of paralysis of the body? Well, maybe. But he wasn't suffering merely from amnesia; he had a complete and unblurred set of memories of a life without Celia, as a contented single man running a successful art gallery, living a fulfilling existence, friends, lovers, travel. Arriving in Mexico City three days ago, looking forward to a week of cheerful solitude, warm weather, spicy food, perhaps some interesting new pieces for his collection. How could a stroke build all that into his mind? With such detail, too: the black Ford cab, Chucho the amiable driver, the seventh-floor room at the Hotel Presidente—

"I've left something upstairs," he told Celia. "I'll just run up for it, and then we can go."

From the room he dialed the Presidente. "Mr. Hilgard, please."

"One moment." A long pause. Then: "Please repeat the name."

"Hilgard. Theodore Hilgard. I think he's in room 770." A longer pause.

"I'm sorry, sir. We have no one by that name."

"I see," Hilgard said, not seeing at all, and put the phone down. He stared at himself in the mirror, searching for signs of a stroke, the drooping eyelid, the sagging cheek. Nothing. Nothing. But his face was gray. He looked a thousand years old.

They hailed a cab outside the hotel and went to the Museum of Anthropology. He had been there several times, most recently yesterday afternoon. But from what Celia said it was apparent she had never seen it, which was a new awkwardness for him: he had to pretend he had no familiarity with that very familiar place. As they wandered through it he did his best to feign fresh responses to objects he had known for years, the great Olmec stone heads, the terrifying statue of the goddess Coatlicue, the jade-encrusted masks. Sometimes it was not necessary to feign it. In the Aztec room there was an immense marble stela just to the left of the calendar stone that he could not recall from yesterday's visit, and there was a case of amazing little Olmec figurines of polished jade absolutely new to him, and the Mayan room seemed arranged in an entirely different way. Hilgard found all that impossible to comprehend. Even the huge umbrella-shaped fountain in the museum courtyard was subtly different, with golden spokes now sprouting from it. The cumulative effect of the day's little strangenesses was making him feel giddy, almost feverish: Celia several times asked if he was getting ill.

They had dinner that night at an outdoor café a few blocks from their hotel, and strolled for a long time afterward, returning to their room a little before midnight. As they undressed Hilgard felt new dismay. Was she expecting him to make love? The thought horrified him. Not that she was unattractive, far from it. But he had never been able to go to bed with strangers. A prolonged courtship, a feeling of ease with the other person, of closeness, of real love—that was what he preferred, indeed what he required. Aside from all that, how could he pretend with any success to be this woman's husband? No two men make love quite the same way; in two minutes she'd realize that he was an impostor, or else she'd wonder what he thought he was up to. All the little sexual rituals and adjustments that a couple evolves and permanently establishes were unknown to him. She would be confused or annoyed or possibly frightened if he betrayed complete ignorance of her body's mechanisms.

And until he understood what had happened to him, he was terrified of revealing his sense of displacement from what he still regarded as his real life. Luckily she seemed not to be in an amorous mood. She gave him a quick kiss, a light friendly embrace, and rolled over, pressing her rump against him. He lay awake a long time, listening to her soft breathing and feeling weirdly adulterous in this bed with another man's wife. Even though she was Mrs. Ted Hilgard, all the same—all the same—

He ruled out the stroke theory. It left too much unexplained. Sudden insanity? But he didn't *feel* crazy. The events around him were crazy; but inside his skull he still seemed calm, orderly, precise. Surely true madness was something wilder and more chaotic. If he had not suffered any disruption of his brain or some all-engulfing delusional upheaval, though, what was going on? It was as though some gateway between worlds had opened for him at Teotihuacan, he thought, and in that instant of dizziness he had stepped through into the other Ted Hilgard's universe, and that other Hilgard had stumbled past him into his own world. That sounded preposterous. But what he was experiencing was preposterous, too.

In the morning Celia said, "I've got a solution to the argument over Cuernavaca versus Guadalajara. Let's go to Oaxaca instead."

"Wonderful!" Hilgard cried. "I *love* Oaxaca. We ought to phone the Presidente Convento to see if they've got a room—that's such a splendid hotel, with those old courtyards and—"

She was staring strangely at him. "When were you in Oaxaca, Ted?"

Hesitantly he said, "Why—I suppose—long ago, before we were married—"

"I thought this was the first time you'd ever been in Mexico."

"Did I say that?" His cheeks were reddening. "I don't know what I could have been thinking of. I must have meant this was *our* first trip to Mexico. I mean, I barely remember the Oaxaca trip, years and years and years ago, but I did go there, just for a weekend once—"

It sounded terribly lame. A trip that was only a vague memory, though the mere mention of Oaxaca had made him glow with recollections of a lovely hotel? Celia had registered the inconsistency, but she chose not to probe it. He was grateful for that. But he knew she must be adding up all the little contradictions and false notes in the things he was saying, and sooner or later she was apt to demand an explanation.

Within an hour they had everything arranged, and that afternoon they flew down to Oaxaca. As they checked in at the hotel, Hilgard had a sudden horrified fear that the clerk, remembering him from two years ago, would greet him by name, but that did not happen. Sitting by poolside before dinner, Hilgard and Celia leafed through their guidebooks, planning their Oaxaca excursions—a drive to the ruins at Monte Albán, a trip out to the Mitla site, a visit to the famous Saturday morning market—and once again he found it necessary to pretend little knowledge of a place he knew quite well. He wondered how convincing he was. They had dinner that night at a splendid Basque restaurant on a balcony overlooking the main plaza, and afterward they strolled back slowly to their hotel. The night air was soft and fragrant, and music floated toward them from the plaza bandstand. When they were halfway back, Celia reached for his hand. He forced himself not to pull away, though even that innocent little contact between them made him feel monstrously fraudulent. At the hotel he suggested stopping in the bar for a nightcap, but she shook her head and smiled. "It's late," she said softly. "Let's just go upstairs." At dinner they had had a carafe of sangria and then a bottle of red Mexican wine, and he felt loose jointed and tranquil, but not so tranquil that he did not fear the confrontation that lay just ahead. He halted a moment on the landing, looking toward the glittering pool. By moonlight the heavy purple clusters of bougainvillea climbing the ancient stone walls of the courtyard seemed almost black. Huge hibiscus blossoms were strewn everywhere on the lawn and strange spiky flowers rose from a border of large bizarre succulents. Celia touched his elbow. "Come," she said. He nodded. They went into their room. She turned on a lamp and began to undress. Hilgard's eyes met hers and he saw a host of expressions cross her face in an instant—affection, desire, apprehension, perplexity. She knew something was wrong. Give it a try, Hilgard told himself fiercely. Fake it. Fake it. He ran his hand timidly along her hips, her thighs. No.

"Ted?" she said. "Ted, what's going on?"

"I can't explain. I think I'm losing my mind."

"You've been so strange. Since yesterday."

He took a deep breath. "Yesterday is the first time I ever laid eyes on you in my life."

"*Ted?*"

"It's true. I'm not married. I run a gallery at 60th near Second. I came to Mexico alone last Thursday and I was staying at the Presidente."

"What are you saying, Ted?"

"Yesterday at Teotihuacan I started to walk past the Temple of Quetzalcoatl and I felt a peculiar sensation in my forehead and since then I seem to be somebody else of the same name. I'm sorry, Celia. Do I sound incoherent? I don't think I do. But I know I'm not making any real sense."

"We've been married nine years. We're partners in a marketing research firm, Hilgard & Hilgard, on 57th and Sixth."

"Marketing research. How strange. Do we have children?"

"No. We live in a co-op on 85th, and in the summers we—oh, Ted! *Ted?*"

"I'm so sorry, Celia."

Her eyes in the moonlit darkness were fixed, bright, terrified. There was the acrid smell of fear-sweat in the room, hers, his. She said huskily, "You don't remember any of our life together? Not a thing? In January we went to San Francisco. We stayed at the Stanford Court and it rained all the time and you bought three ivory carvings at a little place across the street from Ghirardelli Square. Last month we got the contract for the Bryce account and you said, 'Fine, let's celebrate by going to Mexico. We've always wanted to go to Mexico and there's no better time than this.' In April we have a big presentation to do in Atlanta, and in May—Ted? Nothing. Ted?"

"Nothing. It's all a blank."

"How scary that is. Hold me, Ted."

"I'm so sorry."

"You don't remember us in bed either?"

"The first time I saw you was two o'clock yesterday afternoon."

"We'll have to fly home tomorrow. There's got to be some kind of therapy—a drug treatment, or maybe even shock—we'll talk to Judith Rose first thing—"

Hilgard felt a shiver of surprise. "Who?"

"You don't remember her either."

"That's just it. I do. I know a Judith Rose. Tall handsome olive-skinned woman with curly black hair, professor of neurobiology at Rockefeller University—"

"At New York Medical," Celia said. "All the rest is right. You see? You haven't forgotten everything! You still remember Judith!"

"She's at Rockefeller," said Hilgard. "I've known her four or five years. She and I were supposed to take this trip to Mexico together, but at the last moment she had to cancel because she got tied up on a grant proposal, and it looked like she'd be busy with that for weeks and weeks, so we decided that I would come down here by myself, and—"

"What are you saying?" Celia asked, amazed.

"Why, Judith and I are lovers, Celia."

She began to laugh. "Oh, no! No, that's too much. You and Judith—"

"We both see other people. But Judith has the priority. Neither one of us is the marrying sort, but we have an excellent relationship of its kind, and—"

"Stop it, Ted."

"I'm not trying to hurt you. I'm just telling you how it is between me and Judith."

"If you want to tell me you've had affairs, I can handle it. I wouldn't even be immensely surprised. But not with Judith. That's too absurd. Nothing's ever certain in this world, but one thing I'm positive of is that Judith doesn't have any lovers. She and Ron are still like honeymooners. She must be the most faithful woman in the world."

"Ron?"

"Ron Wolff," Celia said. "Judith's husband."

He turned away and stared through the window. Hollowly he said, "In the world I live in, Judith is single and so am I, and she's at Rockefeller University, and I don't know any Ron Wolffs. Or any Celias. And I don't do marketing research. I don't know anything about marketing research. I'm forty-two years old and I went to Harvard and I majored in art history, and I was married to someone named Beverly once for a little while and it was a very bad mistake that I didn't intend to make twice, and I feel sorry as hell for spoiling your vacation and screwing up your life but I simply don't know who you are or where you came from. Do you believe any of that?"

"I believe that you need a great deal of help. And I'll do whatever I have to do to see that you get it, Ted. Whatever has happened to you can be cured, I'm sure, with love and patience and time and money."

"I don't think I'm crazy, Celia."

"I didn't use that word. You're the one who talked of

losing your mind. You've had some kind of grotesque mental accident, you've undergone a disturbance of—"

"No," Hilgard said. "I don't think it's anything mental at all. I have another theory now. Suppose that in front of the Temple of Quetzalcoatl there's a mystery place, a—a whirlpool in the structure of the universe, let's say—a gateway, a vortex, whatever you want to call it. Thousands of people walk through it and nothing ever happens to them. But I was the victim of a one-in-a-trillion shot. I went to Mexico in my world and the Ted Hilgard of your world went there at the same time, and we were both at Teotihuacan at the same time, and some immense coincidence brought us both to the whirlpool place simultaneously, and we both went through the gateway and changed places. It could only have happened because our two worlds were touching and he and I were identical enough to be interchangeable."

"That does sound crazy, Ted."

"Does it? Not as crazy as any other theory. Things are different in this world. You, Judith, Ron. The Updike book has a red jacket here. I'm in marketing research instead of art. The museum has a different kind of fountain. Maybe it costs twenty cents to mail a letter instead of eighteen. Everything's *almost* the same, but not quite, and the longer I look, the more differences I see. I have a complete and vivid picture in my mind of the world on the other side of the gateway, down to the littlest details. That can't be just a mental aberration. No aberration is that detailed. How much does it cost to mail a letter?"

"Twenty cents."

"In my world it's eighteen. You see? You see?"

"I don't see anything," Celia said tiredly. "If you can delude yourself into thinking you're entirely different from who you are, you can also very sincerely believe that the postage rate is eighteen cents. They keep changing it all the time anyway. What does that prove? Listen, Ted, we'll go back to New York. We'll try to get you help for this. I want to repair you. I love you. I want you back, Ted. Do you understand that? We've had a wonderful marriage. I don't want it vanishing like a dream."

"I'm so damn sorry, Celia."

"We'll work something out."

"Maybe. Maybe."

"Let's get some sleep now. We're both exhausted."

"That's a fine idea," he said. He touched his hand lightly to her forearm and she stiffened, as though anticipating his caress to be an initiation of lovemaking. But all he was doing was clutching at her as at a rescue line at sea. He squeezed her arm briefly, let go, rolled to the far side of the bed. Tired as he was, he found it hard to fall asleep, and he lay alert a long time. Once he heard her quietly sobbing. When sleep came to him, it was deep and nearly dreamless.

Hilgard would have liked to roam Oaxaca for a few days, enjoying its clear air, lovely old streets and easy, unhurried pace, but Celia was insistent that they start at once on the task of restoring his memory. They flew back to Mexico City on the 11:00 A.M. flight. At the airport Celia learned that there was a flight to New York in mid-afternoon, but Hilgard shook his head. "We'll stay over in Mexico City tonight and take the first plane out in the morning," he said.

"Why?"

"I want to go back to Teotihuacan."

She gasped. "For Christ's sake, Ted!"

"Humor me. I won't leave Mexico without making certain."

"You think you're just going to walk back into another world?"

"I don't know what I think. I just want to check it out."

"And you expect the other Ted Hilgard to come strolling out from behind a pyramid as you vanish?"

She was starting to sound distraught. Calmly he said, "I don't expect anything. It's just an investigation."

"What if you do? What if you vanish into that whirlpool of yours, and he *doesn't* come out, and I'm left without either of you? Answer me that, Ted."

"I think you're beginning to believe my theory."

"Oh, no, Ted, no. But—"

"Look," he said, "if the theory's crazy, then nothing will happen. If it isn't, maybe I'll go back where I belong and the right me will return to this world. Nobody knows. But I can't go to New York until I've checked. Grant me that much. I want you to humor me, Celia. Will you do that?"

In the end she had to yield, of course, and they checked their baggage at the airport and booked a hotel room for the night and a flight for the morning, and then they hired a cab to take them to the Teotihuacan. The driver spoke little English and it was hard to make him understand that they did not intend to spend all afternoon at the pyramids, but only half an hour or less. That seemed unthinkable to him: why would anyone, even two rich gringos, bother driving an hour and a half each way for a half-hour visit? But finally he accepted the idea. He parked at the southernmost parking lot, near the museum, and Celia and Hilgard walked quickly across the road to the Temple of Quetzalcoatl. His throat was dry and his heart was pounding, and she looked equally tense and drawn. He tried to retrace his steps exactly. "I came through this way," he said, "and just around this corner, as I got my first glimpse of the facade—"

"Ted, please don't. Please."

"Do you want to try? Maybe you'll go through it after him."

"Please. Let's not."

"I have to," he said. Frowning, he made his way along the paved walkway, paused as the facade and its fierce serpent-snouts emerged in sight, caught his breath, plunged onward, waiting for the moment of vertigo, that sensation as of a highly localized earthquake. Nothing. He looked back. Celia, pale, grim, arms folded, was staring at him. Hilgard returned and tried it again. "Maybe I was just six inches off that time. A little to the left—" Nothing. Nothing the third time, or the fourth. A few other tourists passed by, staring oddly at him. Back and forth he went, covering every inch. The pathway was narrow; there were only a few possible routes. He felt no vertigo. No gateway in space opened for him. He did not tumble through into his rightful world.

"Please, Ted. Enough."

"Once more."

"This is embarrassing. You look so damned obsessive."

"I want to go where I belong," Hilgard said.

Back and forth. Back and forth. He was beginning to feel embarrassed too. Perhaps she was right: this was mere madness that had possessed his soul. There are no gateways. He could not walk back and forth in front of those horrendous stone faces all afternoon. "Once more," he said, and nothing happened and he turned away. "It doesn't work," he told her. "Or else it works only when one's counterpart is passing through it at the same instant. And that would be impossible to arrange. If I could send him a message—tie it to a rock, toss it through the gateway, tell him to be here tomorrow at nine sharp—"

"Let's go," Celia said.

"All right. Yes." Defeated, dejected, he let her lead him across the dry hot temple courtyard to the waiting taxi. They returned to Mexico City in the full madness of the evening rush hour, saying little to each other. Their hotel room turned out to have two single beds instead of a double. Just as well, Hilgard thought. He felt an immense airless distance between himself and this woman who believed she was his wife. They had a bleak dinner at a Zona Rosa restaurant and went to sleep early, and before daybreak they were up and out and on their way to the airport.

"Maybe when you're in your own home," she said, "you'll begin to get pieces of your memory back."

"Maybe," he said.

But the co-op on East 85th meant nothing to him. It was a handsome apartment, thirty stories up, obviously worth a fortune, and it was furnished beautifully, but it was someone else's house, with someone else's books and clothes and treasures in it. The books included a good many that he also owned, and the clothes fit him, and some of the paintings and primitive artifacts were quite in accordance with his own taste. It was like being in one's twin brother's home, perhaps. But he wandered helplessly and in growing panic from room to room, wondering where his files were, his little hoard of boyhood things, his first editions, his Peruvian pottery collection. Delusions? Phantom memories of a nonexistent life? He was cut off from everything that he thought to be real, and it terrified him. The Manhattan phone book listed no Theodore Hilgard on Third Avenue, and no Hilgard Galleries, either. The universe had swallowed that Ted Hilgard.

"I phoned Judith," Celia said, "and told her something of what happened. She wants to see you first thing tomorrow."

He had been to Judith's Rockefeller University office often enough, just a few blocks east of his gallery. But this was a different Judith and her office was at New York Medical, uptown at the edge of Spanish Harlem. Hilgard walked over to Fifth and caught a bus, wondering if he had to pay his fare with some sort of token in this world, wondering if the Metropolitan Museum was where he remembered it, wondering about Judith. He negotiated the bus problem without difficulty. The gray bulk of the museum still crouched on the flank of Central Park. Upper Fifth Avenue looked more or less untransformed, the Frick Collection building just as dignified as ever, the Guggenheim spiral just as peculiar as ever. And Judith was untransformed also: elegant, beautiful, warm, with the light of that wonderful intelligence gleaming in her eyes. The only thing missing was that certain mischievous sparkle, that subliminal aura of shared intimacies, that acknowledged that they had long been lovers. She greeted him as a friend and nothing more than a friend.

"What in God's name has been going on with you?" she asked at once.

He smiled ruefully. "Between one moment and the

next I seem to have had a total identity transplant. I used to be a bachelor with an art gallery down the block from Bloomingdale's. Now I'm a married man with a marketing research company on 57th Street. And so on. A burst of dizziness at the ruins of Teotihuacan and everything in my life got switched around."

"You don't remember Celia?"

"It isn't just amnesia, if that's where you're heading. I don't remember Celia or anything else having to do with my life here. But I *do* remember a million other things that don't seem to exist any more, a complete reality substructure: phone numbers, addresses, biographical details. You, for instance. The Judith I know is with Rockefeller University. She's single and lives at 382 East 61st Street and her phone number is—you see what I mean? As a matter of fact, you may be the only link between my old life and this one. Somehow I got to know you in both identities. Figure the odds against that."

Judith looked at him with intense, somber concern. "We'll arrange a full battery of neurological tests right away. This sounds like the damnedest mental short circuit I've ever heard of, though I suspect I'll turn up some similar cases in the literature. People who experienced sudden drastic dissociative reactions leading to complete disruption of personality patterns."

"Some sort of schizoid break, is that what you're saying?"

"We don't use terms like schizophrenia or paranoia much any more, Ted. They've been corrupted by popular misconceptions, and they're too imprecise anyway. We know now that the brain is an enormously complex instrument that has capabilities far beyond our rational understanding—I mean freakish stuff like being able to multiply ten-digit numbers in your head—and it's entirely possible that given the right stimulus it can manufacture a perfectly consistent surrogate identity, which—"

"In layman's terms, I'm crazy."

"If you want to use layman's terms," Judith said,

"you're suffering from delusions of an extraordinarily vivid kind."

Hilgard nodded. "Among those delusions, you should know, is that you and I were lovers for the past four years."

She smiled. "I'm not at all surprised. You've been carrying on a lovely little flirtation with me from the moment we met."

"Have we ever been to bed together?"

"Of course not, Ted."

"Have I ever seen you naked?"

"Not unless you've been spying on me."

He wondered how much this Judith differed from his. Risking it, he said, "Then how do I know you have a small surgical scar on your left breast?"

Shrugging, she said, "I had a little benign tumor removed years ago. Celia might have mentioned that to you."

"And I'd know which breast?"

"You might."

"I can tell you six or seven other things about your body that only somebody who's plenty familiar with it would know. I can tell you what your favorite lovemaking position is, and why. I can imitate the sound you make at your climax."

"Oh? Can you?"

"Listen," he said, and did his best to duplicate that strange whining passionate cry he had heard so many times. Judith's playful, challenging smile disappeared. Her lips grew taut and her eyes narrowed and splotches of color came to her cheeks. She glanced away from him.

Hilgard said, "I didn't have a tape recorder under your bed. I haven't been discussing your sexual idiosyncrasies with Ron. I wouldn't even know Ron if I tripped over him in the street. And I'm not reading your mind. How do I know all these things, then?"

She was silent. She moved papers about randomly on her desk. Her hands appeared to be shaking.

"Maybe you're the one with dissociative reactions," he said. "You've forgotten all about our affair."

"You know that's nonsense."

"You're right. Because the Judith Rose I've been to bed with is at Rockefeller University. But I've been to bed with a Judith Rose who's very much like you. Do you doubt that now?"

She made no reply. She was staring at him in an astounded way, and there seemed to be something else in her look, a volatility, an excitement, that led him to think he had somehow reached across the barrier of his lost world to touch her, *this* Judith, to arouse her and kindle in her some simulacrum of the love and passion that he knew they had had in another existence. A sudden wild fantasy erupted in him—getting free of Celia, getting Judith free of Ron, and reconstructing in this unfamiliar world the relationship that had been taken from him. But the idea faded as quickly as it had come. It was foolishness; it was nonsense; it was an impossibility.

She said finally, "Describe what you think happened to you?"

He told her in all the detail he could muster—the vertigo, the feeling of passing through a gateway, the gradual discovery of the wrongness of everything. "I want to believe this is all just a mental illness and that six lithium pills will make everything be right again. But I don't think that's how it is. I think what happened to me may be a lot wilder than a mere schizoid break. But I don't want to believe that. I want to think it's just a dissociative reaction."

"Yes. I'm sure you do."

"What do you think it is, Judith?"

"My opinion doesn't matter, does it? What matters is proof."

"Proof?"

She said, "What were you carrying on you when you experienced your moment of vertigo?"

"My camera." He thought. "And my wallet."

"Which had credit cards, driver's license, all that stuff?"

"Yes," he said, beginning to understand. He felt a stab of fear, cold, intense. Pulling his wallet out, he said, "Here—here—" He drew forth his driver's license. It had the Third Avenue address. He took out his Diner's Club card. Judith laid her own next to it. The cards were of different designs. He produced a twenty-dollar bill. She peered at the signatures on it and shook her head. Hilgard closed his eyes an instant and had a flashing vision of the Temple of Quetzalcoatl, the great heavy snouts of the serpents, the massive stone steps. Judith's face was dark and grim, and Hilgard knew she had forced him to confront the final proof, and he had a sense of a mighty gate swinging shut forever behind him. He was not the victim of any psychosis. He had actually made the crossing, and it was irrevocable. His other life was gone—it was dead. Bitterly he said, "I forged all this stuff, right? While I was down in Mexico City I had it all printed up, counterfeit money, a fake driver's license, to make the hoax look really convincing. Right? Right?" He remembered something else and went burrowing for it in his wallet and found it after a frantic search—Judith's own business card, with Department of Neurobiology, Rockefeller University on it in shining engraved letters. The card was old and worn and creased. She looked at it as though he had put a basilisk in her hand. When she stared at him again, it was with a sad and tender look of pity.

At length she said, "Ted, I'll give you all the help I can."

"What kind of help?"

"Making the adaptation. Learning your role here. Celia and I, between us, ought to be able to fill you in on who you're supposed to be. It's the only thing I can imagine doing now. You're right that lithium won't fix anything."

"No," Hilgard said. "Don't involve Celia."

"We have to."

"No," he said. "She thinks I'm her husband and that

I'm suffering from an unfortunate dissociative reaction, or whatever you call it. If she comes to realize I'm the complete stranger I've been insisting I am, I'm lost. She'll throw me out and try to find ways of getting *him* back. And I have no way to function in this world except in the identity of Theodore Hilgard."

"You *are* Theodore Hilgard."

"Yes, and I intend to go on being him. Doing marketing research and living with Celia and signing my name to checks. You'll help me adapt, yes. You'll have a couple of sessions of therapy with me every week, and you'll tell me where I went to college and what the names of my friends are and who the presidents have been in this world, if they have presidents here. So far as everyone else will know, you're helping me recover from a mysterious mental fog. You won't tell a soul that I don't belong here. And sooner or later I *will* belong here. All right, Judith? You see, I've got no choice. There's no way for me to get back across the barrier. I've managed to prove to one other human being that I'm not crazy, and now I've got to put that behind me and start living the life I've been handed. Will you help me?"

"One condition," she said.

"Which is?"

"You're in love with me. I see that, and I don't blame you because I know you can't help thinking I'm *your* Judith. I'm not. I'm Ron's. Go on flirting with me, go on having fantasies about me, but don't give me any moves, ever. All right? Because you might open up in me something that I don't want opened, do you understand? We remain *friends*. Co-conspirators, even. That's all. Is that agreed?"

Hilgard looked at her unhappily. It was a long while before he could bring himself to say it.

"Agreed," he told her at last.

Celia said, "Judith phoned while you were on the way back. She talked to me for twenty minutes. Oh, Ted—my poor Ted—"

"I'm going to be okay. It'll take time."

"She says these amnesias, these detailed delusions, are extraordinarily rare. You're going to be a textbook case."

"Wonderful. I'm going to need a lot of help from you, Celia."

"Whatever I can do."

"I'm a blank. I don't know who our friends are, I don't know how to practice my profession, I don't even know who *you* are. Everything's wiped out. I'll have to rebuild it all. Judith will do as much as she can, but the real burden, day by day, hour by hour, is going to fall on you.

"I'm prepared for that."

"Then we'll start all over—from scratch. We'll make a go of it. Tonight we'll eat at one of our special restaurants—you'll have to tell me which our special restaurants are—and we'll have the best wine in the house, or maybe a bottle or two of champagne, and then we'll come back here—we'll be like newlyweds, Celia, it'll be like a wedding night. All right?"

"Of course," she said softly.

"And then tomorrow the hard work begins. Fitting me back into the real world."

"Everything will come back, Ted. Don't worry. And I'll give you all the help you need. I love you, Ted. No matter what's happened to you, that hasn't changed. I love you."

He nodded. He took her hands in his. Falteringly, guiltily, with a thick tongue and a numbed heart, he forced himself to get the words out, the words that were his only salvation now, the words that gave him his one foothold on the shores of an unknown continent. "And I love you, Celia," he told the absolute stranger who was his wife.

The Man Who
Floated in Time

There was something shady and sly about him. For one thing he was small and slightly built, and I have an instinctive mistrust of men who stand less than five feet five: they seem too agile and unpredictable, shifty little Napoleons who are apt to come at you from three directions at once. Then, too, his narrow glittery gray eyes, though they did actually make contact with mine, never seemed to be aimed directly at me but rather, somehow, sent a beam of vision hooking around a sharply banked curve even when his face looked at me right square on. I didn't like that. He was about sixty, sixty-five, lean and trim, not well dressed, his gray hair cropped very short and gone at the crown.

"What I do," he said, "is travel in time. I float freely back to other eras."

"Really," I said. "Never forward?"

"Oh, no, never. That's quite impossible. The future doesn't exist. The past is there, solid and real, a *place*, you know, like Des Moines or Wichita. One can go to Wichita if one makes the proper connection. But one can't go to a city that's never been built. It isn't conceivable. Well, perhaps it's conceivable, but it isn't *doable*, do you follow me? I go to the past, though. I've seen Attila the Hun. I've seen Julius Caesar. I wish I could say I went to bed with Catherine the Great, but I didn't, although I had a few vodkas with someone who did. She smelled of garlic, he said, and she took forever to come. You don't believe any of what I'm saying, do you?"

"You're asking me to swallow quite a lot," I said mildly.

He leaned forward in a conspiratorial way. "You're not the kind of man who's easily convinced of the unusual. I can tell. No ancient astronaut stuff for you, no UFO contact stories, no psychic spoon-bendings. That's good. I don't want an easy believer. I want a skeptic to hear me out and test my words and arrive at his own acceptance of the truth his own way. That's all I ask of you, that you don't scoff, that you don't write me off instantly as a crackpot. All right?"

"I'll try."

"Now: what do you feel when I tell you I've traveled in time?"

"Instinctive resistance. An immediate sense that I've got myself mixed up with a crackpot or at best a charming liar."

"Fine. I wouldn't have come to you if I thought you'd react any other way."

"What do you want from me, then?"

"That you listen to me and suspend your disbelief at least now and then and ask me a question or two, probe me, test me, give me the benefit of the doubt long enough to let me get through to you. And then that you help me get my experiences down on paper. I'm old and I'm sick and I'm not going to be here much longer, and I want to leave a memoir, a record, do you see? And I need someone like you to help me."

"Why not write it yourself?" I asked.

"Easy enough to say. But I'm no writer. I don't have the gift. I can't even do letters without freezing up."

"Doing a memoir doesn't require a gift. You simply put down your story on paper, just as though you were telling it to me. Writing's not as hard as nonwriters like to think it is."

"Writing is easy for you," he said, "and time-traveling

is easy for me. And I'm about as capable of writing as you are of traveling in time. Do you see?" He put his hand on my wrist, a gesture of premature intimacy that sent a quick, and quickly suppressed, quiver through my entire arm. "Help me to get my story down, will you? You think I'm a crazy old drunk, and you wish you had never given me minute one of your time, but I ask you to put those feelings aside and accept just for the moment the possibility that this isn't just a mess of lies and fantasies. Can you do that?"

"Go on," I said. "Tell me about yourself."

He said his time-traveling had begun when he was a boy. The technique by which he claimed to be able to unhitch himself from the bonds of the continuum and drift back along the time-line was apparently one that he developed spontaneously, a sort of applied meditation that amounted to artfully channeled fantasizing. Through this process, which he refined and perfected between the ages of eight and eleven, he achieved what I suppose must be called out-of-the-body experiences, in which his psyche, his consciousness, his walking intelligence, vanished into the past while his body remained here, ostensibly asleep.

On his first voyage he found himself in an American city of the colonial era. He had no idea where he was— when he was older, working from his searingly vivid memories of the journey, he was able to identify it as Charleston, South Carolina—but he knew at once, from his third-grade studies, that the powdered wigs and three-cornered hats must mean the eighteenth century. He was there for three days, fascinated at first, then frightened and confused and terribly hungry—

"Hungry?" I said. "A wandering psyche with an appetite?"

"You don't perceive yourself as disembodied," he replied, looking pleased that I had raised an objection. "You feel that you have been quite literally transplanted to the other era. You need to eat, to sleep, to perform bodily functions. I was a small boy lost in a prerevolutionary city. The first night I slept in a forest. In the morning I returned to the city where some people found me, dirty and lost, and took me to a mansion where I was bathed and fed—"

"And given clothes? You must have been in your pajamas."

"No, you are always clothed in the clothing of the era when you arrive," he said. "And equipped with the language of the region and a certain amount of local currency."

"How very convenient. What providential force takes care of those little details?"

He smiled. "Those are part of the illusion. Plainly I have no real coins with me, and of course I haven't magically learned new languages. But the aspect of me that makes the journey has the capacity to lead others to feel that they are receiving true coinage from me; and as my soul makes contact with theirs, they imagine that it is their own language I speak. What I do is not actual bodily travel, you understand. It is astral projection, to use a phrase that I know will arouse hostility in you. My real body, in its pajamas, remained snug in my bed; but the questing *anima*, the roving spirit, arrived fully equipped. Of course the money is dream-money and melts away the moment I go farther from it than a certain range. In my travels I have left angry innkeepers and cheated peddlers and even a few swindled harlots all over the world, I'm afraid. But for the moment what I give them passes as honest coin."

"Yet the astral body must be fed with real food?"

"Indeed. And I think that if the astral body is injured, the sleeping real body feels the pain."

"How can you be sure of that?"

"Because," he said, "I have fallen headlong down temple steps in the Babylon of Hammurabi and awakened to find bruises on my thigh and shoulder. I have slashed myself on vines in the jungles of ancient Cambodia and awakened to see the cuts. I have stood in the snows of Pleistocene Europe shivering with the Neanderthals and awakened with frostbite in July."

There is an Italian saying: *Se non è vero, è ben trovato.* "If it is not true, it is well invented." There was in his eyes and on his thin gray-stubbled face at that moment a look of such passionate conviction, such absolute sincerity, that I began to tremble, hearing him talk of feeling the bite of Pleistocene winds, and for the first time I began to allow myself the possibility of thinking that this man could be something other than a boozy old scamp with a vivid imagination. But I was far from converted.

I said, "Then if through some mischance you were killed when traveling, your real body would perish also?"

"I have every reason to think so," he replied quietly.

He traveled through vast reaches of space and time when he was still a child. Most of the places he visited were bewilderingly alien to him, and he had little idea of where or when he was, but he learned to observe keenly, to note salient details, to bring back with him data that sooner or later would help him to determine what he had experienced. He was a bookish child anyway, and so it caused no amazement when he burrowed feverishly through the *National Geographic* or the *Britannica* or dusty volumes of history. As he grew older and his education deepened, it became easier for him to learn the identity of his destinations; and when he was still older, fully grown, it was not at all difficult for him simply to ask those about him, What is the name of this city? Who is the king here? What is the event of the day? exactly as though he were a traveler newly arrived from a far-off land. For although he had journeyed in the form of a boy at first, his astral self always mirrored his true self, and as he aged, the projection that he sent to the past kept pace with him.

So, then, he visited while still a child the London of the Tudors, where rivers of muck ran in the streets, and he stood at the gates of Peking to watch the triumphal entry of the Great Khan Kublai, and he crept cautiously through the forests of the Dordogne to spy on the encampments of Neolithic huntsmen, and he tiptoed along the brutal brick battlements of a terrifying city of windowless buildings that proved to be Mohenjo-daro on the Indus, and he slipped with awe through the boulevards and plazas of majestic Tenochtitlan of the Aztecs, his pale skin growing sunburned under the heat of the pre-Columbian sun. And when he was older he stood in the frenzied crowd before the bloody guillotine of the Terror, and saw virgins hurled into the sacred well of Chichen Itza, and wandered through the smoldering ruins of Atlanta a week after General Sherman had put it to the torch, and drank thick red wine in a lovely town on the slopes of Vesuvius that may have been Pompeii. The stories rolled from him in wondrous profusion, and I listened to the charming old crank hour after hour, telling me sly tales of a history not to be found in books. Julius Caesar, he said, was a mincing dandy who reeked of vile perfume, and Cleopatra was squat and thick-lipped, and the Israelites of King David's time were brawling, conniving primitives no holier than the desert folk the next tribe over, and the Great Wall of China had been mostly a slovenly rampart of mud, decaying as fast as it was slapped together, and Socrates had never lived at all but was only a convenient pedagogical invention of Plato's, and Plato had charged an enormous fee even for mere conversation. As for the Crusaders, they were more feared by Christians than Saracens, for they raped and stole and sacked mercilessly as they trekked across Europe to the Holy Land; and Alexander the Great had rarely been sober enough to stand upright after the age of twenty-three; and the orchestras of Mozart's time played mostly out of tune on feeble, screechy instruments. All this poured from him in long disjointed monologues, which I interrupted less and less frequently for clarifications and amplifications. He spoke with utter conviction and with total disregard for my disbelief: I was invited to accept his tales as whatever I pleased, gospel revelations or amusing fraud, so long as I listened.

At our fifth or sixth meeting, after he had told me about his adventures among the bare-breasted wenches of Minoan Crete—the maze, he said, was nothing much, just some alleyways and gutters—and in the Constantinople of Justinian and in the vast unpeopled bison-herd lands of ancient North America, I said to him, "Is there any time or place you haven't visited?"

"Atlantis," he said. "I kept hoping to identify the unmistakable Atlantis, but never, never once—"

"Everywhere else, and every era?"

"Hardly. I've had only one lifetime."

"I wondered. I haven't been keeping a tally, but it seems to me it must have taken you eighty or ninety years to see all that you've seen. A week here, a month there—it adds up, doesn't it?"

"Yes."

"And while you're gone, you remain asleep here for weeks or months at a time?"

"Oh, no," he said. "You've misunderstood. Time spent *there* has no relation to elapsed time *here*. I can be gone for many days, and no more than an instant will have passed here. At most, an hour or two. Why, I've taken off on journeys even while I was sitting here talking with you!"

"What?"

"Yesterday, as we spoke of the San Francisco earthquake—between one eye-blink and the next, I spent eighteen hours in some German principality of the fourteenth century."

"And never said a word about it when you returned?"

He shrugged. "You were prickly and unreceptive yesterday, and I was having trouble keeping your sympathies. I felt it would be too stagy to tell you, Oh, by the way, I've just been in Augsburg or Reutlingen or Ulm or whichever it was. Besides, it was a boring trip. I found it so dreary I didn't even trouble to ask the name of the place."

"Then why did you stay for so long?"

"Why, I have no control over that," he said.

"No control?"

"None. I drift away and I stay away however long I must and then I come back. It's been like that from the start. I can't choose my destination, either. I can best compare it to getting into a plane and being spirited off for a vacation of unknown length in an unknown land and not having a word to say about any of it. There have been times when I thought I wouldn't ever come back."

"Did that frighten you?"

"Only when I didn't like where I happened to be," he said. "The idea of spending the rest of my life in some mudhole in the middle of Mongolia or in an igloo in Greenland or—well, you get the idea." He pursed his lips. "Another thing—it happens automatically to me."

"I thought there was a ritual, a meditative process—"

"When I was a child, yes. But in time I internalized it so well that it happens of its own accord. Which is terrifying, because it can come over me anywhere, anytime, like a fit. Did you think there were no drawbacks to this? Did you think it was a lifelong picnic, roving space and time? I've had two or three uncontrolled departures a year since I was twenty. It's been my luck that I haven't fallen down unconscious in the street, or anything like that. Though there have been some great embarrassments."

"How have your explained them?"

"With lies," he said. "You are the first to whom I've told the truth about myself."

"Should I believe that?"

"You are the first," he said with intense conviction. "And that because my time is almost over and I need at last to share my story with someone. Eh? Is that plausible? Do you still think I've fabricated it all?"

Indeed, I had no idea. To treat his story as lies or fantasy was easy enough to do; but for all his shiftiness of expression, there was an odd ring of truth even to his most enormous whoppers. And the wealth of information, the outpouring of circumstantial detail—I suppose a solitary life spent over history books could have explained that, but nevertheless, nevertheless—

And if it was true? What good had it all been? He had written nothing, no anecdotes of his adventures, no revisionist historical essays, no setting down of the philosophical insights that must have grown out of his exploration of thirty thousand years of human history. He had lived a strange and fitful and fragmentary life, flickering in and out of what we call the reality of the everyday world as though he were going to the movies, and bizarre movies they were, a week in Byzantium and a month in old Sumer and an hour among the Pharaohs. A life spent alone, a loveless life by the sound of it, a weird zigzagging chaos of a life such as has been granted no other human being—

If it was true.

And if not? *Se non è vero, è ben trovato.* I listened enraptured. I continued to probe for details of the mechanics of it. His journeys took him anywhere on earth? Anywhere, he said. Once he had arrived in a wasteland of glaciers that he believed from the strangeness of the constellations to have been Antarctica, though it might have been any icy land at a time when the stars were in other places in the sky. Happily that voyage had lasted less than an hour or he would have perished. But there seemed no limits—he might turn up on any continent, he said, and at any time. Or *almost* any time, for I queried him about dinosaurs and the era of the trilobites and the chance that he might find himself some day plunged into the primordial planetary soup of creation, but no, he had never gone back further than the Pleistocene, so far as he could tell, and he did not know why. I wondered also how he had seen so many of the great figures of history, Caesar and Cleopatra and Lincoln and Dante and the rest, when we who live only in today rarely encounter presidents and kings and movie stars in the course of our comings and goings, but he had an answer to that, too, saying that the world had been much smaller in earlier times, cities being deemed great if they had fifty or a hundred thousand people, and the mighty were far more accessible, going out into the marketplace and letting themselves be seen; besides, he had made it his business to seek them out, for what is the point of finding oneself miraculously transported to imperial Rome and coming away without at least a squint at Augustus or Caligula?

So I listened to it all and was caught up in it, and though I will not say that I ever came to believe the literal truth of his claims, I also did not quite disbelieve, and through his rambling discourses I felt the past return to life in an astonishing way. I made time for his visits, cleared all other priorities out of the way when he called to tell me he was coming and, beyond doubt, grew almost dependent on his tales, as though they were a drug, some potent hallucinogen that carried me off into gaudy realms of antiquity.

And in what proved to be his last conversation with me he said, "I could show you how it's done."

The simple words hung between us in the air like dancing swords.

I gaped at him and made no reply.

He said, "It would take perhaps three months of training. For me it was easy, natural, no challenge, but of course I was a child and I had no barriers to overcome. You, with your skepticism, your sophistication, your aloofness—it would be hard for you to master the technique, but I could show you and train you, and eventually you would succeed. Would you like that?"

I thought of watching Caesar's chariot rolling down the Via Flaminia. I thought of clinking canisters with Chaucer in some tavern just outside Canterbury. I thought of penetrating the caves of Lascaux to stare at the freshly painted bulls.

And then I thought of my quiet, orderly life, and how it would be to fall into a narcoleptic trance at unpredictable moments and swing off into the darkness of space and time, and land perhaps in the middle of some hideous massacre or in a season of plague or in a desolate land where no human foot had ever walked. I thought of pain and discomfort and risk, and possible sudden death, and the disruption of patterns of habit, and I looked into his eyes and saw the strangeness there, a strangeness that I did not want to share, and in simple cowardice I said, "I think I would rather not."

A flicker of something like disappointment passed across his features. But then he smiled and stood up and said, "I'm not surprised. But thank you for hearing me out. You were more open-minded than I expected."

He took my hand briefly in his. Then he was gone, and I never saw him again. A few weeks later, I learned of his death, and I heard his soft voice saying "I could show you how it's done," and a great sadness came over me, for although I knew he was a fraud, I knew also that there was a chance that he was not, and if so, I had foreclosed the possibility of infinite wonders for myself. How sad to have refused, I told myself, how pale and gray a thing to have done, how contemptible, really. Yes, contemptible to have refused him out of hand, without even attempting it, without offering him that final bit of credence. For several days I was deeply depressed; and then I went on to other things, as one does, and put him from my mind.

A few weeks after his death one of the big midtown banks called me. They mentioned his name and said they were executors of his estate and told me that he had left something for me, an envelope to be opened only after his death. If I could satisfactorily identify myself, the envelope would be shipped to my bank. So I went through the routine, sending a letter to my bank, which authenticated the signature and forwarded it to *his* bank, and in time my bank informed me that a parcel had come, and I went down to claim it. It was a fairly bulky manila envelope. I had the sudden wild notion that it contained some irrefutable proof of his voyages in time, something like a photograph of Jesus on the cross or a personal letter to my friend from William the Conqueror, but of course that was impossible; he had made it clear that nothing traveled in time except his intangible essence, no possessions, no artifacts. Yet my hand shook as I opened the envelope.

It contained a thick manuscript and a covering note that explained that he had decided, after all, to share with me the secrets of his technique. Without his guidance it might take me much longer to learn the knack, a year or more of diligent application, perhaps, but if I persevered, if I genuinely sought to achieve—

A wondrous dizziness came over me, as though I hung over an infinite abyss by the frailest of fraying threads and was being asked to choose between drab safety and the splendor of the unknown plunge. I felt the temptation.

And for the second time I refused the cup.

I did not read the manuscript. I was too timid for that. Nor did I destroy it, though the idea crossed my mind; but I was too cowardly even for that, I must admit, for I had no wish to bear the responsibility for having cast into oblivion so potent a secret, if potent it really was. I put the sheaf of papers—over which he must have labored with intense dedication, writing being so painfully difficult a thing for him—back into their envelope and sealed it again and put it in my vault, deep down below the bankbooks and the insurance policies and the stock certificates and the other symbols of the barricades I have thrown about myself to make my life secure.

Perhaps the manuscript, like everything else he told me, is mere fantastic nonsense. Perhaps not.

Some day, when life grows too drab for me, when the pleasures of the predictable and safe begin to pall, I will take that envelope from the vault and study its lessons, and if nothing then happens, so be it. But if I feel the power beginning to come to life in me, if I find myself once again swaying above that abyss with the choices within my reach, I hope I will find the courage to sever the thread, to loose all ties and restraints, to say farewell to order and routine, and to send myself soaring into that great uncharted infinite gulf of time.

The Palace at Midnight

The foreign minister of the Empire of San Francisco was trying to sleep late. Last night had been a long one, a wild if not particularly gratifying party at the baths, too much to drink, too much to smoke, and he had seen the dawn come up like thunder out of Oakland 'crost the bay. Now the telephone was ringing. He integrated the first couple of rings nicely into his dream, but the next one began to undermine his slumber, and the one after that woke him up. He groped for the receiver and, eyes still closed, managed to croak, "Christensen here."

"Tom, are you awake? You don't sound awake. It's Morty."

The undersecretary for external affairs. Christensen sat up, rubbed his eyes, ran his tongue around his lips. Daylight was streaming into the room. His cats were glaring at him from the doorway. The little Siamese pawed daintily at her empty bowl and looked up expectantly.

"Tom?"

"I'm up, I'm up! What is it, Morty?"

"I didn't mean to wake you. How was I supposed to know, one in the afternoon—"

"*What is it*, Morty?"

"We got a call from Monterey. There's an ambassador on the way up and you've got to meet with her."

The foreign minister worked hard at clearing the fog from his brain. He was thirty-nine years old and all-night parties took more out of him than they once had.

"You do it, Morty."

"You know I would, Tom. But I can't. You've got to handle this one yourself. It's prime."

"Prime? What kind of prime? Like a great dope deal? Or are they declaring war on us?"

"How would I know the details? The call came in and they said it was prime, Ms. Sawyer must confer with Mr. Christensen. It wouldn't involve dope, Tom. And it can't be war, either. Shit, why would Monterey want to make war on us? They've only got but ten soldiers, I bet, unless they're drafting the Chicanos out of the Salinas *calabozo*, and—"

"All right." Christensen's head was buzzing. "Go easy on the chatter, okay? Where am I supposed to meet her?"

"Berkeley."

"You're kidding."

"She won't come into the city. She thinks it's too dangerous over here."

"What do we do, kill ambassadors and barbecue them? She'll be safe here and she knows it."

"I talked to her. She thinks the city's too crazy. She'll go as far as Berkeley, but that's it."

"Tell her to go to hell."

"Tom, Tom—"

Christensen sighed. "Where in Berkeley will she be?"

"The Claremont, at half past four."

"Jesus," Christensen said. "How did you get me into this? All the way across to the East Bay to meet a lousy ambassador from Monterey! Let her come to San Francisco. This is the Empire, isn't it? They're only a stinking republic. Am I supposed to swim over to Oakland every time an envoy shows up and wiggles a finger? Some bozo from Fresno says boo and I have to haul my ass out to the valley, eh? Where does it stop? What kind of cloud do I have, anyway?"

"Tom—"

"I'm sorry, Morty. I don't feel like a goddamned diplomat this morning."

"It isn't morning any more, Tom. But I'd do it for you if I could."

"All right. All right. I didn't mean to yell at you. You make the ferry arrangements?"

"Ferry leaves at three-thirty. Chauffeur will pick you up at your place at three, okay?"

"Okay." Christensen said. "See if you can find out any more about all this and have somebody call me back in an hour with a briefing, will you?"

He fed the cats, showered, shaved, took a couple of pills, brewed some coffee. At half past two the ministry called. Nobody had any idea what the ambassador might want. Relations between San Francisco and the Republic of Monterey were cordial just now. Ms. Sawyer lived in Pacific Grove and was a member of the Monterey Senate and that was all that was known about her. Some briefing, Christensen thought. He went downstairs to wait for his chauffeur. It was a late autumn day, bright and clear and cool. The rains hadn't begun yet and the streets looked dusty. The foreign minister lived on Frederick Street just off Cole, in an old white Victorian with a small front porch. He settled in on the steps, feeling wide awake but surly, and a few minutes before three his car came putt-putting up, a venerable gray Chevrolet with the arms of imperial San Francisco on its doors. The driver was Vietnamese or maybe Thai. Christensen got in without a word, and off they went at an imperial velocity through the practically empty streets, down to Haight, eastward for a while, then onto Oak, up Van Ness past the palace, where at this moment the Emperor Norton VII was probably taking his imperial nap, and along Geary through downtown to the ferry slip. The stump of the Bay Bridge glittered magically against the sharp blue sky. A small power cruiser was waiting for him. Christensen was silent during the slow dull voyage. A chill wind cut through the Golden Gate and made him huddle into himself. He stared broodingly at the low rounded East Bay hills, dry and brown from a long summer of drought, and thought about the permutations of fate that had transformed an adequate architect into the barely competent foreign minister of this barely competent little nation. The Empire of San Francisco, one of the early emperors had said, is the only country in history that was decadent from the day it was founded.

At the Berkeley marina Christensen told the ferry skipper, "I don't know what time I'll be coming back, so no sense waiting. I'll phone in when I'm ready to go."

Another imperial car took him up the hillside to the sprawling nineteeth-century splendor of the Hotel Claremont, that vast antiquated survivor of all the cataclysms. It was seedy now, the grounds a jungle, ivy almost to the tops of the palm trees, and yet it still looked fit to be a palace, hundreds of rooms, magnificent banquet halls. Christensen wondered how often it had guests. There wasn't much tourism these days.

In the parking plaza outside the entrance was a single car, a black-and-white California Highway Patrol job that had been decorated with the insignia of the Republic of Monterey, a contorted cypress tree and a sea otter. A uniformed driver lounged against it. "I'm Christensen," he told the man.

"You the foreign minister?"

"I'm not the Emperor Norton."

"Come on. She's waiting in the bar."

Ms. Sawyer stood up as he entered—a slender dark-haired woman of about thirty, with cool green eyes—and he flashed her a quick, professionally cordial smile, which she returned just as professionally. He did not feel at all cordial.

"Senator Sawyer," he said. "I'm Tom Christensen."

"Glad to know you." She pivoted and gestured toward the huge picture window that ran the length of the bar.

"I just got here. I've been admiring the view. It's been years since I've been in the Bay Area."

He nodded. From the cocktail lounge one could see the slopes of Berkeley, the bay, the ruined bridges, the still imposing San Francisco skyline. Very nice. They took seats by the window and he beckoned to a waiter, who brought them drinks.

"How was your drive up?" Christensen asked.

"No problems. We got stopped for speeding in San Jose, but I got out of it. They could see it was an official car and they stopped us anyway."

"The bastards. They love to look important."

"Things haven't been good between Monterey and San Jose all year. They're spoiling for trouble."

"I hadn't heard," Christensen said.

"We think they want to annex Santa Cruz. Naturally we can't put up with that. Santa Cruz is our buffer."

He said sharply, "Is that what you came here for, to ask our help against San Jose?"

She stared at him in surprise. "Are you in a hurry, Mr. Christensen?"

"Not particularly."

"You sound awfully impatient. We're still making preliminary conversation, having a drink, two diplomats playing the diplomatic game. Isn't that so?"

"Well?"

"I was telling you what happened to me on the way north. In response to your question. Then I was filling you in on current political developments. I didn't expect you to snap at me like that."

"Did I snap?"

"It sounded like snapping to me," she said.

Christensen took a deep pull of his bourbon and water and gave her a long steady look. She met his gaze imperturbably. She looked annoyed, amused and very very tough. After a time, when some of the red haze of irrational anger and fatigue had cleared from his mind, he said quietly, "I had about four hours sleep last night and I wasn't expecting an envoy from Monterey today.

I'm tired and edgy, and if I sounded impatient or harsh or snappish, I'm sorry."

"It's all right. I understand."

"Another bourbon or two and I'll be properly unwound." He held his empty glass toward the hovering waiter. "A refill for you, too?" he asked her.

"Yes. Please." In a formal tone she said, "Is the Emperor in good health?"

"Not bad. He hasn't really been well for a couple of years, but he's holding his own. And President Morgan?"

"Fine," she said. "Hunting wild boar in Big Sur this week."

"A nice life it must be, President of Monterey. I've always liked Monterey. So much quieter and cleaner and more sensible down there than in San Francisco."

"Too quiet sometimes. I envy you the excitement here."

"Yes. The rapes, the muggings, the arson, the mass meetings, the race wars, the—"

"Please," she said gently.

He realized he had begun to rant. There was a throbbing behind his eyes. He worked to gain control of himself.

"Did my voice get too loud?"

"You must be terribly tired. Look, we can confer in the morning if you'd prefer. It isn't *that* urgent. Suppose we have dinner and not talk politics at all and get rooms here, and tomorrow after breakfast we can—"

"No," Christensen said. "My nerves are a little ragged, that's all. But I'll try to be more civil. And I'd rather not wait until tomorrow to find out what this is all about. Suppose you give me a précis of it now, and if it sounds too complicated, I'll sleep on it and we can discuss it in detail tomorrow. Yes?"

"All right." She put her drink down and sat quite still, as if arranging her thoughts. At length she said, "The Republic of Monterey maintains close ties with the Free

State of Mendocino. I understand that Mendocino and the Empire broke off relations a little while back."

"A fishing dispute, nothing major."

"But you have no direct contact with them right now. Therefore this should come as news to you. The Mendocino people have learned, and have communicated to our representative there, that an invasion of San Francisco is imminent."

Christensen blinked twice. "By whom?"

"The Realm of Wicca," she said.

"Flying down from Oregon on their broomsticks?"

"Please. I'm being serious."

"Unless things have changed up there," Christensen said, "the Realm of Wicca is nonviolent, like all the neopagan states. As I understand it, they tend their farms and practice their little pagan rituals and do a lot of dancing around the maypole and chanting and screwing, and that's it. You expect me to believe that a bunch of gentle goofy witches is going to make war on the Empire?"

She said, "Not war. But definitely an invasion."

"Explain."

"One of their high priests has proclaimed San Francisco a holy place and has instructed them to come down here and build a Stonehenge in Golden Gate Park in time for proper celebration of the winter solstice. There are at least a quarter of a million neopagans in the Willamette Valley and more than half of them are expected to take part. According to our Mendocino man, the migration has already begun, and thousands of Wiccans are spread out between Mount Shasta and Ukiah right now. The solstice is only seven weeks away. The Wiccans may be gentle, but you're going to have a hundred fifty thousand of them in San Francisco by the end of the month, pitching tents all over town."

"Holy Jesus," Christensen muttered, and closed his eyes.

"Can you feed that many strangers? Can you find room for them? Are the people of San Francisco going to meet them with open arms? Is it going to be a festival of love?"

"It'll be a fucking massacre," Christensen said tonelessly.

"Yes. And the witches may be nonviolent but they know how to practice self-defense. Once they're attacked, there'll be rivers of blood in the city, and it won't all be Wiccan blood."

Christensen's head was pounding again. She was absolutely right—chaos, strife, bloodshed. And a merry Christmas to all. He rubbed his aching forehead, turned away from her and stared out at the deepening twilight and the sparkling lights of the city on the other side of the bay. A bleak bitter depression was taking hold of his spirit. He signaled for another round of drinks. Then he said slowly, "They can't be allowed to enter the city. We'll need to close the imperial frontier and turn them back before they get as far as Santa Rosa. Let them build their goddamned Stonehenge in Sacramento if they like." His eyes flickered. He started to assemble ideas. "The Empire might just have enough troops to contain the Wiccans by itself, but I think this is best handled as a regional problem. We'll call in forces from our allies as far out as Petaluma and Napa and Palo Alto. I don't imagine we can expect much help from the Free State or from San Jose. And of course Monterey isn't much of a military power, but still—"

"We are willing to help you," Ms. Sawyer said.

"To what extent?"

"We aren't set up for much actual warfare, no, but we have access to our own alliances from Salinas down to Paso Robles, and we could call up, say, five thousand troops all told."

"That would be very helpful," said Christensen.

"It shouldn't be necessary for there to be any combat. With the imperial border sealed and troops posted along the line from Guerneville to Sacramento, the Wiccans won't force the issue. They'll revise their revelation and celebrate the solstice somewhere else."

"Yes," he said. "I think you're right." He leaned toward her and said, "Why is Monterey willing to help us?"

"We have problems of our own brewing—with San Jose. If we are seen making a conspicuous gesture of solidarity with the Empire, it might discourage San Jose from proceeding with its notion of annexing Santa Cruz, don't you think? That amounts to an act of war against us. Surely San Jose isn't interested in making any moves that will bring the Empire down on its back."

"I see," said Christensen. She wasn't subtle, but she was effective. Quid pro quo, we help you keep the witches out, you help us keep San Jose in line, and all remains well without a shot being fired. These goddamned little nations, he thought, these absurd jerkwater sovereignties, with their wars and alliances and shifting confederations—it was like a game, it was like playground politics. Except that it was real. What had fallen apart was not going to be put back together, not for a long while, and this miniaturized *weltpolitik* was the realest reality there was just now. At least things were saner in Northern California than they were down south where Los Angeles was gobbling everything, but there were rumors that Pasadena had the bomb. Nobody had to contend with that up here. Christensen said, "I'll have to propose all this to the defense ministry, of course. And get the Emperor's approval. But basically I'm in agreement with your thinking."

"I'm so pleased."

"And I'm very glad that you took the trouble to travel up from Monterey to make these matters clear to us."

"Enlightened self-interest," Ms. Sawyer said.

"Mmm. Yes." He found himself studying the sharp planes of her cheekbones, the delicate arch of her eyebrows. Not only was she cool and competent, Christensen thought, but now that the business part of their meeting was over, he was coming to notice that she was a very attractive woman and that he was not as tired as he had thought he was. Did international politics allow room for a little recreational hanky-panky? Metternich hadn't jumped into bed with Talleyrand, nor Kissinger with Indira Gandhi, but times had changed, after all, and—no. *No.* He choked off that entire line of thought. In these shabby days they might all be children playing at being grownups, but nevertheless, international politics still had its code, and this was a meeting of diplomats, not a blind date or a singles-bar pickup. You will sleep in your own bed tonight, he told himself, and you will sleep alone.

All the same he said, "It's past six o'clock. Shall we have dinner together before I go back to the city?"

"I'd love to."

"I don't know much about Berkeley restaurants. We're probably better off eating right here."

"I think that's best," she said.

They were the only ones in the hotel's enormous dining room. A staff of three waited on them as though they were the most important people who had ever dined there. And dinner turned out to be quite decent, he thought—seafood, calamari and abalone and sand dabs and grilled thresher shark, washed down by a dazzling bottle of Napa chardonnay. Even though the world had ended, it remained possible to eat very well in the Bay Area, and the breakdown of society not only had reduced maritime pollution but also had made local seafood much more readily available for local consumption. There wasn't much of an export trade possible with eleven national boundaries and eleven sets of customs barriers between San Francisco and Los Angeles.

Dinner conversation was light, relaxed—diplomatic chitchat, gossip about events in remote territories, reports about the Voodoo principality expanding out of New Orleans and the Sioux conquests in Wyoming and the Prohibition War now going on in what used to be Kentucky. There was a bison herd again on the Great Plains, she said, close to a million head. He told her what he had heard about the Suicide People who ruled between San Diego and Tijuana and about King Barnum & Bailey III who governed in northern Florida with the aid of a court of circus freaks. She smiled and said, "How can they tell the freaks from the ordinary people? The whole world's a circus now, isn't it?" He shook his head and replied, "No, a zoo," and beckoned the waiter for more wine. He did not ask her about internal matters in Monterey, and she tactfully stayed away from the domestic problems of the Empire of San Francisco. He was feeling easy, buoyant, a little drunk, more than a little drunk; to have to answer questions now about the little rebellion that had been suppressed in Sausalito or the secessionist thing in Walnut Creek would only be a bringdown, and bad for the digestion besides.

About half past eight he said, "You aren't going back to Monterey tonight, are you?"

"God, no! It's a five-hour drive, assuming no more troubles with the San Jose highway patrol. And the road's so bad below Watsonville that only a lunatic would drive it at night. I'll stay at the Claremont."

"Good. Let me put it on the imperial account."

"That isn't necessary. We—"

"The hotel is always glad to oblige the government. Please accept their hospitality."

Ms. Sawyer shrugged. "Very well. Which we'll reciprocate when you come to Monterey."

"Fine."

And then her manner suddenly changed. She shifted in her seat and fidgeted and played with her silverware, looking awkward and ill at ease. Some new and big topic was obviously about to be introduced, and Christensen guessed that she was going to ask him to spend the night with her. In a fraction of a second he ran through all the possible merits and demerits of that and came out on the plus side, and had his answer ready when she said, "Tom, can I ask a big favor?"

Which threw him completely off balance. Whatever was coming, it certainly wasn't what he was expecting.

"I'll do my best."

"I'd like an audience with the Emperor."

"What?"

"Not on official business. I know the Emperor talks business only with his ministers and privy councillors. But I want to see him, that's all." Color came to her cheeks. "Doesn't it sound silly? But it's something I've always dreamed of, a kind of adolescent fantasy. To be in San Francisco, to be shown into the imperial throne-room, to kiss his ring, all that pomp and circumstance— I want it, Tom. Just to *be* there, to *see* him—do you think you could manage that?"

He was astounded. The facade of cool, tough compe-tence had dropped away from her, revealing unantic-ipated absurdity. He did not know what to answer.

She said, "Monterey's such a poky little place. It's just a *town*. We call ourselves a republic, but we aren't much of anything. And I call myself a senator and a diplomat, but I've never really been anywhere—San Francisco two or three times when I was a girl, San Jose a few times. My mother was in Los Angeles once, but I haven't been anywhere. And to go home saying that I had seen the Emperor—" Her eyes sparkled. "You're really taken aback, aren't you? You thought I was all ice and microprocessors, and instead I'm only a hick, right? But you're being very nice. You aren't even laughing at me. Will you get me an audience with the Emperor for tomorrow or the day after?"

"I thought you were afraid to go into San Francisco."

She looked abashed. "That was just a ploy. To make you come over here, to get you to take me seriously and put yourself out a little. The diplomatic wiles. I'm sorry about that. The word was that you were snotty, that you had to be met with strength or you'd be impossible to deal with. But you aren't like that at all. Tom, I want to see the Emperor. He does give audiences, doesn't he?"

"In a manner of speaking. I suppose it could be done."

"Oh, would you! Tomorrow?"

"Why wait for tomorrow? Why not tonight?"

"Are you being sarcastic?"

"Not at all," Christensen said. "This is San Francisco. The Emperor keeps weird hours just like the rest of us. I'll phone over there and see if we can be received." He hesitated. "It won't be what you're expecting."

"In what way?"

"The pomp, the circumstance—you're going to be disappointed. You may be better off not meeting him, actually. Stick to your fantasy of imperial majesty. Seriously. I'll get you an audience if you insist, but I don't think it's a great idea."

"Can you be more specific?"

"No."

"I still want to see him. Regardless."

"Let me make some phone calls, then."

He left the dining room and, with misgivings, began arranging things. The telephone system was working sluggishly that evening and it took him fifteen minutes to set the whole thing up, but there were no serious obstacles. He returned to her and said, "The ferry will pick us up at the marina in about an hour. There'll be a car waiting on the San Francisco side. The Emperor will be available for viewing around midnight. I tell you that you're not going to enjoy this. The Emperor is old and he's been sick and he—he isn't a very interesting person to meet."

"All the same," she said. "The one thing I wanted, when I volunteered to be the envoy, was an imperial audience. Please don't discourage me."

"As you wish. Shall we have another drink?"

"How about these instead?" She produced an enameled cigarette case. "Humboldt County's finest. Gift of the Free State."

He smiled and nodded and took the joint from her. It was elegantly manufactured, fine cockleshell paper, gold monogram, igniter cap, even a filter. Everything else has come apart, he thought, but the technology of marijuana is at its highest point in history. He flicked the cap, took a deep drag, passed it to her. The effect was

instantaneous, a new high cutting through the wooze of
bourbon and wine and brandy already in his brain,
clearing it, expanding his limp and sagging soul. When
they were finished with it, they floated out of the hotel.
His driver and hers were still waiting in the parking lot.
Christensen dismissed his, and they took the Republic of
Monterey car down the slopes of Berkeley to the
marina. The boat from San Francisco was late. They
stood around shivering at the ferry slip for twenty
minutes, peering bleakly across at the glittering lights of
the far-off city. Neither of them was dressed for the
nighttime chill, and he was tempted to pull her close and
hold her in his arms, but he did not do it. There was a
boundary he was not yet willing to cross. Hell, he
thought, I don't even know her first name.

It was nearly eleven by the time they reached San
Francisco.

An official car was parked at the pier. The driver
hopped out, saluting, bustling about—one of those
preposterous little civil-service types, doubtless keenly
honored to be taxiing bigwigs around late at night. He
wore the red-and-gold uniform of the imperial dra-
goons, a little frayed at one elbow. The car coughed and
sputtered and reluctantly lurched into life, up Market
Street to Van Ness and then north to the palace. Ms.
Sawyer's eyes were wide and she stared at the ancient
high-rises along Market as though they were cathedrals.
When they came to the Civic Center area she gasped,
obviously overwhelmed by the majesty of everything,
the shattered hulk of Symphony Hall, the Museum of
Modern Art, the great domed enormity of the City Hall,
the Hall of Justice and the Imperial Palace itself,
awesome, imposing, a splendid many-columned building that long ago had been the War Memorial Opera
House. A bunch of imperial cars were parked outside.
With the envoy from the Republic of Monterey at his
elbow, Christensen marched up the steps of the palace
and through the center doors into the lobby, where a
great many of the ranking ministers and plenipoten-

tiaries of the Empire were assembled. "How absolutely marvelous," Ms. Sawyer murmured. Smiling graciously, bowing, nodding, Christensen pointed out the notables, the defense minister, the minister of finance, the minister of suburban affairs, the chief justice, the minister of transportation, and all the rest. At midnight precisely there was a grand flourish of trumpets and the door to the throne room opened. Christensen offered Ms. Sawyer his arm; together they made the long journey down the center aisle and up the ramp to the stage, where the imperial throne, a resplendent thing of rhinestones and foil, glittered brilliantly under the spotlights. Ms. Sawyer was wonderstruck. She pointed toward the six gigantic portraits suspended high over the stage and whispered a question, and Christensen replied, "The first six emperors. And here comes the seventh one."

"Oh," she gasped—but was it awe, surprise, or disgust?

He was in his full regalia, the scarlet robe, the bright green tunic with ermine trim, the gold chains. But he was wobbly and tottering, a clumsy staggering figure, gray-faced and feeble, supported on one side by Mike Schiff, the imperial chamberlain, and on the other by the grand sergeant-at-arms, Terry Coleman. He was not so much leaning on them as being dragged by them. Bringing up the rear of the procession were two sleek, pretty boys, one black and one Chinese, carrying the orb, the scepter and the massive crown. Ms. Sawyer's fingers tightened on Christensen's forearm and he heard her catch her breath as the Emperor, in the process of being lowered into his throne, went boneless and nearly spilled to the floor. Somehow the imperial chamberlain and the grand sergeant-at-arms settled him properly in place, balanced the crown on his head, stuffed the orb and scepter into his trembling hands. "His Imperial Majesty, Norton the Seventh of San Francisco!" cried Mike Schiff in a magnificent voice that went booming up into the highest balcony. The Emperor giggled.

"Come on," Christensen whispered, and led her forward.

The old man was really in terrible shape. It was weeks since Christensen last had seen him, and by now he looked like something dragged from the crypt, slack-jawed, drooling, vacant-eyed, utterly burned out. The envoy from Monterey seemed to draw back; tense and rigid, repelled, unable or unwilling to go closer, but Christensen persisted, urging her onward until she was no more than a dozen feet from the throne. A sickly-sweet odor emanated from the old man.

"What do I do?" she asked in a panicky voice.

"When I introduce you, go forward, curtsy if you know how, touch the orb. Then step back. That's all."

She nodded.

Christensen said, "Your Majesty, the ambassador from the Republic of Monterey, Senator Sawyer, to pay her respects."

Trembling, she went to him, curtseyed, touched the orb. As she backed away, she nearly fell, but Christensen came smoothly forward and steadied her. The Emperor giggled again, a shrill horrific cackle. Slowly, carefully, Christensen guided the shaken and numbed Ms. Sawyer from the stage.

"How long has he been like that?" she asked.

"Two years, three, maybe more. Completely insane. Not even housebroken any more. You could probably tell. I'm sorry. I told you you'd be better off skipping this. I'm enormously sorry, Ms.—Ms.—what's your first name, anyway?"

"Elaine."

"Elaine. Let's get out of here, Elaine. Yes?"

"Yes. Please."

She was shivering. He walked her up the side aisle. A few of the other courtiers were clambering up onto the stage now, one with a guitar, one with a juggler's clubs. The imperial giggle pierced the air again and again, becoming shrill and rasping and wild. The royal levee would probably go on half the night. Emperor Norton VII was one of San Francisco's most popular amusements.

"Now you know," Christensen said.

"How does the Empire function, if the Emperor is crazy?"

"We manage. We do our best without him. The Romans managed it with Caligula. Norton's not half as bad as Caligula. Not a tenth. Will you tell everyone in Monterey?"

"I think not. We believe in the power of the Empire and in the grandeur of the Emperor. Best not to disturb that faith."

"Quite right," said Christensen.

They emerged into the dark clear cold night.

Christensen said, "I'll ride back to the ferry slip with you, before I go home."

"Where do you live?"

"The other way. Out near Golden Gate Park."

She looked up at him and moistened her lips. "I don't want to ride across the bay in the dark alone at this hour of the night. Is it all right if I come home with you?"

"Sure," he said.

She managed a jaunty smile. "You're straight, aren't you?"

"Sure. Most of the time, anyway."

"I thought you were. Good."

They got into the car. "Frederick Street," he told the driver, "between Belvedere and Cole."

The trip took twenty minutes. Neither of them spoke. He knew what she was thinking about—the crazy Emperor, dribbling and babbling under the bright spotlights. The mighty Norton VII, ruler of everything from San Rafael to San Mateo, from Half Moon Bay to Walnut Creek. Such is pomp and circumstance in imperial San Francisco in these latter days of Western civilization. Christensen sent the driver away and they went upstairs. The cats were hungry again.

"It's a lovely apartment," she told him.

"Three rooms, bath, hot and cold running water. Not bad for a mere foreign-minister. Some of the boys have suites at the palace, but I like it better here." He opened the door to the deck and stepped outside. Somehow, now that he was home, the night was not so cold. He thought about the Realm of Wicca, far off up there in green, happy Oregon, sending a hundred fifty thousand kindly Goddess-worshiping neopagans down here to celebrate the rebirth of the sun. A nuisance, a mess, a headache. Tomorrow he'd have to call a meeting of the cabinet, when everybody had sobered up, and start the wheels turning, and probably he'd have to make trips to places like Petaluma and Palo Alto to get the alliance flanged together. Damn. Damn. But it was his job, wasn't it? Someone had to carry the load.

He slipped his arm around the slender woman from Monterey.

"The poor Emperor," she said softly.

"Yes. The poor Emperor. Poor everybody."

He looked toward the east. In a few hours the sun would be coming up over that hill, out of the place that used to be the United States of America and now was a thousand thousand crazy fractured fragmented entities. Christensen shook his head. The Grand Duchy of Chicago, he thought. The Holy Carolina Confederation. The Three Kingdoms of New York. The Empire of San Francisco. No use getting upset—much too late for getting upset. You played the hand that was dealt you and you did your best and you carved little islands of safety out of the night. Turning to her he said, "I'm glad you came home with me tonight." He brushed his lips lightly against hers. "Come. Let's go inside."

A Thousand Paces Along the Via Dolorosa

Hornkastle said to the dapper young Israeli, "When they eat the mushroom, do they think they see God?"

"Far more than that. The mushroom *is* their god. When they eat it, they become one with Him: they become Him. It is the pure *agapé*," Ben-Horin said, "the true Christian feast."

Ben-Horin's voice, light but firm, crisp and clipped, had a dizzying musical quality. A pounding began in Hornkastle's forehead. Being with the Israeli made Hornkastle—a big man, some years older, nearly forty—feel thick and clumsy and slow. And what Ben-Horin was telling him about these Arab tribal rites stirred in him some mysterious hunger, some incomprehensible longing, that baffled and astounded him. He felt woozy. He suspected he might have had too much to drink. He looked up and across, out the big window of the hotel cocktail lounge. Off there to the west Jerusalem was awesome in the late afternoon sunlight. The domes of the two great mosques, one gold and one silver, glittered like globules of molten metal. Hornkastle closed his eyes and put his drink to his lips and said, "Take me to these people."

"Gently, gently. What they do is very illegal in Israel. And they are Arabs, besides—Christian Arabs, who live between worlds here, who are very cautious people at all times."

"I want to go to them."

"And eat their mushroom? And become one with their god?"

Hornkastle said hoarsely, "To study them. To understand them. You know this is my field."

"You want to eat the mushroom," said Ben-Horin.

Hornkastle shrugged. "Maybe." To swallow God, to be possessed by Him, to entangle one's identity with Him—why not? Why not? "How long before I can go to them?" he asked.

"Who knows? A week? Two? Everything here is conditional. The politics, the inflation rate, the weather, even—one takes everything into account. I promise you you'll see them. Until Easter everything is crazy here—pilgrims, tourists, wandering ecstatics—it gets a little like Benares, almost. After Easter, all right? Can you stay that long?"

Hornkastle considered. He was on sabbatical. He had virtually fled Los Angeles, escaping from the wreckage of his life there. It didn't matter when he went back, or if he ever did. But he was gripped with impatience. He said, "I'll stay as long as possible. But please—soon—"

"We must wait for the right moment," said Ben-Horin firmly. "Come, now. My wife is eager to meet you."

They went out into the surprisingly chilly April air. With a lurch and a roar Ben-Horin's tiny orange Datsun took off, down the hill, around the compact medieval splendor of the walled Old City and through New Jerusalem. Ben-Horin was an outrageous driver, screeching through the streets like a racer in the Grand Prix, honking ferociously at his fellow motorists as if they were all retired Nazis. The Israelis must be the most belligerent drivers in the world, Hornkastle thought. Even a cool cosmopolitan type like Ben-Horin, professor of botany, connoisseur of rare fungi, turned into a lunatic behind the wheel. But that was all right. Life had been a roller-coaster ride for Hornkastle for a couple of years now. One more round of loop-the-loop wasn't going to bother him much. Not after three stiff jobs of arrack on the rocks. Not here. Not now.

Ben-Horin lived in a gray-and-blue high-rise, spectacularly situated on a hilltop near the university. It looked stunning from a distance, but once inside Hornkastle noticed that the stucco was cracking, the lobby tiles were starting to fall out, the elevator made disturbing groaning sounds. The Israeli ushered him into a tiny immaculate apartment. "My wife, Geula," said Ben-Horin with a brusque little wave. "Thomas Hornkastle of the University of California, Los Angeles."

She was a surprise—a big woman, inch or two taller than Ben-Horin, probably twenty pounds heavier, with a ripe, if not overripe, look to her. It was hard to imagine these two as man and wife, for Ben-Horin was dry and precise and contained and she was full of vitality, young and pretty, in a way, and overflowing with life. Her eyes were dark and glossy and it seemed to Hornkastle that she was looking at him with outright interest. Probably a figment of the arrack, he decided.

He needed no more drinks, but he had never been good at refusing them, and soon she had a martini-like thing in his hand, something made with Dutch gin and too much vermouth. The conversation was quick, animated, impersonal. Perhaps that was the style here. Ben-Horin and his wife were both well informed about world affairs, though everything seemed to circle back to analyses of the impact of this event or that on Israel's own situation. Possibly, Hornkastle thought, if you live in a very small country that has been surrounded by fanatical enemies for its entire life, you get fixated on local issues. He had been startled, at the international symposium where he had met Ben-Horin last December, to hear an Israeli historian expounding on the Vietnam war in terms of Israel and Syria. "If your government tells you to defend an outpost," he had said, "you go and defend it. You don't argue with your government about the morality of the thing!" With that sort of outlook even the rainfall in Uganda could become a significant domestic political issue.

Somehow he finished his martini and one after that, and then there was wine with dinner, a dry white wine from the Galilee. Hornkastle always drank a little too heavily, especially when he was traveling, but in the last few turbulent years it had started to be a problem, and the way the Ben-Horins kept him topped off could get troublesome. He knew he was on the edge of becoming sloppy and worked hard at staying together. After a time he was just nodding and smiling while they talked, but suddenly—it was late, and now everyone was drinking a corrosive Israeli brandy—she wanted to know about his field of study. He did his best, but his voice sounded slurred even to him. Professor of experimental psychology, he said, here to investigate rumors of archaic cultist practices among the Arabs just south of Jerusalem. "Oh, the mushroom," she said. "You have tried it in California, perhaps?"

"In a minor way. In the course of my research."

"Everyone in California takes drugs all the time. Yes?"

Hornkastle smiled blearily. "Not these days. Not as much as is commonly believed."

"The mushroom here, the *Amanita muscaria*," she said, "is very strong, maybe because it is holy and this is the Holy Land. Stronger than what is in California, I believe. No wonder they call it a god. You want to try it?"

Hazily he imagined she was offering him some right now, and he looked at her in horror and amazement. But Ben-Horin laughed and said, "He is not sure. I will take him to Kidron and he can conduct his own investigation."

"It is very strong," she said again. "You must be careful."

"I will be careful," Hornkastle said solemnly, although the promise sounded hollow to him, for he had been careful so long, careful to a fault, pathologically careful, and now in Israel he felt strangely reckless and terrified of his own potential recklessness. "My interest is scholarly," he said, but it came out *skhollally*, and as he struggled desperately and unsuccessfully to get the word right, Ben-Horin tactfully rescued him with an apology for having an early class the next day. When they said good night Geula Ben-Horin took his hand and, Hornkastle was certain, held it just a moment too long.

In the morning he felt surprisingly fine, almost jaunty, and at midday he set out for the Old City on foot. Entering it, he looked about in wonder. Before him lay the Via Dolorosa, Christ's route to the Crucifixion, and to all sides spread a tangle of alleys, arcades, stairs, tunnels, passageways and bazaars. Hornkastle had been in plenty of ancient cities, but there was something about this one that put it beyond all others. He could touch a paving stone and think, King David walked here or the Emperor Titus or Saladin, and this was where Jesus had staggered to Golgotha under the weight of his own cross.

So, then: up one winding street and down another, getting himself joyously lost—Monastery of the Flagellation, Western Wall, Dome of the Rock, Street of the Chain, a random walk, poking his nose into the *souks* where old hawk-faced men sold sheepskin rugs, pungent spices out of burlap bags, prayer-beads, shawls, hideous blue ceramic things, camel statuettes, unplucked chickens, sides of lamb, brass pots, hookahs, religious artifacts of every sort and, for all Hornkastle knew, merchandise far more sinister than any of that. In a noisy fly-specked market he bought some falafel and a carbonated beverage, and a little farther on, still hungry, he stopped at a place selling charcoal-grilled kebabs. The fascination of the place was like a drug. These timeless faces, men in worn serge suits who wore flowing Bedouin headdresses, young women darting from doorway to doorway, grubby children, dogs blithely licking at spilled God-knows-what in the gutters, old peasant women with refrigerators or television sets strapped to their backs, cries and odors, the periodic amplified songs of the muezzins calling the faithful to the mosques, picturesque squalor everywhere, why, it was like a movie, like time-travel even, except that it was actually happening to him: he was here and now in Old Jerusalem, capital of the world. It was exhilarating and a little intoxicating. And there was that extra little thrill, that *frisson*, of knowing—if he could believe Ben-Horin's story—that the ancient religion still flourished somewhat hereabouts, that there still were those who ate of the sacred mushroom that had been the forbidden fruit of the Tree of Good and Evil, the manna of the Israelites, the hallucinogenic phallic fungus that made one like unto a god. Perhaps that boy with glittering eyes in the dark doorway, that old man leaning against the cobbled wall, that powerful fellow in the tinsmiths' stall—secret mystics, devouring God in rites as old as Sumer, undergoing joyous metamorphoses of the spirit, ecstasies. From the Greek *ekstasis*, the flight of the soul from the body. "You must come to Israel," Ben-Horin had told him last winter at that meeting in Monaco after Hornkastle had read his paper on Siberian mushroom intoxication. "The most surprising things still exist among us, a dozen kilometers from the tourist hotels, and scarcely anyone knows about them, and those that do pretend that nothing is going on."

At 2:00 P.M. Hornkastle emerged from the maze of the Old City at the Damascus Gate. Ben-Horin was already there. "A punctual man," the Israeli said, turning a quick grin on and off. "You feel all right today? Good. Come with me." He led Hornkastle back into the heart of the city. Near the Via Dolorosa he said, "Walk slowly and glance to your left. See the man at the falafel stand? He is one. A user of *tigla'.*"

"Tigla'?"

"The word is Aramaic. The mushroom. A reference to its phallic shape. Are you hungry?"

They approached the falafel stand. The man behind the counter, presiding over basins of bubbling oil, was an Arab, about thirty, with a lean triangular face, wide jutting cheekbones tapering down toward a sharp narrow chin. Hornkastle stared at him flagrantly, peering as though he were a shaman, an oracle, a holy man. Questions boiled and raged in his mind, and he felt once again that urgent hunger, that need to surrender himself and be engulfed by a larger force.

Ben-Horin said something curt and harsh in Arabic, and the falafel seller scooped several of the golden chick-pea balls out of the hot oil, stuffing them into envelopes of pita bread. As he handed one across to Hornkastle, his eyes—dark, faintly hyperthyroid, blood-shot—met the American's and locked on them for a long moment, and Hornkastle flinched and looked down as he took the sandwich. Ben-Horin paid. When they walked away, Hornkastle said, "Does he know you?"

"Of course. But I could hardly speak to him here."

"Because he's an Arab and you're a Jew?"

"Don't be absurd. We're both Israeli citizens. It is because I am a professor at Hebrew University and he's a falafel seller and this is the Old City, where I am an intruder. There are class lines here that neither he nor I should cross. Don't believe all you hear about what an egalitarian country this is."

"Why did you take me to him?"

"To show you," said Ben-Horin, "that there are *tigla'* folk right in the midst of the city. And to show him that you have my sponsorship, for they trust me, after a fashion, and now they are likely to trust you. This must all be done very, very slowly. Come now, my car is near the bus station."

With his usual terrifying intensity Ben-Horin circled the northeast corner of the Old City and headed south out Jericho Road toward the Kidron Valley. Quickly they left the urban area behind and entered a rough, scrubby terrain, rocky and parched. Like a tour guide Ben-Horin offered a rapid commentary. "Over there, Mount Zion, Tomb of David. There, Valley of Hinnom, where in ancient times were the high places where Baal and Moloch were worshipped. Still are, perhaps, but if it's going on, they keep very quiet about it. And here—" dry ravines, stony fields—"Kidron. You follow the valley to its end and you are in the Dead Sea." Hornkastle saw shepherds, a camel or two, stone huts. Ben-Horin turned off on an easterly road, poorly maintained. It was amazing how quickly the land became desert once you were a short way down from cool, hilly Jerusalem. The Israeli pointed ahead toward a scruffy village—a few dozen crude buildings clumped around a couple of tin-roofed stores, one emblazoned with a giant red COCA-COLA sign. "This is the place. We will not stop today, but I will drive slowly through."

The town was dusty, ramshackle, drab. Outside COCA-COLA sat a few old men in jeans, battered pea-jackets and Arab headdresses. A couple of sullen boys glowered at the car. Hornkastle heard a radio playing—was that an old Presley number wailing across the wasteland? He said, "How in God's name did you ever get them to open up to you?"

"A long, slow process."

"What was your secret?"

Ben-Horin smiled smugly. "Science. The Arabs had begun to exhaust their traditional fungus sources. I told them other places to look. My price was entrée into their rites. I pledge you, it took a long time."

"You've had the mushroom yourself?"

"Several times. To show my good faith. I didn't enjoy it."

"Too heavy for you?"

"Heavy? Heavy?" Ben-Horin seemed puzzled by the idiom. Then he said, "The physiological effects were fascinating—the intensifying of colors and textures, the sense of the earth as a breathing organism, the effect of having music turn into flavors and shapes, all the synesthesias, the familiar psychedelic circus. But also very, very powerful, more than I had experienced elsewhere. I began to feel that there truly was a God and He was touching my consciousness. I am willing to perceive the sound of a flute as something with mottled wings, but I am not willing at the age of thirty-one to begin generating a belief in supernatural deities. And when I began to lose sight of the boundaries between God and Ben-Horin, when I began to think of myself as perhaps partaking of the nature of Jesus—" Ben-Horin shook his head. "For me this is no pastime to pursue. Let those who want to be gods, saviors, divine martyrs, whatever, eat their fill of the mushroom. I am content to study its worshipers."

They were well past the village, now, three or four miles into the empty desert. Hornkastle said, "Do you think this cult has simply survived since ancient times, or is it a deliberate modern revival?"

"I have no idea."

"But what do you think?"

"I said I have no idea. Do you?"

Hornkastle shrugged. "Since the whole Near East once was honeycombed with mushroom cultists, I suppose it's possible that one group has hung on. Especially here. I'm familiar with Allegro's notion that Jesus himself never existed, that *Jesus* is just a code word for the sacred mushroom that rises from the ground, the phallic-looking son of God that is eaten and shows the way to the Godhead. And this is Jesus' own turf, after all. But presumably these cults were all suppressed thousands of years ago."

"Presumably."

"It's exciting to think that the belief simply went underground instead. I want to find out."

"With luck you will, my friend."

"Take me into the village?"

"Eventually."

"Why not now? While we're actually here."

"Your impatience will be your ruin, dear Hornkastle. We must move very slowly."

"If you understood how eager I—"

"I do understand. That is why there must be no haste."

They rounded a bend in the road. An Israeli soldier was standing beside an overturned motorbike, signaling for help. Ben-Horin halted and there was a brief colloquy in Hebrew. Then the soldier clambered into the car, apologizing in mild, inexact English as he jammed himself next to Hornkastle and made room for his machine-gun. "We will give him a lift back to Jerusalem," Ben-Horin explained. That put an end to any talk of sacred mushrooms.

As they passed through the village again, Hornkastle noticed that a younger man had emerged from COCA-COLA and stood outside it, arms folded. For an eerie moment Hornkastle thought he was the falafel seller—the same face, wide cheekbones, pointed chin, bulging, brooding eyes—but of course that was unlikely; this must be a cousin, a brother. In these villages everyone has the same genes.

"I will drop you at your hotel," said Ben-Horin.

Itchy, irritating frustration assailed Hornkastle. He wanted much more than this, and he did not want to wait, and if impatience would be his ruin, so be it: he was impatient. He felt irritable, volatile, explosive. With an effort he calmed himself. Ben-Horin was right: only by moving slowly would anything be accomplished. The trouble was he had moved so slowly so long, all through his tame disciplined academic life. Now those disciplines seemed to be breaking down, and he stood on the brink of strangeness, awaiting the dive.

He said, "When will we meet again?"

"In a few days," Ben-Horin replied. "I must deliver a lecture in Haifa tomorrow, and then there are other responsibilities. I will call you."

* * *

The bartender at the hotel recognized Hornkastle and asked him if he wanted arrack again. Hornkastle nodded gloomily and studied the liquor, watching the ice-cubes turn the clear fluid cloudy. Shadows were starting to lengthen over the domes and parapets of the Old City. He was working on his third drink when two tourists came in, obviously mother and daughter, say fifty-five and thirty, good-looking long-legged golden-haired women with delicate slender faces, fragile sharp noses. British, he guessed, from the severe cut of their clothes and from their imperfect, somewhat bucked teeth. Before long he managed to draw them into conversation. British, yes, Claudia and Helena, cool and elegant and self-contained, friendly. Helena, the daughter, asked what he was drinking. "Arrack," he said. "Anise liqueur, like the Greek ouzo, you know? The Turkish raki. Same stuff from Indonesia to Yugoslavia." The daughter ordered one; the mother tried it and called for sherry instead.

Before long the women were on their second drinks and he was ready for his fourth and everyone was a little flushed. There was a pleasant sexual undercurrent to the conversation now, nothing obvious, nothing forced, just there, mature and not unattractive man sitting with two mature women in strange land. Anything might happen. He was fairly certain of the glow in Helena's eyes—that same you-need-but-ask shine that he had imagined he had seen in Geula Ben-Horin's, but this did not seem like imagination. And even the older one had a spark of it. He allowed himself quick foolish fantasies. The mother tactfully excusing herself at the right moment; he and the daughter going off somewhere for dinner, dancing, night of exotic delights, breakfast on the veranda. Or maybe the *daughter* pleading a headache and disappearing, and he and Claudia—why not? She wasn't that much older than he was. Or perhaps both of them at once, something agreeably kinky, one of those nights to treasure forever. They were widows, he learned, their husbands killed in a freak hunting accident in Scotland the previous autumn. Helena spoke matter-of-factly about it, as if being widowed at thirty was no great event. "And now," she said, "mother and I are pilgrims in Jerusalem! We look forward so much to the Easter celebrations. Since the mishap we've felt the presence of God by our sides constantly, and Jesus as a living force." Hornkastle's dreams of a wild threesome upstairs began to fade. They had been Church of England, said Claudia, very high church indeed, but after the mishap they had turned to the Roman faith for solace, and now, in the Holy Land, they would march with other pilgrims along the Via Dolorosa, bearing the cross—

Eventually they asked Hornkastle about himself, and he sketched it all quickly, UCLA, experimental psychology, divorce, sabbatical, hint of severe inner storms, crisis, need to get away from it all. He intended to say nothing about sacred mushrooms, but somehow that slipped out—secret cult, hallucinogens, mysterious village in the desert. His cheeks reddened. "How *fascinating!*" Helena cried. "Will you take us there?" He imagined what Ben-Horin would say about that. He responded vaguely, and she swept onward, bright-eyed, enthusiastic, chattering about drugs. California, mysticism. He began to think he might be able to get somewhere with her after all, and started to angle the conversation back toward dinner, but no, no, they had a prior engagement, dinner at the rectory, was that it? "We must talk again soon," said Claudia, and off they went, and he was alone again.

A suspended time began. He wandered by himself. One night he went down to the Old City—dark, a mysterious and threatening warren of knotted streets and sinister-looking people. He ate at a little Arab place, grilled fish and mashed chick-peas for a few shekels. Afterward he got lost in a deserted area of blank-walled houses. He thought he was being followed—footsteps in the distance, rustling sounds, whispers—but whenever he glanced back, he saw nothing but woebegone lop-eared cats. Somehow he found his way to Jaffa Gate and picked up a taxi.

He rented a car and did standard tourist things, museums and monuments. Jerusalem, he decided, looked a little like Southern California. Not the inner city, God, no, but the environs, the dry tawny rocky hills, the vast open sky, the clusters of flat-faced condominiums and whatnot sprawling over every ridge and crest—he could almost blink and imagine himself somewhere out by Yorba Linda or Riverside. Except that in the middle of it all was the city of David and Solomon and Herod and Pilate, and the place of the cross. Had any of that really happened, he wondered? A slender bearded man lurching up the Via Dolorosa under the weight of the two massive wooden beams? What is it like to carry the cross? What is it like to hang high above the ground in the cool clear springtime air of Jerusalem, waiting for your Father to summon your spirit?

Hornkastle prowled the Old City constantly, getting to know his way around in the maze. His path often took him past the falafel stand. When he bought sandwiches from the Arab, his hand trembled, as if the falafel-seller who had so many times devoured his own god held some awesome numinous power that instilled fear. What wonders had that man seen, what strange heights had he ascended? Hornkastle felt brutally excluded from that arcane knowledge, half as old as time, that the Arab must possess. Looking into his bloodshot eyes, Hornkastle was tempted to blurt out his questions in a rush of *tell me tell me*, but he did not dare, for the Arab would pretend not to speak English and Ben-Horin, when he found out, would simply disown him, and that would be the end of the quest.

From Ben-Horin he continued to hear nothing. At last, unable to contain his impatience, Hornkastle telephoned him at home but got no answer. A call to Ben-Horin's office involved him in a maddening sequence of university switchboard operators; half an hour of persistence got him through at last to someone in Ben-Horin's department who said he had gone to Athens to deliver a lecture.

"Athens? I thought Haifa!"

"No, Athens. He will be back soon."

"Please tell him that Thomas Hornkastle would—" But Hornkastle was holding a dead phone. Break in service or just a hangup? He reminded himself that he was in Asia, that however shiny and modern Israel might look, the mentality here was not necessarily always Western. The idea of trying to call back, of going through all those intermediaries again, was appalling. It would be quicker to drive out there and leave a message on Ben-Horin's desk. Shortly he was on his way, navigating grimly in his flimsy Fiat among the squadrons of Israeli kamikaze drivers. With minor confusions he reached the glossy campus and managed to find a secretary, a trim little Sabra who took his quickly scrawled note and promised to give it to Dr. Ben-Horin tomorrow when he returned from his trip to Geneva. Some communications failures here, Hornkastle thought. He felt like inviting the secretary to lunch. It was absurd; the frustrations of his mushroom chase were translating themselves into random sexual twitches. He got out of there fast, went over to the university library, and used up the afternoon with the five volumes of Farnell's *Cults of the Greek States,* looking for veiled *Amanita* references.

Back at the hotel he ran into Helena and Claudia. They were friendly, even warm, but that moment of unmistakable mutual attraction in the cocktail lounge seemed impossible to recapture, and when he again suggested dining with him, they once more blandly and smoothly refused. To fill their place he found an Episcopalian deacon from Ohio, who suggested an allegedly worthwhile restaurant in East Jerusalem. The Ohio man had come here for Easter services five years in a row. "Overwhelming," he said, nodding forcefully. "When they surge up the Via Dolorosa under those heavy crosses. The pathos, the passion! And then on Holy Saturday, when the Greek patriarch declares the Resurrection, and the cry goes up: *Christos anesti!* Christ is risen! You can't imagine the power of the scene. Bells ringing, people shouting and dancing, everybody going crazy, candles, torches—you'll still be here for it, won't you? You shouldn't miss it!"

Yes, Hornkastle thought bleakly, I will still be here for it and probably for Christmas, too. Restlessness gnawed at him. This night, perhaps, the Arabs were celebrating the eucharist of the magic mushroom, gathered in some cobblestone-walled hut to turn themselves into gods, and he was here in this mediocre restaurant, trapped in the prison of himself, picking at gristly mutton and listening to the raptures of a wide-eyed Midwesterner. He hungered for escape, for the dive into the abyss of the divine, for the whips of oblivion. The Ohioan chattered on and on. Hornkastle, hardly even pretending to listen, wondered about his ex-wife, his ex-house, his ex-life in his far-off ex-city, and asked himself how it had come to pass that in the middle of his journey he had ended up here, scourged by inner demons he barely comprehended. He had no answers.

The next day he phoned the university again, this time getting through quickly to Ben-Horin's department. Yes, yes, Dr. Ben-Horin had returned, he was leaving for Tel-Aviv tomorrow, perhaps you can reach him at home now.

The home number did not answer.

To Hornkastle it was like being released from a vow. In a sudden access of overwhelming anger, he drove out toward the Kidron Valley, toward the village of the *tiqla'* users, eyes throbbing, hands tight to the knobby wheel. In the village all was as it had been: the old men outside the shop with the COCA-COLA sign, two or three boys playing dice in the dust, a radio blaring sleazy music. No one paid any attention as Hornkastle stepped from his car and went into the shop. A dark place, cramped—canned goods, piles of sheets and blankets, a rack of used clothes, and, yes, a squat red Coca-Cola cooler that emitted dull clunking humming sounds. Behind the counter was the Arab who looked just like the falafel-seller. They are brothers, Hornkastle thought: this is Mustafa; the other is Hassan. Abdul and Ibrahim and Ismail are out tending the flocks, and they all look exactly alike. The bulging bloodshot eyes regarded him coldly. Hornkastle said, in a tentative, faltering way, "Do you speak English?"

"Yes. What do you want?"

Probably it was meant as a shopkeeper's *What can I do for you?* but it came out a lot more hostile than that. Hornkastle moistened his lips. "I want—I am here for—I am trying to learn about—" He halted in confusion and chagrin. This was impossibly stupid. Blurt it out, ask blunt questions about an illegal secret cult? How many months had it taken Ben-Horin to establish contact with these people? I'm ruining everything, Hornkastle thought. He trembled and said, astonishing himself, "Do you sell liquor here?"

A flicker of the dark menacing eyes. "You must go to Jerusalem for that."

"Wine? Beer?"

"Not here. You are in the wrong place."

Hornkastle leaned closer. "I am a friend of Professor Ben-Horin. I study the red plant. You understand?" He pantomimed, trying to draw *Amanita muscaria*'s phallic shape in the air with his hand, and realized that it looked exactly like pantomiming masturbation. The Arab's expression did not change. Hornkastle was shaking. "The mushroom. You understand me?" he said in a thick throaty voice.

"You are mistaken. This is not the place.

"I know it is. Have no fear: I'm no policeman. An American, a friend of Ben-Horin's. I want the mushroom. The closeness to God, do you understand? To taste God, to know the feeling of being divine, of being something greater than myself, of—"

"You are sick. I call doctor."

"No. Please. Trust me. In the name of the compassionate Jesus, help me!"

The Arab stared. Some changes seemed to be going on at last behind the swarthy facade. Hornkastle, sweating, swaying, gripped the counter to keep from falling.

"You are American. You want only fun."

"I swear it, no—"

"The mushroom is not for fun."

"The mushroom is holy. I understand that. *It* is holy, *God* is holy, I—I am not holy. I want to be made holy. To be made whole, do you see?" Hornkastle laughed, a little too wildly. I am babbling, he thought. But he seemed to be getting through. He whispered urgently, "I want to be part of something, finally, does that make sense? To enter a world where I feel I belong. And the mushroom will open the gate. I swear to my need. By the compassionate Jesus, by the eyes of Mary, by the Holy Spirit itself—"

"You are crazy," said the Arab.

"Perhaps I am. I don't think so. But do you have to be sane to want to enter into God? I've been on the outside all my life—looking in, looking for the way, trying to pass that gate and never letting myself do it, never willing to take the last chance. You know, I've had mushrooms, in California. But I always took an underdose, I guess, or the mushroom was too mild, because I only got a hint of the experience, the shadow of it, a little light shining through the door to where I stood—" He faltered. "Please," he said, in a small voice.

From the Arab came an enormous unending silence, broken after an eternity by a few quick gruff words: "Come with me."

Hornkastle nodded. They left the store through a side door, and he followed the Arab on and on, out of the little village, toward the rocky hill to the east. There were a few stone huts up there. The elders of the tribe are convened there, Hornkastle decided, and that is the place of the mushrooms, and I will be presented to them and allowed to plead my case, and then—and then—

Sudden intense panic surged through him. He felt a buzzing in his kneecaps and fierce pressure in his bladder and stabbing pain at the back of his skull. He had a vision of himself being called into judgment in one of those huts, the prying, snooping, ignorant American arraigned for poking his nose where it did not belong, and found guilty and taken out behind the hill, two quick thrusts of the dagger and over the edge into the dry ravine. *This is how we deal with meddlers, Frankish dog.* It was absurd. These people might *look* sinister, but it was all in his overheated imagination; they were harmless peasants, simple shepherds and farmers, much closer to God than he would ever be and hardly likely to do evil to a stranger. Yet fear possessed him. Halfway up the hill he turned and ran back toward the village, feeling feverish, dizzy, more than half-crazed. The Arab yelled after him but did not pursue. Somehow Hornkastle managed to start his car, and in chaos, tears streaming from his eyes as they had not done since he was a child, he drove wildly back to the city, past his hotel, out toward the university area. Angry drivers honked and shook fists at him. Near the Knesset building he saw a public telephone and called Ben-Horin's home, expecting nothing. Geùla Ben-Horin answered. "Hornkastle," he blurted. "I must come over at once."

"Of course. Are you all right?"

"Tell me how to get to your place."

It was only five minutes away. He rang her bell and she peered out. A whiff of musky perfume enveloped him; she was wearing a sheer dressing-gown and nothing else, and he was unprepared for that, the absurd, comical, preposterous seductiveness of her, heavy breasts visibly swaying, all that voluptuous Mediterranean flesh. He said, "Your husband—"

"In Tel-Aviv. Come in. What's wrong with you?"

She put a drink in his hand—the foul Israeli brandy—
and he gulped it like medicine, and then a second one.
She was warm, sympathetic, trying to find out what was
the matter; he was barely coherent. Finally, as the
brandy settled him a little, he managed to say, "I've just
been to the mushroom village."

"Ah." She looked grave.

"Begging them to give me some. I couldn't wait for
your husband to get back from wherever the hell he's
been. I stood the waiting as long as I could and then I
went out there. I talked the ear off some Arab, I reeled
off a whole lot of hysterical drivel about wanting to be
one with God, you know, the whole transcendental
thing—" His voice trailed off in shame.

She said, "And they gave you some, and now it is
beginning to upset your mind, is that it? It will be all
right. There will be some hours of great delirium and
then ecstasy and then gradually you will—"

"No, They didn't give me any."

"No?"

"The Arab told me to follow him and started to lead
me toward some huts on the hillside. And I panicked. I
thought it was a trap, that they were going to kill me for
asking too many questions, and I ran back to my car, I
drove, I—I—I fled here. To the only people I know in
Jerusalem."

Her eyes were warm with sorrow and pity and a sort
of love, it seemed to him, and yet her mouth was
quirked in what looked very much like contempt. "I
think you are wrong," she said calmly. "What you were
afraid of was not that they would do harm to you, but
that they really would give you the mushroom."

He blinked. "How can you say that?"

"I think that is so. Often we turn in fear from that
which we desire the most. You were in no danger from
them, and you knew that. You were in danger from
yourself, from your own troubled and tormented soul,
and what you feared was—"

"Please. Stop."

"—not what they would do to you but what you would see when the mushroom allowed you to look within."

"No. Please."

He was shaking again. He could not meet her gaze. She came close to him—she was nearly as tall as he was—and held him, comforting him, murmuring that she was sorry to have upset him when he was already in such a vulnerable state. He pressed himself against her and felt the tension draining from him. He felt like a child, a big foolish child. She was the great soothing mother herself, Isis, Astarte, Ishtar, and the power that she had over him frightened and attracted him all at once; if he could not let himself surrender to the god who was the mushroom, he would at least be capable of losing himself in the goddess who was His mother and consort.

"Come," she said, taking his hand.

Easily she led him to the bedroom and with dreamy willingness he vanished into her warm billowing body, no longer caring, no longer resisting anything. He had no strength left. It was all very quick, too quick, and he collapsed abruptly into deep sleep from which he woke, equally abruptly, finding himself lying in her arms and for a moment not knowing who, how, where.

He stared at her, aghast.

Before he could speak she put her finger to his lips and said softly, "You are feeling better?"

"We shouldn't have—your husband—"

"Life is very risky here. Any day the end might come. We live as though there are no second chances." She winked. "Our little secret, eh?" Helping him up, finding his scattered clothes. "When he gets home I will tell him you called. He has been so busy, running everywhere, lectures, meetings—he has so little time. I am glad you came. About the mushroom village and what happened to you there: fear nothing. They will not harm you."

"Will you tell him I went there?"

"No. He can find that out from you much better."

"What am I going to do, though? I've bungled everything!"

"You are a Christian?" She smiled and touched her lips lightly to his. "Live in the hope of glorious redemption. Even bunglers are forgiven if there is a God. Forgive yourself and He will forgive you too, eh? Eh?" She drew him to her for a brief warm embrace. "Go, now," she whispered. "It will be all right."

For ten minutes Hornkastle sat behind the wheel of his parked car, groggy, stunned, before he could muster enough will to drive. All the manic energy in him was spent; he felt bleak, drained, desolate. All was lost. The sensible thing was to pack up and go to the airport and take the next plane out, but he was too numb even to do that. At the hotel he went to the bar for a few drinks and, in a stupor of guilt and bewilderment, dropped into bed.

He was still sleeping soundly when his telephone rang the next morning. Ben-Horin.

"Is it too early for you?" the Israeli asked.

Sunlight flooded the room. "No, no, I'm up." The hand holding the receiver shook. "Good to hear from you again."

"Will you meet me at eleven by Saint Stephen's Gate?" Ben-Horin said brusquely, icily.

The day was bright and warm. Crowds of tourists swarmed about the Old City: the climax of the Easter season was at hand. From a distance of twenty yards Hornkastle could feel the anger radiating from Ben-Horin, and it was all he could manage to force himself to approach the little Israeli.

Ben-Horin said, "How could you have done it?"

"Sheer idiotic spinelessness. She gave me a couple of drinks, and I was already overwrought, I guess, and—"

In amazement Ben-Horin said, "What in the name of Mohammed are you talking about?"

"I—she—" He could not say it.

Ben-Horin shook his head furiously. "You lunatic, how could you *possibly* have gone to the village after all my warnings about moving cautiously? You have done me harm that is perhaps irreparable. This morning I went to see Yasin, the falafel-peddler—he pretended not to know me. As if I am police. I could hardly believe it when Geula said you had been to the village. Now they want nothing more to do with either of us. My relationship with them is severed and possibly cannot be rebuilt. How could you? The discourtesy, Hornkastle, the absolute stupidity—"

"I couldn't reach you for four days. I thought you were avoiding me, God knows why. Finally the frustration built up and built up and I *had* to talk to those people, *had* to, so I—"

"How very stupid that was."

"Yes. I know. Even as I was doing it, I knew it was a mistake, but I simply went through with it anyway, like a dumb schoolboy, I suppose, and even worse, when they were about to *give* me the damned mushroom—I'm sure that's what they were going to do—I panicked, I bolted—" Hornkastle rubbed his aching forehead. "Can you forgive me?"

"Forgiveness is not the issue. I want nothing more to do with you. You may have crippled my own research."

"All right."

"I advise you not to try to return to the village."

"I'm planning to leave Israel as soon as I can."

"Probably there will be no flights available until after the Easter holiday. But while you are still here, keep away from those people."

"Yes," Hornkastle said meekly.

"I take no responsibility for what will happen to you if you approach them again."

"There's no chance of that."

"I wish I had never invited you here. I want never to hear your name again."

Ben-Horin turned with military precision and strode away.

Hornkastle felt shame and weariness and a deep sense of loss. It was ended now, the quest, the timid tentative adventure. Out there in the Judaean desert are people acting out the ancient love-feast, communing with a god older than Rome, and he would never know a thing of it now. Slowly, defeatedly, he made his way back to the hotel. I'll call El Al tomorrow, he thought—they'll be open on Good Friday, won't they?—and get the hell out of here, back to the real world, back to all that I wanted to flee.

But there was still tonight and he could not bear to be alone. Recklessly he phoned the room of the English-women—what did he have to lose?—and Claudia answered. Would they join him for dinner? He had asked twice before; maybe he was making a pest of himself and they would tell him to get lost. But no. A lovely idea, she said. Did he have a place in mind? Hornkastle said, "How about right here? At half past seven?"

They both looked beautiful—fine clothes, pale skins, fluffy blonde hair. He loved the British sound of their serene voices. Helena's gauzy blouse revealed fine collar-bones, a delicate bosom. Had she been with a man, he wondered, since the unfortunate hunting mishap? Mother and daughter were heavy drinkers, and Hornkastle matched them two for one, so that things rapidly grew blurred, and he was only dimly aware of his food; he hoped he was being brilliant, suspected he was merely being boorish, and hardly cared. They were tolerating him.

"And your mushroom research?" the mother asked. "How has that been going?"

Painful recollection nearly sobered him. "I've botched it," he said, and as they leaned toward him, eagerly, sympathetically, he poured out his miserable shabby tale of the illicit visit, the conversation with the Arab, the pathetic, inglorious retreat. "I see now that what I was looking for here," he said, "was not just a nice little bit of folk-anthropopharmacology to write up for the *Journal*, but an actual mystic experience, a real communion, and as often happens when you want something too badly, you handle things clumsily, you reach too soon, you blunder—" He paused. "And now it will never happen."

"No," said Claudia. "You will have what you seek."

He half expected her to pull a glowing red *Amanita* mushroom from her tiny purse.

"Impossible now," he said mournfully.

"No. This is the city of divine grace, of redemption. You will have a second chance at whatever you hope to attain. I am quite sure of that."

He thought of Geula Ben-Horin saying, *We live as though there are no second chances.* But maybe for Israelis, living in a state of constant war, things were different. Geula had also said, *Live in the hope of glorious redemption,* and now Claudia had said the same thing. Perhaps. Perhaps. He gave the British woman a bland hopeful smile. But he was without hope.

It was well past eleven by the time the last brandies were gone, and then, without any subtlety at all, Hornkastle asked Helena to spend the night with him, and she, smiling beatifically at her mother as though the barbaric American had just done the most wonderfully *characteristic* thing, as if he had performed one of his tribal dances for her, thanked him for the offer and pleasantly refused—no second chances there, not even a first one—and they left him to deal with the check.

He sat in the restaurant until they told him it was closing. Somehow he managed to persuade his waiter to sell him a whole bottle of arrack from the bar stock and he took it to his room and through the night he methodically emptied it.

By taxi the next morning he descended to the Old City, where a vast horde of pilgrims had gathered to reenact the Savior's final thousand paces along the Via Dolorosa from the place of condemnation to the place of His interment. It looked like the crowd outside a college football game on Saturday afternoon. There were souvenir-sellers, mischievous boys, peddlers of snacks, police and soldiers, television cameramen—and also brown-robed friars, nuns of a dozen orders, priests, people costumed as Roman legionaries carrying spears, a queue of Japanese in clerical clothes with three cameras apiece.

Hornkastle walked in a lurching, shambling way that evidently had an effect on people, for the mob parted before him wherever he went, and soon he was deep in the city's tangled streets. Occasionally hands passed lightly over his body—pickpockets, no doubt, but that was unimportant. He saw Arabs with wide tapering faces everywhere, bloodshot hyperthyroid eyes.

A small boy tapped his knee and took him by the hand. Hornkastle allowed himself to be led, and found himself shortly at Yasin's falafel stand. Hornkastle felt like cringing before the Arab, who surely knew—they all knew everything—of his numbskull journey to the village, of his half-crazed pleadings and bizarre flight. But there was no condemnation on Yasin's face. He was grinning broadly, bowing, making Hornkastle welcome to the Holy Land, to Jerusalem, to the Via Dolorosa, to his own humble falafel stand on the morning of Christ's Passion. Yasin handed Hornkastle a bulging sandwich.

"I have no money," Hornkastle muttered.

The Arab beamed and shook his head. "My gift! Christ will rise!"

His eyes found Hornkastle's and lingered there a long while in what was almost a kind of communion itself. Hornkastle had no idea of what was being communicated, but it left him with a sense of warmth, of trust, of faith. Perhaps Claudia was right, that this is the city of divine grace, of second chances. He thanked Yasin and gobbled the sandwich as if he had not eaten in weeks.

Let it begin soon, he prayed. At last: let it begin.

The boy was still at his side. He had the village face, too, triangular, but his eyes were gentler. Hornkastle realized that the boy had appointed himself his guide. All right. They ploughed together through the hordes and eventually came to the courtyard of the Omarieh School, where a sign proclaimed the First Station of the Cross. Pilate had sentenced Jesus here. The crowd was flowing up the Via Dolorosa here, slowly, ecstatically, praying in many languages, singing, chanting. Wherever Hornkastle looked, he saw pilgrims tottering under immense wooden crosses, gasping and struggling and staggering. His head throbbed. He felt light-headed, giddy, weightless. He let himself be swept along, to the place where Jesus first had fallen—marked by a broken column—and then up the narrow, killingly steep Via Dolorosa through an Arab bazaar. Claudia and Helena, or two women just like them, were nearby, reading out of a guidebook. You were right, he said to them, not bothering to use words. This *is* the city of second chances. "The Fourth Station," said the younger. "Where Jesus met his fainting Mother. This church is Our Lady of the Spasm. The Fifth: Simon of Cyrene carried the cross here. The Sixth, where Veronica wiped the face of Jesus." It was a hard climb now. Hornkastle felt rivulets of sweat on his body.

He was amazed how intense colors were becoming, how bright everything looked, how strange. The walls of the ancient houses seemed furry and were undulating slightly. The voices of those about him dwindled and swelled, dwindled and swelled, as though some amplifier were being turned up and down. Marching beside him was Ben-Horin, implausibly wearing a friar's cassock. He leaned close and in his crisp, cutting way whispered into Hornkastle's ear, "So you study the ceremony after all. Perhaps at last you learn a thing or two." Out of a doorway came Geula Ben-Horin with some sort of Halloween costume on, stripes and splotches of green and scarlet and brilliant yellow. A succubus, perhaps. She winked at Hornkastle and shimmied her hips. "Put this in your thesis," she murmured, throaty voiced, a kosher Mae West. The two Israelis danced around him, melted and flowed, and were gone. Hornkastle pawed at his eyes. He would have fallen, for his legs were growing swollen and rubbery, but the press of the crowd was too tight. "This is the Seventh Station, where Jesus fell the second time," said the cool clear voice behind him, and the tones echoed and reverberated until they were tolling like gongs. Just ahead a dozen Arabs in dark blue suits were singing some ominous hymn as they hauled their cross along; he perceived the words of the song as individual gleaming blades that severed each instant from the next. "And here," said the woman, "Jesus spoke to the compassionate daughters of Jerusalem. This is where He fell the third time. We are nearly at the end of the Via Dolorosa. The last five stations are within the Church of the Holy Sepulchre."

Hornkastle felt the ancient paving stones squirming and sliding beneath his feet. He stumbled and would have pitched headlong but the blue-suited Arabs caught him, laughing and cheering now, and passed him from hand to hand, tossed him about like a sack of old clothes, moved him uphill. He saw a woman in an upper window making the sign of the cross at him and throwing kisses. The hymn was unbearably loud.

His back was pressed up against the Arabs' enormous wooden cross. He saw clearly, as though he were at a movie, how a dozen men with the same triangular face and fierce swollen eyes were holding him in place and driving in the nails. It was not the nails that bothered him but the sound of the hammer blows, which rang in his head with clamorous frenzy. Hornkastle went limp and let it happen to him. A voice as mighty as that of Zeus cried, "Help him, he's having a fit!" But Hornkastle simply smiled and shook his head. All was well. Push me, kick me, do whatever you want to me. I am yours. God is in me, he thought. God is everywhere, but especially He is within me. He could taste the fiery presence of the Godhead on his lips, his tongue, deep in his belly. They had the cross upright now. "Make room! Get him out of here before he's trampled!" No. No. There are still five more Stations of the Cross, are there not? We have not reached the end of the Via Dolorosa. Hornkastle felt utterly tranquil. This is the true *ekstasis*, the parting of the soul from the body. He closed his eyes.

* * *

When he returned to consciousness, he found himself lying in a hospital bed with a placid sweet-faced nun watching him. His arms were rigidly outstretched, his fingers were tightly coiled, the palms of his hands seemed to be on fire, and wave upon wave of nausea swept across his middle. From far away came the sound of wild bells ringing and the roar of mad voices crying a rhythmic slogan over and over.

To the nun he said faintly, "What are they shouting? I can't make it out." She touched his blazing forehead lightly and replied, *"Christos, anesti, Christos anesti,* Christ is risen!"

At the Conglomeroid Cocktail Party

I am contemporary. I am conglomeroid. I am post-causal, contra-linear, pepto-modern. To be anything else is to be dead, nezpah? Is to be a fossil. A sense of infinite potential and a stance of infinite readiness: that's the right philosophy for our recombinant era. Alert to all possibilities, holding oneself always in an existentially pliant posture.

So when quasi-cousin Spinifex called and said, "Come to my fetus-party tonight," I accepted unhesitatingly. Spinifex lives in Wongamoola on the slopes of Dandenongs, looking across into Melbourne. I happened to be in Gondar on my way to Lalibela when his call came. "Mortissa and I have a new embryo," said Spinifex. "We want everyone to help us engineer it. There'll be a contest for the best design. The whole crowd's coming, and some new people." *Some new people.* Could I resist? It's not such a big deal to go from Ethiopia to Australia for a fetus-party. Two hours, with transfers. I was on the pop-chute in half a flick. Pop to Addis, pop to Delhi, pop to Singapore, pop to Melbourne, pop pop pop pop and I was there. *Some new people.* Irresistible. That was the night I met Domitilla.

Spinifex and Mortissa live in a great golden egg on jeweled stilts, with oscillator windows and three captive rainbows moored overhead. In his current Shaping, Spinifex is aquatic, a big jolly blue dolphinoid with spangled red flukes, and spends most of his time in his moat. Mortissa's latest Shaping is more traditionally conglomeroid, no single identifiable style, a bit of tapir and a bit of giraffe and some very high-precision machine-tooled laminations, altogether elegant. I blew kisses to them both.

About thirty guests had already arrived. I knew most of them. There was Hapshash in his ten-year-old Shaping, the carpeted look, last word in splendor then. Negresca still in her tortoise-cum-chinchilla, and Holy Mary looking sublime in the gilded tubular body that becomes her so well. There is a tendency among the ultra-elite to keep the same Shaping longer and longer, with Hapshash the outstanding example of that. At first I thought it was a sign of the recent economic dreariness, but lately I was coming to understand it as a significant underground trend: out of fashion is height of fashion. That sort of thing requires one to stay really aware. When Melanoleum came slithering up to me, she asked me at once how I liked her new Shaping. She looked exactly as she had the last time, a year ago at the big potlatch in Joburg—tendrils, iridescence, lateral oculars, high-spectrum pulse-nodes. For an instant I was baffled, and I came close to telling her I had already *seen* this Shaping, and then I caught on, comprehending that she had just had herself Shaped *exactly like her last Shaping*, which carried Hapshash's gambit to the next level of subtlety, and I hugged her with all my arms and said, "It's brilliant, love, it's devastating!"

"I knew you'd pick up," she said. "Have you seen the fetus?"

"I just got here."

"Up there. In the globe."

"Ah. Beautiful!"

They had rigged a crystalline sphere in a gravitycandle's beam, so that it hovered twenty feet above the cocktail altar, and in it the new fetus solemnly swam in a phosphorescent green fluid. It was, I suppose, eleven or twelve weeks old, a little alien-looking fish with a big furrowed forehead, altogether weird but completely normal, a standard human fetus with no genetic reprogramming at all. Prenatal engineering is too terribly tacky for people like Mortissa and Spinifex, naturally. Let the standard folk do that, going to the cheap-jack helixers to get their offsprings' clubfeet and sloping chins and bandy legs cleaned up ahead of time, so that they can look just like everybody else when they come squirting out of the womb. That's not our way.

Melanoleum said, "The design contest starts in half an hour. Do you have a good one ready?"

"I expect to. What's the prize?"

"A month with anyone at the party," she said. "Do you know Domitilla?"

I had heard of her, naturally—last season's hot debutante, making the party circuit from San Francisco to the Seychelles. But I had been going the other way last season. Suddenly she was at my elbow, a dazzling child in a blaze of cold blue fire. It was her only garment, and under that chilly radiance I saw a slim furry form, five small breasts, sleek muscular thighs, vertebrae elongated to form the underpinning for a webbed sail down her back—an inspired conglomeroid of wolverine and dinosaur. My hearts thundered and my lymph congealed. She noted instantly the power she had over me, and her fiery cloak flared to double volume, a dazzling nimbus that briefly enfolded me and dizzied me with the scent of ozone. She was no more than nineteen, and I was ninety-three, existentially pliant, ready to be overwhelmed. I congratulated her on her ingenuity.

"My fifth Shaping," she said. "I'll be getting a new one soon, I think."

"Your *fifth*?" I considered Hapshash and Negresca and Holy Mary, trendily clinging to their old bodies. "So quickly? Don't. This one is extraordinary."

"I know," she said. "That's why it's time for a new one. Oh, look, the fetus is trying to get born!"

Indeed the little pseudo-fish that my quasi-cousins had conceived was making violent but futile efforts to escape its gleaming tank. We applauded. The servants took that as their signal to come among us with hors d'oeuvres: five standard humans, big and stupid and docile, bearing glittering food-fabrics on platinum trays. We did our dainty best; the trays were bare in no time and back came the standards with a second round, caviars of at least a dozen creatures and sweet-meats and tiny cocktail-globules to rub on our tongues and all the rest. And then Spinifex heaved himself out of the moat with a great jovial flapping of flippers that splashed everyone, and a beveled screen descended and hovered in midair and it was time for the contest. Domitilla was still at my side.

"I've heard about you," she said in a voice like shaggy wine. "I thought I'd meet you at the moon-party. Why weren't you there?"

"I never go there," I said.

"Oh. Of course. Do you know who's going to win the contest?"

"Is it rigged?"

"Aren't they all?" she asked. "*I* know who." She laughed.

Mortissa was on the podium under merciless spotlights that her new Shaping reflected flawlessly. She explained the contest. We were to draw lots and each in turn seize the control-stick and project on the screen our image of what the new child should look like. Judging would be automatic: the design that elicited the greatest amazement would win, and the winner was entitled to choose as companion for a month any of the rest of us. There were two provisos: Spinifex and Mortissa would not be bound to use the winning design if they deemed it life-threatening in any way, and none of the designs could be used by the contestants for future Shapings of their own. The lots were drawn and we took our turns:

Hapshash, Melanoleum, Mandragora, Peachbloom, Hannibal—

The designs ranged from brilliant to merely clever. Hapshash proposed a sort of jeweled amoeba; Peachbloom conjured up a hybrid Spinifex-Mortissa, half dolphin, half machine; Melanoleum's concept was out of the Greek myths, Medusa hair and Poseidon tail; my onetime para-wife Nullamar invented a geometrical shape, rigid and complex, that gave us all headaches; and my own contribution, entirely improvised, involved two slender tapering shells that parted to reveal a delicate and sinuous being, virtually translucent. I was surprised at my own inspiration and felt instant regret for having thrown away something so beautiful that I might well have worn myself someday. It caused a stir and I suspected I would win, and I knew who I would choose as my prize. What, I wondered, did Domitilla have as her entry? I glanced toward her and smiled, and she returned the smile with an airy rippling of her flaming cloak.

The contest went on and on. Hungering for victory, I grew tense, apprehensive, gloomy, despondent. Candelabra's design was spectacular, and Mingimang's was fascinatingly perplexing, and Vishnu's was awesomely cunning. Some, indeed, seemed almost beyond the capacity of contemporary genetic engineering to accomplish. I saw no hope of winning, and my month with Domitilla seemed in jeopardy. Her own turn came last. She took the podium, grasped the stick, closed her eyes, sent her thought-projection to the screen with an intensity of effort that turned her fiery mantle bright yellow and sent it arching out to expose her blue-black furry nakedness.

On the screen a standard human form appeared.

Not quite standard, for it was hermaphrodite, round rosy-nippled breasts above and male genitals below. Yet it was the old basic body other than that, the traditional pre-Shaping shape, used now only by the unfortunate billions of the serving classes. I gasped, and I was not

alone. It's no easy thing to amaze a group so worldly as
we, but we were transfixed with amazement, dumb-
struck by Domitilla's bizarre notion. Was she mocking
us? Was she merely naive? Or was she so far beyond our
level of sophistication that we couldn't comprehend her
motives? Trays clattered to the ground, drinks were
spilled, we coughed and wheezed and muttered. The
meters that were judging the contest whirled and
flashed. No doubt of the winner: Domitilla had plainly
provoked the most intense surprise, and that was the
criterion. The party was at the edge of scandal. But
Mortissa was equal to the moment.

"The winner, of course, is Domitilla," she said calmly.
"We salute her for the audacity of her design. But my
husband and I regard it as hazardous to the life of our
child to give it the standard form for its first Shaping
because of the possibility of misunderstanding by its
playmates, and so we invoke our right to choose another
entry, and we select that of our quasi-cousin Sandalphon, so remarkable for its combination of subtlety and
strength."

"Well done!" Melanoleum called, and I did not know
whether she was cheering Mortissa for her astuteness or
Domitilla for her boldness or me for the beauty of my
design. "Well done!" cried Vishnu, and Candelabra and
Hannibal took it up, and the tensions of the party
dissolved into a kind of forced jubilation that swiftly
became the real thing.

"The prize!" someone shouted. "Who's the prize?"

Spinifex thumped his huge fins. "The prize! The
prize!"

Mortissa beckoned to Domitilla. She stepped forward,
small and fragile-looking but not in the least vulnerable,
and said in a clear, cool voice, "I choose Sandalphon."

We left the party within the hour and popped to San
Francisco, where Domitilla lived alone in a spherical pod
of a house suspended by spider-cables a mile above the
bay.

I had my wish. And yet she frightened me, and I don't frighten easily.

Her fiery mantle engulfed me. She was nineteen, I was ninety-three, and she ruled me. In that frosty blue radiance I was helpless. Five Shapings, and only nineteen! Her eyes were narrow and cat-yellow, and there were worlds of strangeness in them that made me feel like a mud-flecked peasant. "The famous Sandalphon," she whispered. "Would you have picked me if you had won? Yes, I know you would. It was all over your face. How long have you had this Shaping?"

"Four years."

"Time for a new one."

I started to say that Hapshash and the other leaders of our set were traveling in the other direction, that the fashionable thing was to keep one's old Shaping; but that seemed idiocy to me now as I lay in her arms with her dense harsh fur rubbing my scales. She was the new thing, the terrifying, inexorable voice of the dawning day, and what did our modes matter to her? We made love, my worlds of experience against her tigerish youthful vitality, and there, at least, I think I matched her stroke for stroke. Afterward she showed me holograms of her first four Shapings. One by one her earlier selves stepped from the projector and pirouetted before me: the form her parents had given her that she had kept for nine years, and then the second Shaping that one always tends to cling to through puberty, and the two of her adolescence. They were true conglomeroid Shapes, a blending of images out of all the biological spectrum, a bit of butterfly and a bit of squid, a tinge of reptile and a hint of insect, the usual genetic fantasia that our kind adores, but a common thread bound them all, and her current Shape as well. That was the compactness of her body, the taut narrowness of her slender frame, powerful but minimal, like some agile little carnivore, mink or mongoose or marten. When we redesign ourselves, we can be any size we like, whale-mighty or cat-small, within certain basic limitations imposed by the need to house a human-sized brain in the frame that the gene-splicers build for us; but Domitilla had opted always to construct her fantasies on the splendid little armature with which she had come into the world. That too was ominous. It spoke of a persistence, a self-sufficiency, that is not common.

"Which of them do you like best?" she asked, when I had seen them all.

I stroked her strong smooth thighs, "This one. How tight your fur lies against your skin! How beautiful the sail is on your back! You've brought out your deepest self."

"How would you know my deepest self after two hours?"

"Don't underestimate me." I touched my lips to hers. "Part hunting-cat, part dinosaur—the metaphor's perfect."

"Let's make love again. Then we'll pop to Jerusalem."

"All right."

"And then Tibet."

"Certainly."

"And Baltimore."

"Baltimore?"

"Why not?" she said. "Hold me tighter. Yes. Yes."

"Do I get only a month with you?"

"Thirty days. Those were the terms of the contest."

"Do you always abide by terms?"

"Always," she said.

We popped to Jerusalem at dawn, and then to Tibet, and then, yes, to Baltimore. And many more places in the thirty days. She was trying to exhaust me, thinking that nineteen has some superiority over ninety-three, but there, at least, she had misjudged things; at each Shaping we are renewed, you know. I loved her beyond measure, though she terrified me. What did I fear? What does anyone fear most? That in a vulnerable moment someone will say, "I understand what a fraud you are: I have seen all your facades fall away: I know the truth about you." I would not say such a thing to

Melanoleum, nor Nullamar to me, nor any of us to any of us, but yet I felt Domitilla wouldn't hesitate to flay me down to the core beneath the Shapings if that suited her whim, and I lived in dread of that, and I always will.

On the thirtieth day she said goodbye.

"Please," I said. "Another week."

"Those were the terms."

"Even so."

"If we refuse to honor contracts, all society collapses."

"Have I bored you?" Foolish question, inviting destruction.

"Not nearly as much as I thought you would," she replied, and I loved her for it, having expected worse. "But I have other things to do. My new Shaping, Sandalphon."

"You won't. What you are now is too beautiful to discard."

"What I will be next will surpass it."

"I beg you—stay as you are a little longer."

"I undergo engineering tomorrow at dawn," she said, "at the gene-surgery in Katmandu."

Arguing with her was hopeless. We had our last night, a night of miracles, and while I slept she vanished, and the walls of the world fell in on me. I hurried out to my friends, and was houseguest in turn with Nullamar and Mandragora and Melanoleum and Candelabra, and not one of them said the name of Domitilla to me, and at the end of the year I went to Spinifex and Mortissa to admire the new child in the graceful shell of my happy designing, and then, despondent, I popped to Katmandu. All year long a new Domitilla had been emerging from the altered genetic material of the previous one, and now her Shaping was nearly complete. They wouldn't let me see her, but they sent messages in, and she agreed to my request to have dinner with her on the day of her coming-forth. That was still a month away. I could have gone anywhere in the world, but I stayed in Katmandu, staring at the mountains, thinking that my month of Domitilla had gone by in a flick and this month of waiting was taking an eternity; and then it was the day.

The inner door opened and nurses came out, standard humans, and an orderly or two and then the surgeon and then Domitilla. I recognized her at once, the same wiry armature as ever. The new body she wore was the one she had designed for the child of Spinifex and Mortissa. A standard human frame, mortifyingly human, the body of a servant, of a hewer of wood and drawer of water, except that it glowed with the inner fire that burned in Domitilla and that no member of the lower orders could conceivably have. And she was different from the standards in another way, for she was naked, and she had used the hermaphrodite design, breasts above, male organs below. I felt as if I had been kicked; I wanted to clutch my gut and double over. Her eyes gleamed.

"Do you like it?" she asked, mocking me.

I was unable to look. I turned and tried to run, but she called after me, "Wait, Sandalphon!"

Trembling, I halted. "What do you want?"

"Tell me if you like it?"

"The terms of the contest bound you not to use any of the designs," I said bitterly. "You claimed always to abide by terms."

"Always. Except when I choose not to." She spread her arms. "What do you think? Tell me you like it and I'm yours for tonight!"

"Never, Domitilla."

She touched her groin. "Because of *this?*"

"Because of you," I said. I shivered. "How could you do it? A standard, Domitilla. A *standard!*"

"You poor old fool," she said.

Again I turned, and this time she let me go. I traveled to Madagascar and Turkey and Greenland and Bulgaria, and her images blazed in my mind, the wolverine-girl I had loved and the grotesque thing she had become. Gradually the pain grew less. I went in for a new Shaping, despite Hapshash and his coterie, and came out simpler, more sleek, less conglomeroid. I felt better, then. I was recovering from her.

A year went by. At a party in Oaxaca I told the story, finally, to Melanoleum, stunning in her new streamlined form. "If I had it all to do over," I would," I said, "One has to remain in an existentially pliant posture, of course. One must keep alert to all possibilities. And so I have no regrets. But yet—but yet—she hurt me so badly, love—"

"Look over there," said Melanoleum.

I followed her glance, past Hapshash and Mandragora and Negresca, to the slender, taut-bodied stranger scooping fish from the pond: beetle-wings, black and yellow, luminescent spots glowing on thighs and forearms, cat-whiskers, needle-sharp fangs. She looked toward me and our eyes met, a contact that seared me, and she laughed and her laughter shriveled me with post-causal mockery, contra-linear scorn. In front of them all she destroyed me. I fled. I am fleeing still. I may flee her forever.

Our Lady of the Sauropods

21 ***August. 0750 hours.*** Ten minutes since the module meltdown. I can't see the wreckage from here, but I can smell it, bitter and sour against the moist tropical air. I've found a cleft in the rocks, a kind of shallow cavern, where I'll be safe from the dinosaurs for a while. It's shielded by thick clumps of cycads, and in any case it's too small for the big predators to enter. But sooner or later I'm going to need food, and then what? I have no weapons. How long can one woman last, stranded and more or less helpless, aboard a habitat unit not quite five hundred meters in diameter that she's sharing with a bunch of active, hungry dinosaurs?

I keep telling myself that none of this is really happening. Only I can't quite convince myself of that.

My escape still has me shaky. I can't get out of my mind the funny little bubbling sound the tiny powerpak made as it began to overheat. In something like fourteen seconds my lovely mobile module became a charred heap of fused-together junk, taking with it my communicator unit, my food supply, my laser gun and just about everything else. And but for the warning that funny little sound gave me, I'd be so much charred junk now, too. Better off that way, most likely.

When I close my eyes, I imagine I can see Habitat

Vronsky floating serenely in orbit a mere 120 kilometers away. What a beautiful sight! The walls gleaming like platinum, the great mirror collecting sunlight and flashing it into the windows, the agricultural satellites wheeling around it like a dozen tiny moons. I could almost reach out and touch it. Tap on the shielding and murmur, "Help me, come for me, rescue me." But I might just as well be out beyond Neptune as sitting here in the adjoining Lagrange slot. No way I can call for help. The moment I move outside this cleft in the rock I'm at the mercy of my saurians and their mercy is not likely to be tender.

Now it's beginning to rain—artificial, like practically everything else on Dino Island. But it gets you just as wet as the natural kind. And clammy. Pfaugh.

Jesus, what am I going to do?

0815 hours.   The rain is over for now. It'll come again in six hours. Astonishing how muggy, dank, thick, the air is. Simply breathing is hard work, and I feel as though mildew is forming on my lungs. I miss Vronsky's clear, crisp, everlasting springtime air. On previous trips to Dino Island I never cared about the climate. But, of course, I was snugly englobed in my mobile unit, a world within a world, self-contained, self-sufficient, isolated from all contact with this place and its creatures. Merely a roving eye, traveling as I pleased, invisible, invulnerable.

Can they sniff me in here?

We don't think their sense of smell is very acute. Sharper than a crocodile's, not as good as a cat's. And the stink of the burned wreckage dominates the place at the moment. But I must reek with fear-signals. I feel calm now, but it was different as I went desperately scrambling out of the module during the meltdown. Scattering pheromones all over the place, I bet.

Commotion in the cycads. *Something's coming in here!*

Long neck, small birdlike feet, delicate grasping hands. Not to worry. Struthiomimus, is all—dainty dino, fragile, birdlike critter barely two meters high. Liquid golden eyes staring solemnly at me. It swivels its head from side to side, ostrichlike, click-click, as if trying to make up its mind about coming closer to me. *Scat!* Go peck a stegosaur. Let me alone.

The struthiomimus withdraws, making little clucking sounds.

Closest I've ever been to a live dinosaur. Glad it was one of the little ones.

0900 hours. Getting hungry. What am I going to eat?

They say roasted cycad cones aren't too bad. How about raw ones? So many plants are edible when cooked and poisonous otherwise. I never studied such things in detail. Living in our antiseptic little L5 habitats, we're not required to be outdoors-wise, after all. Anyway, there's a fleshy-looking cone on the cycad just in front of the cleft, and it's got an edible look. Might as well try it raw, because there's no other way. Rubbing sticks together will get me nowhere.

Getting the cone off takes some work. Wiggle, twist, snap, tear—*there*. Not as fleshy as it looks. Chewy, in fact. Like munching on rubber. Decent flavor, though. And maybe some useful carbohydrate.

The shuttle isn't due to pick me up for thirty days. Nobody's apt to come looking for me, or even think about me, before then. I'm on my own. Nice irony there: I was desperate to get out of Vronsky and escape from all the bickering and maneuvering, the endless meetings and memoranda, the feinting and counterfeinting, all the ugly political crap that scientists indulge in when they turn into administrators. Thirty days of blessed isolation on Dino Island! An end to that constant dull throbbing in my head from the daily infighting with Director Sarber. Pure research again! And then the meltdown, and here I am cowering in the bushes wondering which comes first, starving or getting gobbled.

* * *

0930 hours. Funny thought just now. Could it have been sabotage?

Consider. Sarber and I, feuding for weeks over the issue of opening Dino Island to tourists. Crucial staff vote coming up next month. Sarber says we can raise millions a year for expanded studies with a program of guided tours and perhaps some rental of the island to film companies. I say that's risky both for the dinos and the tourists, destructive of scientific values, a distraction, a sellout. Emotionally the staff's with me, but Sarber waves figures around, showy fancy income-projections, and generally shouts and blusters. Tempers running high, Sarber in lethal fury at being opposed, barely able to hide his loathing for me. Circulating rumors—designed to get back to me—that if I persist in blocking him, he'll abort my career. Which is malarkey, of course. He may outrank me, but he has no real authority over me. And then his politeness yesterday. (*Yesterday?* An aeon ago.) Smiling smarmily, telling me he hopes I'll rethink my position during my observation tour on the island. Wishing me well. Had he gimmicked my power-pak? I guess it isn't hard if you know a little engineering, and Sarber does. Some kind of timer set to withdraw the insulator rods? Wouldn't be any harm to Dino Island itself, just a quick, compact, localized disaster that implodes and melts the unit and its passenger, so sorry, terrible scientific tragedy, what a great loss. And even if by some fluke I got out of the unit in time, my chances of surviving here as a pedestrian for thirty days would be pretty skimpy, right? Right.

It makes me boil to think that someone's willing to murder you over a mere policy disagreement. It's barbaric. Worse than that: it's tacky.

1130 hours. I can't stay crouched in this cleft forever. I'm going to explore the island and see if I can find a better hideout. This one simply isn't adequate for anything more than short-term huddling. Besides, I'm not as spooked as I was right after the meltdown. I realize now that I'm not going to find a tryannosaur hiding behind every tree. And tyrannosaurs aren't going to be much interested in scrawny stuff like me.

Anyway I'm a quick-witted higher primate. If my humble mamalian ancestors seventy million years ago were able to elude dinosaurs well enough to survive and inherit the earth, I should be able to keep from getting eaten for the next thirty days. And with or without my cozy little mobile module, I want to get out into this place, whatever the risks. Nobody's ever had a chance to interact this closely with the dinos before.

Good thing I kept this pocket recorder when I jumped from the module. Whether I'm a dino's dinner or not, I ought to be able to set down some useful observations.

Here I go.

1830 hours.   Twilight is descending now. I am camped near the equator in a lean-to flung together out of tree-fern fronds—a flimsy shelter, but the huge fronds conceal me, and with luck I'll make it through to morning. That cycad cone doesn't seem to have poisoned me yet, and I ate another one just now, along with some tender new fiddleheads uncoiling from the heart of a tree-fern. Spartan fare, but it gives me the illusion of being fed.

In the evening mists I observe a brachiosaur, half-grown but already colossal, munching in the treetops. A gloomy-looking triceratops stands nearby and several of the ostrichlike struthiomimids scamper busily in the underbrush, hunting I know not what. No sign of tyrannosaurs all day. There aren't many of them here, anyway, and I hope they're all sleeping off huge feasts somewhere in the other hemisphere.

What a fantastic place this is!

I don't feel tired. I don't even feel frightened—just a little wary.

I feel exhilarated, as a matter of fact.

Here I sit peering out between fern fronds at a scene

out of the dawn of time. All that's missing is a pterosaur or two flapping overhead, but we haven't brought those back yet. The mournful snufflings of the huge brachiosaur carry clearly even in the heavy air. The struthiomimids are making sweet honking sounds. Night is falling swiftly and the great shapes out there take on dreamlike primordial wonder.

What a brilliant idea it was to put all the Olsen-process dinosaur-reconstructs aboard a little L5 habitat of their very own and turn them loose to recreate the Mesozoic! After that unfortunate San Diego event with the tyrannosaur, it became politically unfeasible to keep them anywhere on earth, I know, but even so this is a better scheme. In just a little more than seven years Dino Island has taken on an altogether convincing illusion of reality. Things grow so fast in this lush, steamy, high— CO_2 tropical atmosphere! Of course, we haven't been able to duplicate the real Mesozoic flora, but we've done all right using botanical survivors, cycads and tree ferns and horsetails and palms and gingkos and auracarias, and thick carpets of mosses and selaginellas and liverworts covering the ground. Everything has blended and merged and run amok: it's hard now to recall the bare and unnatural look of the island when we first laid it out. Now it's a seamless tapestry in green and brown, a dense jungle broken only by streams, lakes and meadows, encapsulated in spherical metal walls some two kilometers in circumference.

And the animals, the wonderful fantastic grotesque animals—

We don't pretend that the real Mesozoic ever held any such mix of fauna as I've seen today, stegosaurs and corythosaurs side by side, a triceratops sourly glaring at a brachiosaur, struthisomimus contemporary with iguanodon, a wild unscientific jumble of Triassic, Jurassic and Cretaceous, a hundred million years of the dinosaur reign scrambled together. We take what we can get. Olsen-process reconstructs require sufficient fossil DNA to permit the computer synthesis, and we've been able to find that in only some twenty species so far. The wonder is that we've accomplished even that much: to replicate the complete DNA molecule from battered and sketchy genetic information millions of years old, to carry out the intricate implants in reptilian host ova, to see the embryos through to self-sustaining levels. The only word that applies is *miraculous*. If our dinos come from eras millions of years apart, so be it: we do our best. If we have no oterosaur and no allosaur and no archaeopteryx, so be it: we may have them yet. What we already have is plenty to work with. Some day there may be separate Triassic, Jurassic and Cretaceous satellite habitats, but none of us will live to see that, I suspect.

Total darkness now. Mysterious screechings and hissings out there. This afternoon, as I moved cautiously, but in delight, from the wreckage site up near the rotation axis to my present equatorial camp, sometimes coming within fifty or a hundred meters of living dinos, I felt a kind of ecstasy. Now my fears are returning, and my anger at this stupid marooning. I imagine clutching claws reaching for me, terrible jaws yawning above me.

I don't think I'll get much sleep tonight.

22 August. 0600 hours. Rosy-fingered dawn comes to Dino Island, and I'm still alive. Not a great night's sleep, but I must have had some, because I can remember fragments of dreams. About dinosaurs, naturally. Sitting in little groups, some playing pinochle and some knitting sweaters. And choral singing, a dinosaur rendition of *The Messiah* or maybe Beethoven's Ninth.

I fell alert, inquisitive, and hungry. Especially hungry. I know we've stocked this place with frogs and turtles and other small-size anachronisms to provide a balanced diet for the big critters. Today I'll have to snare some for myself, grisly though I find the prospect of eating raw frog's legs.

I don't bother getting dressed. With rain showers programmed to fall four times a day, it's better to go naked anyway. Mother Eve of the Mesozoic, that's me!

And without my soggy tunic I find that I don't mind the greenhouse atmosphere half as much.

Out to see what I can find.

The dinosaurs are up and about already, the big herbivores munching away, the carnivores doing their stalking. All of them have such huge appetites that they can't wait for the sun to come up. In the bad old days when the dinos were thought to be reptiles, of course, we'd have expected them to sit there like lumps until daylight got their body temperatures up to functional levels. But one of the great joys of the reconstruct project was the vindication of the notion that dinosaurs were warm-blooded animals, active and quick and pretty damned intelligent. No sluggardly crocodilians these! Would that they were, if only for my survival's sake.

1130 hours.   A busy morning. My first encounter with a major predator.

There are nine tyrannosaurs on the island, including three born in the past eighteen months. (That gives us an optimum predator-to-prey ratio. If the tyrannosaurs keep reproducing and don't start eating each other, we'll have to begin thinning them out. One of the problems with a closed ecology—natural checks and balances don't fully apply.) Sooner or later I was bound to encounter one, but I had hoped it would be later.

I was hunting frogs at the edge of Cope Lake. A ticklish business—calls for agility, cunning, quick reflexes. I remember the technique from my girlhood— the cupped hand, the lightning pounce—but somehow it's become a lot harder in the last twenty years. Superior frogs these days, I suppose. There I was, kneeling in the mud, swooping, missing, swooping, missing; some vast sauropod snoozing in the lake, probably our diplodocus; a corythosaur browsing in a stand of gingko trees, quite delicately nipping off the foul-smelling yellow fruits. Swoop. Miss. Swoop. Miss. Such intense concentration on my task that old T. rex could have tiptoed right up behind me, and I'd never have noticed. But then I felt a

subtle something, a change in the air, maybe, a barely
perceptible shift in dynamics. I glanced up and saw the
corythosaur rearing on its hind legs, looking around
uneasily, pulling deep sniffs into that fantastically elaborate bony crest that houses its early-warning system.
Carnivore alert! The corythosaur obviously smelled
something wicked this way coming, for it swung around
between two big gingkos and started to go galumphing
away. Too late. The treetops parted, giant boughs
toppled, and out of the forest came our original
tyrannosaur, the pigeon-toed one we call Belshazzar,
moving in its heavy, clumsy waddle, ponderous legs
working hard, tail absurdly swinging from side to side. I
slithered into the lake and scrunched down as deep as I
could go in the warm oozing mud. The corythosaur had
no place to slither. Unarmed, unarmored, it could only
make great bleating sounds, terror mingled with defiance, as the killer bore down on it.

I had to watch. I had never seen a kill.

In a graceless but wondrously effective way, the
tyrannosaur dug its hind claws into the ground, pivoted
astonishingly, and, using its massive tail as a counter-
weight, moved in a ninety-degree arc to knock the
corythosaur down with a stupendous sidewise swat of its
huge head. I hadn't been expecting that. The corythosaur dropped and lay on its side, snorting in pain and
feebly waving its limbs. Now came the coup de grace
with hind legs, and then the rending and tearing, the
jaws and the tiny arms at last coming into play. Burrowing chin-deep in the mud, I watched in awe and weird
fascination. There are those among us who argue that
the carnivores ought to be segregated into their own
island, that it is folly to allow reconstructs created with
such effort to be casually butchered this way. Perhaps in
the beginning that made sense, but not now, not when
natural increase is rapidly filling the island with young
dinos. If we are to learn anything about these animals, it
will only be by reproducing as closely as possible their
original living conditions. Besides, would it not be a

cruel mockery to feed our tyrannosaurs on hamburger and herring?

The killer fed for more than an hour. At the end came a scary moment: Belshazzar, blood-smeared and bloated, hauled himself ponderously down to the edge of the lake for a drink. He stood no more than ten meters from me. I did my most convincing imitation of a rotting log; but the tyrannosaur, although it did seem to study me with a beady eye, had no further appetite. For a long while after he departed, I stayed buried in the mud, fearing he might come back for dessert. And eventually there was another crashing and bashing in the forest—not Belshazzar this time, though, but a younger one with a gimpy arm. It uttered a sort of whinnying sound and went to work on the corythosaur carcass. No surprise: we already knew that tyrannosaurs had no prejudices against carrion.

Nor, I found, did I.

When the coast was clear, I crept out and saw that the two tyrannosaurs had left hundreds of kilos of meat. Starvation knoweth no pride and also few qualms. Using a clamshell for my blade, I started chopping away.

Corythosaur meat has a curiously sweet flavor—nutmeg and cloves, dash of cinnamon. The first chunk would not go down. You are a pioneer, I told myself, retching. You are the first human ever to eat dinosaur meat. *Yes, but why does it have to be raw?* No choice about that. Be dispassionate, love. Conquer your gag reflex or die trying. I pretended I was eating oysters. This time the meat went down. It didn't stay down. The alternative, I told myself grimly, is a diet of fern fronds and frogs, and you haven't been much good at catching the frogs. I tried again. Success!

I'd have to call corythosaur meat an acquired taste. But the wilderness is no place for picky eaters.

23 August. 1300 hours. At midday I found myself in the southern hemisphere, along the fringes of Marsh Marsh about a hundred meters below the equator.

Observing herd behavior in sauropods—five brachiosaurs, two adult and three young, moving in formation,
the small ones in the center. By "small" I mean only
some ten meters from nose to tail-tip. Sauropod appetites being what they are, we'll have to thin that herd
soon, too, especially if we want to introduce a female
diplodocus into the colony. *Two* species of sauropods
breeding and eating like that could devastate the island
in three years. Nobody ever expected dinosaurs to
reproduce like rabbits—another dividend of their being
warm-blooded, I suppose. We might have guessed it,
though, from the vast quantity of fossils. If that many
bones survived the catastrophes of a hundred-odd
million years, how enormous the living Mesozoic population must have been! An awesome race in more ways
than mere physical mass.

I had a chance to do a little herd-thinning myself just
now. Mysterious stirring in the spongy soil right at my
feet, and I looked down to see triceratops eggs hatching!
Seven brave little critters, already horny and beaky,
scrabbling out of a nest, staring around defiantly. No
bigger than kittens, but active and sturdy from the
moment of birth.

The corythosaur meat has probably spoiled by now. A
more pragmatic soul very likely would have augmented
her diet with one or two little ceratopsians. I couldn't do
it.

They scuttled off in seven different directions. I
thought briefly of catching one and making a pet out of
it. Silly idea.

25 August. 0700 hours. Start of the fifth day. I've
done three complete circumambulations of the island.
Slinking around on foot is fifty times as risky as cruising
around in a module, and fifty thousand times as
rewarding. I make camp in a different place every night.
I don't mind the humidity any longer. And despite my
skimpy diet, I feel pretty healthy. Raw dinosaur, I know
now, is a lot tastier than raw frog. I've become an expert

scavenger—the sound of a tyrannosaur in the forest now stimulates my salivary glands instead of my adrenals. Going naked is fun, too. And I appreciate my body much more, since the bulges that civilization puts there have begun to melt away.

Nevertheless, I keep trying to figure out some way of signaling Habitat Vronsky for help. Changing the position of the reflecting mirrors, maybe, so I can beam an SOS? Sounds nice, but I don't even know where the island's controls are located, let alone how to run them. Let's hope my luck holds out another three and a half weeks.

27 August. 1700 hours. The dinosaurs know that I'm here and that I'm some extraordinary kind of animal. Does that sound weird? How can great dumb beasts *know* anything? They have such tiny brains. And my own brain must be softening on this protein-and-cellulose diet. Even so, I'm starting to have peculiar feelings about these animals. I see them *watching* me. An odd knowing look in their eyes, not stupid at all. They stare and I imagine them nodding, smiling, exchanging glances with each other, discussing me. I'm supposed to be observing them, but I think they're observing me, too, somehow.

This is crazy. I'm tempted to erase the entry. But I'll leave it as a record of my changing psychological state if nothing else.

28 August. 1200 hours. More fantasies about the dinosaurs. I've decided that the big brachiosaur—Bertha—plays a key role here. She doesn't move around much, but there are always lesser dinosaurs in orbit around her. Much eye contact. *Eye contact between dinosaurs?* Let it stand. That's my perception of what they're doing. I get a definite sense that there's communication going on here, modulating over some wave that I'm not capable of detecting. And Bertha seems to be a central nexus, a grand totem of some sort, a—a switchboard? What am I talking about? What's happening to me?

30 August. 0945 hours. What a damned fool I am! Serves me right for being a filthy voyeur. Climbed a tree to watch iguanodons mating at the foot of Bakker Falls. At climatic moment the branch broke. I dropped twenty meters. Grabbed a lower limb or I'd be dead now. As it is, pretty badly smashed around. I don't think anything's broken, but my left leg won't support me and my back's in bad shape. Internal injuries too? Not sure. I've crawled into a little rock-shelter near the falls. Exhausted and maybe feverish. Shock, most likely. I suppose I'll starve now. It would have been an honor to be eaten by a tyrannosaur, but to die from falling out of a tree is just plain humiliating.

The mating of iguanodons is a spectacular sight, by the way. But I hurt too much to describe it now.

31 August. 1700 hours. Stiff, sore, hungry, hideously thirsty. Leg still useless and when I try to crawl even a few meters, I feel as if I'm going to crack in half at the waist. High fever.

How long does it take to starve to death?

1 Sep. 0700 hours. Three broken eggs lying near me when I awoke. Embryos still alive—probably stegosaur—but not for long. First food in forty-eight hours. Did the eggs fall out of a nest somewhere overhead? Do stegosaurs make their nests in trees, dummy?

Fever diminishing. Body aches all over. Crawled to the stream and managed to scoop up a little water.

1330 hours. Dozed off. Awakened to find haunch of fresh meat within crawling distance. Struthiomimus drumstick, I think. Nasty sour taste, but it's edible. Nibbled a little, slept again, ate some more. Pair of stegosaurs grazing not far away, tiny eyes fastened on me. Smaller dinosaurs holding a kind of conference by some big cycads. And Bertha Brachiosaur is munching away in Ostrom Meadow, benignly supervising the whole scene.

This is absolutely crazy.

I think the dinosaurs are taking care of me.

2 Sep.   0900 hours.   No doubt of it at all. They bring eggs, meat, even cycad cones and tree-fern fronds. At first they delivered things only when I slept, but now they come hopping right up to me and dump things at my feet. The struthiomimids are the bearers—they're the smallest, most agile, quickest hands. They bring their offerings, stare me right in the eye, pause as if waiting for a tip. Other dinosaurs watching from the distance. This is a coordinated effort. I am the center of all activity on the island, it seems. I imagine that even the tyrannosaurs are saving choice cuts for me. Halluncination? Fantasy? Delirium of fever? I feel lucid. The fever is abating. I'm still too stiff and weak to move very far, but I think I'm recovering from the effects of my fall. With a little help from my friends.

1000 hours.   Played back the last entry. Thinking it over. I don't *think* I've gone insane. If I'm insane enough to be worried about my sanity, how crazy can I be? Or am I just fooling myself? There's a terrible conflict between what I think I perceive going on here and what I know I ought to be perceiving.

1500 hours.   A long, strange dream this afternoon. I saw all the dinosaurs standing in the meadow and they were connected to one another by gleaming threads, like the telephone lines of olden times, and all the threads centered on Bertha. As if she's the switchboard, yes. And telepathic messages were traveling. An extrasensory hookup, powerful pulses moving along the lines. I dreamed that a small dinosaur came to me and offered me a line and, in pantomime, showed me how to hook it up, and a great flood of delight went through me as I made the connection. And when I plugged it in, I could feel the deep and heavy thoughts of the dinosaurs, the slow rapturous philosophical interchanges.

When I woke, the dream seemed bizarrely vivid, strangely real, the dream-ideas lingering as they sometimes do. I saw the animals about me in a new way. As if this is not just a zoological research station, but a community, a settlement, the sole outpost of an alien civilization—an alien civilization native to earth.

Come off it. These animals have minute brains. They spend their days chomping on greenery, except for the ones that chomp on other dinosaurs. Compared with dinosaurs, cows and sheep are downright geniuses.

I can hobble a little now.

3 Sep.   0600 hours.   The same dream again last night, the universal telepathic linkage. Sense of warmth and love flowing from dinosaurs to me.

Fresh tyrannosaur eggs for breakfast.

5 Sep.   1100 hours.   I'm making a fast recovery. Up and about, still creaky but not much pain left. They still feed me. Though the struthiomimids remain the bearers of food, the bigger dinosaurs now come close, too. A stegosaur nuzzled up to me like some Goliath-sized pony, and I petted its rough scaly flank. The diplodocus stretched out flat and seemed to beg me to stroke its immense neck.

If this is madness, so be it. There's community here, loving and temperate. Even the predatory carnivores are part of it: eaters and eaten are aspects of the whole, yin and yang. Riding around in our sealed modules, we could never have suspected any of this.

They are gradually drawing me into their communion. I feel the pulses that pass between them. My entire soul throbs with that strange new sensation. My skin tingles.

They bring me food of their own bodies, their flesh and their unborn young, and they watch over me and silently urge me back to health. Why? For sweet charity's sake? I don't think so. I think they want something from me. I think they need something from me.

What could they need from me?

6 Sep. 0600 hours. All this night I have moved slowly through the forest in what I can only term an ecstatic state. Vast shapes, humped monstrous forms barely visible by dim glimmer, came and went about me. Hour after hour I walked unharmed, feeling the communion intensify. Until at last, exhausted, I have come to rest here on this mossy carpet, and in the first light of dawn I see the giant form of the great brachiosaur standing like a mountain on the far side of Owen River.

I am drawn to her. I could worship her. Through her vast body surge powerful currents. She is the amplifier. By her are we all connected. The holy mother of us all. From the enormous mass of her body emanate potent healing impulses.

I'll rest a little while. Then I'll cross the river to her.

0900 hours. We stand face to face. Her head is fifteen meters above mine. Her small eyes are unreadable. I trust her and I love her.

Lesser brachiosaurs have gathered behind her on the riverbank. Farther away are dinosaurs of half a dozen other species, immobile, silent.

I am humble in their presence. They are representatives of a dynamic, superior race, which but for a cruel cosmic accident would rule the earth to this day, and I am coming to revere them.

Consider: they endured for a hundred forty million years in ever-renewing vigor. They met all evolutionary challenges, except the one of sudden and catastrophic climate change against which nothing could have protected them. They multiplied and proliferated and adapted, dominating land and sea and air, covering the globe. Our own trifling, contemptible ancestors were nothing next to them. Who knows what these dinosaurs might have achieved if that crashing asteroid had not blotted out their light? What a vast irony: millions of years of supremacy ended in a single generation by a chilling cloud of dust. But until then—the wonder, the grandeur—

Only beasts, you say? How can you be sure? We know just a shred of what the Mesozoic was really like, just a slice, literally the bare bones. The passage of a hundred million years can obliterate all traces of civilization. Suppose they had language, poetry, mythology, philosophy? Love, dreams, aspirations? No, you say, they were beasts, ponderous and stupid, that lived mindless bestial lives. And I reply that we puny hairy ones have no right to impose our own values on them. The only kind of civilization we can understand is the one we have built. We imagine that our own trivial accomplishments are the determining case, that computers and spaceships and broiled sausages are such miracles that they place us at evolution's pinnacle. But now I know otherwise. Humanity has done marvelous things, yes. But we would not have existed at all had this greatest of races been allowed to live to fulfill its destiny.

I feel the intense love radiating from the titan that looms above me. I feel the contact between our souls steadily strengthening and deepening.

The last barriers dissolve.

And I understand at last.

I am the chosen one. I am the vehicle. I am the bringer of rebirth, the beloved one, the necessary one. Our Lady of the Sauropods am I, the holy one, the prophetess, the priestess.

Is this madness? Then it is madness.

Why have we small hairy creatures existed at all? I know now. It is so that through our technology we could make possible the return of the great ones. They perished unfairly. Through us, they are resurrected aboard this tiny glove in space.

I tremble in the force of the need that pours from them.

I will not fail you, I tell the great sauropods before me, and the sauropods send my thoughts reverberating to all the others.

20 September. 0600 hours. The thirtieth day. The shuttle comes from Habitat Vronsky today to pick me up and deliver the next researcher.

I wait at the transit lock. Hundreds of dinosaurs wait with me, each close beside the nest, both the lions and the lambs, gathered quietly, their attention focussed entirely on me.

Now the shuttle arrives, right on time, gliding in for a perfect docking. The airlocks open. A figure appears. Sarber himself! Coming to make sure I didn't survive the meltdown, or else to finish me off.

He stands blinking in the entry passage, gaping at the throngs of placid dinosaurs arrayed in a huge semicircle around the naked woman who stands beside the wreckage of the mobile module. For a moment he is unable to speak.

"Anne?" he says finally. "What in God's name—"

"You'll never understand," I tell him. I give the signal. Belshazzar rumbles forward. Sarber screams and whirls and sprints for the airlock, but a stegosaur blocks the way.

"No!" Sarber cries, as the tyrannosaur's mighty head swoops down. It is all over in a moment.

Revenge! How sweet!

And this is only the beginning. Habitat Vronsky lies just 120 kilometers away. Elsewhere in the Lagrange belt are hundreds of other habitats ripe for conquest. The earth itself is within easy reach. I have no idea yet how it will be accomplished, but I know it will be done and done successfully, and I will be the instrument by which it is done.

I stretch forth my arms to the mighty creatures that surround me. I feel their strength, their power, their harmony. I am one with them, and they with me.

The Great Race has returned, and I am its priestess. Let the hairy ones tremble!

Gianni

"**B**ut why not Mozart?" Hoaglund said, shaking his head. "Schubert, even? Or you could have brought back Bix Beiderbecke, for Christ's sake, if you wanted to resurrect a great musician."

"Beiderbecke was jazz," I said. "I'm not interested in jazz. Nobody's interested in jazz except you."

"And people are still interested in Pergolesi in the year 2008?"

"*I* am."

"Mozart would have been better publicity. You'll need more funding sooner or later. You tell the world you've got Mozart sitting in the back room cranking out a new opera, you can write your own ticket. But what good is Pergolesi? Pergolesi's totally forgotten."

"Only by the proletariat, Sam. Besides, why give Mozart a second chance? Maybe he died young, but it wasn't all *that* young, and he did his work, a ton of work. Gianni died at twenty-six, you know. He might have been greater than Mozart if he'd had another dozen years."

"Johnny?"

"Gianni. Giovanni Battista. Pergolesi. He calls himself Gianni. Come meet him."

"Mozart, Dave. You should have done Mozart."

"Stop being an idiot," I said. "When you've met him, you'll know I did the right thing. Mozart would have been a pain in the neck, anyway. The stories I've heard about Mozart's private life would uncurl your wig. Come on with me."

I led him down the long hallway from the office past the hardware room and the timescoop cage to the airlock separating us from the semidetached motel unit out back where Gianni had been living since we scooped him. We halted in the airlock to be sprayed. Sam frowned and I explained, "Infectious microorganisms have mutated a lot since the eighteenth century. Until we've got his resistance levels higher, we're keeping him in a pretty sterile environment. When we first brought him back, he was vulnerable to anything—a case of the sniffles would have killed him, most likely. Plus he was a dying man when we got him, one lung lousy with TB and the other one going."

"Hey," Hoaglund said.

I laughed. "You won't catch anything from him. It's in remission now, Sam. We didn't bring him back at colossal expense just to watch him die."

The lock opened and we stepped into the monitoring vestibule, glittering like a movie set with bank upon bank of telemetering instruments. The day nurse, Claudia, was checking diagnostic readouts. "He's expecting you, Dr. Leavis," she said. "He's very frisky this morning."

"Frisky?"

"Playful. You know."

Yes. Tacked to the door of Gianni's room was a card that hadn't been there yesterday, flamboyantly lettered in gaudy, free-flowing baroque script:

GIOVANNI BATTISTA PERGOLESI

Jesi, January 3 1710—Pozzuoli, March 17 1736
Los Angeles, Dec. 20 2007—.
Genuis At Work!!!!
Per Piacere, Knock Before You enter!

"He speaks English?" Hoaglund asked.

"Now he does," I said. "We gave him tapesleep the first week. He picks things up fast, anyway." I grinned. "Genius at work, eh? Or *genuis*. That's the sort of sign I would have expected Mozart to put up."

"They're all alike, these talents," Hoaglund said.

I knocked.

"*Chi va là?*" Gianni called.

"Dave Leavis."

"*Avanti, dottore illustrissimo!*"

"I thought you said he speaks English," Hoaglund murmured.

"He's frisky today, Claudia said, remember?"

We went in. As usual he had the blinds tightly drawn, shutting out the brilliant January sunlight, the yellow blaze of acacia blossoms just outside the window, the enormous scarlet bougainvillea, the sweeping hilltop vista of the valley and the mountains beyond. Maybe scenery didn't interest him—or, more likely, he preferred to keep his room a tightly sealed little cell, an island out of time. He had had to absorb a lot of psychic trauma in the past few weeks: it must give you a hell of a case of jet-lag to jump 271 years into the future.

But he looked lively, almost impish—a small man, graceful, delicate, with sharp, busy eyes, quick, elegant gestures, a brisk, confident manner. How much he had changed in just a few weeks! When we fished him out of the eighteenth century, he was a woeful sight, face lined and haggard, hair already gray at twenty-six, body gaunt, bowed, quivering. He looked like what he was, a shattered consumptive a couple of weeks from the grave. His hair was still gray, but he had gained ten pounds; the veils were gone from his eyes; there was color in his cheeks.

I said, "Gianni, I want you to meet Sam Hoaglund. He's going to handle publicity and promotion for our project. *Capisce?* He will make you known to the world and give you a new audience for your music."

He flashed a brilliant smile. "*Bene*. Listen to this."

The room was an electronic jungle, festooned with gadgetry: a synthesizer, a telescreen, a megabuck audio library, five sorts of data terminals and all manner of other things perfectly suited to your basic eighteenth-century Italian drawing room. Gianni loved it all and was mastering the equipment with astonishing, even frightening, ease. He swung around to the synthesizer, jacked it into harpsichord mode and touched the keyboard. From the cloud of floating minispeakers came the opening theme of a sonata, lovely, lyrical, to my ear unmistakably Pergolesian in its melodiousness, and yet somehow weird. For all its beauty there was a strained, awkward, *suspended* aspect to it, like a ballet performed by dancers in galoshes. The longer he played, the more uncomfortable I felt. Finally he turned to us and said, "You like it?"

"What is it? Something of yours?"

"Mine, yes. My new style. I am under the influence of Beethoven today. Haydn yesterday, tomorrow Chopin. I try everything, no? By Easter I get to the ugly composers. Mahler, Berg, Debussy—those men were *crazy*, do you know? Crazy music, so ugly. But I will learn."

"Debussy ugly?" Hoaglund said quietly to me.

"Bach is modern music to him," I said. "Haydn is the voice of the future."

Gianni said, "I will be very famous."

"Yes. Sam will make you the most famous man in the world."

"I was very famous after I—died." He tapped one of the terminals. "I have read about me. I was so famous that everybody forged my music, and it was published as Pergolesi, do you know that? I have played it, too, this 'Pergolesi.' *Merda,* most of it. Not all. The *concerti armonici,* not bad—not mine, but not bad. Most of the rest, trash." He winked. "But you will make me famous while I live, eh? Good. Very good." He came closer to us and in a lower voice said, "Will you tell Claudia that the gonorrhea, it is all cured?"

"What?"

"She would not believe me. I said, The doctor swears it, but she said, "No, it is not safe; you must keep your hands off me; you must keep everything else off me.""

"Gianni, have you been molesting your nurse?"

"I am becoming a healthy man, *dottore*. I am no monk. They sent me to live with the *cappuccini* in the monastery at Pozzuoli, yes, but it was only so the good air there could heal my consumption, not to make me a monk. I am no monk now and I am no longer sick. Could you go without a woman for three hundred years?" He put his face close to Hoaglund's, gave him a bright-eyed stare, leered outrageously. "You will make me very famous. And then there will be women again, yes? And you must tell them that the gonorrhea, it is entirely cured. This age of miracles!"

Afterward Hoaglund said to me, "And you thought Mozart was going to be too much trouble?"

When we first got him, there was no snappy talk out of him of women or fame or marvelous new compositions. Then he was a wreck, a dazed wraith, hollow, burned out. He wasn't sure whether he had awakened in heaven or in hell, but whichever it was left him alternately stunned and depressed. He was barely clinging to life, and we began to wonder if we had waited too long to get him. Perhaps it might be wiser, some of us thought, to toss him back and pick him up from an earlier point, maybe summer of 1735, when he wasn't so close to the grave. But we had no budget for making a second scoop, and also we were bound by our own rigid self-imposed rules. We had the power to yank anybody we liked out of the past—Napoleon, Genghis Khan, Jesus, Henry the Eighth—but we had no way of knowing what effects it might have on the course of history if we scooped up Lenin while he was still in exile in Switzerland, say, or collected Hitler while he was still a paperhanger. So we decided *a priori* to scoop only someone whose life and accomplishments were entirely behind him, and who was so close to the time of his natural death that his disappearance would not be likely to unsettle the fabric of the universe. For months I lobbied to scoop Pergolesi, and I got my way, and we took him out of the monastery eighteen days before his official date of death. Once we had him, it was no great trick to substitute a synthetic cadaver, who was duly discovered and buried, and so far as we have been able to tell, no calamities have resulted to history because one consumptive Italian was put in his grave two weeks earlier than the encyclopedia used to say he had been.

Yet it was touch and go at first, keeping him alive. Those were the worst days of my life, the first few after the scooping. To have planned for years, to have expended so many gigabucks on the project, and then to have our first human scoopee die on us anyway—

He didn't, though. The same vitality that had pulled sixteen operas and a dozen cantatas and uncountable symphonies and concerti and masses and sonatas out of him in a twenty-six-year lifespan pulled him back from the edge of the grave now, once the resources of modern medicine were put to work rebuilding his lungs and curing his assorted venereal diseases. From hour to hour we could see him gaining strength. Within days he was wholly transformed. It was almost magical, even to us. And it showed us vividly how many lives were needlessly lost in those archaic days for want of the things that are routine to us—antibiotics, transplant technology, micro-surgery, regeneration therapy.

For me those were wondrous days. The pallid, feeble young man struggling for his life in the back unit was surrounded by a radiant aura of accumulated fame and legend built up over centuries: he was *Pergolesi*, the miraculous boy, the fountain of melody, the composer of the awesome *Stabat Mater* and the rollicking *Serva Padrona*, who in the decades after his early death was ranked with Bach, with Mozart, with Haydn, and whose most trivial works inspired the whole genre of light opera. But his own view of himself was different: he was a weary, sick, dying young man, poor pathetic Gianni, the failure, the washout, unknown beyond Rome and Naples and poorly treated there, his serious operas neglected cruelly, his masses and cantatas praised but rarely performed, only the comic operas that he dashed off so carelessly winning him any acclaim at all—poor Gianni, burned out at twenty-five, destroyed as much by disappointment as by tuberculosis and venereal disease, creeping off to the Capuchin monastery to die in miserable poverty. How could he have known he was to be famous? But we showed him. We played him recordings of his music, both the true works and those that had been constructed in his name by the unscrupulous to cash in on his posthumous glory. We let him read the biographies and critical studies and even the novels that had been published about him. Indeed, for him it must have been precisely like dying and going to heaven, and from day to day he gained strength and poise, he waxed and flourished, he came to glow with vigor and passion and confidence. He knew now that no magic had been worked on him, that he had been snatched into the unimaginable future and restored to health by ordinary human beings, and he accepted that and quickly ceased to question it. All that concerned him now was music. In the second and third weeks we gave him a crash course in post-Baroque musical history. Bach first, then the shift away from polyphony—*"Naturalmente,"* he said, "it was inevitable, I would have achieved it myself if I had lived"—and he spent hours with Mozart and Haydn and Johann Christian Bach, soaking up their complete works and entering a kind of ecstatic state. His nimble, agile mind swiftly began plotting its own directions. One morning I found him red-eyed with weeping. He had been up all night listening to *Don Giovanni* and *Marriage of Figaro*. "This Mozart," he said. "You bring him back, too?"

"Maybe someday we will," I said.

"I kill him! You bring him back, I strangle him, I trample him!" His eyes blazed. He laughed wildly. "He is wonder! He is angel! He is too good! Send me to his time, I kill him then! No one should compose like that! Except Pergolesi. He would have done it."

"I believe that."

"Yes! This *Figaro*—1786—I could have done it twenty years earlier! Thirty! If only I get the chance. Why this Mozart so lucky? I die, he live—why? Why, *dottore?*"

His love-hate relationship with Mozart lasted six or seven days. Then he moved on to Beethoven, who I think was a little too much for him, overwhelming, massive, crushing, and then the romantics, who amused him—"Berlioz, Tchaikovsky, Wagner, all lunatics, *dementi, pazzi,* but they are wonderful. I think I see what they are trying to do. Madmen! Marvelous madmen!"— and quickly on to the twentieth century, Mahler, Schoenberg, Stravinsky, Bartok, not spending much time with any of them, finding them all either ugly or terrifying or simply incomprehensibly bizarre. More recent composers, Webern and the serialists, Penderecki, Stockhausen, Xenakis, Ligeti, the various electronicists and all that came after, he dismissed with a quick shrug, as though he barely recognized what they were doing as music. Their fundamental assumptions were too alien to him. Genius though he was, he could not assimilate their ideas, any more than Brillat-Savarin or Escoffier could have found much pleasure in the cuisine of another planet. After completing his frenzied survey of everything that had happened in music after his time, he returned to Bach and Mozart and gave them his full attention.

I mean *full* attention. Gianni was utterly incurious about the world outside his bedroom window. We told him he was in America, in California, and showed him a map. He nodded casually. We turned on the telescreen and let him look at the landscape of the early twenty-first century. His eyes glazed. We spoke of automobiles, planes, flights to Mars. Yes, he said, *meraviglioso, miracoloso,* and went back to the Brandenburg concerti. I realize now that the lack of interest he showed in the modern world was a sign neither of fear nor of shallowness, but rather only a mark of priorities. What Mozart had accomplished was stranger and more interesting to him than the entire technological revolution. Technology was only a means to an end, for Gianni—push a button, you get a symphony orchestra in your bedroom: *miracoloso!*——and he took it entirely for granted. That the *basso continuo* had become obsolete thirty years after his death, that the diatonic scales would be demoted from sacred constants to inconvenient anachronisms a century or so later, was more significant to him than the fusion reactor, the interplanetary spaceship, or even the machine that had yanked him from his deathbed into this brave new world.

In the fourth week he said he wanted to compose again. He asked for a harpsichord. Instead we gave him a synthesizer. He loved it.

In the sixth week he began asking questions about the outside world, and I realized that the tricky part of our experiment was about to begin.

Hoaglund said, "Pretty soon we have to reveal him. It's incredible we've been able to keep it quiet this long."

He had an elaborate plan. The problem was twofold: letting Gianni experience the world, and letting the world perceive that time-travel as a practical matter involving real human beings—no more frogs and kittens hoisted from last month to this—had finally arrived. There was going to be a whole business of press conferences, media tours of our lab, interviews with Gianni, a festival of Pergolesi music at the Hollywood Bowl with the premiere of a symphony in the mode of Beethoven that he said would be ready by April, et cetera, et cetera, et cetera. But at the same time we would be taking Gianni on private tours of the L.A. area, gradually exposing him to the society into which he had been so unilaterally hauled. The medics said it was safe to let him encounter twenty-first-century microorganisms now. But would it be safe to let him encounter twenty-first-century civilization? He, with his windows sealed and his blinds drawn, his eighteenth-century mind wholly engrossed in the revelations that Bach and Mozart and Beethoven were pouring into it—what would he make of the world of spaceways and slice-houses and overload bands and freebase teams when he could no longer hide from it?

"Leave it all to me," said Hoaglund. "That's what you're paying me for, right?"

On a mild and rainy February afternoon Sam and I and the main physician, Nella Brandon, took him on his first drive through his new reality. Down the hill the back way, along Ventura Boulevard a few miles, onto the freeway, out to Topanga, back around through the landslide zone to what had been Santa Monica, and then straight up Wilshire across the entire heart of Los Angeles—a good stiff jolt of modernity. Dr. Brandon carried her full armamentarium of sedatives and tranks ready in case Gianni freaked out. But he didn't freak out.

He loved it—swinging round and round in the bubbletop car, gaping at everything. I tried to view L.A. through the eyes of someone whose entire life had been spent amid the splendors of Renaissance and Baroque architecture, and it came up hideous on all counts. But not to Gianni. "Beautiful," he sighed. "Wondrous! Miraculous! Marvelous!" The traffic, the freeways themselves, the fast-food joints, the peeling plastic facades, the great fire scar in Topanga, the houses hanging by spider-cables from the hillsides, the occasional superjet floating overhead on its way into LAX—everything lit him up. It was wonderland to him. None of those dull old cathedrals and *palazzi* and marble fountains here—no, everything here was brighter and larger and glitzier than life, and he loved it. The only part he couldn't handle was the beach at Topanga. By the time we got there the sun was out and so were the sunbathers, and the sight of eight thousand naked bodies cavorting on the damp sand almost gave him a stroke. "What is this?" he demanded. "The market for slaves? The pleasure house of the king?"

"Blood pressure rising fast," Nella Brandon said softly, eyeing her wrist-monitors. "Adrenalin levels going up. Shall I cool him out?"

I shook my head.

"Slavery is unlawful," I told him. "There is no king. These are ordinary citizens amusing themselves."

"Nudo! Assolutamente nudo!"

"We long ago outgrew feeling ashamed of our bodies," I said. "The laws allow us to go nude in places like this."

"Straordinario! Incredibile!" He gaped in total astonishment. Then he erupted with questions, a torrent of Italian first, his English returning only with an effort. Did husbands allow their wives to come here? Did fathers permit daughters? Were there rapes on the beach? Duels? If the body had lost its mystery, how did sexual desire survive? If a man somehow did become excited, was it shameful to let it show? And on and on and on, until I had to signal Nella to give him a mild needle. Calmer now, Gianni digested the notion of mass public nudity in a more reflective way; but it had amazed him more than Beethoven, that was plain.

We let him stare for another ten minutes. As we started to return to the car, Gianni pointed to a lush brunette trudging along by the tide-pools and said, "I want her. Get her."

"Gianni, we can't do that!"

"You think I am eunuch? You think I can see these bodies and not remember breasts in my hands, tongue touching tongue?" He caught my wrist. "Get her for me."

"Not yet. You aren't well enough yet. And we can't just *get* her for you. Things aren't done that way here."

"She goes naked. She belongs to anyone."

"No," I said. "You still don't really understand, do you?" I nodded to Nella Brandon. She gave him another needle. We drove on, and he subsided. Soon we came to the barrier marking where the coast road had fallen into the sea, and we swung inland through the place where Santa Monica had been. I explained about the earthquake and the landslide. Gianni grinned.

"Ah, *il terremoto*, you have it here too? A few years ago there was great earthquake in Napoli. You have understood? And then they ask me to write a Mass of Thanksgiving afterward because not everything is destroyed. It is very famous mass for a time. You know it? No? You must hear it." He turned and seized my wrist. With an intensity greater than the brunette had aroused in him, he said, "I will compose a new famous mass, yes? I will be very famous again. And I will be rich. Yes? I was famous and then I was forgotten and then I died and now I live again and now I will be famous again. And rich. Yes? Yes?"

Sam Hoaglund looked over at him and said, "In another couple of weeks, Gianni, you're going to be the most famous man in the world."

Casually Sam poked the button turning on the radio. The car was well equipped for overload and out of the many speakers came the familiar pulsing tingling sounds of Wilkes Booth John doing *Membrane*. The subsonics were terrific. Gianni sat up straight as the music hit him. "What is that?" he demanded.

"Overload," Sam said. "Wilkes Booth John."

"Overload? This means nothing to me. It is a music? Of when?"

"The music of right now," said Nella Brandon.

As we zoomed along Wilshire Sam keyed in the colors and lights too, and the whole interior of the car began to throb and flash and sizzle. Wonderland for Gianni again. He blinked, he pressed his hands to his cheeks, he shook his head. "It is like the music of dreams," he said. "The composer? Who is?"

"Not a composer," said Sam. "A group. Wilkes Booth John, it calls itself. This isn't classical music, it's pop. Popular. Pop doesn't have a composer."

"It makes itself, this music?"

"No," I said. "The whole group composes it. And plays it."

"The orchestra. It is pop and the orchestra composes." He looked lost, as bewildered as he had been since the moment of his awakening, naked and frail, in the scoop cage. "Pop. Such strange music. So simple. It goes over and over again, the same thing, loud, no shape. Yet I think I like it. Who listens to this music? *Imbecili? Infanti?*"

"Everyone," Sam said.

The first outing in Los Angeles not only told us Gianni could handle exposure to the modern world but also transformed his life among us in several significant ways. For one thing, there was no keeping him chaste any longer after Topanga Beach. He was healthy, he was lusty, he was vigorously heterosexual—an old biography of him I had seen blamed his ill health and early demise on "his notorious profligacy"—and we could hardly go on treating him like a prisoner or a zoo animal. Sam fixed him up with one of his secretaries, Melissa Burke, a willing volunteer.

Then, too, Gianni had been confronted for the first time with the split between classical and popular music, with the whole modernist cleavage between high art and lowbrow entertainment. That was new to him and baffling at first. "This *pop*," he said, "it is the music of the peasants?" But gradually he grasped the idea of simple rhythmic music that everyone listened to, distinguished from "serious" music that belonged only to an elite and was played merely on formal occasions. "But *my* music," he protested, "it had tunes, people could whistle it. It was everybody's music." It fascinated him that composers had abandoned melody and made themselves inaccessible to most of the people. We told him that something like that had happened in all of the arts. "You poor crazy *futuruomini*," he said gently.

Suddenly he began to turn himself into a connoisseur

of overload groups. We rigged an imposing unit in his room, and he and Melissa spent hours plugged in, soaking up the waveforms let loose by Scissors and Ultrafoam and Wilkes Booth John and the other top bands. When I asked him how the new symphony was coming along, he gave me a peculiar look.

He began to make other little inroads into modern life. Sam and Melissa took him shopping for clothing on Figueroa Street, and in the *cholo* boutiques he acquired a flashy new wardrobe of the latest Aztec gear to replace the lab clothes he had worn since his awakening. He had his prematurely gray hair dyed red. He acquired jewelry that went flash, clang, zzz, and pop when the mood-actuated sensoria came into play. In a few days he was utterly transformed: he became the perfect young Angeleno, slim, dapper, stylish, complete with the slight foreign accent and exotic grammar.

"Tonight Melissa and I go to The Quonch," Gianni announced.

"The Quonch," I murmured, mystified.

"Overload palace," Hoaglund explained. "In Pomona. All the big groups play there."

"We have Philharmonic tickets tonight," I said feebly.

Gianni's eyes were implacable. "The Quonch," he said.

So we went to The Quonch. Gianni, Melissa, Sam, Sam's slice-junkie livewith, Oreo, and I. Gianni and Melissa had wanted to go alone, but I wasn't having that. I felt a little like an overprotective mother whose little boy wanted to try a bit of freebasing. No chaperones, no Quonch, I said. The Quonch was a gigantic geodesic dome in Pomona Downlevel, far underground. The stage whirled on antigrav gyros, the ceiling was a mist of floating speakers, the seats had pluggie intensifiers, and the audience, median age about fourteen, was sliced out of its mind. The groups performing that night were Thug, Holy Ghosts, Shining Orgasm Revival and Ultrafoam. For this I had spent untold multi-kilogelt to bring the composer of the *Stabat Mater* and *La Serva Padrona* back to life? The kids screamed, the great hall filled with dense, tangible, oppressive sound, colors and lights throbbed and pulsed, minds were blown. In the midst of the madness sat Giovanni Battista Pergolesi (1710–1736), graduate of the Conservatorio dei Poveri, organist of the royal chapel at Naples, *maestro di capella* to the Prince of Stigliano—plugged in, turned on, radiant, ecstatic, transcendent.

Whatever else The Quonch may have been, it didn't seem dangerous, so the next night I let Gianni go there just with Melissa. And the next. It was healthy for both of us to let him move out on his own a little. But I was starting to worry. It wouldn't be long until we broke the news to the public that we had a genuine eighteenth-century genius among us. But where were the new symphonies? Where were the heaven-sent sonatas? He wasn't producing anything visible. He was just doing a lot of overload. I hadn't brought him back here to be a member of the audience, especially *that* audience.

"Relax," Sam Hoaglund said. "He's going through a phase. He's dazzled by the novelty of everything, and also he's having fun for maybe the first time in his life. But sooner or later he'll get back to composing. Nobody steps out of character forever. The real Pergolesi will take control."

Then Gianni disappeared.

Came the frantic call at three in the afternoon on a crazy hot Saturday with Santa Anas blowing and a fire raging in Tujunga. Dr. Brandon had gone to Gianni's room to give him his regular checkup, and no Gianni. I went whistling across town from my house near the beach. Hoaglund, who had come running in from Santa Barbara, was there already. "I phoned Melissa," he said. "He's not with her. But she's got a theory."

"Tell."

"They've been going backstage the last few nights. He's met some of the kids from Ultrafoam and one of the other groups. She figures he's off jamming with them."

"If that's all, then hallelujah. But how do we track him?"

"She's getting addresses. We're making calls. Quit worrying, Dave."

Easy to say. I imagined him held for ransom in some East L.A. dive. I imagined swaggering machos sending me his fingers, one a day, waiting for fifty megabucks' payoff. I paced for half a dreadful hour, grabbing up phones as if they were magic wands, and then came word that they had found him working out with Shining Orgasm Revival in a studio in West Covina. We were there in half the legal time and to hell with the California Highway Patrol.

The place was a miniature Quonch, electronic gear everywhere, the special apparatus of overload rigged up, and Gianni sitting in the midst of six practically naked young uglies whose bodies were draped with readout tape and sonic gadgetry. So was his. He looked blissful and sweaty. "It is so beautiful, this music," he sighed when I collared him. "It is the music of my second birth. I love it beyond everything."

"Bach," I said. "Beethoven. Mozart."

"This is other. This is miracle. The total effect—the surround, the engulf—"

"Gianni, don't ever go off again without telling someone."

"You were afraid?"

"We have a major investment in you. We don't want you getting hurt or into trouble or—"

"Am I a child?"

"There are dangers in this city that you couldn't possibly understand yet. You want to jam with these musicians, jam with them, but don't just disappear. Understood?"

He nodded.

Then he said, "We will not hold the press conference for a while. I am learning this music. I will make my debut next month, maybe. If we can get booking at The Quonch as main attraction."

"This is what you want to be? An overload star?"

"Music is music."

"And you are Giovanni Battista Pergo—" An awful thought struck me. I looked sidewise at Shining Orgasm Revival. "Gianni, you didn't tell them who you—"

"No. I am still secret."

"Thank God." I put my hand on his arm. "Look, if this stuff amuses you, listen to it, play it, do what you want. But the Lord gave you a genius for real music."

"This is real music."

"Complex music. Serious music."

"I starved to death composing that music."

"You were ahead of your time. You wouldn't starve now. You will have a tremendous audience for your music."

"Because I am a freak, yes. And in two months I am forgotten again. *Grazie,* no, Dave. No more sonatas. No more cantatas. Is not the music of this world. I give myself to overload."

"I forbid it, Gianni!"

He glared. I saw something steely behind his delicate and foppish exterior.

"You do not own me, Dr. Leavis."

"I gave you life."

"So did my father and mother. They didn't own me either."

"Please, Gianni. Let's not fight. I'm only begging you not to turn your back on your genius, not to renounce the gift God gave you for—"

"I renounce nothing. I merely transform." He leaned up and put his nose almost against mine. "Let me free. I will not be a court composer for you. I will not give you masses and symphonies. No one wants such things today, not new ones, only a few people who want the old ones. Not good enough. I want to be famous, *capisce?* I want to be rich. Did you think I'd live the rest of my life as a curiosity, a museum piece? Or that I would learn to write the kind of noise they call modern music? Fame is what I want. I died poor and hungry, the books say. *You* die poor and hungry and find out what it is like, and then talk to me about writing cantatas. I will never be poor again." He laughed. "Next year, after I am revealed to the world, I will start my own overload group. We will wear wigs, eighteenth-century clothes, everything. We will call ourselves Pergolesi. All right? All right, Dave?"

He insisted on working out with Shining Orgasm Revival every afternoon. Okay. He went to overload concerts just about every night. Okay. He talked about going on stage next month. Even that was okay. He did no composing, stopped listening to any music but overload. Okay. He is going through a phase, Sam Hoaglund had said. Okay. You do not own me, Gianni had said.

Okay. Okay.

I let him have his way. I asked him who his overload playmates thought he was, why they had let him join the group so readily. "I say I am rich Italian playboy," he replied. "I give them the old charm, you understand? Remember I am accustomed to winning the favors of kings, princes, cardinals. It is how we musicians earned our living. I charm them, they listen to me play, they see right away I am genius. The rest is simple. I will be very rich."

About three weeks into Gianni's overload phase, Nella Brandon came to me and said, "Dave, he's doing slice."

I don't know why I was surprised. I was.

"Are you sure?"

She nodded. "It's showing up in his blood, his urine, his metabolic charts. He probably does it every time he goes to play with that band. He's losing weight, corpuscle formation dropping off, resistance weakening. You've got to talk to him."

I went to him and said, "Gianni, I've stopped giving a damn what kind of music you write, but when it comes to drugs, I draw the line. You're still not completely sound physically. Remember, you were at the edge of *death* just a few months ago, body-time. I don't want you killing yourself."

"You do not own me." Again, sullenly.

"I have some claim on you. I want you to go on living."

"Slice will not kill me."

"It's killed plenty already."

"Not Pergolesi!" he snapped. Then he smiled, took my hand, gave me the full treatment. "Dave, Dave, you listen. I die once. I am not interested in an encore. But the slice, it is essential. Do you know? It divides one moment from the next. You have taken it? No? Then you cannot understand. It puts spaces in time. It allows me to comprehend the most intricate rhythms, because with slice there is time for everything, the world slows down, the mind accelerates. *Capisce?* I need it for my music."

"You managed to write the *Stabat Mater* without slice."

"Different music. For this, I need it." He patted my hand. "You do not worry, eh? I look after myself."

What could I say? I grumbled, I muttered, I shrugged. I told Nella to keep a very close eye on his readouts. I told Melissa to spend as much time as possible with him and keep him off the drug if she could manage it.

At the end of the month Gianni announced he would make his debut at The Quonch on the following Saturday. A big bill—five overload bands, Shining Orgasm Revival playing fourth, with Wilkes Booth John, no less, as the big group of the night. The kids in the audience would skull out completely if they knew that one of the Orgasms was three hundred years old, but of course they weren't going to find that out, so they'd just figure he was a new side-man and pay no attention. Later on Gianni would declare himself to be Pergolesi. He and Sam were already working on the altered PR program. I felt left out, off on another track. But it was beyond my control. Gianni now was like a force of nature, a hurricane of a man, frail and wan though he might be.

We all went to The Quonch for Gianni's overload debut.

There we sat, a dozen or more alleged adults, in that mob of screaming kids. Fumes, lights, colors, the buzzing of gadgetized clothes and jewels, people passing out, people coupling in the aisles, the whole crazy bit, like Babylon right before the end, and we sat through it. Kids selling slice, dope, coke, you name it, slipped among us. I wasn't buying but I think some of my people were. I closed my eyes and let it all wash over me, the rhythms and subliminals and ultrasonics of one group after another, Toad Star, then Bubblemilk, then Holy Ghosts, though I couldn't tell one from the next, and finally, after many hours, Shining Orgasm Revival was supposed to go on for its set.

A long intermission dragged on and on. And on.

The kids, zonked and crazed, didn't mind at first. But after maybe half an hour they began to boo and throw things and pound on the walls. I looked at Sam, Sam looked at me, Nella Brandon murmured little worried things.

Then Melissa appeared from somewhere, tugged at my arm and whispered, "Dr. Leavis, you'd better come backstage. Mr. Hoaglund. Dr. Brandon."

They say that if you fear the worst, you keep the worst at bay. As we made our way through the bowels of The Quonch to the performers' territory, I imagined Gianni sprawled backstage, wired with full gear, eyes rigid, tongue sticking out—dead of a slice overdose. And all our fabulous project ruined in a crazy moment. So we went backstage and there were the members of Shining Orgasm Revival running in circles, and a cluster of Quonch personnel conferring urgently, and kids in full war-paint peering in the back way and trying to get through the cordon. And there was Gianni, wired with full overload gear, sprawled on the floor, shirtless, skin shiny with sweat, mottled with dull purplish spots, eyes rigid, tongue sticking out. Nella Brandon pushed everyone away and dropped down beside him. One of the

Orgasms said to no one in particular, "He was real nervous, man, he kept slicing off more and more, we couldn't stop him, you know—"

Nella looked up at me. Her face was bleak.

"OD?" I said.

She nodded. She had the snout of an ultrahypo against Gianni's limp arm and she was giving him some kind of shot to try to bring him around. But even in A.D. 2008, dead is dead is dead.

It was Melissa who said afterward through tears, "It was his karma to die young, don't you see? If he couldn't die in 1736, he was going to die fast here. He had no choice."

And I thought of the biography that had said of him long ago, "His ill health was probably due to his notorious profligacy." And I heard Sam Hoaglund's voice in my mind saying, "Nobody steps out of character forever. The real Pergolesi will take control." Yes. Gianni had always been on a collision course with death, I saw now; by scooping him from his own era we had only delayed things a few months. Self-destructive is as self-destructive does, and a change of scenery doesn't alter the case.

If that is so—if, as Melissa says, karma governs all— should we bother to try again? Do we reach into yesterday's yesterday for some other young genius dead too soon, Poe or Rimbaud or Caravaggio or Keats, and give him the second chance we had hoped to give Gianni? And watch him recapitulate his destiny, going down a second time? Mozart, as Sam once suggested? Benvenuto Cellini? Our net is wide and deep. All of the past is ours. But if we bring back another, and he willfully and heedlessly sends himself down the same old karmic chute, what have we gained, what have we achieved, what have we done to ourselves and to him? I think of Gianni, looking to be rich and famous at last, lying purpled on that floor. Would Shelley drown again? Would Van Gogh cut off the other ear before our eyes?

Perhaps someone more mature would be safer, eh? El Greco, Cervantes, Shakespeare? But then we might behold Shakespeare signing up in Hollywood, El Greco operating out of some trendy gallery, Cervantes sitting down with his agent to figure tax-shelter angles. Yes? No. I look at the scoop. The scoop looks at me. It is very very late to consider these matters, my friends. Years of our lives consumed, billions of dollars spent, the seals of time ripped open, a young genius's strange odyssey ending on the floor backstage at The Quonch, and for what, for what, for what? We can't simply abandon the project now, can we?

Can we?

I look at the scoop. The scoop looks at me.

The Trouble with Sempoanga

When Helmut Schweid decided to go to Sempoanga for his holiday, he knew the risks, but of course he assumed they didn't apply to him. "You'll pick up a dose of *zanjak* and never get out of quarantine," his friends told him. Helmut laughed. He was a careful man, especially with his body. He would avoid getting *zanjak* by avoiding going to bed with women who had *zanjak:* that was simple enough to manage, wasn't it?

By common agreement Sempoanga was the most beautiful planet in the galaxy. See one sunrise on Sempoanga, everyone said, and you won't care if you never see anything else anywhere. The trouble with Sempoanga was the dismal parasite its humanoid natives harbored. There was only one way to transmit that parasite—by making love. Since the natives of Sempoanga are a good deal less attractive to humans than its sunrises, it is not easy to understand how any human could ever have caught it, but somehow someone had, and it had adapted nicely to human bodies, thriving and multiplying and making itself remarkably contagious, and in the past few years a good many human visitors to Sempoanga had passed it around to one another, with horrendous results. Biologists were working on a cure and hoped they might see results in just a few more years. But meanwhile no one went home from Sempoanga without undergoing tests and if you caught *zanjak*, you stayed quarantined there indefinitely, because the parasite's effect on the human reproductive system was so startling that the future of the entire species might be in jeopardy if it were allowed to spread to the other civilized worlds.

For his first few days on Sempoanga Helmut was so busy experiencing the gorgeous planet itself that he was in no danger of catching any kind of venereal disease, neither the old standbys nor the exotic local specialty. His own world, Waldemar, was a frosty place with a planetwide winter for three-quarters of the year, and on Sempoanga he erupted with great gusto into eternal tropical summer. From dawn to midnight he toured the wonders—Hargillin Falls, where the water is the color of red wine, and Stinivong Chute, a flawless mountain of obsidian at the edge of a lake of phosphorescent pink gas, and The Bubbles, where subterranean psychedelic vapors percolate upward through a shield of porous yellow rock with delightful effect. He ran naked through a grove of voluptuous ferns that wrapped him in their fleshy fronds. He swam in crystalline rivers, eye to eye with vast harmless turtles the size of small islands. And each night he staggered back to his hotel, wonderfully weary, to collapse into his solitary sleep-tube for a few hours.

But after those early greedy gulps of natural marvels, his normal social instincts reasserted themselves. On the fourth day he saw a striking-looking radium-blonde from one of the Rigel worlds at the gravity-ball court. She met his tentative grin with a dazzling one of her own and quickly agreed to have dinner with him. Everything was going beautifully until she excused herself for a moment late in the meal, and the waiter who was bringing the brandies paused to whisper to Helmut, "Watch out for that one. *Zanjak*."

He was stunned. Was she trying to hide it from him, then? No, give her more credit than that: as they strolled through the garden under the light of the five moons she said, "I'd like to spend the night with you. But only if you're already carrying. I am, you know." So that was that. He walked her to her room and kissed her sadly and warmly goodnight, and trembled for a moment as her soft elegant body moved close against his; but he managed to escape without doing anything foolish.

The next night, sitting alone in the hotel cocktail lounge and beginning to feel more than lonely, he noticed another woman noticing him. She was dark-haired and long-legged and perhaps two or three years younger than he was. They exchanged glances and then smiles, and he tapped his empty glass and she nodded and they rose and went to the bar and ritualistically bought each other drinks. Her name was Marbella and she had been on holiday here since last month, escaping from a collapsed six-group on the planet of Tlon. "The divorce is going to take *years*," she told him. "It's a universal-option planet, the six of us come from four different worlds and everybody's home-world laws apply, some of the lawyers aren't even *human*—"

"And you plan to hide out on Sempoanga until it's all over?"

"Can you imagine a better place?"

"Except for—"

"Well, yes, there's *that*. But every paradise has its little snake, after all." Quickly she shifted topics. "I saw you this morning at the puff-glider field. You looked like you wanted to try it."

"How is it done?" he asked. Helmut had watched hotel guests clambering into huge fungoid puff-balls, which immediately broke free of their moorings and went drifting out across golden Lake Mangalole in what looked like guided flight.

"Would you like me to teach you? It's a matter of controlling the puffer's hydrogen-synthesis. Stroke it one way and it gets more buoyant, another and it sinks. And you learn how to ride the thermals and all. Where did you say you were from?"

"Waldemar."

"Brr," she said. "Are you free for dinner tonight?"

He liked her forthright, aggressive ways. They arranged to meet for dinner and to try the puff-gliders in the morning. What might happen in between was left undiscussed, but once again Helmut found himself confronting the problem of *zanjak*. She had been here more than long enough to pick up an infection, and, coming out of a turbulent marriage, it was hardly likely that she had been chaste in this sensuous place. On the other hand, if she did carry the parasite, she would certainly tell him about it ahead of time, as the other woman had. There was bound to be an etiquette about such things.

Over dinner they spoke of her complex marriage and his simpler, but ultimately just as disastrous, one, and briefly of his work and hers and of his planet and hers, and then of the splendors of Sempoanga. He liked her very much. And the gleam in her eyes told him he was making the right impression.

When he invited her to his room, though, she turned him down—warmly and graciously and with what seemed like genuine regret, explaining that this was the last night of her five-day contraceptive holiday; she was fertile as a mink just now and feared giving way to temptation. She seemed sincere. "There'll be other nights, you know," she said, and her smile left him with no doubts.

In the morning they met at the puff-glider field and she taught him quickly and expertly how to control the great organisms. Within an hour they were off and soaring. They crossed the lake, landed on the slopes of jag-toothed Mount Monolang for a lunch of sun-grilled fish and wineberries and ran laughing toward a glistening stream for a dip. Later, when they lay sunning themselves on shelves of glassy rock, he studied her bare body as surreptitiously as possible for signs of *zanjak*— some swelling around the thighs, perhaps, or maybe little puckered red marks below the navel, anything at all that seemed irregular. Nothing visible, at any rate. The pamphlet on *zanjak* that the hotel had thoughtfully left beside his bed had told him there were no external symptoms, but he was uneasy all the same.

It would have been simple enough to drift into lovemaking on this secluded hillside, but his uncertainties held him back, nor did she try to take the initiative. Eventually they dressed and resumed their glider-journey. They halted again to visit a village of natives—flat-faced warty creatures with furry mothlike antennae, so ugly that Helmut wondered what sort of tourist could have been desperate enough to catch the original parasite from one of *them*—and then in late afternoon, strolling hand in hand in fields of mildly aphrodisiac blossoms, they slipped into one of those low-toned, earnest, intimate conversations that only people who are about to become lovers engage in. "What a lovely day this has been," she told him when they were heading back to the hotel.

That night she asked him to her room. Two themes marched through his mind as they undressed. One was his admiration for her beauty, her warmth and intelligence, her desirability. And the other was *zanjak, zanjak, zanjak.*

What to do? By dimmed light he came to her. He imagined himself saying, "Forgive me, Marbella, but I need to know. That terrible parasite—that monstrous disease—" And he could see her turning bleak and furious as he blurted his tactless questions, demanding icily whether he thought she were the sort of woman who might deliberately hide from him anything so ghastly and shoving him into the hall, slamming the door, screaming curses after him—

He faltered. She smiled. Her eyes were bright with desire and refusing her was absurd. He drew her into his arms.

They were inseparable, night and day, the rest of the week. He had no illusions: this was only a resort-planet romance, and when his time was up he would go back to

Waldemar and that would be the end of it. But it was wondrous while it lasted. She was a fine companion, and she appeared to be altogether in love with him, sincerely and a little worrisomely so. He was already rehearsing the speech he was going to have to make after breaking the news to her that business responsibilities would not permit him to extend his Sempoangan holiday beyond the five days that remained.

Then one drowsy morning as they were lying in bed he felt a dismaying internal twitch, as if some tiny supple creature were trying to swim downsteam in his urethra.

He said nothing to her. But after breakfast he invented the need to put a call through to his firm on Waldemar and, in terror, got himself off to the hotel medical office, where a blandly unsympathetic doctor processed him through the diagnostat and told him he had *zanjak*. "You see those little red flecks in your urine? Just a couple of microns in diameter. They're symptomatic. And this blood sample—it's loaded with *zanjak* excreta."

Helmut shivered. "I can't have had it more than a couple of days. Perhaps because we've detected it so soon—"

"Sorry. It doesn't work that way."

"What do I do now?" he asked tonelessly.

The doctor was already tapping data into a terminal. "We put you on the master list, first. That slaps a hold on your passport. You know about the quarantine, don't you? If your home world is covered by the covenant, your government will pay the expenses of transferring your funds and a certain quantity of your possessions to Sempoanga. You can live in the hotel as long as you can afford to, of course. After that, you're entitled to a rent-free room at the Quarantine Center, which is on the southern continent in a very pleasant region where the fishing is said to be superb. You'll be asked to take part in the various test programs for cures, but otherwise you'll be left alone."

"I don't believe this," Helmut muttered.

"These harsh measures are absolutely necessary, of course. You must realize that. The parasite has passed through your genitourinary tract and has taken up residence in your bloodstream, where it's busy filling you with threadlike reproductive bodies known as micro-filariae. Whenever you have sexual relations with a woman—or with another man, for that matter, or with any mammalian organism at all—you'll inevitably transmit microfilariae. If the organism you infect is female, the microfilariae will travel in a few weeks to the ovaries, infiltrate unfertilized eggs and impose their own genetic material by a process we call pseudofertilization, causing the eggs to mature into hybrids, part *zanjak* and part host-species. What appears to be a normal pregnancy follows, though the term is only about twelve weeks in human hosts; offspring are born in litters, adapted quite cunningly to penetrate whatever ecosphere they find themselves in."

"All right. Don't tell me any more."

"No need to. You see the picture. These things could take over the universe if they ever got beyond Sempoanga."

"Then Sempoanga should be closed to interplanetary travel!"

"Ah, but this is a major resort area! Besides, the quarantine is one hundred percent effective. If only new tourists were not so careless or unethical as they seem to be, we would isolate all cases in a matter of weeks and after that—"

"I thought I was being careful!"

"Not careful enough, it seems."

"And you? Don't *you* worry about getting it?"

The doctor gave Helmut a scathing look. "When I was a small child, I learned quickly not to put my fingers into electrical sockets. I conduct my sexual activities with the same philosophy. Good morning, Mr. Schweid. I'll have your quarantine documents sent round to your room when they're ready."

Numbed, staggering, Helmut wandered in a lurching

dazed way over the hotel's vast grounds, looking for
Marbella. He felt unclean and outcast; he could not bear
to look at any of the other guests who amiably greeted
him as he went by; he yearned to thrust his fouled body
into a vat of corrosive acid. Infected! Quarantined!
Exiled, maybe forever, from his home! No. No. It went
beyond all comprehension. That he, that precise and
intelligent and meticulous man, with his insurance
policies and his alarm systems and his annual medical
checkups, should—should have—

He found her watching a game of body-tennis, caught
her by the wrist from behind and whispered savagely,
"I've got *zanjak!*"

She looked at him, startled. "Of course you do, love."

"You say it so casually? You let me believe you were
clean!"

"Yes. Certainly. I knew you were already infected,
even if you didn't. Since you apparently didn't know it
yourself then, you'd never have gone to bed with me if I
admitted I was carrying. And I wanted you so much,
love. I'd have told any kind of harmless little lie then for
the sake of—"

"Wait a minute. What do you mean, you knew I was
already carrying?"

"That blonde bitch from Rigel, the night before you
and I met—I saw the two of you together at dinner. I
had my eye on you even then, you know. And I could tell
that that unscrupulous little tramp would conceal from
you that she was carrying. When I saw you go off to her
room with her, I knew you'd be joining the club."

Icily he said, "I didn't sleep with her, Marbella."

"What? But I was sure—"

"You were, were you?" He laughed bitterly. "I walked
her home and she told me she was a carrier and I kissed
her goodnight and went away. You can't catch it from a
kiss, can you? *Can you?*"

"No," she said in a very small voice.

"So you knowingly and shamelessly gave me a hideous
incurable disease because you had decided I had been

dumb enough to sleep with someone who was carrying it. I guess you were right about that, in a way."

She turned away, looking stricken. "Helmut, please— if you knew how sorry I am—"

"No sorrier than I am. Do you realize I'm quarantined here, and maybe for life?"

She shrugged. "Well, yes. So am I. There are worse places to spend one's life."

"I ought to kill you!"

She began to tremble. "I suppose I'd deserve it. Oh, Helmut—I was so completely fascinated by you—I didn't want to take the slightest risk of losing you. I should have waited until the infection I thought you got from *her* had showed itself. Then it wouldn't have mattered. But I couldn't wait—I tried, I couldn't—and I figured that we'd fall in love and by the time your *zanjak* showed it would be all right for me to admit that I had it, too."

He was silent a long moment. Then he said, "Maybe you figured that even if I *didn't* have it, you'd give it to me, by way of making absolutely sure I'd be stuck here on Sempoanga?"

"No. I swear it." There was shock and horror in her eyes. "You have to believe me, Helmut!"

"I could really kill you now," he said, and for an instant he thought he would. But instead he turned and fled, running in long loping, crazy strides, across the field of octopus palms and down a garden of electric orchids that flashed indignant lights at him and rang their bells, and through a swamp of warm sticky mud filled with little furry snakes, and up the side of Stinivong Chute, thinking he might throw himself over the edge. But halfway up he yielded to exhaustion and fell to the ground and lay there panting and gasping for what seemed like hours. When he returned to his room at dusk, there was a thick packet of documents beside his bed—his responsibilities and rights under the quarantine, how to transfer assets from his home world, pros and cons of applying for Sempoangan citizenship, and much more. He skimmed it quickly and tossed it aside before he was midway through. Thinking about such things was impossible now. He closed his eyes and pressed his face against his pillow, and suddenly scenes from Waldemar burned in his mind: the Great Glacier at Christmas, the ice-yacht races, the warm well-lit tunnels of his city, his snug dome-roofed home, his last night in it with Elissa, his trim little office with the rows of communicator panels—

He would never see any of that again, and it was all so stupid, so impossibly dumb, that he could not believe it.

He could not go to the dining room for dinner that evening. He ordered a meal from room service but left it untouched and nibbled a little of it the next morning after a night of loathsome dreams. That day he wandered at random, alone, getting used to what had happened to him. It was a magnificent day, the sky pink and soft, the flame-trees glowing, but it was all lost on him now. Even though this place might be paradise, he was condemned to dwell in it, and paradise on that basis was not very different from hell.

For two days he haunted the hotel grounds like his own ghost, speaking to no one. He didn't see Marbella again until the third evening after the *zanjak* had emerged in him. To break free of his depression he had gone to the cocktail lounge, and she was there, alone, apparently brooding. She brightened when he appeared, but he glared coldly at her and went past, to the bar. A newcomer was sitting there by herself, an attractive fragile-looking woman with large dark eyes and frosted auburn hair. Deliberately, maliciously, Helmut made a point of picking her up in front of Marbella. Her name was Sinuise; she came from a planet called Donegal; like so many others here, she was trying to forget a bad marriage. When they left the cocktail lounge together, Helmut could feel Marbella's eyes on him and it was like being skewered with hard radiation.

He and Sinuise dined and danced and drifted toward the evening's inevitable conclusion. In the casino he spotted Marbella again, watching them somberly from a distance. "Come," he said to the woman from Donegal. "Let's go for a walk." He slipped his arm over her shoulder. She was delicate and lovely and beyond doubt she was hungry for warmth and closeness, and he knew that he need only ask and she would go to his room with him. But as they strolled down the leafy paths he knew he could not do it. To carry his revenge on Marbella to the point of giving *zanjak* to an unsuspecting woman— no. No.

Under the rustling fronds of a limberwillow tree, he kissed her long and lovingly, and when he released her he said, "It's been a beautiful evening, Sinuise."

"Yes. For me also."

"Perhaps we'll go puff-gliding tomorrow."

"I'd like that. But—tonight—I thought—"

"I can't. Not with you, I have *zanjak*, you know. And unless you've already got it also—"

Her face seemed to crumple. The great dark eyes swam with tears. He took her hand lightly, but a convulsive quiver of disappointment and anguish ran through her, and she pulled away and fled from him, sobbing.

"I'm sorry," he called after her. "More than you can imagine!"

Marbella was still in the casino, still alone. She looked astonished that he had returned. He shot her a venomous look and headed for the gravity-dice table, and in fifteen minutes managed to lose half the money he was carrying. He thought of lovely little Sinuise alone in her bed. He thought of Helmut Schweid, infested by bizarre alien organisms. He thought of Marbella, her energy, her passionate little cries, her quick wit and sly humor. Perhaps she was telling the truth, he thought bleakly. Perhaps she genuinely thought I had picked up a dose from the blonde from Rigel.

Besides, what choice do I have now?

Slowly, wearily, he made his way across the huge room. Marbella was playing five-chip cargo in a reckless way. He watched her lose her stake. Then he lightly touched her arm.

"You win," he said.

They stayed together at the hotel another eight days, and then, because his money was gone and he would not take any from her, they moved to the Quarantine Center. It was, he quickly discovered, just as beautiful as the hotel, with glorious natural features every bit as strange and wonderful. They shared a small cabin and spent their days swimming and fishing and their nights making love. Over the next ten weeks Marbella's breasts grew heavy and her belly began to swell; but when her time came she would not go to the Quarantine Center hospital. Instead she bore her Sempoangan young behind the cabin, a litter of sleek little creatures like tiny green otters, ten or fifteen of them that came sliding out of her without effort. Helmut dug a pit and shoveled them all in, and after she had rested for an hour or so they went down to the beach to watch the translucent waves lapping against the azure sand. He thought of the snows of Waldemar, and of his home there, his lovers, his friends, and it all seemed terribly long ago and more than a million light-years far away.

How They Pass the Time in Pelpel

"**Y**ou know," Dan Britton said, pointing to a particularly sinister-looking ash-gray cactus on the nursery bench, "all these plants have stories, and some of them are damned strange stories. I don't mean botanical stories. I mean that all these peculiar plants that we grow here in California and that we take pretty much for granted had to be discovered by someone in some nasty corner of the world and collected and brought back and propagated and distributed. And in the process of all that, odd things have occasionally happened to the people who went out and found those plants." He picked up the ash-gray cactus. It was strange even as cacti go, not only because of its deathly color but because of the glossy black spines, heavy and menacing, running in rigidly aligned vertical rows down its sides. "*Copiapoa cinerea*," said Britton, "from the Atacama Desert in northern Chile. This one and most of the others you'll see are descended from the parent plants that I collected thirty years ago in the Atacama, between Pelpel and Sabroso. I ought to tell you that story some time."

Britton is a compact, weather-beaten-looking man who for the last dozen years or so has run a little nursery in Santa Barbara. That's a quiet town, and he leads a quiet life, selling fuchsias and pelargoniums and chrysanthemums to the local gardeners. But his own enthusiasms run to stranger stuff—proteas and tree aloes and cycads and such—and you can find those things on sale there, too. Now and then he sells one, for in Santa Barbara's gentle climate you can grow almost anything, and a few people thereabouts like to experiment with horticultural strangenesses. Britton never pushes that sort of merchandise, though. He knows that the people who want exotic plants will find them themselves, and the other kind will only mistreat them anyway. He lets the customers do as they please. I don't think running a nursery really interests him. Being around plants, yes: that's what he's done ever since he was a boy. When he was younger, he had a considerable reputation as a field botanist, venturing into remote and unappetizing places, mainly in South America, and coming back with enough unknown cacti and succulents and bromeliads and whatnot to give himself a distinct, if minor, niche in the history of botanical exploration. That's all behind him now, of course. He seems content to be keeping the locals supplied with the standard pretty merchandise that they like, and goes his own way in most things.

Business was slow that winter day, and he closed the nursery about half past four. I was staying overnight. We drove in silence past Mission Santa Barbara and into the foothills where he has his small house, modest adobe surrounded by awesome specimens of botanical rarities. On the way in I saw in his cactus garden a giant clump of the ash-gray *Copiapoa cinerea* that somehow I had never noticed before. Britton nodded. "From the Quebrada Pelpel, east of the town. One of my original specimens, in fact. The Greek told me where to look for them."

"The Greek?"

"It's a long story," Britton said.

He opened a bottle of chilled chenin blanc and we settled on his patio to watch twilight descend on Santa Barbara. An odd winter light made the red-tiled rooftops look almost pink, and fog was beginning to encroach on the harbor. But the air was mild, and the garden surrounding us was lush with blooming things, two enormous aloes sending up giant red spikes and a row of nine-foot-high proteas ablaze with implausibly intricate blossoms and a rare Mexican yucca unfolding a torrent of white flowers. We were halfway through the wine before either of us spoke. Then Britton said, "The Atacama Desert—it must be the driest place in the world. Three, four, five years at a time without any rain, and then maybe an inch, and then dry for two or three more years. But yet there are plants there. They live on the winter fog, the *camanchaca*, and nothing else." He looked straight at me, and his eyes are intense and piercing, but he seemed to be seeing through me into a sere and horrid realm of dryness almost beyond my comprehension. "This happened in January or February of 1952, when I was collecting along the South American coast for the university, trying to make some sense out of the genus *Copiapoa*, which as you may know was at that time very poorly understood and in desperate need of revision—"

My headquarters down there was in Pelpel, a parched little fishing village on the coast a couple of hundred kilometers south of Antofagasta. These days, for all I know, it's a magnificent resort with a high-rise Hilton and a racetrack and six casinos, but I doubt it very much. Back then it was utterly dismal—a thousand people or so living mainly in tin-roofed shacks. Dust blowing everywhere. The water supply was piped in for a few hours every other day. If you went inland a little way, up on the ridges back of town where there's a little fog condensation, you found some cactus growing, but in the town itself nothing at all could grow. You can't imagine how dreary and drab it was. The center of social life was a bleak scruffy plaza that was bordered by a squalid old hotel, and across the way from that a beer parlor and pool hall that was run by a Greek named Panagiotis. The Greek's place had a loudspeaker that blared music into the plaza every evening, and the big event was the grand promenade: single women going around the plaza in one direction, single men in the other, and eventually some couples would form and go off together for the night, and the next night it would all start over.

I was the only guest in the hotel, and from the way people stared at me when I arrived, I suspect that I was the first guest in seven or eight years. The place was clean enough—an old German woman ran it, and she spent hours every day dusting and sweeping—but the beams were dry and shrunken, the plaster was cracking, the roof was a sounding-board that rattled miserably every time the wind blew. My room was upstairs, and I was delighted to find a shower next door—a shower of sorts, anyway, with an overhead bag and a pull—chain. But when I tried to use it, nothing came out but a trickle of sand. Obviously it hadn't held water in a long time. Pelpel was strictly basin-and-sponge-bath territory.

But I didn't mind. I was young and not very concerned with comfort, and I was glad enough to have a roof over my head at all. What really mattered to me were the *Copiapoas* in the hinterlands, not the luxuries available in Pelpel. And I wasn't in Pelpel long before I found out where the *Copiapoas* were.

The Greek helped me. He was the only person in town who showed the slightest warmth toward me. The others simply gave me cold blank stares and tight-lipped scowls, behind which lay an apparent instant hostility that I suppose was the natural response of these hard-bitten people—forlorn dwellers in a desolate land—to an intruder, and outsider, a fortunate *Norteamericano* who had come to them out of the cozy world of hot and cold running water, air-conditioning and Technicolor movies. The fact that I spoke only the most basic Spanish at that time, and spoke it with a California/Mexican accent that must have seemed ludicrous, barbarous, and close to unintelligible to these Chileans, did not make it easier for me to win friends in Pelpel.

At least there was Panagiotis. I thought at first that his

friendliness was just a professional trait, the standard good-fellowship that any tavern keeper tends to develop, or else that it was only his irrepressible Greek exuberance that led him to greet me with a big toothy smile, whereas I got nothing but sullen frosty scowls from the rest of them. Probably those factors did figure into it to some degree. But also I think he genuinely took a liking to me—that he saw me not as over-privileged and condescending ambassador from a civilization of unimaginable and unattainable marvels, but rather as I really was, a young and rather shy botanist who was voluntarily making a long uncomfortable journey into their disagreeable environment for the sake of bringing back scientific information. I suppose Panagiotis was clever enough to see that what the others must have interpreted as haughtiness and arrogance was actually just the product of my shyness and my difficulties with their language.

I went out into the high county east of the town the first day and came back almost empty-handed. Obviously I am not a person who finds deserts depressing, but this one weighed on my spirits as no other had ever done. It was stark and drab, just bare rock and sand in dull tones of brown and yellow, and dry beyond belief. The desiccated ground was virtually lifeless, no shrubs, no cacti, not even the tiny ground-hugging plants you find in nearly any desert—nothing. Nothing. I could have been on the moon. I wandered for hours in emptiness, growing more discouraged as the day waned. Even though the desert gained in beauty in late afternoon when the sun no longer bleached all color from it and the bare ravines turned dark and mysteriously rich, I sank into a somber, self-pitying mood. It was a mistake to come here, I told myself. I should be up by Iquique, perhaps, or inland on the slopes of the Andes where plant life is more abundant. But of course the whole point of this expedition was to explore this barren and virtually unknown coastal strip, which had not been properly studied by botanists since the pioneering work of Philippi almost a hundred years before.

The afternoon winds stirred up great black clouds of dust, which had the merit of providing me with a spectacular sunset as I trudged back to Pelpel. The rays of the late sun, filtering through the murk and haze, turned from brilliant yellow to a pale violet, and then through a stunningly complex series of ever deeper purples until, suddenly, there was gray and then black. Just before it became dark, I stumbled over what I thought was a rock, and for some reason looked back to discover that I had tripped on an isolated specimen of *Copiapoa cinerea*, a single unbranched plant with short sparse spines, growing, God alone knew why, just a couple of kilometers from town. It was the only plant of interest I had seen in the past six or seven hours. I collected it and went hurrying on into Pelpel as night fell.

Dinner was waiting for me at the hotel—everything out of cans, a watery vegetable soup and some kind of meat stew, washed down by thin, bitter red wine. I ate by myself, served in silence by the Indian woman who seemed to be the hotel's only employee. From across the plaza came the raucous sound of music out of the Greek's loudspeaker. When I was done eating, I walked outside and stood in front of the hotel a long while, watching the townsfolk promenade. Mostly they ignored me. Those that did stare at me stared without amiability and essentially without curiosity. I shrugged and went to my room, but that made things even worse—the bare walls, the fissure in the plaster, the single dim light-bulb, the sound of the dry ugly wind. The idea of trying to work or study or even to relax in such a room until it was time to sleep was a dismal one. And so, although I'm not what anyone would call a drinking man, I found myself going across the plaza to the beer-parlor, simply to have some sort of human contact and a bit of cheer on this cheerless evening in this cheerless town.

Some two dozen men were in the place, mostly gathered around the pool-table, a few slouched at the warped and discolored bar. The look I got from them as I appeared in the doorway was so frigid that I nearly turned and fled. But then Panagiotis boomed out, "Hello, *Norteamericano!* You come in! You have drink with us!" It was impossible to refuse.

The Greek was a big thickset man of about fifty, with gleaming buck teeth and a broad conspicuous nose. His black hair was all but gone, combed across his skull in sparse strands between which a freckled and deeply tanned scalp showed through. He spoke a little English and understood my Spanish, and we were able to communicate. First he tapped the bottles around him on the bar—Peruvian *pisco* and various local brandies and rums and some kind of Scotch that was labeled *Hecho in Mexico*, but I shook them off, not wanting anything so strong after having had wine with dinner, and said, "*Hay cerveza?*" Panagiotis laughed and groped under the bar and came up with a dusty bottle of tepid beer. Getting it down was a challenge, and after that I drank *pisco*.

He introduced me to the other men at the bar. The very tall, almost skeletal one with the sunken burning eyes and the knifelike cheekbones was his brother-in-law, Ramon Sotomayor. The fat one beyond him was Aguirre, the lawyer, and the one with faded red hair was Nuñez de Prado, the doctor, and that was Mendoza, the pharmacist, and so on. Each, when his name was mentioned, gave me a glum, surly glare and a brief reluctant nod of salutation, and that was all.

And then Panagiotis—who, like everyone else, knew from the moment of my arrival that I was here to collect plants—asked me what I was looking for. Cactus, I said, curving my fingers to pantomime their shapes. I had been out all day, I told him, but I had had *mala suerte*, bad luck, I had found *nada*. Panagiotis listened sympathetically. He conferred with Mendoza and Aguirre in Spanish that was too fast and idiomatic for me to understand, and then began drawing crude maps on bar napkins, accompanying his diagrams with a running commentary in broken English and a kind of pidgin-Spanish. The maps were impossible to understand. I smiled and held up a hand and ran back to the hotel—a little tipsily—and got my own set of charts, and we spread them out on the bar. The others muttered and grumbled as though Panagiotis were giving me the location of secret gold mines, but he paid no attention to them and marked for me the places where I thought I would find what I was after. Then he slapped me on the back and filled my glass for the third or fourth time. He would take no payment. Eventually I got back to my room, head spinning, and not even the strident sounds of the loudspeaker music kept me awake for long.

The next day I started at dawn, going as far as I could in my battered jeep, covering the last few kilometers on foot. The Greek had guided me toward the rough ravines of the Quebrada Pelpel, ten kilometers east of town, where I already knew Philippi had collected in 1854. Sure enough, I found dense stands of *Copiapoa cinerea* there, several different populations including some plants with bizarre crested stems—the only such deformities ever observed in this species. That night I thanked Panagiotis warmly, and he filled me full of *pisco* until I begged him to stop and turned my glass bottom-side up.

And over the days that followed I went south across that silent, ghostly desert into the Sierra Esmeralda, and north along the coastal road to Sabroso, the next town up, and inland along the low plateaus, and I found *cinerea* in a wide range of forms, some with brown spines, some with yellowish ones, some so old they were almost spineless. In the hills above Sabroso I discovered the practically unknown *Copiapoa humilis*, a small plant with roots like turnips, last seen by Philippi in 1860. It's a difficult plant to find, because its dark color is much like that of the surrounding soil, and in times when even the fogs fail it protects itself against desiccation by pulling itself down into the earth until it almost vanishes. After looking in vain for it for hours, I discovered that I had sat right down on one clump of it—fortunately the spines are not very threatening—and thereafter I found plenty of them.

In this time I grew no closer to the people of Pelpel. The only one who as much as spoke to me was Panagiotis, and our conversations were limited by language barriers to the simplest themes. To the others I remained a total alien, unwanted, intrusive, resented. Their blank-eyed disdain was harder for me to take than solitude itself. I felt more comfortable by myself in the midst of a desert all but devoid of life than I did in that town. There was no reason for the locals to love me—they are a strange people, confined by the nature of their country to a narrow and rigid existence in their little oasis—but there wasn't any need for them to treat me as if I had come to steal from them or spy on them. Unless, possibly, they suspected me of secretly being an anthropologist trying to pry into their private ways, for I knew that in these coastal towns some odd customs had evolved out of the mixing of Indian and Spanish blood, a religion in which primitive native rites had been somehow hybridized into the Christian worship, and no doubt they wanted no investigation of that. But I think I never gave them cause to suspect I was anything other than what I said I was.

One afternoon I returned to town after a particularly trying and exhausting field trip, and, barely touching the pathetic dinner the Indian woman set out for me, I went to my room and fell into a deep sleep. A few hours later—it was still early evening—I was awakened by the sound of the Greek's loudspeaker. Booming through the plaza, blurred and distorted by echoes and feedback and the crudity of the equipment, was a man's voice, speaking excitedly and rapidly, delivering what sounded like a news broadcast or, more likely, the commentary on some big sporting event.

Puzzled, I peered out my window. A grand commotion was going on in the plaza. Half the population of

Pelpel seemed to be out there, not just those who made the spooky, silent nightly promenades around the plaza's edge. Hundreds of people were gathered, in groups of ten or a dozen or so, listening intently to the broadcast, occasionally cheering, shaking their heads, pointing at the loudspeaker as if arguing with it. I saw money changing hands, too—men taking crumpled wads of hundred-peso notes from their shirts and giving them to others. Every few minutes some loud outcry from the radio voice brought new cheers and groans from the crowd, and more bills went fluttering back and forth.

I went outside, hoping to find out what was going on. Usually when I appeared all activity halted and the townsfolk gave me looks of dark glowering anger as though I were death at the feast. I was a little hesitant to leave the hotel now, not wanting to sour their festivity. But to my surprise they seemed, for the first time, glad to see me. Some of them waved, some of them grinned, some of them tossed their hats in the air. "*Norteamericano!*" they cried. "*Hola, Norteamericano! Viva! Viva!*" What was all *that* about? They surrounded me, coming up close, peering right into my face and winking, slapping me on the back like old friends. The change of attitude was absolute and dramatic. And also a little frightening. I've studied some anthropology. I began to wonder whether I had been chosen for the starring role in some grim municipal ritual that was to be the peak of this mystifying event. I glanced around for the Greek, looking for explanations, but he was nowhere in sight, and the crowd was too thick for me to get across the plaza to his cantina.

Amid all the chaos I stood still and listened, desperately trying to make sense out of the broadcast. And gradually I began to understand a little of it. The announcer was naming local towns—Santa Catalina, Casabindo, San Antonio, Placilla— which I recognized as dusty little way-stations along the inland roads. And he was calling off names—Godoy, de la Gasca, Lezaeta, Alejandro. I gathered that some sort of automobile race was going on out there. In the harsh and forbidding wastelands of the Atacama Desert, under a black moonless sky, men were roaring across the pitted and parched terrain in motorcars, and here in Pelpel frantic wagering was going on over the ultimate outcome and, so it seemed, over the separate stages of the race.

As I listened with growing comprehension I realized that one of the drivers was an American. *El Norteamericano*, the announcer kept saying, was doing very well. *El Norteamericano* was showing great skill. *El Norteamericano* was demonstrating true virtuosity on the dangerous track. And every time the announcer mentioned this unknown countryman of mine, the townspeople around me grinned and cheered and waved at me, and made V-for-victory signs, as if they were rooting for him as a way of making amends for their coldness toward me. They pointed and shouted something at me again and again that at first I was unable to understand, until I picked up the verb *vencer* drifting to me like a word out of a vivid dream, and realized that they were telling me, "You will win!" *Me?*

So frenzied and feverish was the scene that only slowly did I start to consider the baffling, inexplicable, downright impossible aspects of what I was hearing.

The road they were racing on was the same one that I had driven so many times in the past ten or twelve days—a miserable, hopeless washboard track that ran along the coast from Pelpel to Sabroso, then curved inland, practically disappearing into the dust and rocky subsoil, and hooked up briefly with the Pan-American Highway. That road was a killer even for jeeps. What kind of supernatural shocks and springs did the racing cars have? How could the drivers possibly be moving at the speeds the announcer was talking about? Just to get from Placilla to San Antonio was a harrowing half-day project, with pebbles clanging against your oil pan every foot of the way. It was absurd to think of that narrow scratchy dirt-on-dirt track as a racecourse.

Another little mystery was how the announcer was

getting his information. In rapid-fire narrative he was giving continous reports on at least a dozen drivers spread out between Sabroso and Pelpel. I suppose that could have been done by posting him in a helicopter above the scene, but this was thirty years ago, remember, when helicopters were still rare, especially in out-of-the-way corners of Chile. Perhaps observers stationed along the course were phoning in a steady flow of news that the announcer was deftly weaving together to create his running account, but there weren't even any telephones in the town, let alone out there in the open wastelands. Radio communication? Perhaps. Smoke signals, for all I knew, or a semaphore relay? One guess was as good as another. The whole thing didn't make sense.

It was just as hard to figure out where the broadcast was coming from. Radio stations simply didn't exist in these parts. The music that Panagiotis played through his loudspeaker every night came from ancient phonograph records. There were radio stations in the south down by Valparaiso and Santiago, hundreds of miles away, but their signals didn't get up here. The nearest northern station was probably even further, in Lima, but the curve of the continent put the wall of the Andes between us and it. Short wave, then? Well, maybe. Or maybe some fluky transmission out of the Valparaiso station, although it was hard to see why they would want to devote hours of valuable air-time to an obscure automobile race in a sleepy pocket of the desert.

When I looked toward the northern side of the plaza where the road from Placilla came in, I saw the biggest puzzle of all. A length of sturdy twine, gaudily bedecked with red and green and yellow streamers, had been strung across the road to mark what was obviously the finish line. Boys were stationed on either side of the street with Chilean flags atop long poles, no doubt to wave in the victor's face as he came thundering down the home stretch. How, though, could they expect to conclude the long race right in the middle of Pelpel? A mere fifty or sixty feet behind the finish line was the high brick wall of the church. Did anyone seriously think that a car speeding through the line was going to be able to brake in time to avoid hitting that wall? I thought I must be mistaken, that this was no finish line but merely some kind of ceremonial halting point to which the winner would coast after passing the true finish line somewhere outside of town. But no, this certainly was decked out the way the terminus of a motor race ought to be decked out, and the townspeople were carefully keeping the road in front of it clear, as if they expected cars to go zooming into the plaza at any instant. And some of them were staring expectantly into the blackness of the night beyond the floodlit plaza, trying to make out the headlights of the finishers as they approached the end of the race.

Mystery on mystery. Bewildering, dreamlike, almost hallucinatory—I could make no sense out of any of it. This alien ritual left me feeling more thoroughly alone and out of place in Pelpel than ever before.

And yet, in the giddy and tense carnival atmosphere of the moment, nearly everyone was cheerful and friendly. They clustered around me, offering me drinks, cigarettes, rough *macho* handshakes, splay-toothed grins, winks, nudges. Through the air came the crackling boom of the loudspeaker, the voice furry and distorted, calling out the twists and surprises of the race. It was all but impossible for me to comprehend. Was that Alejandro in the lead, now? Or the *Norteamericano?* Was he saying that Lezaeta's car had gone spinning off the track passing the quebrada? And had someone else overturned just outside Sabroso? It was dreamlike, yes, eerie, confusing—little blips and fragments of information, alternating with static, cheering, shouting, and torrents of the bewildering local dialect. The crowd was wholly caught up in it, following each event of the race with wild excitement. They seemed to be making bets constantly—not just on the ultimate winner, so far as I could tell, but on who would be in the lead at certain key points along the course, and even on who would get through the race without a spin-out or a stall—and the hundred-peso notes were going swiftly from hand to hand. Whenever the *Norteamericano* racer was mentioned, the cheering grew more intense and the people surrounding me laughed and clapped as if to tell me that they liked me more and more because my valiant countryman was performing so well. I wondered who this American racer might be and what he was doing in these parts and whether he would make it safely to Pelpel that evening. It had been too many weeks since I had had a coherent conversation with someone whose language I understood.

The race appeared to be reaching its climax now.

Sotomayor, the Greek's brother-in-law, came swaggering up out of the chaos. He loomed ominously over me, at least a foot taller than I am, though I doubt he weighed a hundred forty pounds—a knifeblade of a man, matador-thin, cold, unfathomable. He glowered at me and said icily, "You will not win."

I had no idea what to say.

"You will lose," he said, as though he felt he needed to clarify his first statement.

I shrugged. He was drunk and wobbling, and I was so captivated by the sudden and unexpected friendliness of everyone else around me that I resented having Sotomayor spoil the mood of cordiality. Something possessed me and I tugged my wallet out of my pocket. In a reckless way—on this expedition I had no funds to waste—I pulled out five hundred-peso notes. The Chilean peso was then worth something like three cents, so a hundred pesos was no great fortune, but I could hardly stand to lose even the fifteen dollars that the five bills represented. Nevertheless I glared up at Sotomayor and said, "On the *Norteamericano* to win. *Cinco cientos.*"

"You bet with me?"

"I bet, yes."

Sotomayor laughed. With a vast flamboyant gesture of his great spidery arms he drew forth a purse from a money belt and counted out *ten* hundred-peso notes,

holding each one up so that I could count along with
him. His eyes gleamed mockingly in the glaring light of
the plaza lamps. He was giving me odds of two to one,
unasked—a gesture of contempt, of humiliation. He
swept my bills from my hand, folded them into the ten
he was holding, wrapped them all in a wad and handed
them to fat Aguirre, the lawyer, who stood nearby and
somehow had been appointed keeper of the stakes in
that moment.

The crowd was screaming. It was all but impossible to
make out the announcer's words now.

I said to Aguirre, "Do you know where the racers are
at this minute?"

He pointed past the finish line and vaguely up the
dark highway. "Two kilometers from Pelpel."

Even on that dreadful road it wouldn't take long to
cover two kilometers. The race was almost over. The
screaming was frantic. Along with everyone else I
looked toward the finish line. I still was unable to
understand how the race could possibly end in Pelpel; I
imagined the leading drivers barreling down the narrow
road, passing between the tin-roofed shacks, roaring
across the finish line into the plaza, smashing willy-nilly
into the church wall, piling up in a great flaming mound
of wreckage, car upon car upon car—

Sudden silence. The voice of the announcer, cracking
with the strain: "Alejandro . . . Godoy . . . *Norteamericano* . . . Alejandro . . . *Norteamericano* . . .
Norteamericano . . . *Norteamericano primero* . . ."

Silence.

Everyone frozen, peering out into the night.

"*Norteamericano* wins! Alejandro second! Godoy
third!"

Wins? How? Where?

At the far side of the plaza they were tearing down the
finish line, pulling off the streamers, fluttering them like
banners, and the two flag-bearers were capering about,
waving the flags. A mad celebration was beginning, a

wild crazy leaping and prancing. But where were the cars?

The road was empty. The race was over and no one had arrived in Pelpel.

I began to understand, but I could not believe that I understood what I thought I understood. I had to find Panagiotis. In the madness of the plaza, with everyone going berserk and hundred-peso notes flapping about like confetti, it was not easy to get to the far side, but I pushed and elbowed my way across and finally entered the cantina. The Greek sat wearily slouched behind the bar, face shiny with sweat, eyes glossy, a drink in one hand and a microphone in the other. He smiled and nodded when he saw me.

"You drove well," he said.

"I?"

"Very well. We are proud of you."

I sat down facing him. "The race was inaginary?" I asked.

"*No le entiendo.*"

"Imaginary. You made it up. You invented it. You sat here all evening with that microphone, pretending that a race was going on out in the desert, right?"

"Yes."

"And the *Norteamericano* who was racing—he was me?"

"Yes."

"And the people believe all this?" They think there really was a race?"

Panagiotis grinned. "In Pelpel life is very quiet. This is the most real race we have. This is how we pass the time in Pelpel. The people of Pelpel understand what is real and what is not real, better than you think."

"How—often do you have a race?"

"Whenever we need it. Perhaps every two, three months. Sometimes more often. We did this now, in your honor."

"And let me win?"

"Because you would be more popular in Pelpel," said Panagiotis. "You did not have many friends here. Now everyone is your friend in Pelpel."

"Except Sotomayor," I said.

And just then, as if on cue, Sotomayor and his cronies entered the tavern. There was a black gleam in Sotomayor's eyes that I hope never to see again anywhere. He looked at me with loathing and at his brother-in-law with absolute rage, and said something quick and curt in Spanish that I could not understand but which made a sound like the spitting out of teeth. He pointed to me, to Panagiotis, to the microphone. It was very quiet in the cantina. The pharmacist, Mendoza, laughed nervously, but it did not break the tension.

"You have made me a fool," said Sotomayor to Panagiotis.

The Greek replied, "Only a fool can make a fool. But here, Ramon. Let us drink together and make amends."

He swung around and picked up the bottle of *pisco*. When he turned back to face the rest of us, a small shiny snub-nosed pistol had appeared in Sotomayor's hand, and Panagiotis' mouth made a silent little O of amazement, and Sotomayor shot him once, drilling a small startling hole in the center of the Greek's broad, sloping freckled forehead.

Aguirre put a thick wad of hundred-peso notes into my hand. I had won my bet with Sotomayor, after all. Then he and Mendoza and Nuñez de Prado and Ramon Sotomayor turned and walked out of the bar, leaving me alone with the dead Panagiotis.

Britton paused and poured the last of the chenin blanc into my glass and his. Night had fallen over Santa Barbara and the lights of boats sparkled in the marina and I heard distant foghorns. After a moment Britton said, "The next morning I packed up my *Copiapoas* and left town. The Plaza was absolutely deserted, and the only traces of the events of the night before were the shreds and tatters of the colored streamers. I never found out what happened to Sotomayor. And now, I suppose, they have some other way of passing the time in Pelpel."

Waiting for
the Earthquake

It was eleven weeks and two days and three hours—plus or minus a little—until the earthquake that was going to devastate the planet, and suddenly Morrissey found himself doubting that the earthquake was going to happen at all. The strange notion stopped him in his tracks. He was out strolling the shore of the Ring Ocean, half a dozen kilometers from his cabin, when the idea came to him. He turned to his companion, an old fux called Dinoov who was just entering his postsexual phase, and said in a peculiar tone, "What if the ground doesn't shake, you know?"

"But it will," the aborigine said calmly.

"What if the predictions are *wrong*?"

The fux was a small elegant blue-furred creature, sleek and compact, with the cool all-accepting demeanor that comes from having passed safely through all the storms and metamorphoses of a fux's reproductive odyssey. It raised itself on its hind legs, the only pair that remained to it now, and said, "You should cover your head when you walk in the sunlight at flare time, friend Morrissey. The brightness damages the soul."

"You think I'm crazy, Dinoov?"

"I think you are under great stress."

Morrissey nodded vaguely. He looked away and stared westward across the shining blood-hued ocean,

212

narrowing his eyes as though trying to see the frosty crystalline shores of Farside beyond the curve of the horizon. Perhaps half a kilometer out to sea he detected glistening patches of bright green on the surface of the water—the spawning bloom of the balloons. High above those dazzling streaks a dozen or so brilliant iridescent gasbag-creatures hovered, going through the early sarabandes of their mating dance. The quake would not matter at all to the balloons. When the surface of Medea heaved and buckled and crumpled, they would be drifting far overhead, dreaming their transcendental dreams and paying no attention.

But maybe there will be no quake, Morrissey told himself.

He played with the thought. He had waited all his life for the vast apocalyptic event that was supposed to put an end to the thousand-year-long human occupation of Medea, and now, very close to earthquake time, he found a savage perverse pleasure in denying the truth of what he knew to be coming. No earthquake! No earthquake! Life will go on and on and on! The thought gave him a chilling prickling feeling. There was an odd sensation in the soles of his feet, as if he were standing with both his feet off the ground.

Morrissey imagined himself sending out a joyful message to all those who had fled the doomed world: *Come back, all is well, it didn't happen! Come live on Medea again!* And he saw the fleet of great gleaming ships swinging around, heading back, moving like mighty dolphins across the void, shimmering like needles in the purple sky, dropping down by the hundred to unload the vanished settlers at Chong and Enrique and Pellucidar and Port Medea and Madagozar. Swarms of people rushing forth, tears, hugs, raucous laughter, old friends reunited, the cities coming alive again! Morrissey trembled. He closed his eyes and wrapped his arms tight around himself. The fantasy had almost hallucinatory power. It made him giddy, and his skin, bleached and leathery from a lifetime under the ultraviolet flares of the twin suns, grew hot and moist. *Come home, come home, come home! The earthquake's been canceled!*

He savored that. And then he let go of it and allowed the bright glow of it to fade from his mind.

He said to the fux, "There's eleven weeks left. And then everything on Medea is going to be destroyed. Why are you so calm, Dinoov?"

"Why not?"

"Don't you *care?*"

"Do you?"

"I love this place," Morrissey said. "I can't bear to see it all smashed apart."

"Then why didn't you go home to Earth with the others?"

"Home? Home? This is my home. I have Medean genes in my body. My people have lived here for a thousand years. My great-grandparents were born on Medea and so were *their* great-grandparents."

"The others could say the same thing. Yet when earthquake time drew near, they went home. Why have you stayed?"

Morrissey, towering over the slender little being, was silent a moment. Then he laughed harshly and said, "I didn't evacuate for the same reason that you don't give a damn that a killer quake is coming. We're both done for anyway, right? I don't know anything about Earth. It's not my world. I'm too old to start over there. And you? You're on your last legs, aren't you? Both your wombs are gone, your male itch is gone, you're in that nice quiet burned-out place, eh, Dinoov?" Morrissey chuckled. "We deserve each other. Waiting for the end together, two old hulks."

The fux studied Morrissey with glinting, unfathomable, mischievous eyes. Then he pointed downwind, toward a headland maybe three hundred meters away, a sandy rise thickly furred with bladdermoss and scrubby yellow-leaved anglepod bushes. Right at the tip of the cape, outlined sharply against the glowing sky, were a couple of fuxes. One was female, six-legged, yet to bear her first litter. Behind her, gripping her haunches and readying himself to mount, was a bipedal male, and even at this distance Morrissey could see his frantic, almost desperate movements.

"What are they doing?" Dinoov asked.

Morrissey shrugged. "Mating."

"Yes. And when will she drop her young?"

"In fifteen weeks."

"Are they burned out?" the fux asked. "Are they done for? Why do they make young if destruction is coming?"

"Because they can't help—"

Dinoov silenced Morrissey with an upraised hand. "I meant the question not to be answered. Not yet, not until you understand things better. Yes? Please?"

"I don't—"

"—understand. Exactly." The fux smiled a fuxy smile. "This walk has tired you. Come now: I'll go with you to your cabin."

They scrambled briskly up the path from the long crescent of pale blue sand that was the beach to the top of the bluff, and then walked more slowly down the road, past the abandoned holiday cabins toward Morrissey's place. Once this had been Argoview Dunes, a bustling shoreside community, but that was long ago. Morrissey in these latter days would have preferred to live in some wilder terrain where the hand of man had not weighed so heavily on the natural landscape, but he dared not risk it. Medea, even after ten centuries of colonization, still was a world of sudden perils. The unconquered places had gone unconquered for good reason; and, living on alone since the evacuation, he needed to keep close to some settlement, with its stores of food and materiel. He could not afford the luxury of the picturesque.

In any case the wilderness was rapidly reclaiming its own now that most of the intruders had departed. In the early days this steamy low-latitude tropical coast had been infested with all manner of monstrous beasts.

Some had been driven off by methodical campaigns of extermination and others, repelled by the effluvia of the human settlements, had simply disappeared. But they were starting to return. A few weeks ago Morrissey had seen a scuttlefish come ashore, a gigantic black-scaled tubular thing, hauling itself onto land by desperate heaves of its awesome curved flippers and actually digging its fangs into the sand, biting the shore to pull itself onward. They were supposed to be extinct. By a fantastic effort the thing had dug itself into the beach, burying all twenty meters of its body in the azure sand, and a couple of hours later hundreds of young ones that had tunnelled out of the mighty carcass began to emerge, slender beasts no longer than Morrissey's arm that went writhing with demonic energy down the dunes and into the rough surf. So this was becoming a sea of monsters again. Morrissey had no objections. Swimming was no longer one of his recreations.

He had lived by himself beside the Ring Ocean for ten years in a little low-roofed cabin of the old Arcan wing-structure design that so beautifully resisted the diabolical Medean winds. In the days of his marriage, when he had been a geophysicist mapping the fault lines, he and Nadia and Paul and Danielle had had a house on the outskirts of Chong on Northcape within view of the High Cascades, and had come here only in winter; but Nadia had gone to sing cosmic harmonies with the serene and noble and incomprehensible balloons, and Danielle had been caught in the Hotlands at double-flare time and had not returned, and Paul, tough old indestructible Paul, had panicked over the thought that the earthquake was only a decade away, and between Darkday and Dimday of Christmas week had packed up and boarded an Earthbound ship. All that had happened within the space of four months, and afterward Morrissey found he had lost his fondness for the chilly air of Northcape. So he had come down to Argoview Dunes to wait out the final years in the comfort of the humid tropics, and now he was the only one left in the shore-side community. He had brought persona-cubes of Paul and Nadia and Danielle with him, but playing them turned out to be too painful, and it was a long time since he had talked with anyone but Dinoov. For all he knew, he was the only one left on Medea. Except, of course, the fuxes and the balloons. And the scuttlefish and the rock demons and the wingfingers and the not-turtles and all of those.

Morrissey and Dinoov stood silently for a time outside the cabin, watching the sunset begin. Through a darkening sky mottled with the green and yellow folds and streaks of Medea's perpetual aurora, the twin suns Phrixus and Helle—mere orange red daubs of feeble light—drifted toward the horizon. In a few hours they would be gone, off to cast their bleak glow over the dry-ice wastelands of Farside. There could never be real darkness on the inhabited side of Medea, though, for the oppressive great sullen bulk of Argo, the huge red-hot gas-giant planet whose moon Medea was, lay just a million kilometers away. Medea, locked in Argo's grip, kept the same face turned toward her enormous primary all the time. From Argo came the warmth that made life possible on Medea, and also a perpetual dull reddish illumination.

The stars were beginning to come out as the twin suns set.

"See there," Dinoov said. "Argo has nearly eaten the white fires."

The fux had chosen deliberately archaic terms, folk-astronomy; but Morrissey understood what he meant. Phrixus and Helle were not the only suns in Medea's sky. The two orange-red dwarf stars, moving as a binary unit, were themselves subject to a pair of magnificent blue-white stars, Castor A and B. Though the blue-white stars were a thousand times as far from Medea as the orange-red ones were, they were plainly visible by day and by night, casting a brilliant icy glare. But now they were moving into eclipse behind great Argo, and soon—

eleven weeks, two days, one hour, plus or minus a little—they would disappear entirely.

And how, then, could there not be an earthquake?

Morrissey was angry with himself for the pathetic soft-headedness of his fantasy of an hour ago. No earthquake? A last-minute miracle? The calculations in error? Sure. Sure. If wishes were horses, beggars might ride. The earthquake was inevitable. A day would come when the configuration of the heavens was exactly *thus*, Phrixus and Helle positioned *here*, and Castor A and B *there*, and *there* and *there*, and Argo as ever exerting its inexorable pull above the Hotlands, and when the celestial vectors were properly aligned, the gravitational stresses would send a terrible shudder through the crust of Medea.

This happened every 7,160 years. And the time was at hand.

Centuries ago, when the persistence of certain apocalyptic themes in fux folklore had finally led the astronomers of the Medea colony to run a few belated calculations of these matters, no one had really cared. Hearing that the world will come to an end in five or six hundred years is much like hearing that you yourself are going to die in another fifty or sixty: it makes no practical difference in the conduct of everyday life. Later, of course, as the seismic tickdown moved along, people began to think about it more seriously, and beyond doubt it had been a depressive factor in the Medean economy for the past century or so. Nevertheless, Morrissey's generation was the first that had confronted the dimensions of the impending calamity in any realistic way. And in one manner or another the thousand-year-old colony had melted away in little more than a decade.

"How quiet everything is," Morrissey said. He glanced at the fux. "Do you think I'm the only one left, Dinoov?"

"How would I know?"

"Don't play those games with me. Your people have

ways of circulating information that we were only just beginning to suspect. You know."

The fux said gravely, "The world is large. There were many human cities. Probably some others of your kind are still living here, but I have no certain knowledge. You may well be the last one."

"I suppose. Someone had to be."

"Does it give you satisfaction, knowing you are last?"

"Because it means I have more endurance, or because I think it's good that the colony has broken up?"

"Either," said the fux.

"I don't feel a thing," Morrissey said. "Either way. I'm the last, if I'm the last, because I didn't want to leave. That's all. This is my home and here I stay. I don't feel proud or brave or noble for having stayed. I wish there wasn't going to be an earthquake, but I can't do anything about that, and by now I don't think I even care."

"Really?" Dinoov asked. "That's not how it seemed a little while ago."

Morrissey smiled. "Nothing lasts. We pretend we build for the ages, but time moves and everything fades and art becomes artifacts and sand becomes sandstone, and what of it? Once there was a world here and we turned it into a colony. And now the colonists are gone and soon the colony will be gone and this will be a world again as our rubble blows away. And what of it?"

"You sound very old," said the fux.

"I am very old. Older even than you."

"Only in years. Our lives move faster than yours, but in my few years I have been through all the stages of my life, and the end would soon be coming for me even if the ground were not going to shake. But you still have time left."

Morrissey shrugged.

The fux said, "I know that there are starships standing fueled and ready at Port Medea. Ready to go, at the push of a button."

"Are you sure? Ships ready to go?"

"Many of them. They were not needed. The Ahya have seen them and told us."

"The balloons? What were they doing at Port Medea?"

"Who understands the Ahya? They wander where they please. But they have seen the ships, friend Morrissey. You could still save yourself."

"Sure," Morrissey said. "I take a flitter thousands of kilometers across Medea, and I singlehandedly give a starship the checkdown for a voyage of fifty light-years, and then I put myself into coldsleep and I go home all alone and wake up on an alien planet where my remote ancestors happened to have been born. What for?"

"You will die, I think, when the ground shakes."

"I will die, I think, even if it doesn't."

"Sooner or later. But this way, later."

"If I had wanted to leave Medea," Morrissey said, "I would have gone with the others. It's too late now."

"No," said the fux. "There are ships at Port Medea. Go to Port Medea, my friend."

Morrissey was silent. In the dimming light he knelt and tugged at tough little hummocks of stickweed that were beginning to invade his garden. Once he had landscaped this place with exotic shrubs from all over Medea, everything beautiful that was capable of surviving the humidity and the rainfall of the Wetlands, but now as the end drew near, the native plants of the coast were closing in, smothering his lovely whiptrees and dangletwines and flamestripes and the rest, and he no longer was able to hold them back. For minutes he clawed at the sticky stoloniferous killers, baleful orange against the tawny sand, that suddenly were sprouting by his doorway.

Then he said, "I think I will take a trip, Dinoov."

The fux looked startled. "You'll go to Port Medea?"

"There, yes, and other places. It's years since I've left the Dunes. I'm going to make a farewell tour of the whole planet." He was amazed himself at what he was saying. "I'm the last one here, right? And this is almost the last chance, right? And it ought to be done, right?

Saying good-bye to Medea. Somebody has to make the rounds, somebody has to turn off the lights. Right? Right. Right. Right. And I'm the one."

"Will you take the starship home?"

"That's not part of my plan. I'll be back here, Dinoov. You can count on that. You'll see me again, just before the end. I promise you that."

"I wish you would go home," said the fux, "and save yourself."

"I will go home," Morrissey answered. "To save myself. In eleven weeks. Plus or minus a little."

Morrissey spent the next day, Darkday, quietly—planning his trip, packing, reading, wandering along the beach front in the red twilight glimmer. There was no sign all day of Dinoov or indeed of any of the local fuxes, although in mid-afternoon a hundred or more balloons drifted by in tight formation, heading out to sea. In the darkness their shimmering colors were muted, but still they were a noble sight, huge taut globes trailing long coiling ropy organs. As they passed overhead Morrissey saluted them and said quietly, "A safe flight to you, cousins." But of course the balloons took no notice of him.

Toward evening he drew from his locker a dinner that he had been saving for some special occasion, Madagozar oysters and filet of vandaleur and newly ripened peeperpods. There were two bottles of golden red Palinurus wine left and he opened one of them. He drank and ate until he started to nod off at the table; then he lurched to his cradle, programmed himself for ten hours' sleep, about twice what he normally needed at his age, and closed his eyes.

When he woke it was well along into Dimday morning, with the double sun not yet visible but already throwing pink light across the crest of the eastern hills. Morrissey, skipping breakfast altogether, went into town and ransacked the commissary. He filled a freezercase with provisions enough to last him for three months, since he had no idea what to expect by way of supplies elsewhere on Medea. At the landing strip where commuters from Enrique and Pellucidar once had parked their flitters after flying in for the weekend, he checked out his own, an '83 model with sharply raked lines and a sophisticated moire-pattern skin, now somewhat pitted and rusted by neglect. The powerpak still indicated a full charge—ninety-year half-life; he wasn't surprised—but just to be on the safe side he borrowed an auxiliary pak from an adjoining flitter and keyed it in as a reserve. He hadn't flown in years, but that didn't worry him much: the flitter responded to voice-actuated commands, and Morrissey doubted that he'd have to do any manual overriding.

Everything was ready by mid-afternoon. He slipped into the pilot's seat and told the flitter, "Give me a systems checkout for extended flight."

Lights went on and off on the control panels. It was an impressive display of technological choreography, although Morrissey had forgotten what the displays signified. He called for verbal confirmation, and the flitter told him in a no-nonsense contralto that it was ready for takeoff.

"Your course," Morrissey said, "is due west for fifty kilometers at an altitude of five hundred meters, then north-northeast as far as Jane's Town, east to Hawkman Farms, and southwest back to Argoview Dunes. Then without landing, head due north by the shortest route to Port Kato. Got it?"

Morrissey waited for takeoff. Nothing happened.

"Well?" he said.

"Awaiting tower clearance," said the flitter.

"Consider all clearance programs revoked."

Still nothing happened. Morrissey wondered how to key in a program override. But the flitter evidently could find no reason to call Morrissey's bluff, and after a moment takeoff lights glowed all over the cabin, a low humming came from aft. Smoothly the little vehicle retracted its wind-jacks, gliding into flight position, and spun upward into the moist, heavy, turbulent air.

He had chosen to begin his journey with a ceremonial circumnavigation of the immediate area—ostensibly to be sure that his flitter still could fly after all these years, but he suspected also that he wanted to show himself aloft to the fuxes of the district, to let them know that at least one human vehicle still traversed the skies. The flitter seemed all right. Within minutes he was at the beach, flying directly over his own cabin—it was the only one whose garden had not been overtaken by jungle scrub—and then out over the dark, tide-driven ocean. Up north then to the big port of Jane's Town, where tourist cruisers lay rusting in the crescent harbor, and inland a little way to a derelict farming settlement where the tops of mighty gattabangus trees, heavily laden with succulent scarlet fruit, were barely visible above swarming strangler vines. And then back, over sandy scrubby hills, to the Dunes. Everything below was desolate and dismal. He saw a good many fuxes, long columns of them in some places, mainly six-leg females and some four-leg ones, with males leading the way. Oddly, they all seemed to be marching inland toward the dry Hotlands, as though some sort of migration were under way. Perhaps so. To a fux the interior was holier than the coast, and the holiest place of all was the great jagged central peak that the colonists called Mount Olympus, directly under Argo, where the air was hot enough to make water boil and only the most specialized of living creatures could survive. Fuxes would die in that blazing terrible highland desert almost as quickly as humans, but maybe, Morrissey thought, they wanted to get as close as possible to the holy mountain as the time of the earthquake approached. The coming round of the earthquake cycle was the central event of fux cosmology, after all—a millenial time, a time of wonders.

   He counted fifty separate bands of migrating fuxes. He wondered whether his friend Dinoov was among them. Suddenly he realized how strong was his need to find Dinoov waiting at Argoview Dunes when he returned from his journey around Medea.

The circuit of the district took less than an hour. When the Dunes came in view again, the flitter performed a dainty pirouette over the town and shot off northward along the coast.

The route Morrissey had in mind would take him up the west coast as far as Arca, across the Hotlands to Northcape and down the other coast to tropical Madagozar before crossing back to the Dunes. Thus he would neatly touch base wherever mankind had left an imprint on Medea.

Medea was divided into two huge hemispheres separated by the watery girdle of the Ring Ocean. But Farside was a glaciated wasteland that never left Argo's warmth, and no permanent settlements had ever been founded there, only research camps, and in the last four hundred years very few of those. The original purpose of the Medea colony had been scientific study, the painstaking exploration of a wholly alien environment, but, of course, as time goes along original purposes have a way of being forgotten. Even on the warm continent human occupation had been limited to twin arcs along the coasts from the tropics through the high temperate latitudes, and timid incursions a few hundred kilometers inland. The high desert was uninhabitable, and few humans found the bordering Hotlands hospitable, although the balloons and even some tribes of fuxes seemed to like the climate there. The only other places where humans had planted themselves was the Ring Ocean, where some floating raft-cities had been constructed in the kelp-choked equatorial water. But during the ten centuries of Medea the widely scattered human enclaves had sent out amoeboid extensions until they were nearly continuous for thousands of kilometers.

Now, Morrissey saw, that iron band of urban sprawl was cut again and again by intrusions of dense underbrush. Great patches of orange and yellow foliage already had begun to smother highways, airports, commercial plazas, residential suburbs.

What the jungle had begun, he thought, the earthquake would finish.

On the third day Morrissey saw Hansonia Island ahead of him, a dark orange slash against the breast of the sea, and soon the flitter was making its approach to the airstrip at Port Kato on the big island's eastern shore. Morrissey tried to make radio contact but got only static and silence. He decided to land anyway.

Hansonia had never had much of a human population. It had been set aside from the beginning as an ecological-study laboratory, because its population of strange life-forms had developed in isolation from the mainland for thousands of years, and somehow it had kept its special status even in Medea's boom years.

A few groundcars were parked at the airstrip. Morrissey found one that still held a charge, and ten minutes later he was in Port Kato.

The place stank of red mildew. The buildings, wicker huts with thatched roofs, were falling apart. Angular trees of a species Morrissey did not know sprouted everywhere, in the streets, on rooftops, in the crowns of other trees. A cool hard-edged wind was blowing out of Farside. Two fuxes, four-leg females herding some young six-leggers, wandered out of a tumbledown warehouse and stared at him in what surely was astonishment. Their pelts were so blue they seemed black—the island species, different from mainlanders.

"You come back?" one asked. Local accent, too.

"Just for a visit. Are there any humans here?"

"You," said the other fux. He thought they laughed at him. "Ground shake soon. You know?"

"I know," he said.

They nuzzled their young and wandered away.

For three hours Morrissey explored the town, holding himself aloof from emotion, not letting the rot and decay and corruption get to him. It looked as if the place had been abandoned at least fifty years. More likely only five or six, though.

Late in the day he entered a small house where the town met the forest and found a functioning persona-cube setup.

The cubes were clever things. You could record yourself in an hour or so—facial gestures, motion habits, voice, speech patterns. Scanners identified certain broad patterns of mental response and coded those into the cube, too. What the cube playback provided was a plausible imitation of a human being, the best possible memento of a loved one or friend or mentor, an electronic phantom programmed to absorb data and modify its own program, so that it could engage in conversation, ask questions, pretend to be the person who had been cubed. A soul in a box, a cunning device.

Morrissey jacked the cube into its receptor slot. The screen displayed a thin-lipped man with a high forehead and a lean, agile body. "My name is Leopold Brannum," he said at once. "My specialty is xenogenetics. What year is this?"

"It's '97, autumn," Morrissey said. "Ten weeks and a bit before the earthquake."

"And who are you?"

"Nobody particular. I just happen to be visiting Port Kato and I felt like talking to someone."

"So talk," Brannum said. "What's going on in Port Kato?"

"Nothing. It's pretty damned quiet here. The place is empty."

"The whole town's been evacuated?"

"The whole planet, for all I know. Just me and the fuxes and the balloons still around. When did you leave, Brannum?"

"Summer of '92," said the man in the cube.

"I don't see why everyone ran away so early. There wasn't any chance the earthquake would come before the predicted time."

"I didn't run away," Brannum said coldly. "I left Port Kato to continue my research by other means."

"I don't understand."

"I went to join the balloons," Brannum said.

Morrissey caught his breath. The words touched his soul with wintry bleakness.

"My wife did that," he said after a moment. "Perhaps you know her now. Nadia Dutoit—she was from Chong, originally—"

The face on the screen smiled sourly. "You don't seem to realize," Brannum said, "that I'm only a recording."

"Of course. Of course."

"I don't know where your wife is now. I don't even know where *I* am now. I can only tell you that wherever we are, it's in a place of great peace, of utter harmony."

"Yes. Of course." Morrissey remembered the terrible day when Nadia told him that she could no longer resist the spiritual communion of the aerial creatures, that she was going off to seek entry into the collective mind of the Ahya. All through the history of Medea some colonists had done that. No one had ever seen any of them again. Their souls, people said, were absorbed, and their bodies lay buried somewhere beneath the dry ice of Farside. Toward the end the frequency of such defections had doubled and doubled and doubled again, thousands of colonists every month giving themselves up to whatever mystic engulfment the balloons offered. To Morrissey it was only a form of suicide; to Nadia, to Brannum, to all those other hordes, it had been the path to eternal bliss. Who was to say? Better to undertake the uncertain journey into the great mind of the Ahya, perhaps, than to set out in panicky flight for the alien and unforgiving world that was Earth. "I hope you've found what you were looking for," Morrissey said. "I hope she has."

He unjacked the cube and went quickly away.

* * *

He flew northward over the fog-streaked sea. Below him were the floating cities of the tropical waters, that marvelous tapestry of rafts and barges. That must be Port Backside down there, he decided—a sprawling intricate tangle of foliage under which lay the crumbling splendors of one of Medea's greatest cities. Kelp choked the waterways. There was no sign of human life down there and he did not land.

Pellucidar, on the mainland, was empty also. Morrissey spent four days there, visiting the undersea gardens, treating himself to a concert in the famous Hall of Columns, watching the suns set from the top of Crystal Pyramid. That last evening dense drifts of balloons, hundreds of them, flew oceanward above him. He imagined he heard them calling to him in soft sighing whispers, saying, *I am Nadia. Come to me. There's still time. Give yourself up to us, dear love. I am Nadia.*

Was it only imagination? The Ahya were seductive. They had called to Nadia, and ultimately Nadia had gone to them. Brannum had gone. Thousands had gone. Now he felt the pull himself, and it was real. For an instant it was tempting. Instead of perishing in the quake, life eternal—of a sort. Who knew what the balloons really offered? A merging, a loss of self, a transcendental bliss—or was it only delusion, folly, had the seekers found nothing but a quick death in the icy wastes? *Come to me. Come to me.* Either way, he thought, it meant peace.

I am Nadia. Come to me.

He stared a long while at the bobbing shimmering globes overhead, and the whispers grew to a roar in his mind.

Then he shook his head. Union with the cosmic entity was not for him. He had sought no escape from Medea up till now, and now he would have none. He was himself and nothing but himself, and when he went out of the world he would still be only himself. And then, only then, the balloons could have his soul. If they had any use for it.

* * *

It was nine weeks and a day before the earthquake when Morrissey reached sweltering Enrique, right on the equator. Enrique was celebrated for its Hotel Luxe, of legendary opulence. He took possession of it's grandest suite, and no one was there to tell him no. The air conditioning still worked, the bar was well stocked, the hotel grounds still were manicured daily by fux gardeners who did not seem to know that their employers had gone away. Obliging servomechanisms provided Morrissey with meals of supreme elegance that would each have cost him a month's earnings in the old days. As he wandered through the silent grounds, he thought how wonderful it would have been to come here with Nadia and Danielle and Paul. But it was meaningless now, to be alone in all this luxury.

Was he alone, though? On his first night, and again the next, he heard laughter in the darkness, borne on the thick dense sweet-scented air. Fuxes did not laugh. The balloons did not laugh.

On the morning of the third day, as he stood on his nineteenth-floor veranda, he saw movements in the shrubbery at the rim of the lawn. Five, seven, a dozen male fuxes, grim two-legged engines of lust, prowling through the bushes. And then a human form! Pale flesh, bare legs, long unkempt hair! She streaked through the underbrush, giggling, pursued by fuxes.

"Hello!" Morrissey called. "Hey! I'm up here!"

He hurried downstairs and spent all day searching the hotel grounds. Occasionally he caught glimpses of frenzied naked figures, leaping and cavorting far away. He cried out to them, but they gave no sign of hearing him.

In the hotel office Morrissey found the manager's cube and turned it on. She was a dark-haired young woman, a little wild-eyed. "Hey, is it earthquake time yet?" she asked.

"Not quite yet."

"I want to be around for that. I want to see this stinking hotel topple into a million pieces."

"Where have you gone?" Morrissey asked.

She snickered. "Where else? Into the bush. Off to hunt fuxes. And to be hunted." Her face was flushed. "The old recombinant genes are still pretty hot, you know? Me for the fuxes and the fuxes for me. Get yourself a little action, why don't you? Whoever you are."

Morrissey supposed he ought to be shocked. But he couldn't summon much indignation. He had heard rumors of things like this already. In the final years before the cataclysm, he knew, several sorts of migration had been going on. Some colonists opted for the exodus to Earth and some for the surrender to the Ahya soul-collective, and others chose the simple reversion to the life of the beast. Why not? Every Medean, by now, was a mongrel. The underlying Earth stock was tinged with alien genes. The colonists looked human enough, but they were in fact mixed with balloon or fux or both. Without the early recombinant manipulations the colony could never have survived, for human life and native Medean organisms were incompatible, and only by genetic splicing had a race been brought forth that could overcome that natural biological enmity. So now, with doom-time coming near, how many colonists had simply kicked off their clothes and slipped away into the jungles to run with their cousins the fuxes? And was that any worse, he wondered, than climbing in panic aboard a ship bound for Earth or giving up your individuality to merge with the balloons? What did it matter which route to escape was chosen? But Morrissey wanted no escape. Least of all into the jungles, off to the fuxes.

He flew on northward. In Catamount he heard the cube of the city's mayor tell him, "They've all cleared out, and I'm going next Dimday. There's nothing left here." In Yellowleaf a cubed biologist spoke of genetic drift, the reversion of the alien genes. In Sandy's Mishigos,

Morrissey could find no cubes at all, but eighteen or twenty skeletons lay chaotically on the broad central plaza. Mass immolation? Mass murder, in the final hours of the city's disintegration? He gathered the bones and buried them in the moist, spongy ochre soil. It took him all day. Then he went on, up the coast as far as Arca, through city after city.

Wherever he stopped, it was the same story—no humans left, only balloons and fuxes, most of the balloons heading out to sea and most of the fuxes migrating inland. He jacked in cubes wherever he found them, but the cube-people had little new to tell him. They were clearing out, they said: one way or another they were giving up on Medea. Why stick around to the end? Why wait for the big shudder? Going home, going to the balloons, going to the bush—clearing out, clearing out, clearing out.

So many cities, Morrissey thought. Such an immense outpouring of effort. We smothered this world. We came in, we built our little isolated research stations, we stared in wonder at the coruscating sky and the double suns and the bizarre creatures. And we transformed ourselves into Medeans and transformed Medea into a kind of crazy imitation of Earth. And for a thousand years we spread out along the coasts wherever our kind of life could dig itself in. Eventually we lost sight of our purpose in coming here, which in the beginning was to *learn*. But we stayed anyway. We just stayed. We muddled along. And then we found out that it was all for nothing, that with one mighty heave of its shoulders this world was going to cast us off, and we got scared and packed up and went away. Sad, he thought. Sad and foolish.

He stayed at Arca a few days and turned inland, across the hot, bleak desert that sloped upward toward Mount Olympus. It was seven weeks and a day until the quake. For the first thousand kilometers or so he still could see encampments of migrating fuxes below him, slowly making their way into the Hotlands. Why, he wondered, had they permitted their world to be taken from them? They could have fought back. In the beginning they could have wiped us out in a month of guerrilla warfare. Instead they let us come in, let us make them into pets and slaves and flunkies while we paved the most fertile zones of their planet, and whatever they thought about us they kept to themselves. We never even knew their own name for Medea, Morrissey thought. That was how little of themselves they shared with us. But they tolerated us here. Why? Why?

The land below him was furnace-hot, a badland streaked with red and yellow and orange, and now there were no fuxes in sight. The first jagged foothills of the Olympus scarp knobbed the desert. He saw the mountain itself rising like a black fang toward the heavy low-hanging sky-filling mass of Argo. Morrissey dared not approach that mountain. It was holy and it was deadly. Its terrible thermal updrafts could send his flitter spinning to ground like a swatted fly; and he was not quite ready to die.

He swung northward again and journeyed up the barren and forlorn heart of the continent toward the polar region. The Ring Ocean came into view, coiling like a world-swallowing serpent beyond the polar shores, and he kicked the flitter higher, almost to its maximum safety level, to give himself a peek at Farside, where white rivers of CO_2 flowed through the atmosphere and lakes of cold gas filled the valleys. It seemed like six thousand years ago that he had led a party of geologists into that forbidding land. How earnest they had all been then! Measuring fault lines, seeking to discover the effects the quake would have over there. As if such things mattered when the colony was doomed by its own hand anyway. Why had he bothered? The quest for pure knowledge, yes. How futile that quest seemed to him now. Of course, he had been much younger then. An aeon ago. Almost in another life. Morrissey had planned to fly into Farside on this trip, to bid formal farewell to the scientist he had been, but he changed his mind. There was no need. Some farewells had already been made.

He curved down out of the polar regions as far south as Northcape on the eastern coast, circled the wondrous red-glinting sweep of the High Cascades, and landed on the airstrip at Chong. It was six weeks and two days to the earthquake. In these high latitudes the twin suns were faint and feeble even though the day was a Sunday. The monster Argo itself, far to the south, appeared shrunken. He had forgotten the look of the northern sky in his ten years in the tropics. And yet, and yet, had he not lived thirty years in Chong? It seemed like only a moment, as all time collapsed into this instant of now.

Morrissey found Chong painful. Too many old associations, too many cues to memory. Yet he kept himself there until he had seen it all, the restaurant where he and Danielle had invited Nadia and Paul to join their marriage, the house on Vladimir Street where they had lived, the Geophysics Lab, the skiing lodge just beyond the Cascades. All the footprints of his life.

The city and its environs were utterly deserted. For day after day Morrissey wandered, reliving the time when he was young and Medea still lived. How exciting it had all been then! The quake was coming someday—everybody knew the day, down to the hour—and nobody cared except cranks and neurotics, for the others were too busy living. And then suddenly everyone cared, and everything changed.

Morrissey played no cubes in Chong. The city itself, gleaming, a vast palisade of silver thermal roofs, was one great cube for him, crying out the tale of his years.

When he could take it no longer, he started his southward curve around the east coast. There were four weeks and a day to go.

His first stop was Meditation Island, the jumping-off point for those who went to visit Virgil Oddums's fantastic and ever-evolving ice sculptures out on Farside. Four newlyweds had come here, a billion years ago, and had gone, laughing and embracing, off in icecrawlers to see the one miracle of art Medea had produced. Morrissey found the cabin where they all had stayed. It had faded and its roof was askew. He had thought of spending the night on Meditation Island, but he left after an hour.

Now the land grew rich and lush again as he passed into the upper tropics. Again he saw balloons by the score letting themselves be wafted toward the ocean, and again there were bands of fuxes slowly journeying inland, driven by he knew not what sense of ritual obligation as the quake came near.

Three weeks two days five hours. Plus or minus.

He flew low over the fuxes. Some were mating. That astounded him—that persistence in the face of calamity. Was it merely the irresistible biological drive that kept the fuxes coupling? What chance did the newly engendered young have to survive? Would their mothers not be better off with empty wombs when the quake came? They all knew what was going to happen, and yet they mated. And yet they mated. It made no sense to Morrissey.

And then he thought he understood. The sight of those coupling fuxes gave him an insight into the Medean natives that explained it all, for the first time. Their patience, their calmness, their tolerance of all that had befallen them since their world had become Medea. Of course they would mate as the catastrophe drew near! They had been waiting for the earthquake all along, and for them it was no catastrophe. It was a holy moment, a purification—so he realized. He wished he could discuss this with Dinoov. It was a temptation to return at once to Argoview Dunes and seek out the old fux and test on him the theory that just had sprung to life in him. But not yet. Port Medea, first.

The east coast had been settled before the other, and the density of development here was intense. The first two colonies—Touchdown City and Medeatown—had long ago coalesced into the urban smear that radiated outward from the third town, Port Medea. When he was still far to the north, Morrissey could see the gigantic peninsula on which Port Medea and its suburbs sprawled: the tropic heat rose in visible waves from it, buffeting his little flitter as he made his way toward that awesome, hideous concrete expanse.

Dinoov had been right. There were starships waiting at Port Medea—four of them, a waste of money beyond imagination. Why had they not been used in the exodus? Had they been set aside for emigrants who had decided instead to run with the rutting fuxes or give their souls to the balloons? He would never know. He entered one of the ships and said, "Operations directory."

"At your service," a bodiless voice replied.

"Give me a report on ship status. Are you prepared for a voyage to Earth?"

"Fueled and ready."

"Everything operational."

Morrissey weighed his moves. So easy, he thought, to lie down and go to sleep and let the ship take him to Earth. So easy, so automatic, so useless.

After a moment he said, "How long do you need to reach departure level?"

"One hundred sixty minutes from moment of command."

"Good. The command is given. Get yourself ticking and take off. Your destination is Earth and the message I give you is this: *Medea says good-bye. I thought you might have some use for this ship. Sincerely, Daniel F. Morrissey. Dated Earthquake Minus two weeks one day seven hours.*"

"Acknowledged. Departure-level procedures initiated."

"Have a nice flight," Morrissey told the ship.

He entered the second ship and gave it the same command. He did the same in the third. He paused before entering the last one, wondering if there were other colonists who even now were desperately racing toward Port Medea to get aboard one of these ships before the end came. To hell with them, Morrissey thought. They should have made up their minds sooner. He told the fourth ship to go home to Earth.

On his way back from the port to the city, he saw the four bright spears of light rise skyward, a few minutes apart. Each hovered a moment, outlined against Argo's colossal bulk, and shot swiftly into the aurora-dappled heavens. In sixty-one years they would descend onto a baffled Earth with their cargo of no one. Another great mystery of space to delight the tale tellers, he thought. The Voyage of the Empty Ships.

With a curious sense of accomplishment he left Port Medea and headed down the coast to the sleek resort of Madagozar, where the elite of Medea had amused themselves in tropic luxury. Morrissey had always thought the place absurd. But it was still intact, still purring with automatic precision. He treated himself to a lavish holiday there. He raided the wine cellers of the best hotels. He breakfasted on tubs of chilled spikelegs caviar. He dozed in the warm sun. He bathed in the juice of gilliwog flowers. And he thought about absolutely nothing at all.

The day before the earthquake he flew back to Argoview Dunes.

"So you chose not to go home after all," Dinoov said.

Morrissey shook his head. "Earth was never my home. Medea was my home. I went home to Medea. And then I came back to this place because it was my last home. It pleases me that you're still here, Dinoov."

"Where would I have gone?" the fux asked.

"The rest of your people are migrating inland. I think it's to be nearer the holy mountain when the end comes. Is that right?"

"That is right."

"Why have you stayed, then?"

"This is my home, too. I have so little time left that it matters not very much to me where I am when the ground shakes. But tell me, friend Morrissey: was your journey worth the taking?"

"It was."

"What did you see? What did you learn?"

"I saw Medea, all of it," Morrissey said. "I never realized how much of your world we took. By the end we covered all the land that was worth covering, didn't we? And you people never said a word. You stood by and let it happen."

The fux was silent.

Morrissey said, "I understand now. You were waiting for the earthquake all along, weren't you? You knew it was coming long before we bothered to figure it out. How many times has it happened since fuxes first evolved on Medea? Every 7160 years the fuxes move to high ground and the balloons drift to Farside and the ground shakes and everything falls apart. And then the survivors reappear with new life already in the wombs and build again. How many times has it happened in fux history? So you knew when we came here, when we built our towns everywhere and turned them into cities, when we rounded you up and made you work for us, when we mixed our genes with yours and changed the microbes in the air so we'd be more comfortable here, that what we were doing wouldn't last forever, right? That was your secret knowledge, your hidden consolation, that this, too, would pass. Eh, Dinoov? And now it has passed. We're gone and the happy young fuxes are mating. I'm the only one of my kind left except for a few naked crazies in the bush."

There was a glint in the fux's eyes. Amusement? Contempt? Compassion? Who could read a fux's eyes?

"All along," Morrissey said, "you were all just waiting for the earthquake. Right? The earthquake that would make everything whole again. Well, now it's almost upon us. And I'm going to stand here alongside you and wait for the earthquake, too. It's my contribution to inter-species harmony. I'll be the human sacrifice. I'll be the one who atones for all that we did here. How does that sound, Dinoov? Is that all right with you?"

"I wish," the fux said slowly, "that you had boarded one of those ships and gone back to Earth. Your death will give me no pleasure."

Morrissey nodded. "I'll be back in a few minutes," he said, and went into his cabin.

The cubes of Nadia and Paul and Danielle sat beside the screen. Not for years had he played them, but he jacked them into the slots now, and on the screen appeared the three people he had most loved in all the universe. They smiled at him, and Danielle offered a soft greeting, and Paul winked, and Nadia blew a kiss. Morrissey said, "It's almost over now. Today's earthquake day. I just wanted to say good-bye, that's all. I just wanted to tell you that I love you and I'll be with you soon."

"Dan—" Nadia said.

"No. You don't have to say anything. I know you aren't really there, anyway. I just wanted to see you all again. I'm very happy right now."

He took the cubes from their slots. The screen went dark. Gathering up the cubes, he carried them outside and carefully buried them in the soft moist soil of his garden. The fux watched him incuriously.

"Dinoov?" Morrissey called. "One last question."

"Yes, my friend?"

"All the years we lived on Medea, we were never able to learn the name by which you people called your own world. We kept trying to find out, but all we were told was that it was taboo, and even when we coaxed a fux into telling us the name, the next fux would tell us an entirely different name, so we never knew. I ask you a special favor now, here at the end. Tell me what you call your world. Please. I need to know."

The old fux said, "We call it Sanoon."

"Sanoon? Truly?"

"Truly," said the fux.

"What does it mean?"

"Why, it means the World," said Dinoov. "What else?"

"Sanoon," Morrissey said. "It's a beautiful name."

The earthquake was thirty minutes away—plus or minus a little. Sometime in the past hour the white suns had disappeared behind Argo. Morrissey had not noticed that. But now he heard a low rumbling roar, and then he felt a strange trembling in the ground, as though something mighty were stirring beneath his feet and would burst shortly into wakefulness. Not far offshore terrible waves rose and crashed.

Calmly Morrissey said, "This is it, I think."

Overhead a dozen gleaming balloons soared and bobbed in a dance that looked much like a dance of triumph.

There was thunder in the air and a writhing in the heart of the world. In another moment the full force of the quake would be upon them and the crust of the planet would quiver and the first awful tremors would rip the land apart and the sea would rise up and cover the coast. Morrissey began to weep, and not out of fear. He managed a smile. "The cycle's complete, Dinoov. Out of Medea's ruins Sanoon will rise. The place is yours again at last."

Not Our Brother

Halperin came into San Simón Zuluaga in late October, a couple of days before the fiesta of the local patron saint, when the men of the town would dance in masks. He wanted to see that. This part of Mexico was famous for its masks, grotesque and terrifying ones portraying devils and monsters and fiends. Halperin had been collecting them for three years. But masks on a wall are one thing, and masks on dancers in the town plaza quite another.

San Simón was a mountain town about halfway between Acapulco and Taxco. "Tourists don't go there," Guzmán López had told him. "The road is terrible and the only hotel is a Cucaracha Hilton—five rooms, straw mattresses." Guzmán ran a gallery in Acapulco where Halperin had bought a great many masks. He was a suave, cosmopolitan man from Mexico City, with smooth dark skin and a bald head that gleamed as if it had been polished. "But they still do the Bat Dance there, the Lord of the Animals Dance. It is the only place left that performs it. This is from San Simón Zuluaga," said Guzmán, and pointed to an intricate and astonishing mask in purple and yellow depicting a bat with outspread leathery wings that was at the same time somehow also a human skull and a jaguar. Halperin would have paid ten thousand pesos for it, but Guzmán was not interested in selling. "Go to San Simón," he said. "You'll see others like this."

240

"For sale?"

Guzmán laughed and crossed himself. "Don't suggest it. In Rome, would you make an offer for the Pope's robes? These masks are sacred."

"I want one. How did you get this one?"

"Sometimes favors are done. But not for strangers. Perhaps I'll be able to work something out for you."

"You'll be there, then?"

"I go every year for the Bat Dance," said Guzmán. "It's important to me. To touch the real Mexico, the old Mexico. I am too much a Spaniard, not enough an Aztec; so I go back and drink from the source. Do you understand?"

"I think so," Halperin said. "Yes."

"You want to see the true Mexico?"

"Do they still slice out hearts with an obsidian dagger?"

Guzmán said, chuckling, "If they do, they don't tell me about it. But they know the old gods there. You should go. You would learn much. You might even experience interesting dangers."

"Danger doesn't interest me a whole lot," said Halperin.

"Mexico interests you. If you wish to swallow Mexico, you must swallow some danger with it, like the salt with the tequila. If you want sunlight, you must have a little darkness. You should go to San Simón." Guzmán's eyes sparkled. "No one will harm you. They are very polite there. Stay away from demons and you will be fine. You should go."

Halperin arranged to keep his hotel room in Acapulco and rented a car with four-wheel drive. He invited Guzmán to ride with him, but the dealer was leaving for San Simón that afternoon, with stops en route to pick up artifacts at Chacalapa and Hueycantenango. Halperin could not go that soon. "I will reserve a room for you at the hotel," Guzmán promised, and drew a precise road map for him.

The road was rugged and winding and barely paved,

and turned into a chaotic dirt-and-gravel track beyond Chichihualco. The last four kilometers were studded with boulders like the bed of a mountain stream. Halperin drove most of the way in first gear, gripping the wheel desperately, taking every jolt and jounce in his spine and kidneys. To come out of the pink-and-manicured Disneyland of plush Acapulco into this primitive wilderness was to make a journey five hundred years back in time. But the air up here was fresh and cool and clean, and the jungle was lush from recent rains, and now and then Halperin saw a mysterious little town half-buried in the heavy greenery: dogs barked, naked children ran out and waved, leathery old Nahua folk peered gravely at him and called incomprehensible greetings. Once he heard a tremendous thump against his undercarriage and was sure he had ripped out his oil pan on a rock, but when he peered below everything seemed to be intact. Two kilometers later, he veered into a giant rut and thought he had cracked an axle, but he had not. He hunched down over the wheel, aching, tense, and imagined that splendid bat mask, or its twin, spotlighted against a stark white wall in his study. Would Guzmán be able to get him one? Probably. His talk of the difficulties involved was just a way of hyping the price. But even if Halperin came back empty-handed from San Simón, it would be reward enough simply to have witnessed the dance, that bizarre, alien rite of a lost pagan civilization. There was more to collecting Mexican masks, he knew, than simply acquiring objects for the wall.

In late afternoon he entered the town just as he was beginning to think he had misread Guzmán's map. To his surprise it was quiet imposing, the largest village he had seen since turning off the main highway—a great bare plaza ringed by stone benches, marketplace on one side, vast heavy-walled old church on the other, giant gnarled trees, chickens, dogs, children running about everywhere, and houses of crumbling adobe spreading up the slope of a gray flat-faced mountain to the right.

and down into the dense darkness of a barranca thick with ferns and elephant-ears to the left. For the last hundred meters into town an impenetrable living palisade of cactus lined the road on both sides, unbranched spiny green columns that had been planted one flush against the next. Bougainvillea in many shades of red and purple and orange cascaded like gaudy draperies over walls and rooftops.

Halperin saw a few old Volkswagens and an ancient ramshackle bus parked on the far side of the plaza and pulled his car up beside them. Everyone stared at him as he got out. Well, why not? He was big news here, maybe the first stranger in six months. But the pressure of those scores of dark amphibian eyes unnerved him. These people were all Indians, Nahuas, untouched in any important way not only by the twentieth century but by the nineteenth, the eighteenth, all the centuries back to Moctezuma. They had nice Christian names like Santiago and Francisco and Jesús, and they went obligingly to the iglesia for mass whenever they thought they should, and they knew about cars and transistor radios and Coca-Cola. But all that was on the surface. They were still Aztecs at heart, Halperin thought. Timetravelers. As alien as Martians.

He shrugged off his discomfort. Here *he* was the Martian, dropping in from a distant planet for a quick visit. Let them stare: he deserved it. They meant no harm. Halperin walked toward them and said, *"Por favor, donde está el hotel del pueblo?"*

Blank faces. *"El hotel?"* he asked, wandering around the plaza. *"Por favor. Donde?"* No one answered. That irritated him. Sure, Nahuatl was their language, but it was inconceivable that Spanish would be unknown here. Even in the most remote towns *someone* spoke Spanish. *"Por favor!"* he said, exasperated. They melted back at his approach as though he were ablaze. Halperin peered into dark cluttered shops. *"Habla usted Español?"* he asked again and again, and met only silence. He was at the edge of the marketplace, looking into a chaos of fruit stands, tacos stands, piles of brilliant serapes and flimsy sandals and stacked sombreros, and booths where vendors were selling the toys of next week's Day of the Dead holiday, candy skeletons and green banners emblazoned with grinning red skulls. *"Por favor?"* he said loudly, feeling very foolish.

A woman in jodhpurs and an Eisenhower jacket materialized suddenly in front of him and said in English, "They don't mean to be rude. They're just very shy with strangers."

Halperin was taken aback. He realized that he had begun to think of himself as an intrepid explorer, making his way with difficulty through a mysterious primitive land. In an instant she had snatched all that from him, both the intrepidity and the difficulties.

She was about thirty, with close-cut dark hair and bright, alert eyes, attractive, obviously American. He struggled to hide the sense of letdown her advent had created in him and said, "I've been trying to find the hotel."

"Just off the plaza, three blocks behind the market. Let's go to your car and I'll ride over there with you."

"I'm from San Francisco," he said. "Tom Halperin."

"That's such a pretty city. I love San Francisco."

"And you?"

"Miami," she said. "Ellen Chambers." She seemed to be measuring him with her eyes. He noticed that she was carrying a couple of Day of the Dead trinkets—a crudely carved wooden skeleton with big eyeglasses, and a rubber snake with a gleaming human skull of white plastic, like a cue-ball, for a head. As they reached his car she said, "You came here alone?"

Halperin nodded. "Did you?"

"Yes," she said. "Come down from Taxco. How did you find this place?"

"Antiquities dealer in Acapulco told me about it. Antonio Guzmán López. I collect Mexican masks."

"Ah."

"But I've never actually seen one of the dances."

"They do an unusual one here," she said as he drove down a street of high, ragged, mud-colored walls, patched and plastered, that looked a thousand years old. "Lord of the Animals, it's called. Died out everywhere else. Pre-Hispanic shamanistic rite, invoking protective deities, fertility spirits."

"Guzmán told me a little about it. Not much. Are you an anthropologist?"

"Strictly amateur. Turn left here." There was a little street, an open wrought-iron gateway, a driveway of large white gravel. Set back a considerable distance was a squat, dispiriting hovel of a hotel, one story, roof of chipped red tiles in which weeds were growing. Not even the ubiquitous bougainvillea and the great clay urns overflowing with dazzling geraniums diminished its ugliness. Cucaracha Hilton indeed, Halperin thought dourly. She said, "This is the place. You can park on the side."

The parking lot was empty. "Are you and I the only guests?" he asked.

"So it seems."

"Guzmán was supposed to be here. Smooth-looking man, bald shiny head, dresses like a financier."

"I haven't seen him," she said. "Maybe his car broke down."

They got out, and a slouching fourteen-year-old mozo came to get Halperin's luggage. He indicated his single bag and followed Ellen into the hotel. She moved in a sleek, graceful way that kindled in him the idea that she and he might get something going in this forlorn place. But as soon as the notion arose, he felt it fizzling: she was friendly, she was good-looking, but she radiated an offputting vibe, a noli-me-tangere sort of thing, that was unmistakable and made any approach from him inappropriate. Too bad. Halperin liked the company of women and fell easily and uncomplicatedly into liaisons with them wherever he traveled, but this one puzzled him. Was she a lesbian? Usually he could tell, but he had no reading on her except that she meant him to keep his distance. At least for the time being.

The hotel was grim, a string of lopsided rooms arranged around a weedy courtyard that served as a sort of lobby. Some hens and a rooster were marching about, and a startling green iguana, enormous, like a miniature dinosaur, was sleeping on a branch of a huge yellow-flowered hibiscus just to the left of the entrance. Everything was falling apart in the usual haphazard tropical way. Nobody seemed to be in charge. The mozo put Halperin's suitcase down in front of a room on the far side of the courtyard and went away without a word.

"You've got the one next to mine," Ellen said. "That's the dining room over there and the cantina next to it. There's a shower out in back and a latrine a little further into the jungle."

"Wonderful."

"The food isn't bad. You know enough to watch out for the water. There are bugs but no mosquitoes."

"How long have you been here?" Halperin asked.

"Centuries," she said. "I'll see you in an hour and we'll have dinner, okay?"

His room was a whitewashed irregular box, smelling faintly of disinfectant, that contained a lumpy narrow bed, a sink, a massive mahogany chest of drawers that could have come over with the Spaniards, and an ornate candlestick. The slatted door did not lock and the tile-rimmed window that gave him an unsettling view of thick jungle close outside was without glass, an open hole in the wall. But there was a breathtaking mask mounted above the bed, an armadillo-faced man with a great gaping mouth, and next to the chest of drawers was a weatherbeaten but extraordinary helmet mask, a long-nosed man with an owl for one ear and a coyote for another, and over the bed was a double mask, owl and pig, that was finer than anything he had seen in any museum. Halperin felt such a rush of possessive zeal that he began to sweat. The sour acrid scent of it filled the room. Could he buy these masks? From whom? The dull-eyed mozo? He had done all his collecting through galleries; he had no idea how to go about acquiring masks from natives. He remembered Guzmán's warning about not trying to buy from them. But these masks must no longer be sacred if they were mere hotel decorations. Suppose, he thought, I just *take* that owl-pig when I check out, and leave three thousand pesos on the sink. That must be a fortune here. Five thousand, maybe. Could they find me? Would there be trouble when I was leaving the country? Probably. He put the idea out of his mind. He was a collector, not a thief. But these masks were gorgeous.

He unpacked and found his way outside to the shower—a cubicle of braided ropes, a creaking pipe, yellowish tepid water—and then he put on clean clothes and knocked at Ellen's door. She was ready for dinner. "How do you like your room?" she asked.

"The masks make up for any little shortcomings. Do they have them in every room?"

"They have them all over," she said.

He peered past her shoulder into her room, which was oddly bare, no luggage or discarded clothes lying around, and saw two masks on the wall, not as fine as his but fine enough. But she did not invite him to take a close look, and closed the door behind her. She led him to the dining room. Night had fallen some time ago, and the jungle was alive with sounds, chirpings and rachetings and low thunking booms and something that sounded the way the laughter of a jaguar might sound. The dining room, oblong and lit by candles, had three tables and more masks on the wall, a devil face with a lizard for a nose, a crudely carved mermaid, and a garish tiger-hunter mask. He wandered around studying them in awe, and said to her, "These aren't local. They've been collected from all over Guerrero."

"Maybe your friend Guzmán sold them to the owner," she suggested. "Do you own many?"

"Dozens. I could bore you with them for hours. Do you know San Francisco at all? I've got a big old three-

story Victorian in Noe Valley and there are masks i
every room. I've collected all sorts of primitive art, bu
once I discovered Mexican masks they pushed every
thing else aside, even the Northwest Indian stuff. Yo
collect too, don't you?"

"Not really. I'm not an acquirer. Of things, at any rate
I travel, I look, I learn, I move on. What do you do whe
you aren't collecting things?"

"Real estate," he said. "I buy and sell houses. An
you?"

"Nothing worth talking about," she said.

The mozo appeared, silently set their table, brough
them, unbidden, a bottle of red wine. Then a tureen o
albóndigas soup, and afterward tortillas, tacos, a decen
turkey molé. Without a word, without a change o
expression.

"Is that kid the whole staff?" Halperin asked.

"His sister is the chambermaid. I guess his mother i
the cook. The patrón is Filiberto, the father, but he'
busy getting the fiesta set up. He's one of the importan
dancers. You'll meet him. Shall we get more wine?"

"I've had plenty," he said.

They went for a stroll after dinner, skirting th
jungle's edge and wandering through a dilapidate
residential area. He heard music and handclappin
coming from the plaza but felt too tired to see what wa
happening there. In the darkness of the tropical nigh
he might easily have reached for Ellen and drawn he
against him, but he was too tired for that, too, and sh
was still managing to be amiable, courteous, but distant
She was a mystery to him. Moneyed, obviously. Di
vorced, widowed young, gay, what? He did not precisel
mistrust her, but nothing about her seemed quite t
connect with anything else.

About nine-thirty he went back to his room, toppled
down on the ghastly bed, and dropped at once into a
deep sleep that carried him well past dawn. When he
woke, the hotel was deserted except for the boy. "Cómo s
llama?" Halperin asked, and got an odd smouldering

look, probably for mocking a mere mozo by employing the formal construction. *"Elustesio,"* the boy muttered. Had Elustesio seen the *Norteamericano señorita?* Elustesio hadn't seen anyone. He brought Halperin some fruit and cold tortillas for breakfast and disappeared. Afterward Halperin set out on a slow stroll into town.

Though it was early, the plaza and surrounding marketplace were already crowded. Again Halperin got the visiting-Martian treatment from the townsfolk—fishy stares, surreptitious whispers, the occasional shy and tentative grin. He did not see Ellen. Alone among these people once more, he felt awkward, intrusive, vulnerable; yet he preferred that, he realized, to the curiously unsettling companionship of the Florida woman.

The shops now seemed to be stocking little except Day of the Dead merchandise, charming and playful artifacts that Halperin found irresistible. He had long been attracted to the imagery of brave defiance of death that this Mexican version of Halloween, so powerful in the inner life of the country, called forth. Halperin bought a yellow papier-mâché skull with brilliant flower-eyes and huge teeth, an elegant little guitar-playing skeleton and a bag of grisly, morbid marzipan candies. He stared at the loaves of bread decorated with skulls and saints in a bakery window. He smiled at a row of sugar coffins with nimble skeletons clambering out of them. There was some extraordinary lacquer work on sale too, trays and gourds decorated with gleaming red-and-black patterns. By mid-morning he had bought so much that carrying it was a problem, and he returned to the hotel to drop off his purchases.

A blue Toyota van was parked next to his car and Guzmán, looking just as dapper in khakis as he always did in his charcoal gray suits, was rearranging a mound of bundles in it. "Are you enjoying yourself?" he called to Halperin.

"Very much. I thought I'd find you in town when I got here yesterday."

"I came and went again, to Tlacotepec, and I returned. I have bought good things for the gallery." He nodded toward Halperin's armload of toy skulls and skeletons. "I see you are buying too. Good. Mexico needs your help."

"I'd rather buy one of the masks that's hanging in my room," Halperin said. "Have you seen it? Pig and owl, and carved like—"

"Patience. We will get masks for you. But think of this trip as an experience, not as a collecting expedition, and you will be happier. Acquisitions will happen of their own accord if you don't try to force them, and if you enjoy the favor of *amo tokinwan* while you are here."

Halperin was staring at some straw-wrapped wooden statuettes in the back of the van. "*Amo tokinwan?* Who's that?"

"The Lords of the Animals," said Guzmán. "The protectors of the village. Perhaps protectors is not quite the right word, for protectors are benevolent, and *amo tokinwan* often are not. Quite dangerous sometimes, indeed."

Halperin could not decide how serious Guzmán was. "How so?"

"Sometimes at fiesta time they enter the village and mingle. They look like anyone else and attract no special attention, and they have a way of making the villagers think that they belong here. Can you imagine that, seeing a stranger and believing you have known him all your life? Beyond doubt they are magical."

"And they are what? Guardians of the village?"

"In a sense. They bring the rain; they ward off the lightning; they guard the crops. But sometimes they do harm. No one can predict their whims. And so the dancing, to propitiate them. Beyond doubt they are magical. Beyond doubt they are something very other. *Amo tokinwan.*"

"What does that mean?" Halperin asked.

"In Nahuatl it means, 'Not our brother,' of different substance. Alien. Supernatural. I think I have met them do you know? You stand in the plaza watching the dancers, and there is a little old woman at your elbow or a boy or a pregnant woman wearing a fine rebozo, and everything seems all right, but you get a little too close and you feel the chill coming from them, as though they are statues of ice. So you back away and try to think good thoughts." Guzmán laughed. "Mexico! You think I am civilized because I have a Rolex on my wrist? Even I am not civilized, my friend. If you are wise you will not be too civilized while you are here, either. They are not our brother, and they do harm. I told you you will see the real Mexico here, eh?"

"I have a hard time believing in spirits," Halperin said. "Good ones and evil ones alike."

"These are both at once. But perhaps they will not bother you." Guzmán slammed shut the door of the van. "In town they are getting ready to unlock the masks and dust them and arrange them for the fiesta. Would you like to be there when that is done? The mayordomo is my friend. He will admit you."

"I'd like that very much. When?"

"After lunch." Guzmán touched his hand lightly to Halperin's wrist. "One word, first. Control your desire to collect. Where we go today is not a gallery."

The masks of San Simón were kept in a locked storeroom of the municipal building. Unlocking them turned out to be a solemn and formal occasion. All the town's officials were there, Guzmán whispered: the alcalde, the five alguaciles, the regidores, and Don Luis Gutiérrez, the mayordomo, an immense mustachioed man whose responsibility it was to maintain the masks from year to year, to rehearse the dancers and to stage the fiesta. There was much bowing and embracing. Most of the conversation was in Nahuatl, which Halperin did not understand at all, and he was able to follow very little of the quick, idiosyncratic Spanish they spoke either, though he heard Guzmán introduce him as an important *Norteamericano* scholar and tried thereafter to look important and scholarly. Don Luis produced an enormous old-fashioned key, thrust it with a flourish into the door and led the way down a narrow, musty corridor to a large white-walled storeroom with a ceiling of heavy black beams. Masks were stacked everywhere, on the floor, on shelves, in cupboards. The place was a museum. Halperin, who could claim a certain legitimate scholarly expertise by now in this field, recognized many of the masks as elements in familiar dances of the region, the ghastly faces of the Diablo Macho Dance, the heavy-bearded elongated Dance of the Moors and Christians masks, the ferocious cat-faces of the Tigre Dance. But there were many that were new and astounding to him, the Bat Dance masks, terrifying bat-winged heads that all were minglings of bat characters and other animals, bat-fish, bat-coyote, bat-owl, bat-squirrel, and some that were unidentifiable except for the weird outspread rubbery wings, bats hybridized with creatures of another world, perhaps. One by one the masks were lifted, blown clean of dust, admired, passed around, though not to Halperin. He trembled with amazement at the power and beauty of these bizarre wooden effigies. Don Luis drew a bottle of mescal from a niche and handed it to the alcalde, who took a swig and passed it on; the bottle came in time to Halperin, and without a thought for the caterpillar coiled in the bottom of the bottle he gulped the fiery liquor. Things were less formal now. The high officials of the town were laughing, shuffling about in clumsy little dance steps, picking up gourd rattles from the shelves and shaking them. They called out in Nahuatl, all of it lost on Halperin, though the words *amo tokinwan* at one point suddenly stood out in an unintelligible sentence, and someone shook rattles with curious vehemence. Halperin stared at the masks but did not dare go close to them or try to touch them. This is not a gallery, he reminded himself. Even when things got so uninhibited that Don Luis and a couple of the others put masks on and began to lurch about the room in a weird lumbering polka Halperin remained tense and controlled. The mesca bottle came to him again. He drank, and this time his discipline eased; he allowed himself to pick up a wondrous bat mask, phallic and with great staring eyes. The carving was far finer than on the superb one he had seen at Guzmán's gallery. He ran his fingers lovingly over the gleaming wood, the delicately outlined ribbed wings. Guzmán said, "In some villages the Bat Dance was a Christmas dance, the animals paying homage to little Jesus. But here it is a fertility rite, and therefore the bat is phallic. You would like that mask, no?" He grinned broadly. "So would I, my friend. But it will never leave San Simón."

Just as the ceremony appeared to be getting rowdy, it came to an end: the laughter ceased, the mescal bottle went back to its niche, the officials grew solemn again and started to file out. Halperin, in schoolboy Spanish, thanked Don Luis for permitting him to attend, thanked the alcalde, thanked the alguaciles and the regidores. He felt flushed and excited as he left the building. The cache of masks mercilessly stirred his acquisitive lust. That they were unattainable made them all the more desirable, of course. It was as though the storeroom were a gallery in which the smallest trifle cost a million dollars.

Halperin caught sight of Ellen Chambers on the far side of the plaza, sitting outside a small café. He waved to her and she acknowledged it with a smile.

Guzmán said, "Your traveling companion?"

"No. She's a tourist down from Taxco. I met her yesterday."

"I did not know any other Americans were here for the fiesta. It surprises me." He was frowning. "Sometimes they come, but very rarely. I thought you would be the only *extranjero* here this year."

"It's all right," said Halperin. "We gringos get lonely for our own sort sometimes. Come on over and I'll introduce you."

Guzmán shook his head. "Another time. I have

business to attend to. Commend me to your charmin
friend and offer my regrets."

He walked away. Halperin shrugged and crossed th
plaza to Ellen, who beckoned him to the seat opposi
her. He signaled the waiter. "Two margaritas," he sai

She smiled. "Thank you, no."

"All right. One."

"Have you been busy today?" she asked.

"Seeing masks. I salivate for some of the things th
have in this town. I find myself actually thinking
stealing some if they won't sell to me. That's shockin
I've never stolen anything in my life. I've always paid n
own way."

"This would be a bad place to begin, then."

"I know that. They'd put the curse of the mummy o
me, or the black hand, or God knows what. The sign
Moctezuma. I'm not serious about stealing masks. But
do want them. Some of them."

"I can understand that," she said. "But I'm le
interested in the masks than in what they represent. Th
magic character, the transformative power. When the
put the masks on, they *become* the otherworldly bein
they represent. That fascinates me. That the mas
dissolves the boundary between our world and *theirs*

"*Theirs?*"

"The invisible world. The world the shaman know
the world of the were-jaguars and were-bats. A carve
and painted piece of wood becomes a gateway into th
world and brings the benefits of the supernatural. Tha
why the masks are so marvelous, you know. It isn't ju
an aesthetic thing."

"You actually believe what you've just said?" Halperi
asked.

"Oh, yes. Yes, definitely."

He chose not to press the point. People believed a
sorts of things, pyramid power, yoghurt as a cure fo
cancer, making your plants grow by playing Bach
them. That was all right with him. Just now he foun
her warmer, more accessible, than she had been befor

and he had no wish to offend her. As they strolled back to the hotel, he asked her to have dinner with him, imagining hopefully that that might lead somewhere tonight, but she said she would not be eating at the hotel this evening. That puzzled him—where else around here could she get dinner, and with whom?—but of course he did not probe.

He dined with Guzmán. The distant sound of music could be heard, shrill, alien. "They are rehearsing for the fiesta," Guzmán explained. The hotel cook outdid herself, preparing some local freshwater flatfish in a startlingly delicate sauce that would have produced applause in Paris. Filiberto, the patrón, came into the dining room and greeted Guzmán with a bone-crushing *abrazo*. Guzmán introduced Halperin once again as an important *Norteamericano* scholar. Filiberto, tall and very dark-skinned, with cheekbones like blades, showered Halperin with effusive courtesies.

"I have been admiring the masks that decorate the hotel," Halperin said, and waited to be invited to buy whichever one took his fancy, but Filiberto merely offered a dignified bow of thanks. Praising individual ones, the owl-pig, the lizard-nose, also got nowhere. Filiberto presented Guzmán with a chilled bottle of a superb white wine from Michoacán, crisp and deliciously metallic on the tongue; he spoke briefly with Guzmán in Nahuatl; then, saying he was required at the rehearsal, he excused himself. The music grew more intense.

Halperin said, "Is it possible to see the rehearsal after dinner?"

"Better to wait for the actual performance," said Guzmán.

Halperin slept poorly that night. He listened for the sound of Ellen Chambers entering the room next door, but either he was asleep when she came in or she was out all night.

And now finally the fiesta was at hand. Halperin spent the day watching the preparations: the stringing of colored electric lights around the plaza, the mounting of huge papier-mâché images of monsters and gods and curious spindly-legged clowns, the closing down of the shops and the clearing away of the tables that displayed their merchandise. All day long the town grew more crowded. No doubt people were filtering in from the outlying districts, the isolated jungle farms, the little remote settlements on the crest of the sierra. Through most of the day he saw nothing of Guzmán or Ellen, but that was all right. He was quite accustomed now to being here, and the locals seemed to take him equally for granted. He drank a good deal of mescal at one cantina or another around the plaza and varied it with the occasional bottle of the excellent local beer. As the afternoon waned, the crowds in the plaza grew ever thicker and more boisterous, but nothing particular seemed to be happening, and Halperin wondered whether to go back to the hotel for dinner. He had another mescal instead. Suddenly the fiesta lights were switched on, gaudy, glaring, reds and yellows and greens, turning everthing into a psychedelic arena, and then at last Halperin heard music, the skreeing bagpipe sound of bamboo flutes, the thump of drums, the whispery, dry rattle of tambourines, the harsh punctuation of little clay whistles. Into the plaza came ten or fifteen boys, leaping, dancing cartwheels, forming impromptu human pyramids that promptly collapsed, to general laughter. They wore no masks. Halperin, disappointed and puzzled, looked around as though to find an explanation and discovered Guzmán, suave and elegant in charcoal gray, almost at his elbow. "No masks?" he said. "Shouldn't they be masked?"

"This is only the beginning," said Guzmán.

Yes, just the overture. The boys cavorted until they lost all discipline and went pell-mell across the plaza and out of sight. Then a little old man, also unmasked, tugged three prancing white goats caparisoned with elaborate paper decorations into the center of the plaza and made them cavort, too. Two stilt-walkers fought a mock duel. Three trumpeters played a hideous discord dant fanfare and got such cheers that they played it again and again. Guzmán was among those who cheered. Halperin, who had not eaten, was suddenly captured by the aroma from a stand across the way where an old woman was grilling tacos on a brazier and a tin griddle. He headed toward her, but paused on the way for a tequila at an improvised cantina someone had set up on the streetcorner, using a big wooden box as the bar. He saw Ellen Chambers in the crowd on the far side of the plaza and waved, but she did not appear to see him, and when he looked again he could not find her.

The music grew wilder and now, at last, the first masked dancers appeared. A chill ran through him at the sight of the nightmare figures marching up the main avenue, bat-faced ones, skull-faced ones, grinning devils, horned creatures, owls, jaguars. Some of the masks were two or three feet high and turned their wearers into malproportioned dwarfs. They advanced slowly, pausing often to backtrack, circling one another, kicking their legs high, madly waving their arms. Halperin, sweating, alert, aroused, realized that the dancers must have been drinking heavily, for their movements were jerky, ragged, convulsive. As they came toward the plaza he saw that they were herding four figures in white robes and pale human-faced masks before them, and were chanting something repetitively in Nahuatl. He caught that phrase again, *amo tokinwan*. Not our brother.

To Guzmán he said, "What are they saying?"

"The prayer against the *amo tokinwan*. To protect the fiesta, in case any of the Lords of the Animals actually are in the plaza tonight."

Those around Halperin had taken up the chant now.

"Tell me what it means," Halperin said.

Guzmán said, chanting the translation in a rhythm that matched the voices around them: *"They eat us! They are—not our brother. They are worms, wild beasts. Yes!"*

Halperin looked at him strangely. "'They eat us?'" he said. "Cannibal gods?"

"Not literally. Devourers of souls."

"And these are the gods of these people?"

"No, not gods. Supernatural beings. They lived here before there were people, and they naturally retain control over everything important here. But not gods as Christians understand gods. Look, here come the bats!"

They eat us, Halperin thought, shivering in the warm humid night. A new phalanx of dancers was arriving now, half a dozen bat-masked ones. He thought he recognized the long legs of Filiberto in their midst. Darkness had come and the dangling lights cast an eerier, more brilliant glow. Halperin decided he wanted another tequila, a mescal, a cold cerveza, whatever he could find quickest. *Not our brother.* He excused himself vaguely to Guzmán and started through the crowd. *They are worms, wild beasts.* They were still chanting it. The words meant nothing to him, except *amo tokinwan,* but from the spacing, the punctuation, he knew what they were saying. *They eat us.* The crowd had become something fluid now, oozing freely from place to place; the distinction between dancers and audience was hard to discern. *Not our brother.* Halperin found one of the little curbside cantinas and asked for mescal. The proprietor splashed some in a paper cup and would not take his pesos. A gulp and Halperin felt warm again. He tried to return to Guzmán but no longer saw him in the surging, frenzied mob. The music was louder. Halperin began to dance—it was easier than walking—and found himself face to face with one of the bat-dancers, a short man whose elegant mask showed a bat upside down, in its resting position, ribbed wings folded like black shrouds. Halperin and the dancer, pushed close together in the press, fell into an inadvertent pas de deux. "I wish I could buy that mask," Halperin said. "What do you want for it? Five thousand pesos? Ten thousand? *Habla usted Español?* No? Come to the hotel with the mask tomorrow. You follow? *Venga mañana.*" There was no reply. Halperin was not even certain he had spoken the words aloud.

He danced his way back across the plaza. Midway he felt a hand catch his wrist. Ellen Chambers. Her khaki blouse was open almost to the waist and she had nothing beneath it. Her skin gleamed with sweat, as if it had been oiled. Her eyes were wide and rigid. She leaned close to him and said, "Dance! Everybody dances! Where's your mask?"

"He wouldn't sell it to me. I offered him ten thousand pesos, but he wouldn't—"

"Wear a different one," she said. "Any mask you like. How do you like mine?"

"Your mask?" He was baffled. She wore no mask.

"Come! Dance!" She moved wildly. Her breasts were practically bare and now and then a nipple flashed. Halperin knew that that was wrong, that the villagers were cautious about nudity and a *gringa* especially should not be exhibiting herself. Drunkenly he reached for her blouse, hoping to button one or two of the buttons, and to his chagrin his hand grazed one of her breasts. She laughed and pushed herself against him. For an instant she was glued to him from knees to chest, with his hand wedged stupidly between their bodies. Then he pulled back, confused. An avenue seemed to have opened around them. He started to walk stumblingly to some quieter part of the plaza, but she caught his wrist again and grinned a tiger-grin, all incisors and tongue. "Come on!" she said harshly.

He let her lead him. Past the tacos stands, past the cantinas, past a little brawl of drunken boys, past the church, on whose steps the dancer in the phallic bat mask was performing, juggling pale green fruits and now and then batting one out into the night with the phallus that jutted from his chin. Then they were on one of the side streets, blind crumbling walls hemming them on both sides and cold moonlight the only illumination. Two blocks, three, his heart pounding, his lungs protesting. Into an ungated courtyard of what looked like an abandoned house, shattered tumbledown heaps of masonry everywhere and a vining night-blooming cactus growing over everything like a tangle of terrible green snakes. The cactus was in bloom and its vast white trumpetlike flowers emitted a sickly sweet perfume, overpoweringly intense. He wanted to gag and throw up, but Ellen gave him no time, for she was embracing him, pressing herself fiercely against him, forcing him back against a pile of shattered adobe bricks. In the strange moonlight her skin glistened and then seemed to become transparent, so that he could see the cage of her ribs, the flat long plate of her breastbone, the throbbing purplish heart behind it. She was all teeth and bones, a Day of the Dead totem come to life. He did not understand and he could not resist. He was without will. Her hands roamed him, so cold they burned his skin, sending up puffs of steam as her icy fingers caressed him. Something was flowing from him to her, his warmth, his essence, his vitality, and that was all right. The mescal and the beer and the tequila and the thick musky fragrance of the night-blooming cereus washed through his soul and left it tranquil. From far away came the raw dissonant music, the flutes and drums, and the laughter, the shouts, the chants. *They eat us.* Her breath was smoke in his face. *They are worms, wild beasts.* As they embraced one another, he imagined that she was insubstantial, a column of mist, and he began to feel misty himself, growing thinner and less solid as his life-force flowed toward her. Now for the first time he was seized by anguish and fright. As he felt himself being pulled from his body, his soul rushing forth and out and out and out, helpless, drawn, his drugged calm gave way to panic. *They are—not our brother.* He struggled, but it was useless. He was going out swiftly, the essence of him quitting his body as though she were reeling it in on a line. Bats fluttered above him, their faces streaked with painted patterns, yellow and green and brilliant ultramarine. The sky was a curtain of fiery bougainvillea. He was losing the struggle. He was too weak to resist or even to care. He could no longer hear himself breathe

He drifted freely, floating in the air, borne on the wings of the bats.

Then there was confusion, turmoil, struggle. Halperin heard voices speaking sharply in Spanish and in Nahuatl, but the words were incomprehensible to him. He rolled over on his side and drew his knees to his chest and lay shivering with his cheek against the warm wet soil. Someone was shaking him. A voice said in English, "Come back. Wake up. She is not here."

Halperin blinked and looked up. Guzmán was crouched above him, pale, stunned-looking, his teeth chattering. His eyes were wide and tensely fixed.

"Yes," Guzmán said. "Come back to us. Here. Sit up, let me help you."

The gallery-owner's arm was around his shoulders. Halperin was weak and trembling, and he realized Guzmán was trembling too. Halperin saw figures in the background—Filiberto from the hotel and his son Elustesio, the mayordomo Don Luis, the alcalde, one of the alguaciles.

"Ellen?" he said uncertainly.

"She is gone. *It* is gone. We have driven it away."

"It?"

"*Amo tokinwan.* Devouring your spirit."

"No," Halperin muttered. He stood up, still shaky, his knees buckling. Don Luis offered him a flask; Halperin shook it away, then changed his mind, reached for it, took a deep pull. Brandy. He walked four or five steps, getting his strength back. The reek of the cactus-flowers was nauseating. He saw the bare ribs again, the pulsating heart, the sharp white teeth. "No," he said. "It wasn't anything like that. I had too much to drink— maybe ate something that disagreed with me—the music, the scent of the flowers—"

"We saw," Guzmán said. His face was bloodless. "We were just in time. You would have been dead."

"She was from Miami—she said she knew San Francisco—"

"These days they take any form they like. The woman

from Miami was here two years ago, for the fiesta. She vanished in the night, Don Luis says. And now she has come back. Perhaps next year there will be one who looks like you and talks like you and sniffs around studying the masks like you, and we will know it is not you, and we will keep watch. Eh? You should come back to the hotel now. You need to rest."

Halperin walked between them down the walled streets. The fiesta was still in full swing, masked figures capering everywhere, but Guzmán and Don Luis and Filiberto guided him around the plaza and toward the hotel. He thought about the woman from Miami, and remembered that she had had no car and there had been no luggage in her room. *They eat us.* Such things are impossible, he told himself. *They are worms, wild beasts.* And next year would there be a diabolical counterfeit Halperin haunting the fiesta? *They are—not our brother.* He did not understand.

Guzmán said, "I promised you you would see the real Mexico. I did not think you would see as much of it as this."

Halperin insisted on inspecting her hotel room. It was empty and looked as if it had not been occupied for months. He stretched out on his bed fully clothed, but he did not particularly want to be left alone in the darkness, and so Guzmán and Filiberto and the others took turns sitting up with him through the night while the sounds of the fiesta filled the air. Dawn brought a dazzling sunrise. Halperin and Guzmán stepped out into the courtyard. The world was still.

"I think I'll leave here now," Halperin said.

"Yes. That would be wise. I will stay another day, I think."

Filiberto appeared, carrying the owl-pig mask from Halperin's room. "This is for you," he said. "Because that you were troubled here, that you will think kindly of us. Please take it as our gift."

Halperin was touched by that. He made a little speech of gratitude and put the mask in his car.

Guzmán said, "Are you well enough to drive?"

"I think so. I'll be all right once I leave here." He shook hands with everyone. His fingers were quivering. At a very careful speed he drove away from the hotel, through the plaza, where sleeping figures lay sprawled like discarded dolls, and mounds of paper streamers and other trash were banked high against the curb. At an even more careful speed he negotiated the cactus-walled road out of town. When he was about a kilometer from San Simón Zuluaga he glanced to his right and saw Ellen Chambers sitting next to him in the car. If he had been traveling faster, he would have lost control of the wheel. But after the first blinding moment of terror came a rush of annoyance and anger. "No," he said. "You don't belong in here. Get the hell out of here. Leave me alone." She laughed lightly. Halperin felt like sobbing. Swiftly and unhesitatingly he seized Filiberto's owl-pig mask, which lay on the seat beside him, and scaled it with a flip of his wrist past her nose and out the open car window. Then he clung tightly to the wheel and stared forward. When he could bring himself to look to the right again, she was gone. He braked to a halt and rolled up the window and locked the car door.

It took him all day to reach Acapulco. He went to bed immediately, without eating, and slept until late the following afternoon. Then he phoned the Aeromexico office.

Two days later he was home in San Francisco. The first thing he did was call a Sacramento Street dealer and arrange for the sale of all his masks. Now he collects Japanese netsuke, Hopi kachina dolls, and Navaho rugs. He buys only through galleries and does not travel much any more.

The Regulars

It was the proverbial night not fit for man nor beast, black and grim and howling, with the rain coming on in sidewise sheets. But in Charley Sullivan's place everything was as cozy as an old boot, the lights dim, the heat turned up, the neon beer-signs sputtering pleasantly, Charley behind the bar, filling them beyond the Plimsoll line, and all the regulars in their regular places. What a comfort a tavern like Charley Sullivan's can be on a night that's black and grim and howling!

"It was a night like this," said the Pope to Karl Marx, "that you changed your mind about blowing up the stock exchange, as I recall. Eh?"

Karl Marx nodded moodily. "It was the beginning of the end for me as a true revolutionary, it was." He isn't Irish, but in Charley Sullivan's everybody picks up the rhythm of it soon enough. "When you get too fond of your comforts to be willing to go out into a foul gale to attack the enemies of the proletariat, it's the end of your vocation, sure enough." He sighed and peered into his glass. It held nothing but suds, and he sighed again.

"Can I buy you another?" asked the Pope. "In memory of your vocation."

"You may indeed," said Karl Marx.

The Pope looked around. "And who else is needy? My turn to set them up!"

The Leading Man tapped the rim of his glass. So did Ms. Bewley and Mors Longa. I smiled and shook my

264

head, and the Ingenue passed also, but Toulouse-Lautrec, down at the end of the bar, looked away from the television set long enough to give the signal. Charley efficiently handed out the refills—beer for the apostle of the class struggle, Jack Daniels for Mors Longa, Valpolicella for the Pope, scotch and water for the Leading Man, white wine for Ms. Bewley, Perrier with slice of lemon for Toulouse-Lautrec, since he had had the cognac the last time and claimed to be tapering off. And for me, Myers on the rocks. Charley never needs to ask. Of course, he knows us all very well.

"Cheers," said the Leading Man, and we drank up, and then an angel passed by, and the long silence ended only when a nasty rumble of thunder went through the place at about 6.3 on the Richter scale.

"Nasty night," the Ingenue said. "Imagine trying to elope in a downpour like this! I can see it now, Harry and myself at the boathouse, and the car—"

"Harry and *I*," said Mors Longa. " 'Myself' is reflexive. As you well know, sweet."

The Ingenue blinked sweetly. "I always forget. Anyway, there was Harry and I at the boathouse, and the car was waiting, my cousin's old Pierce-Arrow with the—"

—bar in the back seat that was always stocked with the best imported liquors, I went on silently, just a fraction of a second ahead of her clear high voice, *and all we had to do was drive ninety miles across the state line to the place where the justice of the peace was waiting—*

I worked on my rum. The Leading Man, moving a little closer to the Ingenue, tenderly took her hand as the nasty parts of the story began to unfold. The Pope wheezed sympathetically into his wine, and Karl Marx scowled and pounded one fist against the other, and even Ms. Bewley, who had very little tolerance for the Ingenue's silliness, managed a bright smile in the name of sisterhood.

"—the rain, you see, had done something awful to the car's wiring, and there we were, Harry on his knees in the mud trying to fix it, and me half-crazy with

excitement and impatience, and the night getting worse
and worse, when we heard dogs barking and—"

—*my guardian and two of his men appeared out of the
night*—

We had heard it all fifty times before. She tells it every
horrid rainy night. From no one else do we tolerate any
such repetition—we have our sensibilities, and it would
be cruel and unusual to be forced to listen to the same
fol-de-rol over and over and over—but the Ingenue is a
dear sweet young thing, and her special foible it is to
repeat herself, and she and she alone gets away with it
among the regulars at Charley Sullivan's. We followed
along, nodding and sighing and shaking our heads at all
the appropriate places, the way you do when you're
hearing Beethoven's Fifth or Schubert's *Unfinished*, and
she was just getting around to the tempestuous climax,
her fiancé and her guardian in a fight to the death,
illuminated by baleful flashes of lightning, when there
was a crack of real lightning outside, followed almost
instantly by a blast of thunder that made the last one
seem like the sniffle of a mosquito. The vibrations shook
three glasses off the bar and stood Charley Sullivan's
framed photos of President Kennedy and Pope John
XXIII on their corners.

The next thing that happened was the door opened
and a new customer walked in. And you can imagine
that we all sat to attention at that, because you would
expect only the regulars to be populating Charley's place
in such weather, and it was a genuine novelty to have a
stranger materialize. Well timed, too, because without
him we'd have had fifteen minutes more of the tale of
the Ingenue's bungled elopement.

He was maybe thirty-two or a little less, roughly
dressed in heavy-duty Levis, a thick black cardigan, and
a ragged pea-jacket. His dark unruly hair was soaked
and matted. On no particular evidence I decided he was
a merchant sailor who had just jumped ship. For a
moment he stood a little way within the door, eyeing us
all with that cautious look a bar-going man has when he

comes to a new place where everyone else is obviously a long-time regular; and then he smiled, a little shyly at first, more warmly as he saw some of us smiling back. He took off his jacket, hung it on the rack above the jukebox, shook himself like a drenched dog, and seated himself at the bar between the Pope and Mors Longa. "Jesus," he said, "what a stinking night! I can't tell you how glad I was to see a light burning at the end of the block."

"You'll like it here, brother," said the Pope. "Charley, let me buy this young man his first."

"You took the last round," Mors Longa pointed out. "May I, Your Holiness?"

The Pope shrugged. "Why not?"

"My pleasure," said Mors Longa to the newcomer. "What will it be?"

"Do they have Old Bushmill here?"

"They have everything here," said Mors Longa. "*Charley* has everything. Our host. Bushmill for the lad, Charley, and a double, I think. And is anyone else ready?"

"A sweetener here," said the Leading Man. Toulouse-Lautrec opted for his next cognac. The Ingenue, who seemed to have forgotten that she hadn't finished telling her story, waved for her customary rye and ginger. The rest of us stood pat.

"What's your ship?" I asked.

The stranger gave me a startled look. "*Pequod Maru,* Liberian flag. How'd you know?"

"Good guess. Where bound? D'ye mind?"

He took a long pull of his whiskey. "Maracaibo, they said. Not a tanker. Coffee and cacao. But I'm not going. —ah—resigned my commission. This afternoon, very suddenly. Jesus, this tastes good. What a fine warm place this is!"

"And glad we are to see you," said Charley Sullivan. "We'll call you Ishmael, eh?"

"Ishmael?"

"We all need names here," said Mors Longa. "This

gentlman we call Karl Marx, for example. He's socially
conscious. That's Toulouse-Lautrec down there by the
tube. And you can think of me as Mors Longa."

Ishmael frowned. "Is that an Italian name?"

"Latin, actually. Not a name, a sort of a phrase. *Mors
longa, vita brevis*. My motto. And that's the Ingenue, who
needs a lot of love and protection, and this is Ms. Bewley,
who can look after herself, and—"

He went all around the room. Ishmael appeared to be
working hard at remembering the names. He repeated
them until he had them straight, but he still looked a
little puzzled. "Bars I've been in," he said, "it isn't the
custom to make introductions like this. Makes it seem
more like a private party then a bar."

"A family gathering, more like," said Ms. Bewley.

Karl Marx said, "We constitute a society here. It is not
the consciousness of men that determines their existence, but on the contrary their social existence determines their consciousness. We look after one another in
this place."

"You'll like it here," said the Pope.

"I do. I'm amazed how much I like it." The sailor
grinned. "This may be the bar I've been looking for all
my life."

"No doubt but that it is," said Charley Sullivan. "And a
Bushmill's on me, lad?"

Shyly Ishmael pushed his glass forward, and Charley
topped it off.

"So friendly here," Ishmael said. "Almost like—
home."

"Like one's club, perhaps," said the Leading Man.

"A club, a home, yes," said Mors Longa, signaling
Charley for another bourbon. "Karl Marx tells it truly
we care for each other here. We are friends, and we
strive constantly to amuse one another and protect one
another, which are the two chief duties of friends. We
buy each other drinks, we talk, we tell stories to while
away the darkness."

"Do you come here every night?"

"We never miss a one," Mors Longa said.

"You must know each other very well by this time."

"Very well. Very, very well."

"The kind of place I've always dreamed of," Ishmael said wonderingly. "The kind of place I'd never want to leave." He let his eyes pan in a slow arc around the whole room, past the jukebox, the pool table, the dart board, the television screen, the tattered 1934 calendar that had never been changed, the fireplace, the piano. He was glowing, and not just from the whiskey. "Why would anyone ever want to leave a place like this?"

"It is a very good place," said Karl Marx.

Mors Longa said, "And when you find a very good place, it's the place where you want to remain. Of course. It becomes your club, as our friend says. Your home away from home. But that reminds me of a story, young man. Have you ever heard about the bar that nobody actually ever does leave? The bar where everyone stays forever, because they couldn't leave even if they wanted to? Do you know that one?"

"Never heard it," said Ishmael.

But the rest of us had. In Charley Sullivan's place we try never to tell the same story twice, in order to spare each other's sensibilities, for boredom is the deadliest of afflictions here. Only the Ingenue is exempt from that rule because it is her nature to tell her stories again and again, and we love her all the same. Nevertheless, it sometimes happens that one of us must tell an old and familiar story to a newcomer; but though at other times we give each other full attention, it is not required at a time such as that. So the Leading Man and the Ingenue wandered off for a tête-à-tête by the fireplace, and Karl Marx challenged the Pope to a round of darts, and the others drifted off to this corner or that until only Mors Longa and the sailor and I were still at the bar, I drowsing over my rum and Mors Longa getting that faraway look and Ishmael, leaning intently forward, saying, "A bar where nobody can ever leave? What a strange sort of place!"

"Yes," said Mors Longa.

"Where is there such a place?"

"In no particular part of the universe. By which I mean it lies somewhere outside of space and time as we understand those concepts, everywhere and nowhere at once, although it looks not at all alien or strange, apart from its timelessness and its spacelessness. In fact, it looks, I'm told, like every bar you've even been in in your life, only more so. The proprietor's a big man with black Irish in him, a lot like Charley Sullivan here, and he doesn't mind setting one up for the regulars now and then on the house, and he always gives good measure and keeps the heat turned up nicely. And the wood is dark and mellow and well polished, and the railing is the familiar brass, and there are the usual two hanging ferns and the usual aspidistra in the corner next to the spittoon, and there's a dart board and a pool table and all those other things that you find in bars of the kind that this one is. You understand me? This is *a perfectly standard sort of bar*, but it doesn't happen to be in New York City or San Francisco or Hamburg or Rangoon or in any other city you're likely to have visited, though the moment you walk into this place you feel right at home in it."

"Just like here."

"Very much like here," said Mors Longa.

"But people never leave?" Ishmael's brows furrowed. *"Never?"*

"Well, actually, some of them do," Mors Longa said. "But let me talk about the other ones first, all right? The regulars, the ones who are there *all the time*. You know, there are certain people who absolutely never go into bars, the ones who prefer to do their drinking at home or in restaurants before dinner or not at all. But then there are the bar-going sorts. Some of them are folks who just like to drink, you know, and find a bar a convenient place to get their whistles wetted when they're en route from somewhere to somewhere else. And there are some who think drinking's a social act, eh? But you also find people in bars, a lot of them, who go to the place because there's an emptiness in them that needs to be filled, a dark, cold, hollow space, to be filled not just with good warm bourbon, you understand, but a mystic and invisible substance that emanates from others who are in the same way, people who somehow have had a bit of their souls leak away from them by accident and need the comfort of being among their own kind. Say, a priest who's lost his calling or a writer who's forgotten the joy of putting stories down on paper or a painter to whom all colors have become shades of gray or a surgeon whose scalpel-hand has picked up a bit of a tremor or a photographer whose eyes don't quite focus right any more. You know the sort, don't you? You find a lot of that sort in bars. Something in their eyes tells you what they are. But in this particular bar that I'm talking about, you find *only* that sort, good people, decent people, but people with that empty zone inside them. Which makes it even more like all the other bars there are, in fact the Platonic ideal of a bar, if you follow me, a kind of three-dimensional stereotype populated by flesh-and-blood clichés, a sort of perpetual stage-set, do you see? Hearing about a place like that where everybody's a little tragic, everybody's a bit on the broken side, everyone is a perfect bar-type, you'd laugh; you'd say it's unreal; it's too much like everybody's idea of what such a place ought to be like to be convincing. Eh? But all stereotypes are rooted firmly in reality, you know. That's what makes them stereotypes, because they're exactly like reality, only more so. And to the people who do their drinking in the bar I'm talking about, it isn't any stereotype and they aren't clichés. It's the only reality they have, the realest reality there is, for them, and it's no good sneering at it, because it's their own little world, the world of the archetypical saloon, the world of the bar regulars."

"Who never leave the place," said Ishmael.

"How can they? Where would they go? What would they do on a day off? They have no identity except inside the bar. The bar is their life. The bar is their universe. They have no business going elsewhere. They simply stay where they are. They tell each other stories and they work hard to keep each other happy, *and for them there is no world outside*. That's what it means to be a regular, to be a Platonic ideal. Every night the bar and everything in it vanishes into a kind of inchoate gray mist at closing time, and every morning when it's legal to open the bar comes back, and meanwhile the regulars don't go anywhere except into the mist, because that's all there is, mist and then bar, bar and then mist. Platonic ideals don't have daytime jobs and they don't go to Atlantic City on the weekend and they don't decide to go bowling one night instead of to their bar. Do you follow me? They stay there the way the dummies in a store window stay in the store window. Only they can walk and talk and feel and drink and do everything else that window dummies can't do. And that's their whole life, night after night, month after month, year after year, century after century—maybe till the end of time."

"Spooky place," said Ishmael with a little shudder.

"The people who are in that bar are happier than they could possibly be anywhere else."

"But they never leave it. Except you said some of them do, and you'd be telling me about those people later."

Mors Longa finished his bourbon, and, unbidden, Charley Sullivan gave him one more and set another rum in front of me and an Irish for the sailor. For a long while Mors Longa studied his drink. Then he said, "I can't really tell you much about the ones who leave, because I don't know much about them. I intuit their existence logically, is all. You see, from time to time there's a newcomer in this bar that's outside of space and time. Somebody comes wandering in out of the night, the way you did here tonight, and sits down and joins the regular crowd and, bit by bit, fits right in. Now, obviously, if every once in a while somebody new drops in, and nobody ever leaves, then it wouldn't take more than a little for the whole place to get terribly crowded, like Grand Central at commuter time, and what kind of a happy scene would that make? So I conclude that sooner or later each of the regulars very quietly must disappear, must just vanish without anybody's knowing it, maybe go into the john and never come out, something like that. And not only does no one ever notice that someone's missing, but *no one remembers that that person was ever there*. Do you follow? That way the place never gets too full."

"But where do they go, once they disappear from the bar that nobody ever leaves, the bar that's outside of space and time?"

"I don't know," said Mors Longa quietly. "I don't have the foggiest idea." After a moment he added, "There's a theory, though. Mind you, only a theory. It's that the people in the bar are really doing time in a kind of halfway house, a sort of purgatory, you understand, between one world and another. And they stay there a long, long time, however long a time it is until their time is up, and then they leave, but they can only leave when their replacement arrives. And immediately they're forgotten. The fabric of the place closes around them, and nobody among the regulars remembers that once there used to be a doctor with the d.t.'s here, say, or a politician who got caught on the take, or a little guy who sat in front of the piano for hours and never played a note. But everybody has a hunch that that's how the system works. And so it's a big thing when somebody new comes in. Every regular starts secretly wondering, Is it me who's going to go? And wondering too, Where am I going to go, if I'm the one?"

Ishmael worked on his drink in a meditative way. "Are they afraid to go, or afraid that they won't?"

"What do you think?"

"I'm not sure. But I guess most of them would be afraid to go. The bar's such a warm and cozy and comforting place. It's their whole world and has been for a million years. And now maybe they're going to go somewhere horrible—who knows?—but for certain they're going to go somewhere *different*. I'd be afraid of that. Of course, maybe if I'd been stuck in the same place for a million years, no matter how cozy, I'd be ready to move along when the chance came. Which would you want?"

"I don't have the foggiest," said Mors Longa. "But that's the story of the bar where nobody leaves."

"Spooky," said Ishmael.

He finished his drink, pushed the glass away, shook his head to Charley Sullivan, and sat in silence. We all sat in silence. The rain drummed miserably against the side of the building. I looked over at the Leading Man and the Ingenue. He was holding her hand and staring meaningfully into her eyes. The Pope, hefting a dart, was toeing the line and licking his lips to sharpen his aim. Ms. Bewley and Toulouse-Lautrec were playing chess. It was the quiet part of the evening, suddenly.

Slowly the sailor rose and took his jacket from the hook. He turned, smiled uncertainly, and said, "Getting late. I better be going." He nodded to the three of us at the bar and said, "Thanks for the drinks. I needed those. And thanks for the story, Mr. Longa. That was one strange story, you know?"

We said nothing. The sailor opened the door, wincing as cold sheets of rain lashed at him. He pulled his jacket tight around him and, shivering a little, stepped out in the darkness. But he was gone only a moment. Hardly had the door closed behind him but it opened again and he stumbled back in, drenched.

"Jesus," he said, "it's raining worse than ever. What a stinking night! I'm not going out into that!"

"No," I said. "Not fit for man nor beast."

"You don't mind if I stay here until it slackens off some, then?"

"Mind? Mind?" I laughed. "This is a public house, my friend. You've got as much right as anyone. Here. Sit down. Make yourself to home."

"Plenty of Bushmill's left in the bottle, lad," said

Charley Sullivan. "I'm a little low on cash," Ishmael muttered.

Mors Longa said, "That's all right. Money's not the only coin of the realm around here. We can use some stories we haven't heard before. Let's hear the strangest story you can tell us, for openers, and I'll undertake to keep you in Irish while you talk. Eh?"

"Fair enough," said Ishmael. He thought a moment. "All right. I have a good one for you. I have a really good one if you don't mind them weird. It's about my uncle Timothy and his tiny twin brother, that he carried around under his arm all his life. Does that interest you?"

"Most assuredly it does," I said.

"Seconded," said Mors Longa. He grinned with a warmth I had not seen on his face for a long time. "Set them up," he said to Charley Sullivan. "On me. For the house."

Jennifer's Lover

Finch had married very young—he had been only twenty-three, and Jennifer even younger—and even so he hoped they would live happily ever after. Marriage had been back in fashion for a few years, then, but all the same it was unusual to do it so early, and friends and relatives warned them of the risks. Get out and live in the adult world for a while, they said. There's plenty of time later for settling down.

But marrying was more than a matter of fashion for Finch. He had since adolescence felt himself to be a basically married person. Like one of the primordial creatures of Plato's *Symposium* is how he saw himself—a twofold being that somehow had been divided and could not be happy until it had been reunited with its missing half. He searched diligently until he found Jennifer, who seemed to be that separated segment of himself; and then he quickly took care to join her securely to him once again. They settled in a sleek and snug Connecticut suburb. He sold portable computer terminals for a dynamic little hi-tech outfit in Bridgeport, and she worked for a publishing company in Greenwich, and before long they had a daughter named Samantha and a son named Jason, after which Jennifer quit her job and began doing some volunteer work at the local museum. Their parents, who had been pretty wild items in their own day, doing dope and marching for peace and trashing campuses, were amazed at the way everything had come around full circle in just one generation.

Finch was on the road a lot, making sales calls in a territory that stretched from Rhode Island to Delaware, and occasionally he wondered if Jennifer might some-day amuse herself with a lover. But the idea was really too alien to make sense to him. Even when he was away from home three or four nights in a row, sleeping in drab motels in New Jersey or Pennsylvania, he saw no need to go outside his warm and secure marriage, and he imagined Jennifer felt the same way. He wondered if that was naive and decided it wasn't. As a couple they were complete, a single entity, a unity. Naturally the early raptures were only warm memories now, but the expectable cooling of passion had been followed by deep friendship. They were together even when they were apart; a lover would be a superfluity; Finch told himself that if he learned Jennifer had been unfaithful to him, he would not so much be jealous as merely mystified.

And of course there were the children to bind them always. Samantha was already beautiful at seven, a slim golden creature who was as apt to speak French as English. She awed them both, and they were immensely proud of her precocious elegance. Jason, not quite six, was of a different substance, a stolid and literal person whose toys were made of microprocessors and LEDs. He had his father's love of technology, and Finch saw in him a chance to create what he himself had not managed to be—a genuinely original scientific intellect rather than a peddler of other people's inventions. Whenever he returned from a long trip he brought gifts for everyone, a book or a record for Jennifer, something pretty for Samantha, and invariably a computer game or mechan-ical puzzle for Jason. They were splendid children, and he and Jennifer often congratulated one another on having produced them.

At a computer showroom in Philadelphia one rainy autumn afternoon, Finch bought a wonderful toy for Jason, a little synthesizer that played lively tunes when you tapped out signals in a binary code. Not only would it develop Jason's musical skills—and that side of the brain needed to be trained too, Finch thought—but it would sharpen his ability to count in binary. It was so expensive that he felt guilty and eased his conscience by getting the new supercassette of *Die Meistersinger* for Jennifer and a sweater of some glittering furry fabric for Samantha; but on the long drive home he thought only of Jason creating buoyant melodies out of skeins of binary digits.

Jason accepted it politely but seemed not very interested. He watched as Finch demonstrated it, and when it was his turn he generated a few fragmentary atonal squawks. Then a call from Jennifer's parents interrupted things, and afterward, Finch noticed, the child wandered off to his room without taking the synthesizer with him. That was disappointing, but Finch reminded himself that six-year-olds had a way of being preoccupied with one thing at a time, and possibly Jason's preoccupation of the moment was so compelling that even a wondrous new device could not gain much of a grip on his attention.

After dinner, feeling a little miffed, Finch took the synthesizer to Jason's room and found him hunched over an odd glowing thing the size of a large marble. When he saw Finch enter, the boy disingenuously pushed it into the clutter on his tabletop and pretended to be busy with his holographic viewer. "You left this in the living room," Finch said, giving him the synthesizer. Jason took it and obligingly hit the keys in his mild, obedient way, but he looked uncomfortable and impatient. Finch said, pointing at the little glowing thing, "What's that?"

"Nothing much."

"It's very pretty. Mind if I see it?"

Jason shrugged. He generated a jagged screeching tune. Finch picked up the sphere. Jason looked even more restless.

"What does it do?" Finch asked.

"You press it in places. It turns colors. You have to get it the same color all over."

"Rubik's Cube," Finch said. "An old idea brought up to date, I guess." He put his fingertips to the sphere and watched in surprise as colors of eerie indefinable hues came and went, blending, shifting. Touch it a certain way and there were stripes; another and there were triangular patterns; another and the surface of the sphere burst into thick, brilliant, throbbing patches of color, almost like a Van Gogh landscape. He had never seen anything like it. "Where'd you get it?" he asked. "Jennifer buy it for you?"

"No."

"Grandpa Finch send it?"

"No."

Finch felt himself growing annoyed. "Then who gave it to you?"

The child looked momentarily troubled, tugging at his lower lip, twisting his head at a peculiar angle. Then he began to contemplate the synthesizer, and the old serene Jason, imperturbable, studious, returned.

"Nort gave it to me," he said.

"Nort?"

"*You* know."

"I don't. Who's Nort?"

Jason was manipulating the synthesizer, quickly getting the hang of it, making something close to a tune emerge. He had dismissed Finch from his awareness as thoroughly as though Finch had been transported to Pluto. Gently Finch said, "You aren't answering me. Who's Nort?"

"He plays with me sometimes."

Finch decided to drop it. Jason would tell him about Nort in his own good time, he supposed. Meanwhile the boy was mastering the synthesizer with gratifying swiftness; no point distracting him from that. Finch picked up the sphere again, stroked it so that it went through a whole new series of color changes, and brought it almost to the single hue that apparently one was meant to achieve. But he did something wrong and kicked it into a geometrical pseudo-Mondrian pattern instead. A clever gadget, he thought, and went off to find Jennifer and to catch up on local gossip. The mysterious Nort quickly slipped from his mind, and he might never have thought of him again at all if Samantha had not remarked, when he was in her room to say good night to her, "I'm glad you're back. I don't like Nort, really. I hope he doesn't come here any more."

Very calmly Finch said, "Oh, he was here again?"

"Two days, this time. Tell him not to come, will you?"

"I don't know if I can do that. You know who Nort is, after all, don't you?"

"Sure. *Maman's* nephew. A nephew is something like a brother, *n'est ce pas?*"

"A little bit," said Finch. He kissed her lightly. "I'll see what I can do about Nort, all right? And if he comes back when I'm gone, you tell me about it, sweet. I don't think I like him either. But let's not say anything about this to *maman*, okay? She's very fond of her nephew, you know, and it would upset her if she knew that you and I didn't like him."

He paused a moment in the hallway, pressing his forehead against the wall, catching his breath. *Maman's nephew.* Jennifer had no nephews. Finch was trembling. Visiting lovers usually claimed to be uncles, he thought. A nephew? *Jennifer's lover?* It was craziness, a phantasm, a melodrama of a tired mind. Jennifer had no lovers. Finch could visualize their marriage, that abstraction, as a solid concrete thing, a gleaming polished marble sphere rather like Jason's glowing toy, and in the perfection of that sphere there was neither need nor room for lovers. In his own way he would find out who Nort was, he resolved, but above all else he would stay calm. He poured himself a drink and rejoined Jennifer, studying her covertly as if looking for signs of adultery on her forehead, in her cheeks. She was playing *Meistersinger*, humming along with the jollier choruses. When they went to bed, he turned to her as he always did when he came home from a long trip, but he imagined that something strange had descended between them like a curtain of metal links, and he was unable to embrace her. The unknown Nort lay as a barrier in their bed. Finch ran his hands halfheartedly over her breasts and flanks but did nothing else. "You must be very tired," Jennifer whispered.

"I am. All that rain—the traffic skidding around—"

She kissed the tip of his nose. "Get a good night's rest," she said.

He had trouble sleeping. He felt her presence inches away as a pulsating vibration that made his fingers and toes tingle disagreeably. That she might have a lover frightened him, for it meant he held faulty assumptions about their relationship, that his evaluation of reality was defective. And he had to admit that he was upset on a much simpler level: a stranger was creeping into his bed, and he hated that as a violation of his rights. He found his reaction embarrassing. Mere jealousy, he thought, is ugly and stupid and very much beneath me. Nonetheless, beneath him or not, he felt what he felt, and it hurt him keenly.

Eventually he fell asleep, and when he woke to brilliant October sunlight streaming through the blazing leaves of the red maple outside their bedroom everything seemed normal again. Jason was using the synthesizer, getting it to play something that almost might have been *Three Blind Mice*. Finch was intensely pleased by that. At work that day he thought sometimes about Nort, but not in any very painful way—some neighborhood person, he supposed, an artist Jennifer had met at the museum, maybe, who drops around for a drink and some artistic chitchat, most likely gay, gentle, fond of children, harmless. He was much more interested in that peculiar glowing sphere. That night he went into Jason's room to examine it again. Ingenious, the play of colors, the tantalizing way it *almost* went oned as you handled it and then slipped away into patterns. He had no idea how it worked. Sensitive to skin-temperature fluctuations, perhaps, or possibly even pressure-sensitive, though it was solid as a marble. And what generated the changing colors and projected them to the surface? He was tempted to ask Jason to get a second sphere from Nort that he could try to take apart.

The week after next he was up in Boston for three days on his regular monthly trip. The first two went well; but on the evening of the third, as he returned to his motel after an overly winy dinner with a buyer from a Cambridge data-shop chain, the incandescent image of Jennifer getting into bed with Nort suddenly blazed in his soul. The Nort that Finch invented was older than he, perhaps thirty-seven, dark and muscular, with a dancer's supple body and an easy, self-assured manner. Finch bit his lip and tried to force the unwanted vision away, but it grew ever more vivid and ever more graphic, and the pain of it was astonishing. He thought seriously of driving home in the middle of the night. But that would be insane, he realized.

He came home on schedule with the usual gifts, and when he gave Jason his—a little screen on which he could draw with a light-pen—he feared the boy, still enthralled by some phenomenal incomprehensible thing that Nort had just brought him, might snub it. But Jason said nothing about Nort and was instantly fascinated by the screen. Finch felt a surge of relief until Samantha drew him aside, an hour later, to tell him, "He was here again."

"Nort?"

"Oui. Mardi et marcredi."

"Mercredi," he corrected automatically. Her French still had some flaws; but she was only seven. He turned away to hide his look of torment. Two nights, again: Tuesday, Wednesday. He had no idea what he was supposed to do. Confront her with his suspicions and demand an explanation? They had never even had a real quarrel. Swallow his agony and count himself grateful that there was someone here protecting his home and family while he was away? Sure. Sure. In a dull voice

he said, "What do Nort and *maman* do when he's visiting
her?"

"They have dinner after we go to sleep. Then they
stay up late and talk. In the morning he asks us
questions about school and things and tries to be nice to
us."

In the morning. Finch winced.

He forced himself to make love with Jennifer that
evening so she would not suspect that he suspected, but
he was without desire and barely managed to enter her,
which made it all even worse. Guilty herself, she would
want to assume the worst in him, and this uncharacteristic failure of virility after three nights away from her
probably would lead her to think he had been with
women in Boston, which would encourage her to give
herself even more flagrantly to her own lover, which—

In the two weeks before his next road-trip he thought
constantly of what would take place between Jennifer
and Nort while he was away. He was jittery, remote,
short-tempered, and morose; Jennifer seemed to be
trying to please him, but whatever she did was counter-
productive, and he was reduced to pleading business
worries and headaches to keep from having to blurt out
what was really on his mind. He wanted no confronta-
tions with her. The love he bore her should be great
enough to allow scope for a little discreet adultery, and if
it did not, well, he would try to work on his attitudes.

But as he drove off toward Hartford under gray
November skies, he imagined Nort's car gliding into the
garage, Nort entering the house, Nort with his hands on
her breasts, Nort leading her toward the bedroom. The
absurd intensity of his obsession alarmed and dismayed
him. But he could not control his feelings. In Hartford
he checked into his motel and drifted like a man in a
haze through his first three calls; he must have seemed
in terrible shape, because everyone commented on the
way he looked; he had two drinks before making his
fourth call, which he never did, and then he canceled

the call and returned to the motel. There he had another drink, ate a hamburger in the coffee shop, and stared unseeingly at the television set until midnight, when he abruptly rose, dressed, stumbled outside, and grimly began to drive homeward. He knew that this was absolute madness. He would let himself into the house and catch them in bed together, and then the three of them would sit down and discuss things. And he had no idea what would happen after that.

Just before two in the morning he parked in front of his house and saw, with perverse satisfaction, that a lamp was lit in the bedroom. Strangely calm, Finch peered through the garage window, but saw only Jennifer's station-wagon inside. So Nort *was* a neighborhood person, Finch thought. She phones him and he walks over here and she lets him in.

Noiselessly Finch unlocked the door, punched in his identity code on the burglar-alarm keyboard, slipped off his shoes, and tiptoed upstairs. His heart pounded with such startling force that he began to fear real damage to it. At the top of the stairs he paused, paralyzed with shame and misgivings. Leave them alone, he told himself. This is unquestionably the most stupid and reckless and self-defeating thing you've done in your life. He was quivering. He did not dare go forward.

"Dale?" Jennifer called from the bedroom. "Dale, is that you? It *better* be you!"

"Me," he croaked, and lurched into the room.

She was alone, sitting up in bed, looking frightened and surprised. Finch, ashen and shaking, still had the presence of mind to scan the room for spoor of Nort, an overlooked wristwatch, a stray sock. Nothing. Jennifer was naked. She slept that way with him, but she had once told him that she always wore pajamas when he was away, for warmth. Certainly Nort was still here. Nobody jumps out a second-floor window to escape an angry husband. In the closet? In the bathroom? Under the bed? Finch knew he had created a preposterous farce.

"I felt ill," he mumbled. "Dizzy—hot flashes—

couldn't be alone. I just climbed into the car and headed for home—to be with you—the kids—"

"Dale, what's the matter? What hurts you?" She was as tense and anguished as he was, but she seemed to be recovering her poise. She got out of bed—were those the red imprints of Nort's fingers on her breasts and thighs?—and pulled on her robe and came to him. "If you were so sick, you shouldn't have tried to drive all the way from Hartford. Why didn't you call first? Why didn't you try to have the motel get you a doctor?" He swayed. His legs felt like concrete. He leaned against her, sniffing for the other man's cologne or even the smell of his sweat, and let Jennifer ease him down to the bed. He wanted to ask her where she had hidden Nort. But the words would not come. She helped him undress and brought him aspirins, and turned the thermostat up because he was shivering so violently, and clasped him in her arms. Her body was so warm and yielding and tender against him that he nearly began to cry. He let himself relax in her embrace, and to his amazement his desires rose and he reached for her. She tried to quiet him, telling him she was too exhausted for any such thing, but there was no halting him and he took her quickly and with uncharacteristic force. Jennifer met his thrusts with a vigor he had not encountered in months. It must be because Nort's done all the foreplay for me, he thought bitterly, and came at once, with a sob, and collapsed against her breast. At once he was asleep, and in the morning it all seemed like a dreadful dream, nothing more. Finch insisted on going back to Hartford and making his rounds, and would hear no objection from Jennifer. But first he went into Samantha's room and, cutting short her expression of surprise at seeing her father return from his trip so soon, asked her bluntly whether Nort had come for dinner the night before.

"Yes," she said. "He was here when I got home from school. Is he still upstairs with *maman?*"

Finch asked himself, as he drove shakily back to

Hartford, whether to seek the advice of friends, his parents, the local minister, a therapist. He had never done any of that. His life had always been an amiable progression toward deeper happiness. By the time he reached the motel, he knew he would consult no one, would take no action at all, would simply wait and see. He would let Jennifer make the next move.

But she said nothing and he said nothing and after his next trip, a brief one, he found Jason with another strange new toy, an arrangement of gleaming wires that crossed and recrossed and seemed to disappear at one juncture into a baffling uncharted dimension, visible only as a dazzling flicker of green light. Yes, the boy said, Nort had given it to him. Finch felt a surge of frantic anger. He was almost desperate now to bring this thing to some sort of resolution, for it was devouring him. Jennifer remained tender and loving and outwardly unchanged. Finch suffered. He could not push his fears and confusions below the threshold of awareness for more than an hour or two at a time; he was losing weight; everyone commented on his frayed and frazzled appearance. He was drowning in the silent turbulence of his altered life.

A second time he returned prematurely from a sales trip, hoping to catch them together. Again the light was on in the bedroom in the middle of the night. Again he stumbled in to find Jennifer flustered but alone. He explained that he was drunk and bewildered. "I think I'm having some sort of a breakdown," he told her, and this time he called in sick and took a week off, though the Christmas holidays were coming and it looked very bad to do that now. Impulsively he went with Jennifer to Bermuda for four days, leaving the children with his parents, and it was like a second honeymoon for them, the pink sandy shore, the palm trees. But the moment they came home his mind was full of Nort again. A few days before Christmas he had to go to Pittsburgh for a meeting, but when still at the airport he was consumed with the awareness that Nort was in his house.

joking amiably with Jason and Samantha. Grimly Finch boarded his plane, sat in a cold funk of silence all the way and, in Pittsburgh, bought a ticket on the next flight back to JFK. A light snowfall had begun, and his car, sitting in the vast lot, looked dainty and virginal in its thin white mantle. He reached home at midnight. The bedroom light was on. Finch let himself in and took the stairs two at a time. Jennifer was sitting up in bed, naked at least to the waist, her bare breasts blazing at him like beacons, and next to her, relaxed, comfortable, his hands clasped behind his head, was a slender, naked young man, perhaps thirty at most, with cool green eyes and dense red hair that clung to his head in a curious caplike way.

Finch felt a kind of relief. "You're Nort?"

"Yes. Is time we finally met, I think, Mr. Dale."

"Mr. *Finch*. Or Dale." Nort had some slight accent. Finch said, "I don't know what the protocol is in a thing like this. I suppose I should be furious and smash things and make threats. But I'm hollow inside by now. I've known about this a long time."

"We know," Jennifer said. "Why else would you have kept coming here trying to catch us in the middle of the night?"

"Twice," said Nort. "This be the third. I thought this time I stay and talk with you."

"You were here the other two times?"

"Certainly. But Jennifer wanted no face-to-face. So when the Dale-detector went off, I did the vanish. You follow?"

Finch stared wearily at his wife. "Jennifer, who is this man and how did he get into our lives?"

"He's my nephew," she said.

"You have no—"

"—eleven generations removed."

"What?"

"A remote descendant in my sister's line. He comes from A.D. 2215. He's here to do research."

Finch thought of the toys Nort had given Jason. His eyes glazed.

Nort said. "I make the field trip, you follow? I do genealogical research, visit the ancestors, family anecdotes. In my era is very important, knowing the history. I have made many journeys over a long span."

"He has my whole family tree," said Jennifer. "I never knew it, but I'm descended from Millard Fillmore and Johann Sebastian Bach and possibly John of Gaunt."

Finch nodded. "That's fascinating."

Nort said, "We do not interfere, you know. We move around like spies, doing our studies and never interacting with the past-folk, out of fear of consequences, of course. But this was an exception. I was captivated by Jennifer instantly."

"Captivated," said Finch bleakly.

"Captivated, yes. We became lovers. It is a kind of incest, I imagine, but is not very serious, outside the direct maternal line, yes? My studies suffer. Now I come only to this year. Jennifer is a wonderful woman. You know?"

"I know, yes." Finch looked toward Jennifer. "I haul my ass over eight states peddling primitive data-processing devices while you amuse yourself with a lover from the twenty-third century. That absolutely captivates me, Jennifer. I can't tell you how—"

"Dale, please. You know I love you. But—but—"

Nort looked troubled. "You are not accepting of this?"

"I am not accepting, no," Finch said.

"But this is the late twentieth century, a decadent time for the marriage custom, and you are sophisticated educated, elite persons. It is my understanding that toleration of nonmarital sexual interpersonation is widespread in your cohort. You are displeased I love you wife?"

"Very," said Finch in a gray voice. He lowered himsel into the chair by the window and said, "You're a hell of guy for keeping a straight face, Nort. I have to admir that. Throughout this whole routine you've been ver

convincing. But I'm worn out, and I can't take any
futuristic rigmarole any more. Please put your clothes
on and go away and don't come back, and leave Jennifer
and me to pick up the pieces of our marriage. Okay?
Because if I catch you here again, I might do something
violent, which is against my nature, and I'll probably
have to divorce Jennifer, which is the last thing in the
world I want to do even now."

"You doubt I am from a future time?"

"I doubt you are from a future time, yes."

Nort climbed out of the bed. Finch noticed a thin
plastic band of some constantly oscillating greenish color
around his left thigh. He touched it and disappeared,
and when he reappeared, a moment later, he was in a
different corner of the room, holding out a folded
newspaper to Finch. Finch glanced at it: the New York
Times for April 16, 2037. The main headline was
something about Pope Sixtus performing Easter services
on the moon. Finch made a little choking sound and
started to scan the other stories, but Nort, with an
apologetic smile, took the paper from him, vanished
again, and reappeared without it, back in the bed. "I
have sorrow," he said softly, "but I am forbidden to let
you inspect the newspaper in detail. Shall I do other
things? What would convince you I am genuine?"

Finch wanted to sob. He shook his head and said,
"Don't bother. I don't need to know. You probably are
what you say you are. Will you go away now? Go annoy
Millard Fillmore."

"I am loving your wife."

"You *have loved* my wife. That's the correct grammar.
It's over. Listen, I'm a ruthless late-twentieth-century
man, and you're on dangerous ground. I have weapons.
If you're killed while on a field trip, will you stay dead in
2215?"

Jennifer said, "Dale, stop talking that way."

"What do you want me to say? He flashes in here like
something out of Buck Rogers, he screws my wife every
time I look the other way, he upsets my daughter and

alienates my son with his crazy future toys, and now I'm supposed to—"

"You mustn't threaten him, Dale. You're behaving *extremely* prehistorically. Haven't you ever had an affair?"

"Never. Not once."

"Those motels—"

"Not once. I suppose you've had plenty, though."

"Two before this one," she said, reddening a little. "I thought you knew. This isn't 1906, after all. They were both absolutely casual."

Finch thought of that polished perfect sphere that was his metaphor for the flawlessness of his relationship with Jennifer. He thought of the two-bodied male-female entities of Plato's *Symposium*. His face was leaden and his hands shook.

She said, "This is more serious, Dale. I'm terribly fond of Nort. I love you as much as ever, but he's shown me other aspects of life, things I never dreamed of, and I'm not talking about sex. I mean spiritual concepts, human potentialities, the—"

"All right," said Finch. "I won't try to compete. I won't shoot him and I won't punch him and I won't do anything else uncivilized. Why don't the two of you get the hell off to A.D. 2215 and carry on the rest of your affair there, okay? Go have a flying fuck in the century after next and let me alone. Okay? Okay? The two of you. *Let—me—*"

Nort disappeared. So did Jennifer.

"Alone," Finch finished weakly. "Jennifer? Jennifer? Where are you? Hey, I wasn't serious! Jennifer! God-damn it, what kind of sadistic stunt is this? Where are you?"

The cruelty of their game astounded him. He waited for them to pop back into the room as Nort had done with the newspaper, but they did not, and as the minutes went by he began to suspect that they were not going to. Numb with disbelief, he prowled the house, searching closets for them. Suddenly horror-struck, he rushed to Jason's room, then to Samantha's, but the children were still there, Jason asleep, Samantha awake and troubled by the shouting she had heard. He picked her up and held her a long moment, and tears came to him. "It's all right," he murmured. "Go back to sleep." He returned to the bedroom and sat there until dawn, waiting for Jennifer.

In the morning he phoned the office to say that severe family problems had forced him to return from Pittsburgh suddenly and that he needed an indefinite leave of absence, with or without pay. His supervisor was wholly understanding, not at all skeptical, as if Finch's voice communicated precisely how stunned and bewildered he was. He managed to deliver the children to school, and then spent the morning by the telephone, hoping to hear from Jennifer. But no word came from her all day. In late afternoon he called his parents to say that Jennifer had gone off somewhere without warning and could they please come early for their holiday visit, because he wasn't sure he could handle all this domestic stuff alone. They arrived the next day and asked blessedly few questions. In their generation, he thought, it must have been the usual thing for marriages to break up without warning.

Jennifer did not come back. He felt like someone who had been given a single wish and had used it stupidly: now she was off in the inconceivable future with Nort. Was that possible? Was this not all some kind of bizarre dream? Apparently not, for on Christmas Eve a note from Jennifer materialized inexplicably on the living-room table, dated 14 Oct 2215 and wishing him happy holidays and assuring him of her love and telling him not to expect her back. "Sometimes you simply have to follow your destiny," she concluded. "I had only a fraction of a second to make my decision and I made it, and maybe I'll regret it, but I did what I had to do. I miss you, darling. And you know how much I miss Samantha and Jason." Next to the note was a little package, with a tag marked Merry Christmas from Nort. It contained a tiny crystal ball that when held close to his eye showed him what looked like an Antarctic landscape, gales howling and placid penguins wandering around on an ice floe. He put it down, and when he picked it up a second time it displayed the Pyramids, with a long line of tourists milling about. Finch flung it against the wall and it cracked in half and turned cloudy. He wished he had not done that.

Getting through the holidays was even more of an ordeal than usual, but his parents were an immense help, and his friends, once they discovered that Jennifer was gone, came magnificently to his aid. He was scarcely alone the whole week, and he suspected that it would not have been hard for him to find company for the night, either, but of course that was out of the question. The children were perplexed by Jennifer's disappearance, but after some disorientation they appeared to adapt, which Finch found more than a little chilling. He hired a housekeeper early in January and, feeling like a sleepwalker, went back to work. Because of the change in his family circumstances, the company took him off the outlying routes, so that he would not have to spend nights away from home.

Some time in early spring he started genuinely to believe that Jennifer had skipped away into the future with her lover. Notes from her arrived now and then, always friendly, with regards for the children and reminders about oiling the furnace and taking the cars in for tune-ups. She said she was having a wonderful time but missed him terribly. There was never any mention of coming back. From time to time, also, little gifts appeared—gadgets, toys, knicknacks of the future. Perhaps they were meant for Jason, but Finch kept them himself, hoarding them in his closet and examining them at night with awe. He had always loved gadgets— computers, remote-control devices, wrist videos, and such—but these seemed more like miracles than gadgets to him, and he ceased to doubt that Nort was what he said he was. Finch hoped another of the crystal balls would turn up, but it never did. He did get something that appeared to tune in the music of the spheres, and another that could be programmed to give him the dreams he wanted, and one that displayed abstract color-fields of a serene unearthly kind.

When summer came, he drifted with surprising ease into a romance with Estelle, the company's PR consultant, and that carried him into late autumn. Gently she extricated herself from the relationship then, but he had learned how to meet and win women once again, and he ran through a lively bachelorhood in the months that followed. The first anniversary of Jennifer's disappearance passed. The notes from her and the gifts from Nort came less frequently and then not at all. He was quite competent at running a family without a wife by now, but he had never lost that old sense of himself as an innately married man, as half of a couple, and so, admitting that Jennifer was never coming back, he filed for divorce and won an uncontested decree. That was the strangest part thus far, the knowledge that he was no longer married to Jennifer. He looked for a new wife in his diligent, serious-minded way and, within six months, found one. Her name was Sharon and she was warm hearted and lovely and rather like Jennifer, though her interests ran more to drama and poetry than to music and painting. She had had an unhappy marriage just after college and had a boy of four, Joshua, very bright. Joshua got along wonderfully with Jason and Samantha, they accepted Sharon readily as their new mother— Jennifer was only a hazy memory to them now—and everything seemed to have worked out for the best. Sometimes Finch called Sharon "Jennifer" when they made love, but she was very understanding about that. Sometimes, too, he woke up drenched with sweat, wondering where he had misplaced his one true wife, his sundered half; but whenever that happened, Sharon held him until he regained his grasp on reality. He moved up nicely in the firm, which was expanding at a remarkable rate, and stayed trim and agile all through his forties. Samantha and Jason turned out well, too:

Jason went to Cal Tech, joined a West Coast company, and invented an information-encapsulating device that made him a stock-option millionaire by the time he was twenty-two. Samantha grew tall and radiant and even more beautiful, pursued her interest in French, and achieved splendid translations of Rabelais and Ronsard and married the French ambassador. Finch saw less and less of his children once they were grown, of course, but they always came home for a family reunion at Christmas. They were with him that afternoon twenty-three years after Jennifer's disappearance when Jennifer reappeared.

Finch did not know who she was, at first. She quite suddenly was *there* in the living room, a handsome, slender, full-breasted young woman of about thirty, with golden hair in tight waves against her scalp, who wore a clinging garment of metallic mesh. She blinked and looked about and gasped as she saw Finch, who was in his mid-fifties and reasonably youthful-looking for his age.

"Dale?" she said doubtfully.

He let his drink clatter to the floor. "No," he said. "It isn't possible. Christ, what are you doing here?"

"I had to come back. Oh, Dale, it's the wrong year, isn't it? I wanted to see the children again!"

"There they are," he said stonily. "Take a look."

"Where—which—"

Jason was there and Samantha, and also Joshua and some of their friends; and obviously Jennifer did not recognize her own. Finch pointed. The stocky broad-shouldered young man with the earnest myopic gaze was Jason. The long-legged, awesomely beautiful woman was Samantha. Jennifer's glossy poise seemed to shatter. She was trembling and close to tears. "I wanted to see the children," she whispered. "They were so small—he was six, she was seven—oh, Dale, I've set the timer wrong! I've made a mess of it, haven't I?"

Samantha, quick as always, was the only other one who understood. She went toward her mother and stared at her as though Jennifer were an intruder from some other planet. Finch had heard that Samantha often used her beauty as a weapon, but he had never before seen it. Jennifer appeared to shrivel before the sleek, dazzling woman she had helped to create. In a low husky voice Samantha said, "You don't belong here now, you know. This is a happy time for us, and we don't need you and we don't want you. Will you go away?"

"Wait," Finch muttered.

Too late. Jennifer, reddening, dismayed, nodded and said to Samantha, "I'm terribly sorry. I'm sorry for everything." She ran from the room. Finch raced after her, out to the hall, but of course she had disappeared. White-faced, Finch returned to the party. He looked toward Sharon, who was both smiling and frowning. He had never told her or anyone else exactly what had become of his first wife.

"Who was that?" Sharon asked amiably. "Some girl-friend of yours, Dale?" There was nothing like jealousy in her voice. She was only mildly curious.

"No—no, nothing like that—"

"I wonder how she got in here. Like coming out of thin air, almost. Strange. Why did she dash away like that?"

"She didn't belong here," Finch said hoarsely. He poured himself another drink. "She was in the wrong time, the wrong place." He glanced at his daughter, who was flushed with triumph. What power she had, what force! All the same, he was starting to regret that Samantha had driven her off so quickly. With a wobbly hand he raised his glass. "Merry Christmas, everybody! Merry, merry, merry Christmas!"

For a few years after that he found himself wondering, as the holiday season approached, whether Jennifer would make another appearance, like some ghost of marriages past coming round again. Had she tired of Nort and Nort's century? Did she yearn for all she had abandoned? Though there was no longer any room in Finch's life for her, he held no grudge after all this time;

he was almost eager to go off and talk with her a little, to find out who she had become, this woman who had once been part of him. But she never again returned. Perhaps she spent her holidays with Millard Fillmore now, he thought. Or singing carols by the blazing Yule log at the fireside of great-great-great-grandpa Johann Sebastian Bach.

Needle in a Timestack

Between one moment and the next the taste of cotton came into his mouth, and Mikkelsen knew that Tommy Hambleton had been tinkering with his past again. The cotton-in-the-mouth sensation was the standard tip-off for Mikkelsen. For other people it might be a ringing in the ears, a tremor of the little finger, a tightness in the shoulders. Whatever the symptom, it always meant the same thing: your time-track has been meddled with, your life has been retroactively transformed. It happened all the time. One of the little annoyances of modern life, everyone always said. Generally, the changes didn't amount to much .

But Tommy Hambleton was out to destroy Mikkelsen's marriage, or, more accurately, he was determined to unhappen it altogether, and that went beyond Mikkelsen's limits of tolerance. In something close to panic he phoned home to find out if he still had Janine.

Her lovely features blossomed on the screen—glossy dark hair, elegant cheekbones, cool sardonic eyes. She looked tense and strained, and Mikkelsen knew she had felt the backlash of this latest attempt too.

"Nick?" she said. "Is it a phasing?"

"I think so. Tommy's taken another whack at us, and Christ only knows how much chaos he's caused this time."

"Let's run through everything."

"All right," Mikkelsen said. "What's your name?"

"Janine."

"And mine?"

"Nick. Nicholas Perry Mikkelsen. You see? Nothing important has changed."

"Are you married?"

"Yes, of course, darling. To you."

"Keep going. What's our address?"

"11 Lantana Crescent."

"Do we have children?"

"Dana and Elise. Dana's five, Elise is three. Our cat's name is Minibelle, and—"

"Okay," Mikkelsen said, relieved. "That much checks out. But I tasted the cotton, Janine. Where has he done it to us this time? What's been changed?"

"It can't be anything major, love. We'll find it if we keep checking. Just stay calm."

"Calm. Yes." He closed his eyes. He took a deep breath. The little annoyances of modern life, he thought. In the old days, when time was just a linear flow from *then* to *now*, did anyone get bored with all that stability? For better or for worse it was different now. You go to bed a Dartmouth man and wake up Columbia, never the wiser. You board a plane that blows up over Cyprus, but then your insurance agent goes back and gets you to miss the flight. In the new fluid way of life there was always a second chance, a third, a fourth, now that the past was open to anyone with the price of a ticket. But what good is any of that, Mikkelsen wondered, if Tommy Hambleton can use it to disappear me and marry Janine again himself?

They punched for readouts and checked all their vital data against what they remembered. When your past is altered through time-phasing, all records of your life are automatically altered too, of course, but there's a period of two or three hours when memories of your previous existence still linger in your brain, like the phantom twitches of an amputated limb. They checked the date of Mikkelsen's birth, parents' names, his nine genetic coordinates, his educational record. Everything seemed right. But when they got to their wedding date the readout said 8 Feb 2017, and Mikkelsen heard warning chimes in his mind. "I remember a summer wedding," he said. "Outdoors in Dan Levy's garden, the hills all dry and brown, the 24th of August."

"So do I, Nick. The hills wouldn't have been brown in February. But I can see it—that hot dusty day—"

"Then five months of our marriage are gone, Janine. He couldn't unmarry us altogether, but he managed to hold us up from summer to winter." Rage made his head spin, and he had to ask his desk for a quick buzz of tranks. Etiquette called for one to be cool about a phasing. But he couldn't be cool when the phasing was a deliberate and malevolent blow at the center of his life. He wanted to shout, to break things, to kick Tommy Hambleton's ass. He wanted his marriage left alone. He said, "You know what I'm going to do one of these days? I'm going to go back about fifty years and eradicate Tommy completely. Just arrange things so his parents never get to meet, and—"

"No, Nick. You mustn't."

"I know. But I'd love to." He knew he couldn't, and not just because it would be murder. It was essential that Tommy Hambleton be born and grow up and meet Janine and marry her, so that when the marriage came apart she would meet and marry Mikkelsen. If he changed Hambleton's past, he would change hers too, and if he changed hers, he would change his own, and anything might happen. Anything. But all the same he was furious. "Five months of our past, Janine—"

"We don't need them, love. Keeping the present and the future safe is the main priority. By tomorrow we'll always think we were married in February of 2017, and it won't matter. Promise me you won't try to phase him."

"I hate the idea that he can simply—"

"So do I. But I want you to promise you'll leave things as they are."

"Well—"

"Promise."

"All right," he said. "I promise."

Little phasings happened all the time. Someone in Illinois makes a trip to eleventh-century Arizona and sets up tiny ripple currents in time that have a tangential and peripheral effect on a lot of lives, and someone in California finds himself driving a silver BMW instead of a gray Toyota. No one minded trifling changes like that. But this was the third time in the last twelve months, so far as Mikkelsen was able to tell, that Tommy Hambleton had committed a deliberate phasing intended to break the chain of events that had brought about Mikkelsen's marriage to Janine.

The first phasing happened on a splendid spring day—coming home from work, sudden taste of cotton in mouth, sense of mysterious disorientation. Mikkelsen walked down the steps looking for his old ginger tomcat, Gus, who always ran out to greet him as though he thought he was a dog. No Gus. Instead a calico female, very pregnant, sitting placidly in the front hall.

"Where's Gus?" Mikkelsen asked Janine.

"Gus? Gus who?"

"Our cat."

"You mean Max?"

"Gus," he said. "Sort of orange, crooked tail—"

"That's right. But Max is his name. I'm sure it's Max. He must be around somewhere. Look, here's Minibelle." Janine knelt and stroked the fat calico. "Minibelle, where's Max?"

"Gus," Mikkelsen said. "Not Max. And who's this Minibelle?"

"She's our cat, Nick," Janine said, sounding surprised.

They stared at each other.

"Something's happened, Nick."

"I think we've been time-phased," he said.

Sensation as of dropping through trapdoor—shock, confusion, terror. Followed by hasty and scary inventory of basic life-data to see what had changed. Everything appeared in order except for the switch of cats. He didn't remember having a female calico. Neither did Janine, although she had accepted the presence of the cat without surprise. As for Gus—Max—he was getting foggier about his name, and Janine couldn't even remember what he looked like. But she did recall that he had been a wedding gift from some close friend, and Mikkelsen remembered that the friend was Gus Stark, for whom they had named him, and Janine was then able to dredge up the dimming fact that Gus was a close friend of Mikkelsen's and also of Hambleton and Janine in the days when they were married, and that Gus had introduced Janine to Mikkelsen ten years ago when they were all on holiday in Hawaii.

Mikkelsen accessed the household callmaster and found no Gus Stark listed. So the phasing had erased him from their roster of friends. The general phone directory turned up a Gus Stark in Costa Mesa. Mikkelsen called him and got a freckle-faced man with fading red hair, who looked more or less familiar. But he didn't know Mikkelsen at all, and only after some puzzling around in his memory did he decide that they had been distantly acquainted way back when, but had had some kind of trifling quarrel and had lost touch with each other years ago.

"That's not how I think I remember it," Mikkelsen said. "I remember us as friends for years, really close. You and Donna and Janine and I were out to dinner only last week, is what I remember, over in Newport Beach."

"Donna?"

"Your wife."

"My wife's name is Karen. Jesus, this has been one hell of a phasing, hasn't it?" He didn't sound upset.

"I'll say. Blew away your marriage, our friendship, and who knows what-all else."

"Well, these things happen. Listen, if I can help you

any way, fella, just call. But right now Karen and I were on our way out, and—"

"Yeah. Sure. Sorry to have bothered you," Mikkelsen told him.

He blanked the screen.

Donna. Karen. Gus. Max. He looked at Janine.

"Tommy did it," she said.

She had it all figured out. Tommy, she said, had never forgiven Mikkelsen for marrying her. He wanted her back. He still sent her birthday cards, coy little gifts, postcards from exotic ports.

"You never mentioned them," Mikkelsen said.

She shrugged. "I thought you'd only get annoyed. You've always disliked Tommy."

"No," Mikkelsen said, "I think he's interesting in his oddball way, flamboyant, unusual. What I dislike is his unwillingness to accept the notion that you stopped being his wife a dozen years ago."

"You'd dislike him more if you knew how hard he's been trying to get me back."

"Oh?"

"When we broke up," she said, "he phased me four times. This was before I met you. He kept jaunting back to our final quarrel, trying to patch it up so that the separation wouldn't have happened. I began feeling the phasings and I knew what must be going on, and I told him to quit it or I'd report him and get his jaunt-license revoked. That scared him, I guess, because he's been pretty well behaved ever since, except for all the little hints and innuendoes and invitations to leave you and marry him again."

"Christ," Mikkelsen said. "How long were you and he married? Six months?"

"Seven. But he's an obsessive personality. He never let's go."

"And now he's started phasing again?"

"That's my guess. He's probably decided that you're the obstacle, that I really do still love you, that I want to spend the rest of my life with you. So he needs to make us unmeet. He's taken his first shot by somehow engineering a breach between you and your friend Gus a dozen years back, a breach so severe that you never really became friends and Gus never fixed you up with me. Only it didn't work out the way Tommy hoped. We went to that party at Dave Cushman's place and I got pushed into the pool on top of you and you introduced yourself and one thing led to another and here we still are."

"Not all of us are," Mikkelsen said. "My friend Gus is married to somebody else now."

"That didn't seem to trouble him much."

"Maybe not. But he isn't my friend any more, either, and that troubles *me*. My whole past is at Tommy Hambleton's mercy, Janine! And Gus the cat is gone too. Gus was a damned good cat. I miss him."

"Five minutes ago you weren't sure whether his name was Gus or Max. Two hours from now you won't know you ever had any such cat, and it won't matter at all."

"But suppose the same thing had happened to you and me as happened to Gus and Donna?"

"It didn't, though."

"It might the next time," Mikkelsen said.

But it didn't. The next time, which was about six months later, they came out of it still married to each other. What they lost was their collection of twentieth-century artifacts—the black-and-white television set and the funny old dial telephone and the transistor radio and the little computer with the typewriter keyboard. All those treasures vanished between one instant and the next, leaving Mikkelsen with the telltale cottony taste in his mouth, Janine with a short-lived tic below her left eye, and both of them with the nagging awareness that a phasing had occurred.

At once they did what they could to see where the alteration had been made. For the moment they both remembered the artifacts they once had owned, and how eagerly they had collected them in '21 and '22, when the craze for such things was just beginning. But there were no sales receipts in their files and already their memories of what they had bought were becoming blurry and contradictory. There was a grouping of glittery sonic sculptures in the corner, now, where the artifacts had been. What change had been effected in the pattern of their past to put those things in the place of the others?

They never really were sure—there was no certain way of knowing—but Mikkelsen had a theory. The big expense he remembered for 2021 was the time-jaunt that he and Janine had taken to Aztec Mexico, just before she got pregnant with Dana. Things had been a little wobbly between the Mikkelsens back then, and the time-jaunt was supposed to be a second honeymoon. But their guide on the jaunt had been a hot little item named Elena Schmidt, who had made a very deter- mined play of Mikkelsen and who had had him con- sidering, for at least half an hour of lively fantasy, leaving Janine for her.

"Suppose," he said, "that on our original time-track we never went back to the Aztecs at all, but put the money into the artifact collection. But then Tommy went back and maneuvered things to get us interested in time-jaunting, and at the same time persuaded that Schmidt cookie to show an interest in me. We couldn't afford both the antiques and the trip; we opted for the trip, Elena did her little number on me, it didn't cause the split that Tommy was hoping for, and now we have some gaudy memories of Moctezuma's empire and no collection of early electronic devices. What do you think?"

"Makes sense," Janine said.

"Will you report him, or should I?"

"But we have no proof, Nick!"

He frowned. Proving a charge of time-crime, he knew, was almost impossible, and risky besides. The very act of investigating the alleged crime could cause an even worse phase-shift and scramble their pasts beyond repair. To enter the past is like poking a baseball bat into a spiderweb: it can't be done subtly or delicately.

"Do we just sit and wait for Tommy to figure out a way to get rid of me that really works?" Mikkelsen asked.

"We can't just confront him with suspicions, Nick."

"You did it once."

"Long ago. The risks are greater now. We have more past to lose. What if he's not responsible? What if he gets scared of being blamed for something that's just coincidence, and *really* sets out to phase us? He's so damned volatile, so unstable—if he feels threatened, he's likely to do anything. He could wreck our lives entirely."

"If *he* feels threatened? What about—"

"Please, Nick. I've got a hunch Tommy won't try it again. He's had two shots and they've both failed. He'll quit it now. I'm sure he will."

Grudgingly Mikkelsen yielded, and after a time he stopped worrying about a third phasing. Over the next few weeks, other effects of the second phasing kept turning up, the way losses gradually make themselves known after a burglary. The same thing had happened after the first one. A serious attempt at altering the past could never have just one consequence; there was always a host of trivial—or not so trivial—secondary shifts, a ramifying web of transformations reaching out into any number of other lives. New chains of associations were formed in the Mikkelsens' lives as a result of the erasure of their plan to collect electronic artifacts and the substitution of a trip to pre-Columbian Mexico. People they had met on that trip now were good friends, with whom they exchanged gifts, spent other holidays, shared the burdens and joys of parenthood. A certain hollowness at first marked all those newly ingrafted old friendships, making them seem curiously insubstantial and marked by odd inconsistencies. But after a time everything felt real again, everything appeared to fit.

Then the third phasing happened, the one that pushed the beginning of their marriage from August to the following February, and did six or seven other troublesome little things, as they shortly discovered, to the contours of their existence.

"I'm going to talk to him," Mikkelsen said.

"Nick, don't do anything foolish."

"I don't intend to. But he's got to be made to see that this can't go on."

"Remember that he can be dangerous if he's forced into a corner," Janine said. "Don't threaten him. Don't push him."

"I'll tickle him," Mikkelsen said.

He met Hambleton for drinks at the Top of the Marina, Hambleton's favorite pub, swiveling at the end of a jointed stalk a thousand feet long rising from the harbor at Balboa Lagoon. Hambleton was there when Mikkelsen came in—a small sleek man, six inches shorter than Mikkelsen, with a slick confident manner. He was the richest man Mikkelsen knew, gliding through life on one of the big microprocessor fortunes of two generations back, and that in itself made him faintly menacing, as though he might try simply to *buy* back, one of these days, the wife he had loved and lost a dozen years ago when all of them had been so very young.

Hambleton's overriding passion, Mikkelsen knew, was time-travel. He was an inveterate jaunter—a compulsive jaunter, in fact, with that faintly hyperthyroid goggle-eyed look that frequent travelers get. He was always either just back from a jaunt or getting his affairs in order for his next one. It was as though the only use he had for the humdrum real-time event horizon was to serve as his springboard into the past. That was odd. What was odder still was where he jaunted. Mikkelsen could understand people who went zooming off to watch the battle of Waterloo, or shot a bundle on a first-hand view of the sack of Rome. If he had anything like Hambleton's money, that was what he would do. But according to Janine, Hambleton was forever going back seven weeks in time, or maybe to last Christmas, or occasionally to his eleventh birthday party. Time-travel as tourism held no interest for him. Let others roam the ferny glades of the Mesozoic: he spent fortunes doubling back along his own time-track, and never went anywhen other. The purpose of Tommy Hambleton's time-travel, it seemed, was to edit his past to make his life more perfect. He went back to eliminate every little contretemps and faux pas, to recover fumbles, to take advantage of the new opportunities that hindsight provides—to retouch, to correct, to emend. To Mikkelsen that was crazy, but also somehow charming. Hambleton was nothing if not charming. And Mikkelsen admired anyone who could invent his own new species of obsessive behavior, instead of going in for the standard hand-washing routines, or stamp-collecting or sitting with your back to the wall in restaurants.

The moment Mikkelsen arrived, Hambleton punched the autobar for cocktails and said, "Splendid to see you, Mikkelsen. How's the elegant Janine?"

"Elegant."

"What a lucky man you are. The one great mistake of my life was letting that woman slip through my grasp."

"For which I remain forever grateful, Tommy. I've been working hard lately to hang on to her, too."

Hambleton's eyes widened. "Yes? Are you two having problems?"

"Not with each other. Time-track troubles. You know, we were caught in a couple of phasings last year. Pretty serious ones. Now there's been another one. We lost five months of our marriage."

"Ah, the little annoyances of—"

"—modern life," Mikkelsen said. "Yes. A very familiar phrase. But these are what I'd call frightening annoyances. I don't need to tell you, of all people, what a splendid woman Janine is, how terrifying it is to me to think of losing her in some random twitch of the time-track."

"Of course. I quite understand."

"I wish I understood these phasings. They're driving us crazy. And that's what I wanted to talk to you about."

He studied Hambleton closely, searching for some trace of guilt or at least uneasiness. But Hambleton remained serene.

"How can I be of help?"

Mikkelsen said, "I thought that perhaps you, with all your vast experience in the theory and practice of time-jaunting, could give me some clue to what's causing them, so that I can head the next one off."

Hambleton shrugged elaborately. "My dear Nick, it could be anything! There's no way of tracing phasing effects back to their cause reliably. All our lives are interconnected in ways we never suspect. You say this last phasing delayed your marriage by a few months? Well, then, suppose that as a result of the phasing you decided to take a last bachelor fling and went off for a weekend in Banff, say, and met some lovely person with whom you spent three absolutely casual and nonsignificant but delightful days, thereby preventing her from meeting someone else that weekend with whom in the original time-track she had fallen in love and married. You then went home and married Janine, a little later than originally scheduled, and lived happily ever after; but the Banff woman's life was totally switched around, all as a consequence of the phasing that delayed your wedding. Do you see? There's never any telling how a shift in one chain of events can cause interlocking upheavals in the lives of utter strangers."

"So I realize. But why should we be hit with three phasings in a year, each one jeopardizing the whole structure of our marriage?"

"I'm sure I don't know," said Hambleton. "I suppose it's just bad luck, and bad luck always changes, don't you think? Probably you've been at the edge of some nexus of negative phases that has just about run its course." He smiled dazzlingly. "Let's hope so, anyway. Would you care for another filtered rum?"

He was smooth, Mikkelsen thought. And impervious. There was no way to slip past his defenses, and even a direct attack—an outright accusation that he was the one causing the phasings—would most likely bring into play a whole new line of defense. Mikkelsen did not intend to risk that. A man who used time-jaunting so ruthlessly to tidy up his past was too slippery to confront. Pressed, Hambleton would simply deny everything and hasten backward to clear away any traces of his crime that might remain. In any case, making an accusation of time-crime stick was exceedingly difficult, because the crime by definition had to have taken place on a track that no longer existed. Mikkelsen chose to retreat. He accepted another drink from Hambleton; they talked in a desultory way for a while about phasing theory, the weather, the stock market, the excellences of the woman they both had married, and the good old days of 2014 or so when they all used to hang out down in dear old La Jolla, living golden lives of wondrous irresponsibility. Then he extricated himself from the conversation and headed for home in a dark and brooding mood. He had no doubt that Hambleton would strike again, perhaps quite soon. How could he be held at bay? Some sort of preemptive strike, Mikkelsen wondered? Some bold leap into the past that would neutralize the menace of Tommy Hambleton forever? Chancy, Mikkelsen thought. You could lose as much as you gained, sometimes, in that sort of maneuver. But perhaps it was the only hope.

He spent the next few days trying to work out a strategy. Something that would get rid of Hambleton without disrupting the frail chain of circumstance that bound his own life to that of Janine—was it possible? Mikkelsen sketched out ideas, rejected them, tried again. He began to think he saw a way.

Then came a new phasing on a warm and brilliantly sunny morning that struck him like a thunderbolt and left him dazed and numbed. When he finally shook away the grogginess, he found himself in a bachelor flat ninety stories above Mission Bay, a thick taste of cotton in his mouth, and bewildering memories already growing thin of a lovely wife and two kids and a cat and a sweet home in mellow old Corona del Mar.

Janine? Dana? Elise? Minibelle?

Gone. All gone. He knew that he had been living in this condo since '22, after the breakup with Yvonne, and that Melanie was supposed to be dropping in about six. That much was reality. And yet another reality still lingered in his mind, fading, vanishing.

So it had happened. Hambleton had really done it, this time.

There was no time for panic or even for pain. He spent the first half hour desperately scribbling down notes, every detail of his lost life that he still remembered, phone numbers, addresses, names, descriptions. He set down whatever he could recall of his life with Janine and of the series of phasings that had led up to this one. Just as he was running dry the telephone rang. Janine, he prayed.

But it was Gus Stark. "Listen," he began, "Donna and I got to cancel for tonight, on account of she's got a bad headache, but I hope you and Melanie aren't too disappointed, and—" He paused. "Hey, guy, are you okay?"

"There's been a bad phasing," Mikkelsen said.

"Uh-oh."

"I've got to find Janine."

"Janine?"

"Janine—Carter," Mikkelsen said. "Slender, high cheekbones, dark hair—you know."

"Janine," said Stark. "Do I know a Janine? Hey, you and Melanie on the outs? I thought—"

"This had nothing to do with Melanie," said Mikkelsen.

"Janine Carter." Gus grinned. "You mean Tommy Hambleton's girl? The little rich guy who was part of the La Jolla crowd ten-twelve years back when—"

"That's the one. Where do you think I'd find her now?"

"Married Hambleton, I think. Moved to the Riviera, unless I'm mistaken. Look, about tonight, Nick—"

"Screw tonight," Mikkelsen said. "Get off the phone. I'll talk to you later."

He broke the circuit and put the phone into search mode, all directories worldwide, Thomas and Janine Hambleton. While he waited, the shock and anguish of loss began at last to get to him, and he started to sweat, his hands shook, his heart raced in double time. I won't find her, he thought. He's got her hidden behind seven layers of privacy networks and it's crazy to think the phone number is listed, for Christ's sake, and—

The telephone. He hit the button. Janine calling, this time.

She looked stunned and disoriented, as though she were working hard to keep her eyes in focus. "Nick?" he said faintly. "Oh, God, Nick, it's you, isn't it?"

"Where are you?"

"A villa outside Nice. In Cap d'Antibes, actually. Oh, Nick—the kids—they're gone, aren't they? Dana. Elise. They never were born, isn't that so?"

"I'm afraid it is. He really nailed us, this time."

"I can still remember—just as though they were real—as though we spent ten years together—oh, Nick—"

"Tell me how to find you. I'll be on the next plane out of San Diego."

She was silent a moment.

"No. No, Nick. What's the use? We aren't the same people we were when we were married. An hour or two more and we'll forget we ever were together."

"Janine—"

"We've got no past left, Nick. And no future."

"Let me come to you!"

"I'm Tommy's wife. My past's with him. Oh, Nick, I'm so sorry, so awfully sorry—I can still remember, a little, how it was with us, the fun, the running along the beach, the kids, the little fat calico cat—but it's all gone, isn't it? I've got my life here, you've got yours. I just wanted to tell you—"

"We can try to put it back together. You don't love Tommy. You and I belong with each other. We—"

"He's a lot different, Nick. He's not the man you remember from the La Jolla days. Kinder, more considerate, more of a human being, you know? It's been ten years, after all."

Mikkelsen closed his eyes and gripped the edge of the couch to keep from falling. "It's been two hours," he said. "Tommy phased us. He just tore up our life, and we can't ever have that part of it back, but still we can salvage something, Janine, we can rebuild, if you'll just get the hell out of that villa and—"

"I'm sorry, Nick." Her voice was tender, throaty, distant, almost unfamiliar. "Oh, God, Nick, it's such a mess. I loved you so. I'm sorry, Nick. I'm so sorry."

The screen went blank.

Mikkelsen had not time-jaunted in years, not since the Aztec trip, and he was amazed at what it cost now. But he was carrying the usual credit cards and evidently his credit lines were okay, because they approved his application in five minutes. He told them where he wanted to go and how he wanted to look, and for another few hundred the makeup man worked him over, taking that dusting of early gray out of his hair and smoothing the lines from his face and spraying him with the good old Southern California tan that you tend to lose when you're in your late thirties and spending more time in your office than on the beach. He looked at least eight years younger, close enough to pass. As long as he took care to keep from running into his own younger

self while he was back there, there should be no
problems.

He stepped into the cubicle and sweet-scented fog
enshrouded him and when he stepped out again it was a
mild December day in the year 2012, with a faint hint of
rain in the northern sky. Only fourteen years back, and
yet the world looked prehistoric to him, the clothing and
the haircuts and the cars all wrong, the buildings heavy
and clumsy, the advertisements floating overhead offering archaic and absurd products in blaring gaudy colors.
Odd that the world of 2012 had not looked so crude to
him the first time he had lived through it; but then the
present never looks crude, he thought, except through
the eyes of the future. He enjoyed the strangeness of it:
it told him that he had really gone backward in time. It
was like walking into an old movie. He felt very calm. All
the pain was behind him now; he remembered nothing
of the life that he had lost, only that it was important for
him to take certain countermeasures against the man
who had stolen something precious from him. He
rented a car and drove quickly up to La Jolla. As he
expected, everybody was at the beach club except for
young Nick Mikkelsen, who was back in Palm Beach
with his parents. Mikkelsen had put this jaunt together
quickly but not without careful planning.

They were all amazed to see him—Gus, Dan, Leo,
Christie, Sal, the whole crowd. How young they looked!
Kids, just kids, barely into their twenties, all that hair, all
that baby fat—he had never before realized how *young*
you were when you were young. "Hey," Gus said, "I
thought you were in Florida!" Someone handed him a
popper. Someone slipped a capsule to his ear and
raucous overload music began to pound against his
cheekbone. He made the rounds, grinning, hugging,
explaining that Palm Beach had been a bore, that he had
come back early to be with the gang. "Where's Yvonne?"
he asked.

"She'll be here in a little while," Christie said.

Tommy Hambleton walked in five minutes after

Mikkelsen. For one jarring instant Mikkelsen thought that the man he saw was the Hambleton of his own time, thirty-five years old, but no: there were little signs, and certain lack of tension in this man's face, a certain callowness about the lips, that marked him as younger. The truth, Mikkelsen realized, is that Hambleton had *never* looked really young, that he was ageless, timeless, sleek and plump and unchanging. It would have been very satisfying to Mikkelsen to plunge a knife into that impeccably shaven throat, but murder was not his style, nor was it an ideal solution to his problem. Instead, he called Hambleton aside, bought him a drink and said quietly, "I just thought you'd like to know that Yvonne and I are breaking up."

"Really, Nick? Oh, that's so sad! I thought you two were the most solid couple here!"

"We were. We were. But it's all over, man. I'll be with someone else New Year's Eve. Don't know who, but it won't be Yvonne."

Hambleton looked solemn. "That's so sad, Nick."

"No. Not for me and not for you." Mikkelsen smiled and nudged Hambleton amiably. "Look, Tommy, it's no secret to me that you've had your eye on Yvonne for months. She knows it too. I just wanted to let you know that I'm stepping out of the picture, I'm very gracefully withdrawing, no hard feelings at all. And if she asks my advice, I'll tell her that you're absolutely the best man she could find. I mean it, Tommy."

"That's very decent of you, old fellow. That's extraordinary!"

"I want her to be happy," Mikkelsen said.

Yvonne showed up just as night was falling. Mikkelsen had not seen her for years, and he was startled at how uninteresting she seemed, how bland, how unformed, almost adolescent. Of course, she was very pretty, close-cropped blonde hair, merry greenish blue eyes, pert little nose, but she seemed girlish and alien to him, and he wondered how he could ever have become so involved with her. But of course all that was before

Janine. Mikkelsen's unscheduled return from Palm Beach surprised her, but not very much, and when he took her down to the beach to tell her that he had come to realize that she was really in love with Hambleton and he was not going to make a fuss about it, she blinked and said sweetly, "In love with Tommy? Well, I suppose I *could* be—though I never actually saw it like that. But I could give it a try, couldn't I? That is, if you truly are tired of me, Nick." She didn't seem offended. She didn't seem heartbroken. She didn't seem to care much at all.

He left the club soon afterward and got an express-fax message off to his younger self in Palm Beach: *Yvonne has fallen for Tommy Hambleton. However upset you are, for God's sake get over it fast, and if you happen to meet a young woman named Janine Carter, give her a close look. You won't regret it, believe me. I'm in a position to know.*

He signed it *A Friend,* but added a little squiggle in the corner that had always been his own special signature-glyph. He didn't dare go further than that. He hoped young Nick would be smart enough to figure out the score.

Not a bad hour's work, he decided. He drove back to the jaunt-shop in downtown San Diego and hopped back to his proper point in time.

There was the taste of cotton in his mouth when he emerged. So it feels that way even when you phase *yourself,* he thought. He wondered what changes he had brought about by his jaunt. As he remembered it, he had made the hop in order to phase himself back into a marriage with a woman named Janine, who apparently he had loved quite considerably until she had been snatched away from him in a phasing. Evidently the unphasing had not happened, because he knew he was still unmarried, with three or four regular compan-ions—Cindy, Melanie, Elena and someone else—and none of them was named Janine. Paula, yes, that was the other one. Yet he was carrying a note, already starting to fade, that said: *You won't remember any of this, but you were married in 2016 or 17 to the former Janine Carter, Tommy Hambleton's ex-wife, and however much you may like your present life, you were a lot better off when you were with her.*

Maybe so, Mikkelsen thought. God knows he was getting weary of the bachelor life, and now that Gus and Donna were making it legal, he was the only singleton left in the whole crowd. That was a little awkward. But he hadn't ever met anyone he genuinely wanted to spend the rest of his life with, or even as much as a year with. So he had been married, had he, before the phasing? Janine? How strange, how unlike him.

He was home before dark. Showered, shaved, dressed, headed over to the Top of the Marina. Tommy Hambleton and Yvonne were in town, and he had agreed to meet them for drinks. Hadn't seen them for years, not since Tommy had taken over his brother's villa on the Riviera. Good old Tommy, Mikkelsen thought. Great to see him again. And Yvonne. He recalled her clearly, little snub-nosed blonde, good game of tennis, trim compact body. He'd been pretty hot for her himself, eleven or twelve years ago, back before Adrienne, before Charlene, before Georgiana, before Nedra, before Cindy, Melanie, Elena, Paula. Good to see them both again. He stepped into the skylift and went shooting blithely up the long swivel-stalk to the gilded little cupola high above the lagoon. Hambleton and Yvonne were already there.

Tommy hadn't changed much—same old smooth slickly dressed little guy—but Mikkelsen was astonished at how time and money had altered Yvonne. She was poised, chic, sinuous, all that baby-fat burned away, and when she spoke there was the smallest hint of a French accent in her voice. Mikkelsen embraced them both and let himself be swept off to the bar.

"So glad I was able to find you," Hambleton said. "It's been years! Years, Nick!"

"Practically forever."

"Still going great with the women, are you?"

"More or less," Mikkelsen said. "And you? Still run

ning back in time to wipe your nose three days ago, Tommy?"

Hambleton chuckled. "Oh, I don't do much of that any more. Yvonne and I were to the Fall of Troy last winter, but the short-hop stuff doesn't interest me these days. I—oh. How amazing!"

"What is it?" Mikkelsen asked, seeing Hambleton's gaze go past him into the darker corners of the room.

"An old friend," Hambleton said. "I'm sure it's she! Someone I once knew—briefly, glancingly—" He looked toward Yvonne and said, "I met her a few months after you and I began seeing each other, love. Of course, there was nothing to it, but there could have been— there could have been—" A distant wistful look swiftly crossed Hambleton's features and was gone. His smile returned. He said, "You should meet her, Nick. If it's really she, I know she'll be just your type. How amazing! After all these years! Come with me, man!"

He seized Mikkelsen by the wrist and drew him, astounded, across the room.

"Janine?" Hambleton cried. "Janine Carter?"

She was a dark-haired woman, elegant, perhaps a year or two younger than Mikkelsen, with cool perceptive eyes. She looked up, surprised. "Tommy? Is that you?"

"Of course, of course. That's my wife, Yvonne, over here. And this—this is one of my oldest and dearest friends, Nick Mikkelsen. Nick—Janine—"

She stared up at him. "This sounds absurd," she said, "but don't I know you from somewhere?"

Mikkelsen felt a warm flood of mysterious energy surging through him as their eyes met. "It's a long story," he said. "Let's have a drink and I'll tell you all about it."

ABOUT THE AUTHOR

ROBERT SILVERBERG was born in New York and makes his home in the San Francisco area. He has written several hundred science fiction stories and over seventy science fiction novels. He has won two Hugo awards and four Nebula awards. He is a past president of the Science Fiction Writers of America. Silverberg's other Bantam titles include *Lord Valentine's Castle, Majipoor Chronicles, The Book of Skulls, Born With the Dead, The World Inside, Thorns, The Masks of Time, Dying Inside, Downward to the Earth, The Tower of Glass, World of a Thousand Colors, Lord of Darkness* and *Valentine Pontifex.*

Read the powerful novels of award-winning author

ROBERT SILVERBERG

One of the most brilliant and beloved science fiction authors of our time, Robert Silverberg has been honored with two Hugo awards and four Nebula awards. His stirring combination of vivid imagery, evocative prose, and rousing storytelling promise his audience a reading experience like no other.

WEST
of
EDEN

Harry Harrison

From a master of imaginative storytelling comes an epic tale of the world as it might have been, a world where the age of dinosaurs never ended, and their descendants clash with a clan of humans in a tragic war for survival . . .